MEDICINEMAN
~1884~

FLATS JUNCTION SERIES
BOOK 4

SARA DAHMEN

MEDICINEMAN 1884

Promontory Press
www.promontorypress.com

ISBN: 978-1-77374-102-4

Cover designed by Edge of Water Design
Typeset by Spica Book Design
Interior Artwork Copyright © 2023 Sara Dahmen
Printed in the United States

0 9 8 7 6 5 4 3 2 1

To my three children
and to John, moja miłość
for without you, where would I belong?

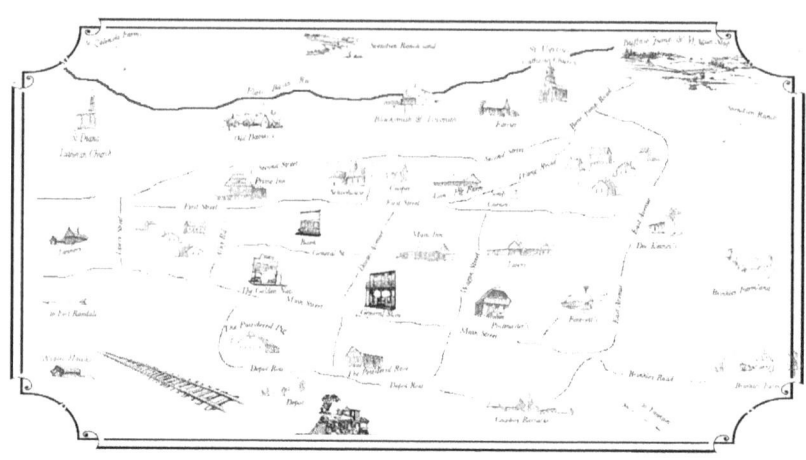

RICE'S
SECTIONAL MAP OF
DAKOTA
TERRITORY.

DRAWN & COMPILED BY FRED STEINBECK

Published for the St. Paul Litho. & Eng. Co.
1881
ST. PAUL MINNESOTA.

Flats Junction
Medicineman
1884

CHAPTER ONE

Jane

July 27, 1883

A Practical Treatise on the Diseases of Women by Thomas Gaillard.

It's likely filled with unmentionable horrors I'll never forget.

I slip a finger under the rusty book cover and yank the digit back quickly. A seam of red pierces the first crease. Frowning, I suck the drop of blood off before it can splatter on my skirt, newly sewn by Widow Hawks only last week and with plenty of fabric along the waist and bodice to accommodate quickly expanding flesh.

Above the roof of Patrick's office, there's a smattering of hammer blows, mismatched and without rhythm. The doctor himself is gone on another case of black measles, but Hardy the blacksmith's apprentice is on the roof in the late afternoon, as is Moses Thompson, who splits his repair hours between our blackened porch and Kate's crumbling General.

I go back to the book. Its the last of the shelf, as I take them down to clean them of old soot and extra dust. It's worse than usual, as the front porch fire during the July Fourth's town festivities a few weeks ago drenched most surfaces with a fine layer of ash. Patrick's office is always dingy at the best of times, a sallow, pale-grey hole with only the one small front window to let in any light. Everything in it is a shade of mushroom or tired brown. Everything, that is, except the books. I envy them their stout fatness, and the words they cuddle between covers. Even in their faded jackets of paisley corduroy or tightly woven tweed, they are lovely and hold more knowledge than I could ever wish to absorb.

Opening the cover more carefully, I am surprised to see this is not only a book. It's filled with debris and folded papers stuffed between pages and haphazardly filed. It is unlike Patrick to be so disorganized with information.

The first is an old patient file – or at least, what I would call a patient file, though it is unlike his current system. This is more notes, observations, and what looks to be questions to himself to check on later. The name at the top is smudged, but it reads *Franklin* clear enough. There is only one Franklin in town, and as I squint to decipher the hurried but distinguishably looped handwriting of my husband, I realize, even without a date on the document, what it is. I quickly put it on the desk so I can file it properly later with the current file.

Ah. But then again, Franklin does not allow the doctor to see him. There is no file for him, nor any of the Jones family.

And another letter, this one from Boston—

"Jane?" Esther Davies stands at the door of the study, her thick black brows raised up and her long mouth, lined with a single deep crevasse, tweaked in gentle, iron patience.

"What?"

"Have you asked your husband if you might go through his personal notes?" She enters the room with simple steps, her feet soundless as always. "I typically left everything in Percy's office to himself."

"That was a generation ago," I say at once, and then feel my back tighten and the oiled muscles slide down the ridges of my spine. "But I hear your meaning. It is typically not done to pry a husband's papers. I just...I sometimes think he means to let me see it all, and glean what I can from his books."

"And that?" she asks, pointing her rounded chin at the letter in my hand. "That is not a book."

"No," I say, rubbing the soft yellow paper between forefinger and thumb. My callouses and fingerprints catch on the suppleness of it. "But I know the name and the man who wrote it. I met his wife myself when I interviewed out east. It is not like I truly pry."

She gives me an arched, incredulous look, scalding and understanding in one swoop. It feels like the sliced glance of a woman who understands yet cannot officially agree. One who will not aid or harm. One who knows more than she says.

There are times I wish that was me.

What would it be, to hold such knowledge in my hands, which none could siphon and steal from me?

"I would finish quickly, then, before Patrick is home," she says, her gaze, black and steady on the letter in my fingers. "You are needed in the kitchen."

A falsehood if ever there was one. If anyone can handle a fire and a meal, it is Widow Hawks herself. But I will not contradict her—I cannot remember if I have ever done so—and she is right. I pry. I know it.

But I also know I must understand all the tiny details of my existence if I am to continue to live in Flats Junction, bear the babe in my womb, love the doctor I married. To turn away from it, to pretend I don't see the papers and the books, is to deny myself my nature. I want to know how the dust squeaked under his boots when he arrived, how deeply he inhaled greasy chimney smoke choked with day-old meat, to ask for directions from one side of town to the other, just as I did when the icy spring winds whipped and I walked the rutted roads. I want to know if he asked Esther about the plants she loved or the medicines she harbored.

Yet this letter is a line to my old life, and to ignore it is to pretend I do not know my name.

"I'll be right behind you," I tell Esther.

She knows it for the lie it is and doesn't move at first.

"Looking for answers in old dusty books is not how you will solve the troubles here in Flats Junction now, Jane," she says to me. "People hate and destroy and burn what they do not know. Or like. It is the same, no matter. Anything difficult or different is met with anger. It is how it always is, no matter where you look. Your husband knows this. He has known it since he became the doctor here. He knew it even as he knew it could mean violence. You must know this now, too."

She walks out, still soundless, and I turn back to the old, burnished letter. There is less pleasure in reading it, now, but I do so defiantly anyway, as if I can fix everything in Flats Junction by unwrapping its history.

Paddy,

I know you had to go, but so fast? You didn't even say good-bye to us. Tara is not pleased that we were only left with a note. You must be sure to write and tell us where to ship mail, especially these blasted medical journals now forwarded to my address by your request. They will pile up something fierce.

You'll come back to Boston, I'm sure, once things in the medical community calm down, and the people move about, you'll see. There's a place for a doctor everywhere in the world, or at least where the people's memories are short. They're long out west, I hear, so return soon, aye? Meanwhile, don't go silent, or I'll think you're dead, and will have to go to the territories or beyond to find you, and you know I'm not cut out for anything so rough.

Always your friend in times of need,

RMH

Then at the back, a braid, small and twisted and fraying on the edges. It is not the glossy raven locks of the woman he'd taken as a lover before he wed me. Nor is it mine, for I have never given him such a thing, though it is still quite in fashion. I did not think Patrick so sentimental as to wish for a token like this.

And lastly, fluttering and old enough to feel slick and soft under my fingers, is a stamped ticket, for the Dakota Southern rail to Vermillion, dated August 19, 1876.

And under that, a fare for a carriage ride, from Vermillion to Fort Randall, Dakota Territories.

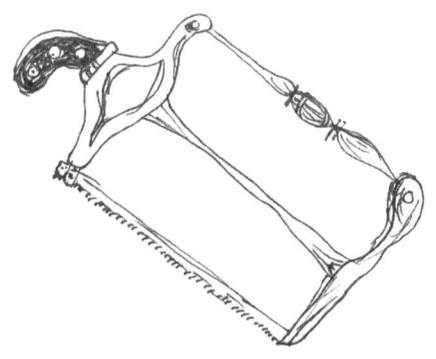

CHAPTER TWO
Patrick

August 22, 1876

As the carriage slowed, the driver shouted a warnin', tellin' all us passengers to stay put.

"It's lookin' right dang'rus ahead!" he yelled down, clearly hopin' the wind would carry his voice through the open window. "I'll pull off a ways t' town, so's if you need vittles or if you're stayin' but I'd righ' drive to Randall wi'out a stop if'n I ca'."

Patrick glanced at Aunt Bonnie. Her narrow face curdled a paste-yellow, but her mouth set in a long line, straight and decisive.

"You'll need to get off, Pat," she said grimly, and he realized, inherently, without questioning, that he knew this already. To hear it said aloud, though, made action necessary, and he began to calculate the likelihood of different injuries.

"Do you think you can hide, dependin' on what we find?" he asked her. "It sounds like some tribes don't care whether you're woman or child – if you're white, they'll kill you. Will you stay out of the way?"

She looked out at the dust again, and nodded once, prim and quick. Patrick nodded in return and pounded on the side of the carriage. Hard. Once, twice.

The driver, a man they'd taken to calling Hitch due to how he was always either hitchin' the horses or hitchin' up his pants—and the fact that his real name was an unpronounceable mouthful of Russian—cussed quick but drove in a wide arc and began to slowly ease up the four horses.

Patrick grabbed their bags. He and Aunt Bonnie had managed to limit themselves over the years, and other than his medical bag and kit they'd given away most of their already meager belongings to make travel easier as they meandered ever further west, lookin' for a place to stay.

A place with no doc.

A place that might have a use for him and his skills.

As he moved, one of the two gentlemen in the seat across made a motion to block the door. His eyes were wide, and his tall black hat tumbled down one side of his head.

"You can't mean to go out there, man. It's madness. Suicide." The man panted, sweat runnin' in rivers in the corners of his ears. He looked ready to bolt, except there was nowhere inside the four-person carriage to run.

Patrick glanced again out the window. "It's my job. My profession. I must help them. To ignore it would be… impossible."

They were nearer Flats Town now, jigglin' closer and bouncin' around the side of it. Even with the chaos of the street, he saw people layin' in the dirt, struck down by arrows or hatchets, he figured. And all filled with pain and sufferin'. They had to get off fast, and let the carriage keep movin' or there might be more injured. He gripped his medical bag tighter, feeling the leather squeeze under the curves of his palms.

Patrick's abilities and knowledge of healin' would not differentiate him at all to the shoutin' natives outside the carriage, and he had absolutely no idea how he would help anyone. He just knew he needed to try. The same as he needed to help every man, woman and child he met and helped back in Boston or under Doctor Burns' watchful eye.

"Sir, I truly must insist. My place as a gentleman. You can't go out there." The top hat man looked frantic, quiverin' in his threadbare suit and sweating rivulets down his unshaved cheeks. Was he frightened for Patrick, or the raid happenin' outside?

There was no time for an answer.

"Now, Aunt Bonnie. I'll help you."

Aunt Bonnie's skirts swirled behind him, like some strong comfortin' presence. Before the blusterin' gentleman could protest further, they squeezed past and leapt as best they could onto the hard earth beside the carriage, stumblin' as they went. The driver screeched at the horses, and they took off, faster than they arrived.

Without pausin', he strode towards what passed for a large street. Everything smelled like dust. Harsh and soft at the same time, smellin' of dirt and wind and sulfur. Immediately to his left, there was a deep groan.

A young man sprawled in the street, his face gazin' straight up to the dirt crusted sky, and blood poolin' around

8

his upper back. Patrick's first thought was alarm, thinkin' a head wound, which were always the worst. But as he drew closer, he realized the puddle wasn't very big or spreadin' very fast, nor was it as close to his head as he'd thought.

Falling to his knees, he turned him over, wishin' he could open his medical bag and examine the boy all at the same time. Thinkin' on Aunt Bonnie, too, he looked up for her, only to see her a few paces back, frozen in fear. She looked green along the edge of her jaw, and he realized this was likely the most blood she'd ever seen.

"Auntie!" he said, lest she forget to hide from the rampagin' around them. "Go!"

She finally twitched, then lowered herself next to him. "I don't know where to go, Patrick. Let me help. I'd prefer to be useful."

The young man moaned again, and the old trace came upon him - a combination of understandin' bodies, sinew, and bone. A clean knowledge, filled with excitement and comfortableness and curiosity. It was a place he went every time he was faced with surgery.

The man's back was covered in sticky blood. Patrick peeled up his shirt to expose an arrow wound to the top shoulder, the stone embedded into the soft tissue right under the blade. Somehow, perhaps with his fall, he had already broken off the shaft, leaving Patrick to explore the open wound to try and see if anythin' was left in the hole.

Luckily for the doctor, the patient was already halfway gone with pain, and didn't seem to mind a finger inside his muscle, pinchin' the fat tissue and probin' against the meat of it. He would sterilize his efforts later. There was no time in the middle of it.

Aunt Bonnie opened the medical bag, and she poised over his tools. He didn't wish to make a bigger laceration to try to find the arrowhead, but there seemed to be nothin' for it. The sooner he popped it out, the sooner he could start to heal him and be sure there'd be less chance of germs wormin' their way in.

"Scalpel," Patrick directed at Aunt Bonnie. She gave a witherin' look, and he tried again. "Knife, auntie."

She carefully selected the proper tool, which he grabbed without thanks. From the sound of the shoutin', firin', and screamin' beyond the far east buildings, they had little time left with the patient before more fightin' would arrive on their street. The pressure of the situation slid into his fingers. Sweat trickled down the back of his neck and around the corners of his ears.

Patrick knew his tools to be clean, so he opened up the small hole into a single line. His bag contained a vial of whiskey, which he never used for his own dabblin', contrary to popular opinion about doctors and Irish ones in particular. He poured it into the wound and onto his finger before stickin' it back in. By sheer luck, the arrowhead was not so deep that it was invisible to his gropin' fingers.

The stone was hard, bumpy and slim, but jagged enough that it didn't slide around as he drew it out. If Patrick had more time, and it didn't cause such injury, he would take a closer look at the craftsmanship.

Meanwhile, the youth fainted with both blood loss and pain. He decided to stitch him later. It was more important to get out of the street.

Pouring another splash of whiskey into the gaping wound, he dragged the man across his shoulder. There was

10

a large General Store, nearby. It was best to get inside, he figured.

Natives tore through the east side of town, circling ever closer. Even with the distance, it was clear some had vivid black and yellow paint on their faces and others did not.

Patrick still knew so little about the territories. So many questions crowded into his mind. *Do they belong on this land? Are they divided or of one mind when it comes to us? Should we turn back to Chicago and leave them their own battles?*

As they crossed the street, more bodies came into focus through the swirling dust. He forced down the panic. *Who to choose first?*

He pounded the door of the General, feelin' the blood of his patient leak into his sleeve, hot and salty. When there was no answer, Patrick pushed hard and forced himself in, startlin' the tall, rail-thin elderly man hidin' behind the counter with an ancient musket across his knees.

"We need a place to take the wounded," Patrick told him.

The man jumped to his feet, and without a word began movin' barrels and pullin' out lumpy sacks of seed and flour. Without time to offer further instruction, Patrick turned on his heel, shoved down another round of panic, and headed back into the street, leavin' Aunt Bonnie to facilitate the creation of a make-shift hospital.

His shoes twisted along the broken ground of the road, hardened by sun and heat and clumped unevenly by wagon wheels and horse's feet.

Suddenly, three Indians reeled past on their horses, firin' backwards while actively pursued by several other natives who were tryin' to aim their pistols while ridin' hard. Patrick broke into a run just as several shots rang out behind. He dove behind barrels next to a saloon to the west of the General, and ducked until they all rode past, screamin' and carryin' on.

When he stuck his head back up, he cast his eye on the nearest body. The man's horse had stopped movin' and stood by its master, which should have tipped him off, but didn't. Another horse tore off, riderless. He headed toward the nearest fallen, just as two ranchers appeared from behind a closed door of the saloon and tried for the horse's reins.

They all shrunk back as a warrior with black lines on his face bore down on the horse, whooped, caught the bridle and shot off after the others, who were hollerin' up on the west side of town. Another holler bore around the street, as if it was on wings. The warrior yellin' rode directly toward them, and Patrick was ashamed to freeze up instead of makin' a run back to the barrel. But this native wasn't carryin' obvious weapons, and instead chased after the wild horse headin' out of town.

Heart poundin', he headed toward the injured, twisting an ankle a bit, and gauged which of the two men in the street could use help most. He tried to ignore how he felt to be a turtle without a shell, vulnerable under a hot sun. The continued shouts and gun firin', marks a skirmish that was clearly not over. He had to hurry or risk gettin' caught up in another round, but Patrick could not stop workin'. He couldn't give up and return to that General Store without savin' the other poor fellows.

Of the two men in the street, one was a native. The warrior was knocked out cold, with superficial wounds at worst. Like the other native calmin' the fallen rancher's horse, this man also had no paint on his face. There was no way to know if he was friend or foe: he was, in that frenzied state of carnage, simply a body that needed to be tended. But the white man had a ball in the leg, a ripped gash that tore deep into the flesh, burrowin' into the bone, which had fractured into splinters throughout the muscle. The arteries gushed. The foot was crushed, and all the ligaments already dirty from the dust of the road. The impact of the destruction felt like a terrible puzzle, a man's life pourin' out, a limb mangled beyond savin'.

Patrick knew he had to amputate.

"She sent me out to help!" The breathless voice sounded utterly terrified, and Patrick looked up to see the proprietor of the nearby General, his white fluffy hair standin' up like a dandelion's puff. Behind the man, her eyes wide and her hands on her hips, was Aunt Bonnie, standin' in the store-front window. The glass had been broken, and she was half reflected in light bouncin' off the shards still holdin' onto the frame.

Patrick turned back to the man and nodded once. "Take him up. I'll need you to hold him down as best you might. The leg has to come off."

The proprietor dragged the man up the stairs with Aunt Bonnie takin' the knees. A trail of bone and blood followed them up, but Patrick couldn't operate yet. There was one more. As he made for the other man's side, arrows rained around the street. One glanced off the rough, thick leather of Patrick's vest, somehow drawn short enough that the hide repelled it. His latest charge was not so lucky, and before he could help the half-sleepin' fellow into the General, an arrow found the man's arm, landin' with a sickenin' thunk.

13

"Jesus, Mary and Joseph!" Patrick shouted. "Confound this place!" Doctorin' by itself while under siege suddenly felt impossible and beyond frustratin'. He was unable to properly concentrate, and a perfectly healthy patient, save for a knock on the head, now had a new injury. From the screamin' and shoutin' to the rollin' injuries that appeared without stop, Patrick wanted to throw up his hands.

By the time he moved the warrior inside, the man had fainted, and the dead weight of him yanked on Patrick's shoulder blades. The General manager didn't make a sound as he deposited the limp body on flour sacks.

He could wait, though.

The amputation had to happen at once, or the man was going to bleed out and die.

The whiskey ran over his tools, and into the wound, though he wished for boilin' water and lye. The patient was incoherent with pain and loss of blood, and the seconds ticked by as fast as his life.

Patrick wearily pulled out the long bone saw and began the murderous task of takin' away the leg from the knee without a moment to think of anesthesia.

"Hold him down," he commanded the General manager, and the man's wiry strength pulled on the arms hard.

There was no way to save a life in a moment like that but to rid a man of the mangled limb, stop the bleedin' and hopefully stave off infection. Patrick promised himself, as he drove the metal into sinew, that he would stay and follow up with his limited amount of carbolic acid. The thought of the future treatment moved him through the grisly act, made worse by the retchin' of his impromptu aid and the initial keenin' scream of the patient.

When he was done, the patient was completely unconscious.

Patrick patched up the leg with a bandage that also acted like a tourniquet just as a small volley of arrows shot across his field of vision. In irritation, without even pausin', he drew out the pistol from his belt and fired it blindly toward the direction of the arrow launchers. The way the pistol jumped in his hand was unfamiliar and bruisin'. He shoved it back and turned to Aunt Bonnie. She stood holdin' the bloody rags and instruments, her breath comin' in short bursts as she looked anywhere but at the severed limb on the floorboards.

"Raise the stump up on the flour sacks. And bind it again over my bandage as tight as you might," he said.

She minced closer, as if afraid amputation was catchin'. "With the fabric?"

"Yes! Hurry!" Patrick told her. "And boil some water, for the love of all things holy."

The warrior was not awake yet. Was it a bad head wound? Had he slept? Too long? Patrick had no notion of time, or how long the operation had taken. He only knew from the yelps and shouts and rising dust clouds that whatever was happenin' outside was still going on.

The arrow lodged into the Indian's forearm, but not too deeply. As Patrick tested the hardiness of the arrow shaft to see if it might be pulled out directly before the glue on it started to disintegrate with the man's blood, the Indian opened his eyes.

"I need to pull this out," Patrick told him, his voice soundin' low and comfortable in spite of the panic he felt ridin' in his marrow. The fact that he would likely not speak English hit too late.

The warrior regarded Patrick for a moment, measurin'. He seemed unperturbed that he had woken up in the General, and his eyes did not leave the doctor's. Then, with great slow deliberation, he reached across and wiggled at the arrow without flinchin'. Patrick watched the shaft bend precariously under his calloused hands, a practiced twist and gentle pull done at once that slowly began to ease out the full piece, arrowhead and all. Patrick's mouth dropped open. *How did he—*

Aunt Bonnie poked the doctor on the arm. "I've the water near boilin', Patrick," she told him quietly.

"Good. Bring some in a clean pot, if you can," he instructed, still in awe over the removal of the arrow. Arrowheads left behind could often fester into infectious wounds, or their removal left such a gape that it too would become incredibly infected. Except the once, when he had been asked to remove an arrowhead long since wedged in a man's back, who was living his life as if nothin' was wrong. He knew the stone was there, but it hadn't bothered him on his daily activities, so he'd allowed it to nearly heal over with new skin. Patrick's appearance in the vicinity had his long-worried wife seek him out and beg interference. He had been convinced the man would survive with the arrowhead buried under layers of thick skin, but the knowledge it was there had been driving his wife out of her mind...

The native had made no sound as he operated on himself, but sweat soon beaded his brow, and poured down his half-bared chest as the last of the arrow came out with a strange, tiny sucking sound – the sound of tissue, blood and muscle protestin'. The man handed Patrick the arrowhead, and made to get up, but the doctor settled him down with a firm press of his hand. He narrowed his eyes, and Patrick felt himself narrowin' his back.

The General manager arrived at Patrick's side, white hair still in a wild puff around his ears and his eyes bugged out. "This here says he's a doc, from out east, Cheech. He likely knows what he's doing."

He apparently understood enough English, then, or at least enough to give a slide glance to the manager and an even more incredulous once-over of Patrick, dismissin' his capabilities with a quirk of the eyebrow that was not so much insolent as skeptical.

"At least let me bind it so you aren't bleedin' all over," Patrick said.

He ignored the doctor, found his legs, and stood anyway. Patrick stood nearly as quick and was fast enough to start wrappin' a bandage around the wound. The warrior paused just long enough for Patrick to tie a haphazard knot in the white linen, the blood arrested at once. No artery or vein, then. That was as best as one could hope.

"Alright, Cheech?" the manager said. "Many thanks to your uncle for grabbing Nels's horse, by the by."

"Yes, he will want it when he wakes." Cheech looked down at the newly amputated leg of the other patient—Nels. In the quiet moment of reflection, arrows zipped in through the open window, slammin' heavily into sacks of grain.

"Lord Almighty!" Aunt Bonnie broke the silence to swear. "They mean to kill us even in here!" She no longer seemed unnerved by all the blood, and her eyes burned somethin' wild.

Cheech turned from the General's door and found her in the deep gloom. He gave a single nod. "Yes. They are Crow."

The second he left, Patrick whirled to the General's man. "What is goin' on?"

"Who are you?" he shot back, seeming to finally find his mettle.

Patrick opened his mouth, but another barrage of shouts, gunfire and subsequent screams rang out. He shot out the door with only the one thought: *Please let there be no further amputations today...*

The shootin' was two streets over, toward the west and nearer the edge of the prairie. The general store manager caught up with the doctor, out of breath, mutterin' and whimperin' when another volley of arrows hit the side of the nearest buildin', all landin' with the same hollow thunk. It was impossible to tell if they aimed for the pair, or just movement in particular – it seemed to come from a densely clustered chunk of trees near the south of the town.

With the increase in shoutin' and screaming' all manner of people decided to make another mad dash back and forth. Most men had guns clenched in tight fists, and the women lifted their skirts beyond their knees to move fast.

On the street to the north of the General, two more men were down and a dog, shot clean through the head. A shout echoed across the space between wooden homes as a woman in dirty leathers pulled herself from the shadows of the smithy. As quick as she appeared, an arm yanked her back.

"Let me go, Berit! That's my husband out there! Tadeusz!" Her voice was clear as a birdsong, filled with anxiety and hysteria.

"You go out there and the next Crow will scoop you up before you can make a sound, and then where will we be?" An older woman's argument turned muddled, and half lost as Patrick focused on the latest casualties. The first – a huge blacksmith – tried to stand as they approached, with little luck. He collapsed back down, hard, and with an angry grunt.

"Here then, use his shoulder as a crutch, and walk back over to the General." Patrick nudged the General manager over to the man's side.

"Seems foolhardy to go to the General when my home is close enough. And truth be it, my weight'll be too much for you, Harry," the smith grouched.

"Best do as the man says," the General man—Harry— said with a shrug.

The smith tossed a look toward the forge, now silent where the woman had called out. Patrick pressed his case as he edged over to the other man, who had woken and started to groan. "If it's not broke, I'll want to check it first thing anyway. It'll be worse for you if you wait and let it swell too big."

Harry gave a hand and staggered under the smith, who looked unconvinced, but hobbled off toward the store.

The doctor's next patient was not nearly as lucky. The man's arm was blown clear out, the flesh a jagged wound and the skin mangled beyond stitchin'. Patrick would have to take it off below the elbow, as the bone was nothing but smashed splinters. If there was time to moan, he would have, as the doctor didn't prefer to take limbs. It wasn't surgery, not the true kind, and the risk of infection, even with the precautions, was always high, with death to follow.

Patrick wiped his brow, sweat and blood mingling, as he lifted up the much smaller, mostly unconscious man. The torn tissue seepedthrough the rag at the end of the grisly, useless limb dribblin' down the side of the doctor's shirt and onto the ground. His collar stuck to his neck, painted itself onto his shoulders and arms with the slickness runnin' across his skin – from the heat, the sun, and the fright all rolled together. Patrick's focus shifted and waned between the injured and his surroundings as he half-dragged his newest patient along, body tense for another round of arrows.

It was the ultimate emergency, one he'd longed for in Boston and had never had the chance to experience in the years of the war, on account of bein' too young. While everythin' was calmer now, Patrick still felt out of control, and was surprised to hear how his voice sounded strong as he gave instructions to Harry and Aunt Bonnie. They jumped, as if Patrick's leadership was the only thread that kept both from giving in to fear.

There was nothin' for waitin' once the water was brought and his tools cleansed. It was best to take the mangled arm while the man was still in a decent faint. Harry didn't retch while Patrick finished the sinew off, snippin' the last of it and foldin' what skin was left over the gushin' hole.

"I saw Abukcheech walking out with a bandage, Harry," the blacksmith mentioned from his corner. "What did he do?"

Harry jerked his head over to Patrick awkwardly. "This one, the doc, wanted to help him pull out an arrow."

The smith snorted, but then his face blanched as he twisted in his seat and noticed the other fellow with the right leg half gone. "*Pierdolić*! What the hell happened to Nels?"

"A woman is here," Patrick said automatically, but the smith simply raised an eyebrow as the doctor propped up his foot and eased off a soot-crusted boot.

"That's very well, doc." The title drawled out speculatively. "My thought is first on Nels, who needs two legs to walk behind a plow."

Patrick's eyes met the smith's as his fingers continued to search under the puffed skin for signs of a sprain or break. "Likely he'd rather have a limp behind a plow than be dead, I wouldn't wonder."

A tilt of the blacksmith's head recognized Patrick's point. "That may be, but you've already taken a saw to two fine men who were whole only minutes ago. Not exactly what anyone expects around here."

The doctor had been in Flats Town perhaps an hour and already he'd been shot at and chopped off limbs. The smith was right. Perhaps it wasn't such an auspicious way to enter a town. Three more stray arrows suddenly found their way in through the large front window, whistling thinly. Instinctively they all ducked. Two hit the floor, one stuck, and the third pinged off a plow in the room's center.

"Still Crow?" Harry asked, and the smith leaned forward to get a better look at the markings along the wooden shaft near him.

"So looks it, if I'm any judge," he said tightly.

Briefly, Patrick wondered...*maybe Aunt Bonnie and I should take the first stage out of Flats Town, instead of checkin' to see if they need a physician. Maybe we ought to circle back east. Or south. Anywhere that isn't Boston.*

"There's no break as far as I can tell," the doctor brought the smith's dark eyes back to me. "But might as well rest up before you go home."

"My wife will be worried," he mentioned, and shifted to stand, then glanced over at the younger man, whose arm

21

was gone. He frowned. "Damn. Much good the dash into the street did to get Franklin in before he got shot by that one with the gun."

Patrick stood as he headed to the door, his hands already crinklin' with dried blood.

The smith stopped mid-limp, turned, and cocked his head. "Mighty kind of you to stop in on a day like today, doc. Good-bye."

It was a dismissal, with expectation loaded into the farewell. Then the smith was gone, back out into the diminishin' foray.

Patient - nels Henderssen

h

Lives at farm south of Flats town

Occupation farmer

aug 22
1896
	amputation of left leg below the knee
	   foot crushed beyond repair or reconstruction
	   bullet tore through the gastrocnemius and shat
	   tered the tibia into seven pieces, plus fragments.
	   Bullet remained buried in a hunk of tibia, while
	   smaller fragments of fthe of ibula buried
	   throughout the muscle
	     tissue. ligaments full of mud, grime and feces
	   from street and animals.
	   amputation given without patient aware.

aug 25	attending nels at the family farm. no sign of pus or infection at site of amputation. wife Clard seems to understand need for cleaning and sterilization. will leave further instructions ~ speak to Percy about nels farm
aug 28	nels on crutches, learning to walk with only one leg. discusses selling the farm and moving to town with his family, wants to try to plow f irst. debating about bringing out a wooden leg? amputation site tender and bruised, but laceration healing and no internal bleeding. ~ nels says he can still feel his missing leg
sept. 1	removal of old catgut stitches but innent went to be safe

jones

removal of right arm from elbow joint after
riad on 22 august '76.
cut at trochlea and capitulum, leaving both
intact and behind.
dislodge torchlear notch and disposed of ulna
and radius and entire crushed hand.

    patient has refused continuing care after loss of arm.

    i had not known his trade was cooper; his business is now
    closed and effectively lost to him.
    would he prefer to have died?

    four months post operation

    Franklin has lost his work; reports of drunkeness
    notice his wife now often sports bruising

    patient will not speak to me. he says he was "best in Flats town"
    and now has no reason to live.
    can someone - kate? help him find work?

        percy gave franklin work to run the train depot;
        hope it pulls him out of his violence
        last thing percy did before getting ill

july 5   franklin helping to rebuild
1885   general and had many hero
    moments during kate's fiire.
    have found a purpose?

        Mikey o'donnell hire franklin?
        woodwork to sell?

CHAPTER THREE

Jane

July 31, 1883

"This is for...what you call the nervousness."

"A sedative, then."

Esther raises her eyebrows. "A fancy word, that, for removing the trouble of an overeager mind."

"You're saying skullcap can be used to make a nerve tonic."

"Yes," she said, her dark eyes meeting mine warmly. "And to remove a headache."

There's a bang and another on the roof above, before another smattering ensues. We both look up, her with amusement and I with no small amount of guilt as the hammering on the shingles continues with the onslaught of Patrick's unpracticed hand.

The doctor did not forbid me to learn the old ways—the medicinals and remedies of the Lakota, and all that

Esther knows in her long-reaching mind. Doing such a thing anyway while he labors in the last of the summer heat feels like a betrayal. I suppose part of me is doing it to make us on even ground, one betrayal cancelling out another. But he has made it clear he does not approve.

I did not expect him to.

He has always been so open-handed with learning, generous beyond my expectations. What other husband would allow his wife to read the medical texts? To offer her his own experiences and let her take on nursing duties even if she is without such an education? I grant that he is more fair-minded than most, open to new ideas to a fault. But he seems set against using what Esther knows in her bones. And I chafe inside my own skin, an itch that has nothing to do with layers of muslin or the pressure of stays against the soft flesh under my armpits. I've been married before, and spent it in silence, hiding a ravenous hunger for words and knowledge. I refuse to let my curiosity go to waste. The doctor knows what type of woman I was when we married. I hid some things from him before our vows to be sure, but never this piece of my nature. For him to expect, now...

I turn away from the scraggly plant, with its curved stalk and bruised, hat-like flowers on my table to pour corn-meal into a scotch bowl. "So it's a good herb, then. One to have on hand."

"It has always been a woman's herb," Esther says, carefully tying the ends together with twine before bringing it over to hang in the window. "If a woman aches at the time of her bleed, or to purify her if needed."

I glance up at the fresh skullcap, where it twists wetly

next to a much drier bundle of coneflowers. "Will it grow in the garden?"

"No. I found this on the banks of the Flats Basin River, in the low part on the way to the Zalenski farms. It needs both the damp as well as the sun."

"I will write this down, so I do not forget," I say, jotting a note on the paper from Patrick's office and bit of graphite lodged in the pocket my worn yellow calico skirt, attached now to a new bodice and with half the tucks taken out. I glance at her as I pour a bit of the honey from the Brinkley's into the cornmeal as I go back to mixing. "You don't mind?"

"Why else would I share with you, Jane? You are the only one who asks."

There's a knock at the front door, interrupting our discussion.

Esther takes the spoon from me, and I brush the last of the bumpy cornmeal grains onto my apron and head into the dim hallway, leaving her to finish pouring it all into the iron skillet for tonight's meal.

A heavy pounding on the roof signals the arrival of more men—and possibly more mouths to feed this evening—but I am grateful for their help and what it means for Patrick. He whistles every night before bed, and I know it's more than fixing the roof and rebuilding the porch. It's impossible to ignore the slow budding of camaraderie from the least likely of sources.

I expect it to be one of said men, hat in hand, meekly asking to stay to sup. Rusty has, twice now, and one night Hardy the blacksmith apprentice did, too, peppering the doctor with all manner of questions unrelated to roofing.

Marie Salomon is at the door, her babe Garik on her hip, and a large basket balanced on the other forearm.

I swallow my surprise and paste on the old city smile, bland and polite, so she will not see how thrilled I am to see her.

"I came over with Thaddeus," she says, looking at me directly. It is always startling to stare into her eyes. She and I share the same color, though that is where our physical similarities end. Still, it sometimes is like peering into a cloudy mirror.

"We heard the loud hammering," I tell her, opening the screen door.

She does not enter, and instead just hands over the basket, which I nearly drop with the unexpected weight. It takes both of my hands to hoist it back up. She juts her chin toward the ceiling. "Seeing as you've been feeding some of my men."

"It was only Hardy, and only the once," I protest.

"He's a growing boy and eats the same as two men some nights." She nods at the basket. "Berit made the most of it, so you'll know it's good, and I put in some of my own bread."

I poke around the cloth over the food, which gives off the faintest heat. Apples and cinnamon folded into tarts, dumplings, and a bowl of meatballs. "It's too much, Marie."

She shrugs and turns to go. "Well, then."

"Wait. Don't leave quite—"

I step out after her despite myself, forgetting the half-rotted burned-out porch. My entire foot goes clean through, up to my ankle, and I fall to the other knee, creating a loud thud as I do. Both hands splay to catch myself from smacking face-first into the blackened planks as Marie's basket crashes next to me, and I cannot stop myself from crying out, sharp and high.

She turns at once, her eyes wide. "Jane!"

There's a crunchy thud next to me as a clumsy body jumps down. "Mrs. Kinney! You hurt?"

I look up into Hardy's sky-blue eyes and earnest cheeks. He reaches for my arms and tries to pull me out, but my fool boot has become wedged under the board itself, and I can feel my bones straining with the pressure.

"Stop," I tell him, sounding breathless even to my own ears. "It's stuck."

"Hold on, I'm comin'." Patrick's voice is behind and above me, and though it's calm, I can hear the note of panic hidden in it. He climbs the last of the way and inches over on the good porch planks until he can kneel at my side. "You alright, Janie? Any pains?"

"No, I'm only caught under the broken board, just right. I think the shoe is making it worse."

"None of the other sort?"

"Other s...oh." Marie stands over us, close enough to overhear. Her forehead smooths and a small, womanly smile twitches at the corner of her mouth.

Another body lowers itself from the ladder behind me, and then Thaddeus blocks half the sunlight as he looms over us. "What's the trouble?"

"Jane's stuck."

"And I think I ruined all the good vittles your wife just brought over."

Thaddeus's eyebrows go up at the tipped basket. Sauce leaks from it, and the turnovers poke out. "Looks like it'll still be edible."

Marie shoves the baby in Thaddeus's arms, carefully pulls the basket close and starts to rearrange it, her hands sticky with juice from the tumbling meatballs, while Patrick discreetly pulls my skirt up to my knees to see the trouble.

It is strange and disjointed to be caught and held, surrounded by those wishing to help. Even though I feel ridiculous and then some, I also cannot help but feel the gentle, golden glow of this camaraderie. It makes me think that I'm no longer quite the outcast.

"Is everything alright?"

All swing to look at Esther except for me and Patrick, who finally finds the troublesome hook on my boot and pops it from the shard of wood below. I'm glad for Esther's distracting presence, as it means no one sees the flush pouring up my neck as Patrick squeezes the delicate and sensual spot behind my knee as he smooths my skirts and hoists me back to the safe part of the porch.

"I see you're still in town," Marie says, with some careful clearing of her throat, her eyes not leaving where Esther stands behind the screen.

"For a little while. Not too long, I should think," Esther says, the music in her lilt flattened slightly.

Patrick and I exchange a look, silent but pleading, but we both of us know now is not the time to turn to Esther and demand other answers. So much is still so unsettled in Flats Junction. So much feels as though it is unbalanced and wobbly. We do not need to have a domestic discussion in broad view of the Salomons, nor Mrs. Molhurst, who is undoubtedly crouched behind her elderberries and listening without shame.

Thaddeus hands little Garik back to Marie with an unreadable glance and nudges Hardy. "Back up on the roof then, boy." The two clamber back up the bouncing ladder, specks of dried mud and old soot spitting from the bottoms of their soles as they go. Marie hands me the hastily re-packed basket and smiles again.

"It is good news, truly, Jane. I'm glad for you." She includes Patrick in her self-dismissal and walks back east toward the combined smith shops with the gait of a woman half her age. I marvel at the strength of her stride before Patrick touches the back of my hand.

"See if you can get some sense into her." He means Esther. As he follows Thaddeus and Hardy to the roof, I straighten my shoulders and feel the tug of the stays along my sides. They will have to be loosened yet again tomorrow. Esther can help me. Esther can do so much for me, for all of us, if only she would see it.

I walk back into the kitchen in time to see her poke the cornbread with a knife to check if it sponges back or sinks. It's nowhere near ready, and I realize she is hiding herself in my presence in the only way she knows. She is nervous for this, too, this unending discussion that has caused much journeying and heartache, and many circular arguments. She perhaps had not meant to make her plans known so soon or so publicly.

"You have decided," I say, fighting the resignation in my sinew, coupled with frustration that would boil to anger in a heartbeat if I let it. "After all this time. After we—after Kate!—went to Fort Randall to bring you back. To beg you back."

"Things have changed since. Things always change. That is the rhythm of living."

"Not all things."

"All things."

I cannot believe I'm arguing with her again and feel inherently I will lose—this time mayhap for good. Widow Hawks—Esther Davies—Kate's mother has always done as she pleases.

"Patrick will be bereft without you. And so will I. You know this, you needn't hear me say it again, but I will. Until you agree that you have a place here."

"I don't. Not anymore. And why should you wish me to stay? I only bring trouble. You are blind if you say I do not."

There is nothing to say to her with this. Nothing at all.

I stand next to her and take the wooden spoon she spins in her well-worn hands. We stand shoulder to shoulder, looking out the fat back window, where the riotous garden gives way to the wavy grasses, which I now know also shows the invisible line between Brinkley and Svendsen grazing land. And in that quiet moment, I dare to speak of the loss that weighs heaviest between us—the one where we both lost a bed, but she lost everything. The fire that remains a mystery, as long as one does not ask too many questions.

"The...your house burned because—"

"I don't wish to discuss that particular fire. Let us discuss this one, which still threatens you and your home. I am a danger to you and Patrick—to him especially, who has struggled from the first day."

"If Bern Masson truly was the one who started the fire here in this house, it likely had much more to do with the fact that I jilted him, and far less to do with you living in it."

Her shoulder rises, in a gesture that echoes Kate. Do certain movements come with the womb, I wonder? Will my

32

babe—should it live—have lips that tremble with emotion, like Patrick? Or be overtly curious, like us both?

"For now, I plan to stay, but only long enough to teach you what I know. Then I feel it is best I return to my people. I have been apart from them so long. It would do my ears good to listen to my language. To breathe the smell of the cookfires under the sky, and the dry paint on the hides."

I cannot begrudge her these losses or yearnings, and I would be an unkind woman to tell her that my ways are just as comforting. Surely she has gotten used to it over the decades? But it is only one look at her moccasins, and the beads woven into the steel plait down her back, to know that she has never forgotten her roots. Why should she? She has never had to do so—not until recently. It was only after Percy's death that it seems she has lost the ability to straddle both worlds. Not for the first time do I wonder what power he held over the town and its people, and how well he played the strings of a puppeteer.

Maybe someday, I will ask. For now, I will steal more moments and more knowledge from her, if she is so willing to offer it. This discussion did not end with utter finalization, and I feel less worried than I did a moment ago.

"Well, you have also brought this," I turn and point to the last herb splayed on the careworn kitchen table. "What does that do?" The tension in the points of my shoulder blades and the pressure of the ceiling seems to lessen as I move.

She smiles in her gentle strong way and reaches for it. "This is *makȟá čhaŋš'iŋhu*. My husband called it skeleton plant, but some say it is the prairie pink. The whole plant is boiled for children with the runs. And the sap can be chewed for no purpose but distraction."

We get no further, because Patrick bounds into the hallway and kitchen before I realize that there was no more pounding above. I'd been so caught up with convincing Esther to stay that I hadn't realized the sounds outside changed. There are no hammer strokes or stomps on the roof. Instead, there are raised voices—men's voices—at our porch, and my entire body tightens with a new but familiar clench.

His body is still moving when his eyes catch up with what he sees. The result is a strange physical draw-up that twists his torso and cheekbones but leaves his arms and legs looking a bit askew. He rights himself in a moment.

"Someone's come to report of a cow sickness. Seems several of Brinkley's are ill—only one or two were when they came up this spring, but it's been spreadin', and faster."

"But Old Henry doesn't like you to see the livestock. Only Mitch does, and—"

"I'm aware of my standing at the Brinkley farmstead, Jane," the doctor says, his eyes still stuck on the herbs Esther holds. "But it's Svendsen's now, too. The illness has jumped to the next ranch. It's like the black measles – no rhyme or reason to it."

"No one can blame you for the black measles, Pat," Esther says softly.

"They can blame me for not fixin' it," he counters, meeting her gaze straight. His fingers twitch at his side, and then he crosses his arms. "That's what you had me stay for— why you and Percy asked me to live in Flats Junction. To heal and fix and save and cure. I'm not doin' well with that where black measles are concerned, and I'm not lookin' forward to a failure with animals. I've always done well there, at least. And now…"

"Will you go?"

"Not to Brinkley's – unless they ask. Just to Danny's when I can."

"It sounds an awful lot of trouble outside for cows," I say, finally really listening to the staccato of men's voices, rising and falling and gaining in number.

"Well, it's not cows. Not now. Look—I want you to bar the back door and keep watch. I have to go to the General."

"Why?" I don't mean to sound icy, but my tone makes him wince, then narrow his eyes.

"Does my wife need all my comin's and goin's, then? I'm to be tied to the apron string, is that it?"

It is unlike him to push back with fire, but then again, I have not been a questioning wife. It is only...I do not understand Kate. I don't know if I ever will. And I will likely never get over the fact that she had expected to marry Patrick herself and begrudges me my gold wedding band.

"No," I say, low. "I am not asking for that, Patrick."

He doesn't move. He stares at the table, then at the herbs hanging to dry.

Both Esther and I wait, frozen. Patrick's silence fills and stifles the room, the unspoken words hanging with great weight around the corners of the windows and crawling across the ceiling. I can feel the old itchiness, brought on by lack of information and being treated as if I cannot handle facts of any kind. It's a familiar scratch, but one I recall more with Henry, in my first marriage. To shoulder the quiet without complaint is not my usual response to Patrick, but he seems distracted again, watching Esther twist the marsh elder, so it's lime-colored seeds spill into a bowl at her hip.

"Jane. I didn't...I had no idea you were still..."

"Learning?" I ask. "I'll take what knowledge I can get." The challenge in my voice jars him. He pulls his body close, smoothing down the shiny leather of his vest and running a hand through his dark hair.

"Fair," he finally relents, and turns his head toward the rising ire outside. "It's only the Army is marchin' through, coming from the prairie and headin' to the Fort and stoppin' at the General, so the word comes. I have to go there before I see to any cattle. They've lots of wounded, which is risin' fears of the Lakota and even the Crow again." He looks at Esther with apology. "I'm sayin' stay in, so you're safe, least until they're gone."

Esther's mouth tightens, but she only nods and stirs the seeds in her bowl. He heads to go, but then turns back and fixes me with those blue eyes, which do not crinkle merrily at the corners as he narrows them.

"Why, Jane?"

The frustration and anger wins more than anything else, and I draw myself up, conscious of the slight round in my belly as I do, but I keep my palms from the bulge and hold them as fists when I meet his look. I will not bow into silence by yet another husband, made worse as this time it's a man who I love.

"Why did *you* want to learn medicine, Patrick? The why is always the same."

CHAPTER FOUR

Patrick

March 2, 1858

When they had first come to Boston, he and Aunt Brónach had squatted in the garden of another crumbly boardinghouse, so she told him. Now they had peelin' narrow walls, and two hooks on the back of the door. Aunt Brónach believed the space had once been the large pantry of the house before it had been converted over, and the floor and walls of the dingy rented room with swollen ceilings still didn't mask the smells of soiled laundry and decayin' onion skins.

Patrick's best mate Michael sprinted past, and he followed with the rest, the mud and muck sprayin' around knees and oozin' into the cracks of any who had shoes. They were all always racin' after the makeshift school let, which perched on the end of Batterymarch and Broad. Mr. Arrott stood in his shoddy black coat and tattered white collar ringin' a brass bell so all the mothers knew school was out. It sounded tinny and yet still appeared too heavy in his long hands. Mr. Arrott looked a slight one, but he could whip a switch across a bottom like no other and they all knew so. It was a good day if one could get through without the touch of it.

After lessons, most boys had to return home to help mams or family with the little ones so more work could be done. They didn't like to speak of it, to be branded babby watchers, but otherwise many couldn't make ends meet. Anyone with work had to do everythin' to keep it, as there was always someone else waitin' in line to take the job instead, and likely for less wages. Aunt Brónach worked for an Ulsterman called McClure, a ship owner out of Belfast and she was his secretary and housekeeper.

Michael beat him running from school, and Patrick forgave him as was the usual.

"'Bye Paddy!" he yelled, headin' over toward his place. Patrick sometimes wished Michael could stay out to roam the street, but Michael had chores. He always had to watch his younger siblings so his mam could deliver laundry to her customers. Sometimes Patrick helped him manage the little ones, if only for more time with Michael, but not today.

Nothing would keep him from this.

A small kitten burrowed inside the box, and he carefully pulled the animal out and onto the bed. The blank, strip-walled room, with the measly bed, small table and two chairs shrouded itself in grey and dust and shadow for all that it was mid-afternoon. Aunt Brónach kept the dust down and the walls washed, but even she couldn't always keep the floor from dried muck and whirls of debris.

Patrick hadn't slept last night worryin' the thing would make a noise. She was sickly and scrawny, and he didn't know how he was going to feed her, but he'd found her alone and mewlin' on a side of the street yesterday and couldn't leave without tryin' to help. He just didn't know how.

Aunt Brónach would be unhappy about it – she'd say the animal would bring diseases and eat too much.

He tucked the kitten under his jacket – it was not so cold yet and anythin' was better than the stench indoors. Stepping around the overflowin' chamber pot outside the neighbor's door, Patrick paused by Mrs. O'Coffey where she sat outside her daughter's door holding the wee babe. The little one had just nursed and slept in wizened hands. Mrs. O'Coffey coughed, and he heard the jumble of voices inside the room – the old one often tried to stay out of the way of her daughter's brood and the MacClancy family they shared the one room with. Every day, Aunt Brónach reminded him that this would be their fate if Mr. McClure stopped payin', but she always said it with a little smile on her face.

Clamberin' outside, he sidestepped two more chamber pots, a splatter of vomit and barely escaped a fight on the bottom floor. The Carroll brothers liked to talk with their fists, especially if they'd been drinkin' all morning.

"What've you got there, laddie?" Mr. Kilbride leaned over as he spat, his worn perch by the doorway creakin'. Patrick opened his coat a bit, watchin' Mr. Kilbride's spit disappear into the sodden, churned earth.

"Ah, now, there's a sweet thing," Mr. Kilbride crooned. "Y'know, if you run her over three streets, and knock at the third house on the left, you might find Mr. O'Byrne. He were a horse doc back in Ireland, one of them fancied vets out of Dublin school, and I'm sure one animal is nearly like the next in terms of fixin'."

"Thank you," Patrick took off for the animal vet at once, not realizin' truly how far away he would go from his usual haunts. Along the soggy streets he took care to leave his eyes down. Only Irish voices scrambled and called all around, but he'd heard enough stories and saw enough in the yards behind the boardinghouses to know that anyone could be a victim of anythin'. Mean livin' led to a lot of mean-hearted people.

A whole section of the street wrapped with worse stench, clogged from near a hundred chamber pots all emptied out in the same place. Everyone skirted around as best they might, but the drunks waded through as if they couldn't smell it. Past half a dozen wooden shacks piled into the first alley, he saw two boys lyin' almost across the path of passersby. Someone tripped over their legs and cursed, then kicked the lads savagely. They looked about Patrick's age, so he wandered closer instead of inching 'round. With a little jolt, he recognized two of his classmates from last year – two of the big boys who hadn't returned after Christmastide. He and Michael had figured maybe they'd found jobs – somethin' far more important than book learnin'. He peered at their faces. Vomit puddled under Seamus, and Danny looked as though he were at death's door. Helpless wonder seized him, but the soft, constant mewin' of the kitten tucked under his arm kept him from stoppin' to see if they were well. They frightened him, truth be told. He didn't know what to do but stare, and Aunt Brónach always believed it rude to do so.

He crossed over another alley, looking for the third house on the left as Mr. Kilbride had minded.

"Oh-ho! What've we got here, lads?" The mockin' voice barely registered as Patrick was too busy checkin' his step in the street and dodgin' brisk-walkin' adults.

40

"Hey you! Boy!"

A foot planted directly in his way but Patrick saw it too late, trippin' heavily into the muck and puddles of the road. His arms gripped the kitten to protect her instinctively, and his shoulder and half his chin grabbed the brunt of the fall.

"Ooo – ya wee crybabby!" The voice above crooned a nasty sneer as his eyes smarted with the sting. "Well, you've got nothin' really to cry on, now, it's just a wee fall."

He fumbled to get up. He didn't ever know what to say to the big boys; they scared him. He and Michael always made it a game to keep out of their way. Anyone taller was considered a threat and the four boys around Patrick now were no different. The one who had tripped his legs leaned in, and the whiskey was sour on his breath.

"No, I'm sure a small boyo like you hasna run into any real badd'uns afore. Not like us." His chest puffed out, and then quick as he pleased he ripped the kitten from Patrick's arms.

"No!" The cry came out voluntarily.

"Now here's a bit of a laugh for us. Come on, lads, to the dogs!"

They raced off, and Patrick tore after them without thinkin', wishin' he were as fast as Michael.

He had to weave among the adults and brawls, but so did the other boys, so they couldn't run as quick as they might. It still was a struggle to keep up, his chest burnin' and eyes stingin' – he had only wanted to help! He just wanted to care for somethin' for once! Why couldn't this one thing be his? The boys shouted to each other and threw insults over their shoulders at him as they peeled ahead. The words hit his face and ached.

The group skidded ahead and jumped down an alley.

"Alrighty, lads, here's the fun!" The oldest and biggest boy opened up a wooden crate. Somethin' scratched and whined inside. As Patrick pushed closer, one of the lads made a kick in his direction, keeping him at bay.

"I want my animal back," he demanded once more, weakly but too angry to stay silent.

"Oh come off it, ya wee piss, we want a bit o' sport." The leader threw the kitten in. Her tiny head plunged over the side of the crate, immediately followed by a snarled growl, a hiss, then the yowlin' of the cat sliced off. The whole crate shook violently as the other animal inside bit and pounced. It took only a few seconds, but the boys crowded around and yelled, pumpin' fists and laughin'. Reachin' in after the rockin' stopped, the big boy pulled out a small scraggly mutt of a dog, his chops still smeared with blood, his tongue lollin' and lickin' at his fur.

The boy found Patrick's eyes and held up his dog under its narrow belly like a trophy, his face full of mocking triumph.

"What're ye starin' at?" Menace cracked his voice, and Patrick backed up.

"Nothin'."

The boys grinned at each other and started to follow his steps. Before he could spin, a girl a full head taller than them all snagged open the holey curtain in the wall. Behind her, a shrill wail rose, the sound of a babby who was just put down.

"Breccan, damnit, get in here and empty your pockets afore I tell mam and da that ya shirked your chores again," she shrieked, stamping her foot and pointing a finger at one of the lads. "Ye were 'sposed to beg all day!"

"Shut it, *deirfiúr*, or I'll tell 'em you left the wee babby alone and joined me!"

Their exchange gave Patrick all the chance he needed to turn and get a head start on the run, and he half expected to hear them poundin' after.

Two streets up, he took a break and looked back. There was no sign of them. Maybe taking his wee cat was all they had wanted, though he was pretty certain they would have found some other torment if they hadn't been interrupted. The relief of their desertion sunk into his bones.

But now what?

Now he had nothin' to worry on. Nothin' to care for. And…the loss of the wee thing, and the way of her dyin'… he wanted to wail. He wanted…Aunt Brónach.

The buildings sagged, rangin' from squalid to only dilapidated, and despite the press of bodies around, few people looked to be doin' much work. The noise swelled again, the roar of voices and shouts, the mess of legs passin' by and the sweet rot of the street's muck. His toes curled in the mud, and though he knew it was likely going to cost a few whacks, mainly he wanted to find Aunt Brónach. It was against the rules to go to McClure's house except in dire emergency, but this felt like one.

There was another brawl he had to swerve around, the sickly sound of fists hitting live meat, the grunt of sluggish male effort as two groups of men grappled. On the sidelines, one slight boy and three women colored with bright face paint and wearin' a few too few clothes for the chilly fall day watched. They all drank pale colored whiskey from a shared bottle.

Rickety wood shacks, crammed together with nothin' but curtains for privacy between them were crowded along one building wall. Most were empty save for the children left behind while their folks went out drinkin' or workin', except one room held a man and woman bouncin' on each other and breathin' funny.

"Make way! Make way for th' doc! *Dhéanamh ar bhealach*! Move or I'll run ya over! *Bogadh*!"

People pushed out of the way, trying to move before hooves came in their direction. A light cab behind a pair of blacks shifted and slid along choppy ruts and deep puddled dips in the street. As it flew by, Patrick saw a small, round man holding onto his cap with one hand, and the other braced his body from tossin' as his driver urged the horses ahead only to yank them up outside a tavern. The little man jumped out with a battered black leather case and trotted inside the tavern. People immediately crowded the leaded glass, pushin' and peerin'. Patrick bent his head under a stained sleeve and poked an eye over the pub's window ledge. Inside, a man laid out on a long table, moanin' and groanin', with a large puddle of blood under him. The little doctor began an exam at once, pushing his fingers into a wound on the head and then quickly grabbing what looked to be a needle and thread. Someone above Patrick said, "Aw, *ag fuck an dochtúir*!" and lewd laughter rose in response. Someone else spit on the window and rubbed to see the operation better, and Patrick ducked back out before any more spittle could land on him.

McClure's was off Batterymarch and High Street: the closest building he could get to the wharves. The closer Patrick walked, the more he smelled the sea. A thick salt taste saturated the air and weighed down the breeze. He didn't mind it but disliked the fishy vomit that lined the sidewalks off the pubs nearby.

Aunt Brónach had always said he would know the proper building by the green paint on the corner, and sure enough, he saw the peelin' wooden decorative pillars straight away. Above the foggy glass windows and faux wood arches, red brick went up three more stories with windows packed tightly along all sides. Many were propped open, with voices callin' to the street or inside, and right above him. A woman reeled in clothes on a line across High Street, her wrinkled hands graspin' mottled socks.

As he opened the building door, a man heaved against it from the other side.

"No ye dinna think so, ye scoundrel! There's proper businessmen what in here an' I don't allow lads free runnin' th' halls. Ye might disrupt business, ye ken?"

He wasn't a child of the slums for nothin'. "Please, sir, please. Me auntie works here—Aunt Brónach. She works for Mr. McClure, the ship man."

"Aunt Brónach? Ach, ye mean sweet Bonnie?"

Bonnie? Patrick didn't know if the Scotsman meant the right woman, but the door quickly opened. The man was broad and squat at the same time, givin' the impression of a barrel with legs stickin' out from under. A beard, shot with early white and the remnants of the past few days lunch spread out over his chest, and small blue eyes puckered from under a dusty brown cap pulled low.

"Bonnie Kinney is yer auntie then, laddie?" For all his shortness, his voice boomed, and his arms crossed as he blocked the way in.

Patrick nodded, starin' up the massive belly roundness.

"Well, speak up, then, what be yer name?"

"Pat—Patrick Kinney, sir," he said, and his voice sounded squeaky. "Aunt Brónach is my great aunt, actually, on my father's side, at that. She's the youngest sister of his da, Carbry Kinney, born two years after me own da."

Suddenly, the doorman laughed loudly, and held up a hand. "Ach, I dinna need yer whole family history, laddie. I ken ye're Bonnie's boy – she said ye might come if ever there be trouble." He leaned down, mirth gone, and looked Patrick straight in the eye. "All be a'right, Paddy? I dinna ken if Bonnie will be able t' see ye straight away."

"I can wait."

"A'right, then, in ye come and up ye go." He ushered Patrick in and slammed the heavy door shut. The change from the outside to the inside of the place was startlin'. Even though the day was overcast and drippy, the relative quiet and oppressive shadows inside were a stark contrast, with the outside drafts still comin' from the chinks in the windows. He went up the stairs alone, feelin' relieved, but also just a little silly. In the safety of the big building, and with a friendly face to greet him, Patrick almost paused midway up the stairs. Maybe he was fine, after all… But the thought of bravin' the streets again alone was too much.

A small iron plate nailed on the center of the door said *McClure Shipping & Co.* Inside, there was a rustle of paper, and then his auntie's voice, though he couldn't make out what she said. The door was not completely shut, and he edged a finger along the seam, nervous to knock and make a sound echo along the deserted dusty hallway.

"Bonnie lass, it's not as though the paperwork matters." Patrick heard a gruff, heavily accented brogue drag, but the sound rang hollow. There was a dry cough and a sniff.

"Ye know as well as me that my name be Irish, so we'll be doubly checked for smuggled Irish bodies."

Patrick peeled a fingernail into the crack, and slowly pried open the door to the office, but it was empty. A wooden desk squatted in the center of the room, chipped and scratched, but covered in important looking lists and documents. He immediately recognized his auntie's handwriting even from a distance, long ago wrought out by the teacher at the hedge school back in Ireland, along with the stories of how her knuckles had smarted from the smacks of the stick. The half-light filtered watery and speckled through the murky leaded glass window, and there was no dust on the small lamps around the space or on the sideboard where a small mean bottle of dark liquor had a place of honor, no doubt for any of Mr. McClure's special clients.

No rug softened the floor, and the high ceilings created heightened sound, so when he heard his auntie's voice it seemed to jump into all the corners of the space – dismembered and eerie.

"Andy, you can't just leave them there."

"What do ye want me to do, lassie? I don't want to lose what I've built. They're watchin' for immigrants harder than ever, an' I lose half a profit when I fill the ships with people – an' then pay the fees and bribes at the harbors both ways." The Ulsterman's accent was a mix of Scottish and Irish. He sounded tired but determined.

"I still say you—" His auntie cut short when Patrick poked his head around the corner. She stood facing the thin wood door that separated the two spaces, and had clean dishes piled precariously on the narrow trestle behind her. Mr. McClure's back was to Patrick, so he could see Mr.

McClure's thinning black and steel hair, smoothed to hide the balding spot on the back of his head. And McClure's hand was on Aunt Brónach's waist.

"Patrick?" Aunt Brónach's eyes widened, and her lips went skinny as she slid away from Mr. McClure. "What are you doin' here? Is somethin' terribly wrong?"

He could tell by the shake of her hands that she was upset, but he didn't know if it was his appearance or her argument with Mr. McClure. Was she in trouble? Was Mr. McClure angry? Worry tumbled into Patrick. Aunt Brónach couldn't lose her job. The idea filled him with a learned dread.

Mr. McClure swung around. His eyes widened too, and then his lined face collapsed on itself as he smiled, and his growly voice grew a notch higher.

"Ach! Now this is your nephew, is that so, Bonnie?" He bent down and shook Patrick's hand, pumpin' it a few times. "Finally I get to meet ye, boyo! About time!"

"He's my great-nephew," Aunt Brónach corrected. "Youngest son of my oldest nephew."

Mr. McClure inclined his head back to acknowledge her, but his eyes were still on Patrick. He was infectiously jovial, not at all like the rigid, particular employer Aunt Brónach spoke of at home.

"So ye say, just a mite specific she is," he winked as if sharin' a joke. He let go and stood straight, his portly frame supported by a broad chest and wide hips.

"So, then, laddie, what can we do for ye?"

"I..." Patrick's eyes darted to Aunt Brónach, who mimicked Mr. McClure's stance, her arms crossed tightly over her bosom.

"Well, out with it, Patrick," she burst. "Is it somethin' of an emergency that you come burstin' in on us? For heaven's sake!"

"Lay easy on the lad, Bonnie," Mr. McClure put a hand on her arm. Aunt Brónach jolted back and continued to pin Patrick with her eyeballs.

"Now, then, boyo, be ye hurt?" Mr. McClure bent down again. His face was shiny and his eyes a soft hazel.

Patrick shook his head, glanced at Aunt Brónach, and then the whole day's story came spillin' out while he kept his eyes on muddy bare feet.

"Did ye cry, boyo?" Mr. McClure asked at the end.

"Only a little, when I fell."

"Then ye won a battle there. Those big boys are trouble if they're not schoolin' or workin' and if they were tippin' whiskey it's worse. And likely they got shoved around by some mick or other and were lookin' to take their anger off."

Finally, Aunt Brónach jumped in. "And just when were you goin' to tell me of the kitten?"

"Bonnie!" Mr. McClure straightened up and turned to face her. "Take a bit of pity."

She burst. "I'm so sorry he's bothered you!" She looked nearly tearful, which was a strange thing. "He—he didn't even *knock*!"

"I'm sorry Aunt Brónach," he said. "I won't come again – not unless the house is burnin' down or so."

Patrick's apology didn't seem to change her. Mr. McClure sighed, and then took the plate off the sideboard with the tea's leftovers. Even though it looked to be just crusts of whatever Aunt Brónach had made him, it seemed a feast.

"Here ye go, Paddy. Set yourself in the office and have a bite while your auntie and I finish up a bit for the day. Just mind ye don't touch the paperwork."

"No sir!" He plunked down on the dusty floorboards and devoured the edges of a rye loaf, boiled potatoes seasoned with a bit of salt, and some sweetly sour kraut. It was a spread of epic imaginin' so he tried to eat slowly and failed. Through the door, he heard Mr. McClure. He didn't do a thing to lower his voice.

"Jesus, Mary and Joseph, Bonnie! Why didn't ye tell me you can't even keep the boy in shoes?"

His aunt's response was quiet, muffled.

"It's not an excuse!" Mr. McClure's boomin' lilt dropped. Patrick leaned back against the desk and closed his eyes, pretending that the food completely filled him up.

And it did, nearly.

As the afternoon went on, it felt like forever to sit and wait for his auntie to finish work, and every time he fidgeted, Aunt Brónach cleared her throat and shot a steely glare. Mr. McClure shook his head a little at her when she did her iron eye, but she paid him no mind at first. It was only after he tutted several times that she rounded on him.

"He's my nephew, Mr. McClure. It's my job to see he behaves properly as so."

"Ye can't begrudge him for breathin', Bonnie" he said, without a bit of rancor in his voice. "Besides, it's nearly time for the evenin' meal. He can help you."

She stopped moving for a moment and raised her eyebrows, as if she disbelieved Patrick would be capable of such an activity, then nodded.

"Patrick, please help me in the kitchen."

50

He stood, grateful to be relieved of the corner confinement. Had he known he'd have been stuck inside and silent he might have reconsidered comin'.

As he moved to the kitchen, a booming knock hit and before Mr. McClure could even rise to answer, the beefy Scotsman from the front door poked his head around.

"So, then, Andy, did the laddie find his auntie?" the doorman's voice filled the whole space.

"He did, MacLaren – thank ye," Mr. McClure smiled at the man, and caught Aunt Brónach's eye with the briefest of winks as she paused between the two rooms. "Kenny, you've come at a good time. Bonnie's just about to put on supper."

The Scotsman came in without another prompt, rubbed his massive stomach and blinked. "Ach, o' course! It be that time again, eh? Well, now, I wouldna want ta put ye out."

"No, no," Mr. McClure pulled up a chair and indicated it. "You're welcome to it, as ye always are. In fact, we'll all eat."

Patrick followed Aunt Brónach into the small kitchen, which was dark and crowded in the far space. The leaded glass window steamed up where the bed was pressed against the wall near it. Aunt Brónach handed over drippin' plates and nodded at a damp towel nearby for the dryin'. It was supposed to be women's work, but he knew not to argue. Even though Aunt Brónach had her eyes on the bin of suds, she watched to ensure he wiped the tin well before stacking the plates together. But he couldn't take his own eyes off the next feast. It was unfathomable to have so much good food in one day. Breakfast was always leftovers from the day before – cold and half hardened in the bottom of the iron skillet because there wasn't time to fully heat it on the community stove downstairs. It was all Patrick ever had for lunch. Aunt Brónach never ate with Patrick at night – she ate instead with Mr. McClure and brought the leftovers home for him and Michael's family. It was part of her pay. And she also refused to eat with everyone else at home on the weekends. She said that it was that she did not enjoy dinin' with so many people at once – most were always ill. It crushed her appetite. In the spring and summer, they could hand off a bit of change or bread leftover from Mr. McClure's to whoever was growin' a narrow garden plot in the makeshift shack piles in the original gardens and get somethin' fresh in return, which she'd mix up in their little room for her and Patrick alone.

Aunt Brónach poured water into a big cast iron kettle on the stove, and shoved it over so the deep inset bottom fit just inside, hiding the small peg legs. As the steam began to filter, she took two lobsters out of a box on the floor and dumped them in. The white mist started to rise from the spider and the screech was both familiar and excitin'. Lobster was trash food, but still tasty, and by the look of the box, there was plenty enough to eat. Soon six lobsters lined up on the board, seared red and ready for choppin'.

"Make the tea, please, Patrick," she said in a low voice.

As he took the box of tea, he thought to ask, "Why do they call you Bonnie?"

She paused for a long moment, stirrin' the soup.

"It is a good American version of my name," she said slowly, and then waved her free hand to indicate he should not be idle while they talked. He took a large spoon of tea leaves out and poured them into the teakettle. The water was so hot that it steamed the underside of his wrist.

"Should I call you that, then?" he wondered. "We are American, after all."

She gave a little smile. "We are that, aye, Patrick."

With her soft eyes, Patrick suddenly felt as though he had been sent to a heavenly respite. There were so few drafts in the space, and the stove had everything heated so beautifully, and the smell of warm, fresh soup and bread was enough to make any lad feel as though he could be nowhere better.

"Gentlemen," Aunt Brónach approached the door between the rooms and nodded. "The food is set and hot if you're ready."

"Of course we are!" Mr. MacLaren bounced to his feet while Mr. McClure came at a leisurely pace. Patrick sat across from Mr. MacLaren and he winked briefly before they began.

Mr. MacLaren especially ate with gusto and made many loud appreciations for the food. "Ye ken more ways t' work a lobster than any woman I've ever met," he praised. "One might believe it's almost a proper thing to eat."

"Well, they are plentiful and inexpensive," she murmured.

"And what of your wee nephew then?" Mr. MacLaren swung his wide head. There were bread crumbles in his beard. "Does he appreciate his auntie's cookin'?"

"Most certain, sir," Patrick said. "I like it even more, when it's hot like this."

"Patrick!" Aunt Brónach scolded.

Mr. McClure put out a hand halfway across the table. "He's only speakin' a truth, Bonnie. There's no offense."

Her face blistered bright red – anger and even embarrassment written across her cheeks, and Patrick kept his head down the rest of the meal, even as the conversation turned to his story of the kitten, and then beyond – to the doctors, like Doc O'Byrne—the one Patrick hadn't found in time.

"Quacks, th' lot o' 'em," Mr. MacLaren said forcefully. "Hangin' shingles at every turn! Why th' other day, I seen one out by the washerwoman! The laundry ladies is sayin' they're medicinals. There's no order to it."

"There's plenty of order to their work," Mr. McClure said. "That is, if you stay in your place."

"Eh?"

"Well, from what my own physician tells me, an allopath man must never speak to a homeopath, and a hospital man thinks he's above them all."

"So they fight amongst theirselves. Is that our trouble?"

"It can be," Mr. McClure said mildly, and winked at Patrick. "Some say if yer doc is a homeopath, an' yer best friend sees a hospital doc, th' two of you can't be friends at all, nor be seen together. A doc makes th' rules on yer business an' more."

"It sounds rather ridiculous," Aunt Brónach said. "And all this over something that's not even a sound profession. Pass the bread 'round again, Patrick."

He did, grabbin' an extra for himself, and kept listenin'.

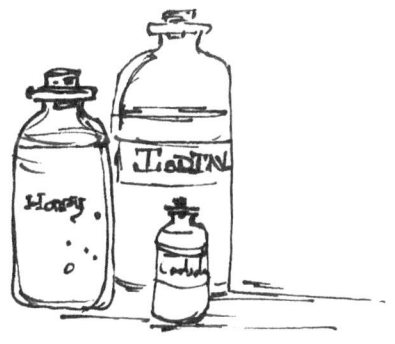

CHAPTER FIVE

Jane

July 31, 1883

Patrick does not come home for lunch, so instead I feed Thaddeus Salomon his wife and mother-in-law's own vittles. Hardy, Thaddeus' apprentice, grows so fast these days that he might be as tall as his master. He shovels food in his mouth so fast I keep waiting for him to choke instead of swallow.

Thaddeus notices the rush as well and smacks the back of his spoon on Hardy's knuckles. "Not so fast, boy, or you'll forget to breathe."

Hardy slows down, which gives me time to slide another slice of Marie's bread onto his plate without fear of getting stabbed by his fork. Thaddeus pours himself another cup of coffee, and then, after a beat, does so for me as well without meeting my eyes. The act itself is familiar and speaks of friendship and intimacy. Yet it feels strange coming from the smith, who has only recently shown his approval of Patrick after years of disdain and foul luck between them.

Esther moves about quietly, making a plate up for herself around us before taking a seat next to me. Hardy doesn't notice, but Thaddeus pauses and frowns. I frown back at him which feels impolite given he is helping us with our porch and front roof, but who is he to judge who eats at my table? Sometimes I get quite exhausted with the stubbornness and lack of tolerance in the west. It was supposed to be much easier here, to blend in and make a new life. I myself believed the same when I first came to the Territories. One would think a place made by menfolk, who are in general less observant of nuances than women are, would be more keen for open-mindedness. But it is not so. Perhaps men are just as particular as women and just don't let on they are so picky. Or perhaps it is the arrival of more women and wives in the west that has changed the patterns. Would it be our prejudices, doled out with catty words and sidelong glances that have renewed the splitting of society? I dislike thinking we would be so harsh on one another.

I give one of those side glances to Esther, who eats with her head down, and am reminded why she is here in my house. Her own daughter shuns her. Maybe women might be to blame for societal rifts – more than we might like to admit. I don't like the idea, but credit must be given if it is due. And to repair it? I suppose if it partially be the fault of the womenfolk, it is up to us to change the ways of it.

Pushing away my plate, I stand with resolution, the hardened leather of my soles clicking on the worn boards under the table.

"You don't like it?" Thaddeus looks from the uneaten food and my face. "But it's not Marya's cooking."

"The food's delicious. It's not that," I say, wincing and rubbing the side of my hip bones with two fingers. I've forgotten the twinges of the first months of pregnancy, and how the womb seems to stretch the width of the pelvis to settle firmly in its cradle.

Thaddeus's eyes follow my movements, but he only grabs his coffee and drinks with his gaze now locked the lip of the tin cup.

"I should go see what's holding Patrick," I tell him, and spare a look in Esther's direction. She eats with a measured pace, not stopping even though I have. "He's missed lunch and might be hungry."

"He's busy," Thaddeus says.

"I'm sure."

"No – busy as a doc can be when a passel of soldiers arrives."

"What? Already?"

"Saw them from the roof right before you called us in to eat. Looks like a whole platoon if I'm any judge. They came down from the northeast, walking on foot and slowly, too."

"So many are wounded!" Hardy finally finds space between bites to speak. "I saw at least a dozen stretchers! You could even hear one or two of them scream if they were bumped too hard. It must be terrible bad."

I refuse to look at Esther for fear she will take my glance as an accusation. Was it her people who did this? They shouldn't be off the reservation now – not without fear of government response. But I know she worries about them – their lack of clothing, of food, of their way of life. It is only natural for the young men to get restless and angry. It is not their way to sit still. I may be a woman born and raised in Massachusetts, but I am not so blinded by my own ways that I cannot understand there are others who have lived—and crave to live—in the way they have always done so.

"He may need help," I say, moving to the pantry to remove my cooking apron and putting on a larger one that better protects more of my dress. It is new for me, and one of the few things in my wardrobe I have sewn myself, as it is a simple design made from old flour sacks. Next to the cone of brown sugar on the middle shelf is another new item that I have only just completed: a rolled bundle in oiled leather filled with bandages and other small necessities Patrick told me to have on hand as a sort of simple nursing kit. Within it is a tiny vial of precious iodine just in case, a bar of home-made soap, and also a tincture of comfrey which is my own addition.

When I turn back to the kitchen, Hardy stands up.

"I'll go with you, Mrs. Kinney."

"No, you won't," Thaddeus counters, places a hand on the boy's shoulder and bodily shoves him back to the bench. "Finish your vittles and then we'll do as much as we can before the sun sets."

"But I want to…I want to see what the doc does. Maybe he'll do another surgery!"

"Why watch the sawbones? We all know he's good with a knife."

Thaddeus's slander makes me wince, but I suppose old habits and names are difficult to forget. Sometimes I want to shake the smith and remind him that Patrick saved Marie's life—that he owes my husband some respect. But then I think of how much Thaddeus has softened—in his own gruff way—toward us, and I must remember to be thankful for even the small graces.

Hardy shoots a frustrated glare at the blacksmith but returns to eating—this time half-heartedly.

Thaddeus now stands instead and rakes his fingers through his dark beard. "It'll be me to take you down to the General." He juts his chin at my stomach. "Wouldn't be right for you to walk alone if you're not…feeling yourself."

"Thank you kindly, but no need." I try not to smile at this example of Thaddeus's softening. "If the doctor is there, I'm sure it will be safe. And I wish to stop in to your own home—see how Kaspar is faring."

Thaddeus shrinks with the mention of his oldest son. "That would be…it's appreciated. We are not sure always if we're applying the medication right. And the pain…if there's something for the pain." His grey eyes meet mine straight on, and the agony there makes shock swirl in my chest. The man is frightened or worried beyond the pale – that much is suddenly clear.

"Is it very bad?" I ask gently.

Thaddeus glowers at his bread and mashes on honey with a fist so tight his scarred knuckles mottle white and pale pink.

"Sometimes…he can't stand it," Hardy says softly. "It's like he's going mad."

It was what we feared with his injury, and I am not surprised by this report – only that it has taken this many days for anyone in the Salomon house to say something. How can that young boy manage such a terrible large burn on his arm without the terrible pain making him scream? I wonder if Marie and Thaddeus blame Kate for it – Kaspar had caught a red-hot timber as Kate's General store burned and is paying the price for his good deed. Kate's store is saved, but his arm may not be. And then where will we be? With another Franklin Jones – a young man in his prime with a lost limb and lost trade, drowning in whiskey?

"I'll stop in after I check on Doctor Kinney," I promise. Thaddeus grunts in response and continues munching on the crispy end of his wife's loaf of bread.

I grab the basket Marie had sent along with the food stuffs, as well as the now-empty crocks to return to her and her mother-in-law. As I reach the screen door and squint into the buttery afternoon sunlight, a touch on my sleeve stops me from pushing through.

It's Esther, moving with the same stealth and soft leather as always. She presses something into my hand, soft and smooth. "For the pain."

"Which kind?"

There is one small crease in the corner of her eyes and two deep ones on each side of her lips when she smiles. "You're learning to ask the right questions."

The corner of my mouth lifts as I try not to grin at her praise—rarely given and all the more thrilling because of it. I open my fingers to stare at the small leather pouch. It's squishy inside, a crinkle and rustle signifying the herbs tucked inside.

"Marie won't go for a talisman," I remind Esther. "She barely tolerates Patrick's usual type of medication, and this is only s—." I stop hard on the next word. *Superstition.* I was about to betray my ill-conceived notions of the Lakota, which I have long since realized are often far from the truth. Half of the time it sounds just that – superstition and old guesses – but I have learned enough that even if Esther and her people do not use Patrick's scientific words, many of their ways are just as effective. Sometimes better. And sometimes I wonder if that's why Patrick won't hear of it. He's won his medical license too dearly to think it unusable.

"It's not a bundle," she says. "It's a tea. The skull-cap again, in a small amount. And *piŋkpá hiŋšmá*—prairie smoke—for a salve. I wish they would let me see the burn. There are other plants to put on the skin. You will look, won't you? And tell me how it shows?"

The idea of peeling back the bandages on Kaspar's oozing arm brings sour bile to the corners of my jaw, tightening it and yet making me wish to spit and gag. I am the doctor's nurse as well as his wife, though, and how else will I learn? I nod, a promise married to the action, and head out, taking care to skirt around the last charred pieces of the porch and stair.

"Jane!" she calls. "Don't forget – do not use the comfrey! Not unless you are sure!"

Sure. Unless I am sure. She says it with such trust, as if I will ever know surety again! I feel my life has been one set of uncertainties for years – ever since Henry Weber died of cancer and left me once again to figure out a path for myself. I believe the only thing I have since been certain of is my marriage to Patrick, and even that is less easy than my first one. With Henry I at least understood my role in society and in his house and knew what he expected of a wife and how to fulfill that role, even if I chafed and rebelled against it as time when on. There was comfort in some of the mundane. Yet I must admit that my life in Flats Junction is worth the constant upheaval, if only because it means I might create my own path. Doing so without the full support of a husband is not something new.

I set out at a brisk pace from the front path, dodging the two youngest Fawcett boys as they run in the center of the street playing hoop and stick. Sadie waves from her backyard. She carries a teapot and two cups into the little summer house behind the big Fawcett home. Through the smudged windows of the little structure, Helena Salomon bends over cascading deep blue satin and a stack of creased papers. There's a part of me that desperately wants the new seamstress of Flats Junction to make me up a new dress with the patterns Helena brought back from out east. Her story is one no one seems to know, though there's something to do with Kate Davies from what little has been said around town on the matter. None of the women are inclined to gossip overmuch, being too afraid of Lara and Sadie to protest any improperness of the young woman traveling east and back unchaperoned. And frankly, most of the women cannot wait for a chance to afford a beautiful dress for Sunday church. But who am I to fool? Patrick and I cannot afford such frivolous things. A doctor's wife should stay to practical fabrics—especially one who wishes to be more nurse than anything else.

Usually Nancy, the postmistress, sits on the front stoop of the post office sorting anything remaining from the previous mail sack to allow her to stop and gossip with anyone passing by, but today she's riveted to the edge of her seat and doesn't even glance as I crunch past on the dusty main road. But when I follow her gaze, I stop short at the edge of Wagon Street and stare, too.

A mess of army men stand about Kate's General store, where it's mostly built, but not finished, the yellow of new planks nailed tightly to old grey ones. The porch is on, but not the overhang, so the men mill under the sun and peer through the square left for a coming pane of glass to comment on Horeb and Gil's game of checkers and share the spit can with Horeb himself. They're all dusty, with dirt crusted boots and torn pant hems. Many sleeves are ripped and sooty, day-old bandages wrap many a limb. The stench of urine and of coppery blood turned old and more like iron mix with coughs and rumbling voices, tossed hats and the clink of weapons. Several of the men wander off in twos and threes towards Yves Gardiner's make-shift tent—the man and his posse have left out ostentatious crocks of what can only be whiskey. Where has that come from? A few others have found Matt Winters's mess hall and several lead horses the long way around to Rusty's livery. There are so many men, and most look rough and unkept. I'm certain much of it has to do with their past skirmishes and long hike to Flats Junction.

I look about for Patrick in the passel of bodies but cannot see him. Instead, I notice Kate flying around with pins dripping from her shiny black hair and the bright yellow of her plaid setting off the natural rouge of her lips. She has snowy bandages under one arm and a battered army canteen in another.

Tightness binds my chest, and I crush Marie's basket to my hip so tightly before I realize I've dented the handle. What is Kate doing? Acting the nurse? This is my role. My job.

My husband.

I shake out the hot ugliness festering in my gut as I stride toward Kate. My first instinct is to rip the bandages out of her hand and chuck the water at her head, but that will only cause more trouble when it's clear these men need help if they will make it the last ten miles to Fort Randall.

I walk up to the nearest injured soldier. He is suspended on a litter strapped between two mules.

"Sir," I say, ignoring Kate's nearness and pretending as if I have not seen her. "Have you seen the doctor yet?"

"He will now." My husband appears, ghost-like and covered in a fine layer of dust, on the others side of the mule.

I try not to smile at him – imagine looking pleased now – and nod. He has no such qualms and grins at me, quick and light, before turning serious eyes on the man.

"Sergeant. How're you feelin'?"

"Damn awful. These pack animals stink. Give me a horse," the man grunts. His eyes roll to me, and the way he holds his neck to do so looks all wrong. "How do, ma'am."

"What's this contraption?" I ask him, hoping to offer some distraction while Patrick beings a gingerly check on the man's body.

"Some lad once heard an old army doc say the donkeys take smaller steps so as to make the ride easier like," he says, wincing every time Patrick shifts him slightly. "I'm strapped in, see, so's not to roll off during travel, but my muscles sure are cramped up."

The mules shift slightly from foot to foot, and the sergeant's forehead pales. His lips go white on the edges.

"Was the journey here difficult since the…since you were all injured? You were able to sleep a little, I hope?" I meet Patrick's eyes as he finishes his exam. He gives a small shake of his head, and frowns.

"Sleep?" the sergeant chortles, then winces. "Oh no. There's the animals tripping along at a right jog and bounce pace, see, and one of the boys got clipped in the face by the rear mule. And then the other day I got rolled off when we hit a rocky part. Oh, and Johnson nearly washed away when we forded the river."

Patrick maneuvers around the donkeys to get in front of the man's face. He seems stiff even to follow the doctor's movements.

"Were you hit?"

"No, fell bad, that's all, doc."

"You've a broken back, or a small fracture at the least," Patrick says calmly. "I've no way to tell if your spine is beyond repair without getting' you down and keepin' you here. You've movement in your feet and toes, so that's well enough. If you'd like to stay on in Flats Junction while I watch things, we can find you a place."

"I need to get to the fort. I'm certain there'll be a doc there who can do the same, if it's all the same to you," the sergeant says.

Patrick nods, and turns away, pulling me along with a touch to my elbow.

"Is there a doctor at Fort Randall?" I ask, wondering how I have not thought to do so before.

"Not that I'm aware of…at least. If there is a doctor, it's not a well-trained one."

I look around, feeling overwhelmed by the sheer number of male bodies sprawled about. Several are smoking pipes, adding additional blue-grey haze to the fluffy curls of dust from extra horses, donkeys and feet all congregating in one area.

"What's the worst of it, Pat?" I try not to gape open-mouthed at another contraption, this one a wooden bed with a wired cage suspended from the side of one of the war horses. The litter carries a man with a face near ripped off from cheek to jaw. The familiar bile rises up again and pools under my tongue.

"It's mostly scrapes, but there are some bullet wounds. The boys coming off the reservation to harry our wagons have completely given up on arrows – it's all guns. The worst of it is they use cylindrical bullets instead of the Army's standard balls. Those long things cause a…create awful tissue damage."

Kate sails across my line of sight once more. This time, she carries a bucket of water and offers it to several of the mules.

"What are you going to do?"

"I'd like to amputate that hand," Patrick says, pointing to a man sitting on the General's front stairs with a wrapped stump looking as if it is already blown off to bits. "It'll turn rancid if it hasn't already."

"Do you have the carbolic acid?"

"Yes, in the spray apparatus." He pats the worn leather bag, "and Kate found an old bottle of iodine."

"Did she?" I narrow my eyes at Kate's back, biting the sour words hanging on the edge of my mouth. "Well, the carbolic will be best for that hand. Unless you have any way to knock him out, he won't let you amputate. And you shouldn't, Patrick. It's already…"

He half-turns to look at me, and the argument from earlier in the kitchen suddenly simmers there, tangible and malignant between us. "Yes, I know. I'm already known for my preference to take a saw or knife. But sometimes it's the only way."

66

"Then let the other doctor – the one at Fort Randall – take the blame this time."

"Jane. You know me better than that. I have to help where I can."

"Sometimes you ought to help yourself," I mutter, and he goes stiff beside me. I inhale, and then wish I hadn't, as the stench of feces has added to the many extra smells. "If he will let you take it, then I suppose you must. Otherwise, be liberal with the acid so maggots don't start."

"It'll sting somethin' fierce. But you're right. A fine plan, Nurse Kinney." He doesn't soften, but his words are not sharp. And the title is new and meant with affection even under the frustration.

Kate strides toward us, looking almost delighted with the chaos. I suddenly realize that I see her most happy when she's surrounded by a maelstrom of drama, and she the calm center. She does not seem to even hear the cacophony of an entire company of men around her. Her liquid eyes are only on Patrick and me, and she parts through the blue wool uniforms as if they cannot touch her.

I pull my husband's attention to myself, though a part of me is embarrassed by my pettiness. Why can I not shut it off? "You shouldn't let them take the injured further in the litters like the one on the horse," I say. "It'll only get worse for them as they go."

"I was just going to say the same," Kate says, placing her body in such a way that her shoulder points at my throat and her chest faces Patrick directly. "They should be carried more carefully. And I'm surprising myself by saying this, but my mother's people have the way of it. A travois would be more comfortable."

I'm at once cut from the conversation. Patrick's eyes light up with the idea, and I'm too proud to ask Kate what she means.

"Doc, have you seen to the worst of them?" A narrow man with a belly too big for his lean hips and small muscles appears at Patrick's side. "We leave tomorrow first light, so's if there's no more, we'll get to the mess."

"Sergeant Major," Patrick turns. How does he know these ranks so easily? "Just the man to see. We're discussin' the best way to finish your journey – for your wounded."

"What's that?"

"A travois. The injured would ride behind the horses – like a pole drag. Safer for people and beasts. If you dismantle your current litters, we could net together some of the old fabric and straps and create a sort of web."

"You know how to make these things?"

"Oh, aye." Patrick hesitates a fraction too long, and his glance strays to Kate. The sergeant major pulls himself up, yanking on a frayed leather belt so it comes up to his navel and sticks. His eyes narrow.

"Seen this done, have you. By what? Her?" He pushes out his lower jaw in Kate's direction, then spits at the dirt to the side of her feet.

Kate's face is stone, and though I struggle through constant conflicting feelings where she is concerned—not the least of which is linked to the past moments in the bedroom that she and my husband share—I cannot help but feel anger. She has provided his men with fresh linen and water, and likely more. And now? Suddenly now he sees her and notes the slant of her eyes and the curve of her nose and her notions are not enough?

The sergeant major shakes his head. "No, man. We won't do nothing those savages do. No siree. The boys can manage on good, solid American litters. I thank you, doc."

He turns off and shouts about finding ale. A large group take off west to the swinging signs of The Golden Nail and, further up and over to First Street, the Prime Inn.

Kate watches the group go, and how several of them stop at Yves's. Coins glint in the afternoon sunlight as the posse likely asks ridiculous fees for the use of their alcohol stores. I turn to Kate, preparing to swallow my rancor and offer her a kinder word, but she spins away before I can make a sound and disappears up the General's stairs. I want to shout after her, my gentleness gone with her abruptness. It's me who's been wronged now, not her. For all her anger at my marriage to Patrick, now it's me who has a right to be cross. Its only...I cannot seem to completely let go of my cultivated Boston ways to truly shout at her in public.

"He'll end up killin' some of his own men," Patrick says, his gaze locked on the sergeant major's skeletal backside. "They can't travel so rough, some of them. Not in their condition."

"Saints preserve them," I breathe, feeling Patrick's distress in my bones. His voice aches with the annoyance and frustration of being unable to fix and cure, and I can only imagine how desperately he wishes to get his hands on some of the injured bodies and hold them down until they are well. "But – do you wish to see to the ones still about?" I nod in the direction of some of the young army men, including the one with the mauled hand.

Patrick sighs, and then seems to see me – truly see me – and snaps upright. "Jane. Let's get you back home. There's nothin' you can do now."

"If you're going to amputate—."

"You said yourself it's a poor notion, and that's assumin' the boy will let me. Come – I'll get you as far as Fawcett's so you're safe."

"I'm off to Marie's, actually," I say, shaking the basket. "And if she'll allow, I'll take a peek at Kaspar."

"Fine then, I'll get you there."

He steers me off and away from the General, taking Davies Avenue and squeezing past Alan Lampton's pig farm to Second Street so we miss the fuss of so many extra bodies milling around the street.

"You'll tell me how it is?" the doctor mutters at the door of the tinshop. "And make a report for the files?"

"Of course."

He spins on the heel of his boot, but I hold him back with a tug on the edge of his vest. It's a private touch, meant to offer a truce. He looks down at me, the blue of his gaze just clear of emotion that I feel brave enough to lift on my toes and kiss him quick and light on the corner of his mouth. He jerks slightly at the affection, and even as I lower back down I can feel heat blooming on my cheeks at the forwardness.

"Mrs. Kinney, I never would have expected it of you. Right here on the street!" There is delight in his voice, and a new twinkle in his eyes.

"I do not like discord between us," I say. "And in the face of so much damage—so many hurt…I do not like us at odds."

His mouth trembles, the lips thinning as they do when he has much on his mind and little to say. But we are indeed on the street, and now is not the time for a deep discussion about our unanticipated and slowly diverging paths of medicinal study.

"I will see you at home," I say, offering him an excuse. "Do be careful."

"All will be steady," he promises, and then walks back toward the General. His loose-limbed walk is the same as always, and he swings his doctor bag with ease. I like to think I've lightened his heart just a bit. If so, then perhaps I am doing well in figuring out some of the wifely ways I wish to have. I will do this marriage better. I suspect it is also much easier to do when a woman loves her husband.

I let myself into Marie's tinshop. She's at the main bench in the middle, which has two large rectangles cut on the long sides. Iron plates punched through with square holes of different sizes are inlayed within the wood of them, and she wrestles out a large anvil-like tool from one of the squares while glancing my way.

"Jane! The boys ate it all, I see."

"It was delicious."

She manages to haul the big stake away and chooses one shaped like a mushroom to replace it. It settles into the hole with ease, making a dull scraping noise as it rattles into place. Marie selects a hammer and picks up a bowl.

"You can set the basket next to my ledger on the counter – I'll take it in to Berit."

"I can take it," I tell her. "It may...maybe I can see how Kaspar is doing."

Marie pauses and looks wary, "He seems to be fine. We're doing the iodine on it, and no fever so far."

"Yes. The iodine." I refrain from asking about it. Patrick and I were shocked to discover the Salomon family had a massive bottle of the stuff the very day Kaspar was injured. He'd asked Thaddeus about it. Kate had offered it up to them, a stunning reveal on a day already so filled with terror and horror that the meaning of it was lost to me until Patrick reminded how there'd been no iodine available for months. Somehow, it had never arrived on the oft-broken trains. He didn't need to say more. Without the iodine, many had died over the winter of 1882 and into 1883. One was Urszula – Marie and Thad's youngest daughter. We agreed, in the deep quiet of our bed, never to mention this to Marie or Thad—or call out Kate's obvious duplicity.

I want to say something now, though, if only because I am rankled by Kate's overeager nursing in my place at the General this morning. But it's no use dragging up old spirits now, and Marie is worried enough over her son.

"Well, why not let me see? I can offer some comfort and maybe a poultice," I say, trying not to wheedle. I'm sure I sound a bit like I am, anyway, so I smile to cover the plead.

It works. Marie sets down the hammer with a small sigh and leads the way through the blacksmith's forge and into the living quarters behind the two combined smith shops. Berit Salomon, Marie's mother-in-law, looks up from kneading on the wide planks of the pitted kitchen table. Her hair has gone white from ice blond, but she still moves with a straight back and still holds her head as queenly as always. In the corner of the room Gerik sleeps on a cot, and makes no twitch or jerk as we enter in a clatter of shoes.

"Marie – Jane," Berit says, and her face bunches into a brilliant smile, forming fine thready wrinkles everywhere. "You didn't need to make a special trip with the basket. The boys could have brought it back."

Marie swallows a snort next to me.

"What?" Berit asks, looking between us.

I suddenly catch the joke and scrunch my nose so I don't giggle.

"It's…could you see Tadeusz carrying a woman's basket across town?" Marie says, her voice thick with suppressed laughter. It spurs on my own unladylike inhale and I tamp it down.

"Well." Berit's smile stretches into a grin. "You have a point."

We all give in to a short bout of hoots before remembering the invalid in the next room over and hushing ourselves as one. The tiny moment, as short as it is, makes me glow as if filled with sunlight. I feel welcome—not only in the Salomon house, but also in Flats Junction. It makes me remember I am not in Boston or Rockport or Gloucester, but where I have wanted to be, since I fell in love with the doctor—here, in the west, where the ways and the possibilities are wider and more free, even if it's small, like snorting a laugh in a kitchen.

"I'll just see how Kaspar is doing," I say once I settle down. The laughter is light and free, as if I can shake off the tendrils of darkness I feel whenever I have dealings with Kate these days.

Leaving the basket next to Berit and removing my little nursing kit from it, I let myself through to the hallway beyond the great room and to the door of the children's room, which now only is for Kaspar and his younger brother Natan. Marie follows me, and twitches at the covers of one of the unused beds on the other side of the room – Helena or Urszula's. I won't ask. It's not my place.

Instead, I turn my attention to Kaspar, who is awake but bleary-eyed.

"And how are we?"

He lifts his arm, which is stained ochre from the iodine and a dull rusty brown of old blood. I frown deeply, the crease between my eyebrows wrinkling my nose tightly, and twist on the bed at the rustle of skirts at the door. Marie enters with a short tray that tinkles, for on it is the dark bottle of iodine itself, as well as a glass of water and a plate of buttered bread.

"Have you been using the same bandages after you clean the wound?" I ask, hoping to stem any accusation from my tone.

Marie hears it anyway, and stops up short, her skirts swooping in front of her as they catch up to the pause. "I—should we not have?"

"No. Never," I say. Unwinding the cloth shows ever more discoloration on the cotton, and I hold my breath against the growing low stench that curdles out from under it. Steeling myself for what I find, I finish the last layer, and am appalled to realize the cotton has become stuck to the flesh, as if the hopeful scar of tissue has welded itself to skin. Kaspar whimpers at last, making the first sound since I've walked in, and he turns his face away into the faded calico of the blanket.

Marie comes closer and puts the tray on Natan's bed. Her wild black hair brushes my cheek as she bends over her son.

"Are you feeling alright, my boy?" she asks, and her voice is low and as kind as I've ever heard it. "No too hot or too cold?"

"Fine, mother," he says. "Fine enough. I just…can't move it without pain."

I gaze with a growing, fuzzy trepidation at the exposed

burn, bubbling where the cloth sticks to it. It will sting and hurt even worse when I take it off, but it must, or it will only fester.

"Marie, I wonder if you and Berit might find some new strips of cloth. Any clean cotton will do, cut into strips. Otherwise, I have some at home." I begin to slowly, ever so slowly, peel back the fabric glued to Kaspar's slowly healing burn. He hisses between his teeth and squeezes his eyes shut. There must be a better way to do this. I open the leather roll of my little kit by pulling on the leather string, and pull out tweezers, properly sanitized in the doctor's surgery since the last use.

As I pick at the fabric in minute pulls, Kaspar whimpers. Marie plants her feet at my side, so close her knee pushes into the side of my thigh. While Kaspar keeps his eyes closed and his breathing shallow, Marie inhales great gusts, and her quivering concern is a tic that makes my neck tighten. My nursing abilities are still uncertain, and an audience makes me twitch. I rotate my shoulder blade and glance up at Marie.

"Are you sure you wish to watch? It is painstaking."

She seems to realize her nearness, and takes a step back, then carefully sits on her other son's bed, moving so she does not spill the tray. "I'm sorry."

My eyes are trained on the glued fabric meshed with pus and skin, but I glance at her quickly. Curiosity beckons and for once I don't tamper with it.

"Sorry? For what?"

Marie offers a small smile filled with blankness instead of true esteem. Her dark eyes go dull, encased in a lost memory. She picks at the rippled skin on the backs of her hands and runs her fingers along deep scars at her wrists.

"I should have remembered. It's not always a nice thing to be observed so closely, or with keen eyes. I have been there myself, years ago, long before I married Thaddeus or even had a tinshop of my own. I did not mean to pry."

"It's no trouble," I say, winded at her explanation. "I'm…only a bit nervous."

"I was, too."

We share another moment of unsteady friendship, all contained in a single glance, and then I go back to concentrating on her son's arm. She watches, but not as closely, and I work hard to avoid causing unnecessary pain to the boy, attempting to avoid any area that has a nice thick scab and pulling at the threads of stained cotton with gentleness.

"Do you suppose…" Marie cuts through the quiet, and then she stills herself, tense and fretful. I am near enough to finishing and don't look up, so she plunges on. "We are hoping he will be able to lift a hammer again. He's not damaged so much that he's lost his trade, has he?"

Kaspar finally opens his eyes and trains his brown-black eyes on me. Pinned between the two gazes, I find myself wanting to reassure, even if it means speculation and lies. But I would be doing no one any favors to guess —not the Salomon family, and certainly not myself or Patrick.

"I don't think he will lose use of the arm," I say slowly. "But the healing…it is…it will take a while. His arm will tire easily. And this…" I run my fingers in the air over the open meat of his arm. "There is still so much that can go wrong. The best thing is for it to close quickly, to allow the skin to heal. There is too much damage for sewing up the skin, but… there are other things."

"Other medicines?" Marie leans forward. "How much does it cost?"

"It's...it's not the kind of thing the doctor orders from out East. It's..." I glance at my little nursing kit, and the bottle of comfrey. The urge to use it, to start knitting the skin together, is overpowering. It would work so well and so quickly, and it would show that Esther and myself have some knowledge of healing, but her warning rattles around in my head and I don't reach for it. "I have some of the old ways, the use of flowers and plants."

Marie now sits up straight and her forehead creases. "Plants?"

I twist to face her fully, opening my palms and bending toward her so tightly that the lump of my womb feels like a brass ball between my hips and rib cage.

"It's the same as a possible remedy for the black measles."

"That's stopped," Marie says swiftly, fear sharpening the corners of her tone. "The bit of epidemic is over."

"Doctor Kinney believes it temporary. It comes and goes with the seasons, as if it lives in the earth or under the hot sun. Whatever it is, it doesn't matter. Esth—Widow Hawks says her people have never been ill from it. They have a way of living that repels the illness. And there are other things, other flowers, that can do much for a sickness. Or a burn."

Marie's eyes float to Kaspar's deep wound, and the bit of color in the high points of her cheekbones fade. "Thaddeus and I...we've sworn off... Do you need to wrap that back up?"

"It can be unbound for a bit," I say. "Have you the clean cloth? It must always—every day—be bound with fresh, clean linen. Without that, the iodine cannot always help."

She nods and stands, beckoning me to follow with one quick, taut jerk of her hand.

I follow her out after a backwards glance at Kaspar, who seems to be both fascinated and disgusted by his own injury, but at least not prone to touch it.

In the short, wide hallway of the Salomon house, made particularly awkward by the way they have added on the bedrooms as their family has grown, Marie spins and pushes into my face. We are not exceptionally tall women and are of a similar enough height that our eyes are matched as she prods a finger in the air between our collarbones.

"You're talking Sioux medicine. Witch doctoring. I won't have that, not in my house, and not for my son."

"I was only speaking of the black measles," I backtrack at once at her ire. "I won't offer—there's nothing I would force upon you for Kaspar's care."

She freezes, her eyes wide. The whites of them, rimmed by very dark lashes, seem to glow in the faded grey of the hallway, where only the one far window lets in the afternoon sun. Her finger drops, and her mouth thins. I expect her to throw me out of the house in a moment, if I say the wrong thing, all our carefully built friendship gone in my too-generous offering of information. Even now, after all these years and all my troubles, I do not seem to know when and how to explain my own reasonings and enthusiasm for digging up any and all medical knowledge.

"I don't want to think about that disease," she says finally. "But I want to know what can be done for my child."

"You and Thaddeus don't trust me. Us," I say. "You

still don't, after everything." It is an accusation, and a disappointment. I had thought that after we saved her life, and that of her new babe Garik, and with Thaddeus and Hardy working on our fire-rotted roof, not to mention a conversation I know Thaddeus had with the doctor about Marie's fertility… I had hoped that we had managed to get past any of their issues with the doctor. "I hope you know – you must know – that the death of your father-in-law, and then later, of Urszula—."

"I don't speak of that, either!" Marie looks wild, suddenly, and grips her left forearm with her right palm, hard and tight. "I don't wish to remember the dead."

"But the doctor—."

"He is a good doctor!" she says, her voice high at the end, and her eyes look glassy. "I understand he is not God, and he is no miracle worker. He pushes his newfangled science too much and is too quick to use a knife or a saw, but he is good. I know the difference!"

Her defense of my husband curdles the words on my tongue, poised there to refute her, and now I must swallow them.

"I don't understand."

"He is not like the old doc," Marie says, and hugs her elbows, forming a cross around her body as she looks at the ground. "He's…a good man."

"Did the doctor before Patrick not do well? Did many die?"

Marie shrugs, still staring daggers into the pitted and uneven floorboards. Her mouth goes even thinner, as if she's sucking all ill will and bad memories back inside of her, pushing it into the depths of her chest.

"He was... Doc Gunnarsen was old. He didn't know the same things as Doc Kinney, and he didn't want to learn—though he didn't take off limbs as quick, either. But...he..." Marie swallows. "He liked his whiskey. It made his hands shake. And his hands..." She shudders and squeezes herself even tighter. "He like to use them, he liked to touch, even when, even during..." Her eyes flash up to meet mine, direct and earnest. "Thaddeus swore he'd never let a doctor touch me again, after Helena's birth. After he walked in and saw Doc Gunnarsen..." She breaks and gives up her explanation, letting her arms fall to her sides. The insides of her palms glow red, marked with the utter tightness she'd gripped her elbows.

I understand enough. So, he was a lout and a drunkard, a quack in the truest sense, and one that liked to grossly fondle his women patients left in his care. He is the reason half the people in Flats Junction fear Patrick, unwilling to give him a chance. He is also the reason Patrick is good for this town, for if given a chance, my husband can show them all that science paired with reason is palatable. A guilty jolt and whisper flits through my mind – I may indeed ruin his chance to do this if I dabble overmuch in Lakota herbal lore. But to leave such knowledge unused...I have to believe there is a marrying of the two sciences.

"I will not ask you to let Doctor Kinney treat Kaspar, but I would hope you'd allow me to try a few things. They are a woman's medicinals. It will not do any harm to try."

Marie inhales slow and deep, and glances back at the bedroom. Before she answers, the door between the kitchen and the bedroom hall bangs open, revealing Thaddeus and Hardy. Thaddeus looks the same—a towering giant with grey-shot dark beard and flinty grey eyes, but Hardy glows, looking oddly angelic.

"Mrs. Kinney!" he gushes at once. "Have you seen? Doc Kinney's got some hospital set up by the General, and he's doing all sorts of healing!"

"I've seen," I say, stopping myself from asking if Kate is still playing nurse for my husband. "I hope he's been able to make some progress."

"Is Kaspar better?" he asks, eagerly craning his neck around my shoulder. "Is the burn healing quick enough?"

"Go get some clean strips of calico from Berit's rag box," Marie says, shooing Hardy back out. "Mrs. Kinney says we need to use new ones each day."

Hardy hurries out, so quick that he catches a toe on the edge of the doorway and flails as he moves. He catches himself just in time, and his voice bounces into the kitchen as the door closes behind him.

Thaddeus rounds on me, crossing his meaty biceps and glowering. "What is it now?"

"Nothing," I say, wishing he had not interrupted so that I could unfold more information out of Marie. "I'm only doing a check and a change of dressing."

"Mm. So then." Thaddeus turns his eyes on Marie. "Wife. The additional army recruits. We should send word with David Fawcett about what we can offer the Fort."

"So many of them...you don't suppose they'll make too many demands?" she asks her husband, her eyebrows rising. "Nothing beyond what can be done, reasonably?"

"You're thinking of Captain Bush, and we won't see his like again, I should think."

I glance between the two of them, lost, until Thaddeus shifts and glances down at me, then at Marie. He shakes out his arms and jams his fists into his broadcloth pockets. Bits of sawdust and small slivers of wood fall from the creases, leftover from his work on my roof.

"One of the old commanders at Fort Randall," he says to me, rightfully interpreting my confused silence. "He was exacting and demanding, but he had us doing some of our finest work." He juts his chin at Marie. "We haven't done like since."

"He was intense, to be sure," Marie says quietly. "I just didn't like all the extra men, sniffing around us women like we were ripe for any taking."

"It won't come to that," Thaddeus says, with the air of a man unused to a challenge for a fight. He swings his big head to take in both of us and frowns. "What, you think I just let those army bastards come 'round on their own privilege? Well. I kept an eye out, even before we wed."

"That explains your constant appearing in my old tin-shop whenever one would stop in."

He folds his arms again, even tighter. "Why shouldn't I? I had my eye on you from the day we met."

Marie's shoulders soften, but I'm filled with questions again. Was it so terrible to have the Army nearby, to protect us civilians from anything that lurks on the wild plains? I did not think they meddled so much with Flats Junction, preferring to look ever westward instead of back at us. Then again, there has been quietness on the prairies since I arrived. Only snippets of tales—like everything else—reaches my ears. The news in Boston was unreliable about this as well as how life truly is in the west, and I sometimes think even when I work to glean information of any kind, I am met with the barriers of half-truths and secrets.

"There are not that many men," I say to both. "Maybe fifty or seventy all told."

"It's the new ones, coming in on the trains over the next month I heard tell of," Thaddeus says, rocking back on his heels. "It's going to change things, having that many more unattached men. We're the closest thing to a real town for those boys, and ten miles isn't that far."

Before we can speculate further, Hardy pops back in, holding faded, dark blue sprigged calico strips in both hands, as if it's an offering at Patrick's Catholic Mass. I take them, careful to pinch only the ends with my forefinger and thumb. He watches me closely, his blue eyes squinting with concentration.

"Why are you holding so?" he asks quickly. "Can't they—."

"Enough. Back out. There's filing to be done in the shop, and you can go fetch Natan from the O'Donnells. They've spent enough time whiling away their afternoon," Thaddeus pushes the tall boy back out. He nods at me and Marie before following Hardy into the kitchen. In the silence of the door shutting, I fill my chest with air and look at Marie, hoping we can restart the conversation of before, if only to recapture our budding friendship.

But she has moved back into Kaspar's bedroom, and the time for speaking plain with another woman is over. I go in as well and use a watered-down wash of carbolic acid and then take a small vial from the leather pouch.

"Let's try to start with this," I say. Uncorking the bottle and shaking it hard, golden, precious gobs of honey come out. "I have a small store from the Brinkley's, and it's rare until their fall harvest of the hives. But it's the best I have to start healing the skin around the burn and keep infection out."

"Not the iodine?" Marie asks, her brow hunching over her eyes. "I thought—."

"The iodine is good. And if you don't have honey, it's better than nothing. I will bring some more over. There are other things to knit the skin together, but…" The bottle of comfrey beckons once again, but I roll it back up with the leather.

"If there is something to help, I would like to know it," Marie says.

Kaspar watches the honey ooze along his arm, and leans back into his pillow. "This is working fine, ma. No pain—not as much as it was. It almost tingles, like a spice."

"Is that usual?" Marie asks sharply.

"I…I suppose so." It's the first time I've used the honey, based on Esther's advice, and while I don't wish to lie, I do not wish to discourage Marie's openness in this moment. It would be worse for all if she forced me to scrape it off, anyway. "Every injury is different."

After wrapping the massive burn back up, taking care around the particularly raw spots, and forcing myself to look with science and a clinical mind on the gaping holes and deep chunks of missing skin, I stand to depart.

"I can check on him in another day or two, if you like," I offer. "Or at the very least, drop off more of the honey and other such items."

Marie's frown has lessened. Kaspar has a fine sheen of sweat on his dewy upper lip, but it is the sweat of daytime and the bandage changing. He seems fit and hale for a boy who has suffered a terrible shock to his body, and I have hope yet that he will heal. The Salomons need him—they need his arm and the knowledge of the forge that Thaddeus has poured into him. For all Hardy is a big strapping lad, he is still clumsy enough with the hammers, and is no real match for Kaspar's skill.

"That will be fine, Jane. I...thank you." She smiles at me. When I leave their home and shop another moment later, I realize I have accomplished exactly what Patrick believes impossible. I have used the old medicines, and I am acting as an actual, useful nurse. It may be that I can save lives, too.

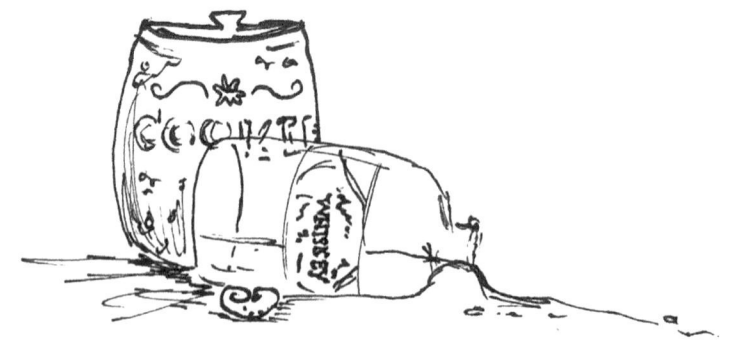

CHAPTER SIX

Patrick

October 9, 1858

"And then, Kara whacked the babby and I near thought he'd fall into the soup and mam started shoutin' and all the while da is sleepin' on the bed like the dead," Michael retold last night's antics as Patrick listened, elbows on the table in the small, tight room Michael's family shared. One could barely walk around the bodies. But none of Michael's brothers or sisters wanted to go out – it was too chilly a mornin'.

Kara, Michael's closest sister in age, smacked her brother in a lazy swat. "Well, he's got to stop standin' on the table, the wee fiend."

Michael's mother burst in, cradling' a basket filled with squashes.

"Why in heaven are all of you in here? Get out!"

No one moved at first, especially the younger three. Patrick nudged Michael. "I should go anyway."

His best friend nodded, then raised his eyebrows with a leer. "Later, then?" He meant the pair of them might creep behind the taverns and see if there were any scraps or bit of booze left in a bottle that could be sold for a coin. Patrick grinned back and shrugged. Kara swept by, and shooed her siblings out to the hallway, and then out to the back of the property to bother all the squatters on the grass outside. As Patrick followed, Michael's mother stopped him.

"Will you be needin' to eat here today, Patrick?" she asked, her mouth drawn up tight. Though Aunt Bonnie tried to send food from Mr. McClure's weekly, it was never quite enough. Still, none of the women seemed inclined to let anyone starve if they'd a way to stop it, and he knew it well. He also knew what trouble it was for them.

"Not likely, thanks," he said, and moved to the front door after a wave to Michael.

There was the first real stiff nip in the air. He felt it the minute he stepped off the stoop. Old Mr. Kilbride huddled against the chill though he still enjoyed the outside, as dedicated as any guard dog. Patrick hesitated, eyeing up the churned mud along the step. It wasn't entirely frozen yet.

"Ach, boyo, it'll do ya good to get used to it," Mr. Kilbride advised. "It'll be all ya know 'til summer."

It didn't take Patrick long to plunge a foot in. He didn't want to waste time. It'd been months since he'd gone to Aunt Bonnie's work, and she had said last night Patrick should arrive in the mornin'. It was a Saturday so he could go care-free, without waitin' on school. Excitement ran like ribbons in his bones. There was a good chance he could eat at Mr. McClure's table.

Aunt Bonnie worked every day but Sunday, so Patrick figured Mr. McClure did too, and this time he was determined to be of some more use to Aunt Bonnie in some way, so Mr. McClure might ask him back yet again. He pulled the much-stitched coat around his shoulders and buttoned it up. Aunt Bonnie had brought it home last week, tight mouthed, but bade him put it on for size and had nodded once, hard and fast, when it fit with some space to grow.

Under his arm crunched the last of his Friday lessons. It was a special report on the biology of the natural systems. Mr. Arrott asked for special recitations at times, and Patrick enjoyed this one more than most – particularly because it was possible to glean some good knowledge from it all as opposed to simple rote of old speeches or some sort of rotted literature.

He walked through the muck, pickin' his way through the previous evenin's vomit and piss. Mainly he just didn't want to stink overmuch when he arrived at Mr. McClure's.

Since his run in with the gang, he hadn't had to walk past their alley and beyond. Even though Patrick was sure they might not remember him, he worried the new coat made him a mark for trouble. He wanted to cross the street to avoid being spotted, but generally crossin' the street was fearsome enough, so he kept his course.

The loss of the kitten still bothered him. He couldn't stop thinkin' he could have made a difference, keepin' her alive. Already he knew he had no mind for math and figures like Mr. McClure and his shipping records, and he wished to settle on a trade so Aunt Bonnie could apprentice him off. He'd stop bein' a burden to her, and soon start to earn wages, then. All the big boys finished up school around Patrick's age, and found some sort of work, and he didn't want to be stuck doing somethin' unskilled all his life – cleaning yards or stables or unloading ships.

Lost in thought, he near passed the alley of his tormentors. Lookin' about carefully, it was the same, as he recognized some of the shacks, but the boys were gone. A few children lolled on the edge of the street. The tallest was thin with overlarge eyes, and it was with a strange pang in his gut that he realized she was the big girl who had scolded one of the boys who had stolen the kitten. Her eyelids were lined with black, and her lips rubbed raw, so they crusted red. She scarcely gave Patrick a glance, and instead shrugged her shoulder out of her dress and made an odd hip jutting sashay onto the street in the path of two men. They paused and raked her with beady, lidless eyes before movin' on, and she sighed went back to her post.

Stopping at the edge of the gloomy shallow alley, he heard a few heavy coughs deep in the bowels of the slatted shacks. There was no babby crying this time. Curiosity bloomed inside his chest. He suddenly wished to go in and see why the broad lusty girl was no longer so, and why the boys were no longer runnin' around, and why all the adults were absent. The why was not too much a mystery when he gave it another moment of thought. Whatever ailment was sweepin' through the little cranny had already killed the babe.

Worst of all, he also knew he would not be able to help.

He put his head down and kept going until he reached Mr. McClure's building. This time, when he knocked, the door was flung open to Mr. MacLaren's enormous, one-armed embrace.

"Ach! Ye have arrived safe – yer auntie will be glad to hear it so!" he boomed. Mr. MacLaren lowered his voice, so likely only the rooms directly around them could hear, instead of the entire building. "She's a worrier, that one, ye ken, a softie for all her crackle." He gave a little push. "Ye ken th' way, laddie."

Patrick ran up the stairs, and only paused to knock on Mr. McClure's office panel. Aunt Bonnie opened it up immediately.

"Patrick. Thank goodness you're here all right." She smiled at him, and Patrick checked at her happiness. It seemed overly bright for Aunt Bonnie. He walked in and held his hat, straightenin' the jacket so Mr. McClure could see it was in good order.

Mr. McClure pointed up a finger, his head bent over long lists on his desk. In the mornin' light, the room was still dark, so candles were lit. He saw the pale pinkish glimmer of skin, round and purposefully hidden under Mr. McClure's slowly disappearin' hair. It was gray around the edges, but the top part of his head, where he was losin' hair, was still black as tar.

Aunt Bonnie and Patrick waited, and the minute he fidgeted, she flicked him with her fingers at the back of the neck. It stung. After a long minute, Mr. McClure took a deep inhale and then looked up and grinned.

"Why, Paddy, you're lookin' more a gentleman now, I'd say. And nearer ready for winter, are ye?"

"For certain, sir," he said, overeager with the attention.

His eyes dropped to Patrick's feet. "Boys do grow fast then, don't they? Well, there's nothin' for it. Today we take you to get some shoes and then we're headin' north."

"Shoes?" Patrick hadn't had a decent pair for over a year. The mornin' walk in the frigid, disgustin' muck made him desire some even more, never mind the coming winter.

90

"Aye, Paddy. I would have thought what I sent along with your auntie covered them, but I know I'm out of touch with costs of children." A shadow crossed his face, and then he grinned widely again. "Your Aunt Bonnie has a wee bit of tea and bread aside for us, and then we'll go."

Patrick wanted to whoop. Shoes and a trip for the weekend! It was a holiday to be sure! He held in the emotion, afraid Aunt Bonnie would nix the whole idea if he acted as a scamp before they'd even left Boston.

They shared a pot of hot, dark black tea and day-old bread. Mr. McClure's tin cup had a worn wedge in the metal, and his thumb slid easily over the mark as if he always held a cup exactly the same and had made a dent.

Afterwards, all three of them marched to straight to the shoe seller on Fulton. He was Scots-Irish like Mr. McClure, and hailed with a hearty: "Hi ye! How's things?"

"Brave and good," Mr. McClure said, releasing Aunt Bonnie's arm to shake the man's hand, then turned to her. "Miss Kinney, this is Mr. MacNulty."

"*Fair faa ye.*" He jerked his head. The man's hands did not stop moving even with the greetin's. Patrick watched him run his fingers over the bottoms of different shoes, picking at places where the uppers and the soles were sewn together.

"How goes the business yourself?" Mr. McClure asked casually, his hands hooked under his vest onto his suspenders.

"'Tis middlin' to be true, Andy. The families I've been usin' to make me goods are some of them closin' up shop – there's competition more an' more now what with the machines they've made an' the factories. They can churn out the boots faster than my folk. A shame to be sure, for all of us."

"Aren't there more jobs then, though, for the Irish?" asked Aunt Bonnie.

"Perhaps," nodded Mr. MacNulty. "But a sad thing for us small folk who've made a livin' thus far this older way."

"Well, we've come to give ye some business," Mr. McClure said smartly, and gestured to Patrick. "This lad needs some shoes for winter."

Mr. MacNulty eyed Patrick's bare feet. "An' some stockin's too, it looks. I keep some on hand for just this."

He yanked a ball of tan wool from under his table and handed it to Aunt Bonnie and then pulled down a pair of shoes danglin' on the pole above him, slung together by their laces. The blackish brown leather gleamed a little, though it was obvious these were second-hand with only a bit of wear.

"Repaired these meself, Andy," he spoke to Mr. McClure directly, but gave the shoes to Aunt Bonnie. She took them in hand and ran her fingers across the bottom soles, where there was a crease along the outer edges, but with plenty of use still in them before needin' fixin'. Patrick didn't care. He was glad to get used shoes – breakin' in a new pair would have meant weeks of aching feet and bleedin' toes.

He stared at his muddy feet, wonderin' if he should put them inside the stockings, but Aunt Bonnie had thought ahead as usual, and pulled out a towel from Mr. McClure's kitchen from her apron pocket.

She bade him sit on a large stone set outside the shoe seller's window to clean him and get him settled. All the while, Patrick listened to Mr. McClure and Mr. MacNulty. It was as if he'd grown up in a matter of weeks, and suddenly cared more and more for what the adults said around him.

Like he was soakin' up knowledge without pause. It some-times made his head swirl.

"Well, and then they says to me, they have bought a sewin' machine to match their rollin' machine, and they think they have a regular little factory inside their house! And I am to pay a higher price at first, but then as they make more, they are to be cheaper. I don't know if they'll really get their money back, but now they can fill orders from both me and three other shoe sellers up the Batterymarch and one at the foot of Beacon Hill."

"Heaven knows what they had to borrow to afford the things." Mr. McClure shook his head. "Sounds a bit of a dangerous investment for small men to make."

"That's what I thought," Mr. MacNulty agreed, now watchin' Aunt Bonnie closely as she slid the shoes on Patrick's feet. "Ah, now, Missus, they're the straight lasts o' course, but the laddie who wore them first had a big foot, so I made them stouter on the cone a wee bit with an extra pad. They'll be more comfortable enough for a smaller boyo like yours."

The shoes still pinched on the corners of Patrick's last toes and the leather squeezed into the tips of his nails. Parts of the heel dug into the smooth backs of his ankles. But they were shoes. The warmth of the stockings and the laced boots gave the impression of bein' cozy and wealthy. Patrick grinned up at Aunt Bonnie, and she smiled back, looking both pleased and satisfied.

"They fit, for sure, with some room for growin' into the spring at the very least," she said. Mr. McClure clucked his tongue and smiled, too, then turned to Mr. MacNulty.

"Well, then, you've a sale, Hugh," he said jovially, and pulled out a note. Patrick had never seen a full dollar before, and stared without manners as he handed it over. What riches. He gave Aunt Bonnie an incredulous bug eye, and she shook her head a little, her lips skinny again. Patrick knew the look—he was to stay silent.

After the transaction ended, Mr. McClure stopped by his office again to pick up a hamper and bag before they walked to the public livery. The wharves along the way smelled of salt and the sea and rot and fish. Patrick happily sloshed along beside his auntie in the new shoes, bubblin' with glee. The shoes would slow him down in the races to and from school, but at least he would have warm feet all winter.

In the bustle and press of people, Patrick heard Mr. McClure say to Aunt Bonnie lowly, "Those shoes weren't so dear, Bonnie. Was the coat?"

"I meant to use some of my next wages on the shoes, truly, Andy. But – well – you know I still wish to learn of the family, at least for Patrick's sake, and I…"

"Ye sent it over to Éireann again, lass, didn't ye?" There was a tiredness to Mr. McClure's voice. Patrick looked up and saw him starin' at Aunt Bonnie with sadness and exasperation.

His aunt put her head down and to the side, watching her step as she tried to pick her way around puddles filled with brown water and oily surfaces.

"I know you think it's foolish, but I have to try."

"It is foolish, ye soft girl," said Mr. McClure, and Patrick thought it was funny to hear Aunt Bonnie called a girl. "The money likely never makes it to them, and just lines pockets of men who promise empty things."

"Why is it so hard to get word of people?" she griped.

"It's hard to say. But don't send away any more money, ye hear me? Not until I make some of my own inquiries to see if there are better ways to hear of our families." Mr. McClure's tone sounded final.

A rented horse and a buggy borrowed from one of Mr. McClure's friends were ready for them. Mr. McClure put Aunt Bonnie up into it first, then Patrick. He moved carefully and slow as he took the reins and moved them into the Boston streets, sweat beadin' on his forehead even with the chilly mornin'.

As the first hour passed, Patrick watched the changin' land with interest. He'd never been outside the city, and the sheer number of trees and land was better than any entertainment he could have imagined. But he also noticed that Mr. McClure drove the horses with unease. He and Aunt Bonnie sat in the front of the small wagon side-by-side, nerves feedin' off of each other as they watched the horse's ears twitch, as if readin' Mr. McClure's stupidity at drivin' a carriage. His obvious discomfort made Patrick a little giggly but also highly alert.

Aunt Bonnie also looked nervous with the journey – the biggest she said she'd ever had since taking the boat from Ireland.

"Well, Paddy, do ye suppose we'll make it?" Mr. McClure tried small talk but ended up pointing out exactly what everyone in the wagon didn't want to think about. He hunched over, looking miserable, and suddenly Patrick snorted. Aunt Bonnie added, with a strange sort of hysterical hiccup. Mr. McClure looked at the two of them like they were a bit touched in the head until he suddenly shook, too. Nerves gettin' out of the way, somehow the horse sensed it stopped pullin' on the reins hard.

The miles melted away as Mr. McClure talked about Ireland, and Aunt Bonnie gave lectures about traditional Irish tales.

Arrivin' in Gloucester, the large main road was at once impressive. Patrick heard the same cry of gulls, as the horse struggled up the steep streets were steep and tight corners. Gloucester's beach gleamed. The tide was low, and the seaweed on the rocks glistened in the deep yellow afternoon light. The extra dust from the road caked heavily on Patrick's skin, and he ached to jump into the small, rockin' waves that bumped along the sand. Over it all, the sea smelled like new salt and fresh kelp, and the wind smelled like water.

Mr. McClure had arranged it to stay with one of his friends, an older shipwright who kept accounts for several of the local operations as he no longer did the actual buildin' of vessels. While Mr. MacHugh didn't give Mr. McClure direct business, his friendship meant Mr. McClure himself was always welcome in Gloucester. Patrick had also been told about Mr. MacHugh's son by a second wife was of an age. The notion of spending time with a strange, wealthy boy was interestin'.

The MacHugh house sat near the top of Washington Street, with painted clapboards weathered against the sea air. Cedar shingles on the roof glimmered a pale grey, and the handful of windows facing the street were polished. Patrick was filled with jealousy—a whole house for one family. And then curiosity crept in. Could he own his own house someday? Could he ever find enough success to afford such a luxury?

Mr. McClure handed Patrick the reins, stoppin' any

further musin'. He took the ropes while eyin' up the hitch, knowin' that should the animal decide to bolt, the narrow piece of fencin' wouldn't hold. Mr. McClure went around to help Aunt Bonnie out. He took her hand and treated her as if she were a fine lady and not his hired help. They went into the house, Aunt Bonnie untied her headscarf and smoothed her hair as they walked. Patrick held onto the leather reins with both hands, starin' at the horse's ears.

"Hey!"

The voice made the horse shift weight, but Patrick actually jumped. He glanced down and saw a young man, two or three years younger.

"Yes?"

"You with McClure?"

Patrick assumed it was Robert, the son of MacHugh. The boy smiled broad, a cheeky sort of grin that was not really so mischievous but full of the genuine happiness of a person who had had very little hardship. Patrick was a little annoyed by the boy's easiness, and ignored him.

"I'm glad he brought you – Patrick, isn't it? He talks about you all the time, and I don't know why he hasn't had you come up before. Finally, someone my age!"

Patrick gave a little smile, and the boy dampened up. He stood, a little awkwardly, as if unsure what to say from there, but was rescued when Mr. McClure came out, hands slidin' into his suspenders.

"Hello there, Bobby! And...well, Patrick. Drive the horse around back and I'll help ye unhitch." He winked. "And then if ye like, go off and enjoy yourself until dusk. Mind, you've strict orders from your aunt to stay completely out of trouble."

Patrick glanced at the sky, noting the slowly sinkin' sun. If he hurried, he'd be able to enjoy the beach for an hour or two before needin' to be back. It really was a holiday.

Robert watched but did not follow around behind the house. There was a strong hitchin' post and a sway-backed mare already munchin' her dinner there. With Mr. McClure's help, the wagon was unhooked and they pushed it off a few yards so the horse wouldn't kick it. Findin' the proper brushes and an extra blanket in the lean-to, Mr. McClure hesitantly brushed down the animal while Patrick put out some hay a bit of oats and then took up another brush. The horse seemed to enjoy the attention, and the steadiness of task felt relaxin'. Patrick wondered what it would be like to take care of animals. Would it be different from bein' curious about people?

With Mr. McClure's approval, Patrick took his leave to the beach without stoppin' into the house. That way, Aunt Bonnie couldn't say no. The way down to the port was steep, and he felt a tug at the tops of his legs as he bent to keep from pitchin' down some of the hill. He smelled the fish, but it was a different smell than the putrid stench of the city wharves. Here it was briny, fresher, and somehow cleaner. Even though Gloucester was a thrivin' city, it still felt younger and crisper.

He picked around a few large buildings. One had a huge sign advertisin' its ice. Patrick moved along south of it, hearin' rumblings inside and the shouts of men within and along the port walkways, where fishing boats of various sizes filled up with what he could only presume to be ice itself. It seemed beyond reason to have ice stored up in a buildin'.

At the long expanse of beach, he inched around shimmerin' seaweed that looked rubbery and wet, even though the tide was low and it had all been sittin' out for hours. There was a jellyfish, globular and completely translucent, mostly flattened with delicate threads in tan and red along the edges, and softened pebbles of many sizes and colors, glitterin' in the tiny lapping waves. He kicked over a large half-broken shell, and revelled in the freedom from work and the constant jut of the wagon ride up.

Under his new shoes, other small shells crunched. The sun was deep yellow, mustard and burnt gold, and cast a brown deepness to the shadows. He shoved his hands into his pockets and looked up into the sun. Its rays filtered across the water, which was nearly black against the brightness in the sky.

A pure, unblemished shell curved like the top of an ear and speckled with pink and blush against a pale white-purple background caught his eye. When he picked it up, he saw a type of hollow on the other side, where the snail itself had made its home.

There was a crack, and Patrick turned around. It was Mr. MacHugh's boy, Robert.

Robert had stopped walkin' along, though, and stared out over the water. There was little breeze, and his cap was pushed high on top of his head. Patrick put his own head down, and kept walkin' heavily, hittin' the shells and rocks with the leather of his shoes. Eventually the drag of water in the sand seeped into his socks. He stopped thinkin' of Robert's unexpected company and stood still, absently rubbin' the back of the shell against his thumb.

The pause didn't last long.

"It's nice, yes?"

Robert inched near, a few yards away, but his voice carried the same easy way that the waves did.

Patrick squinted at the buttery sky, so brilliantly yellow now that the horizon was nearly gone with white light. Why had the boy followed him? He was the son of a gentleman and was still in schoolin' whereas Patrick was soon to have to find work. Robert's hands were unbroken and he did not look hungry or full of cares.

Envy washed over him, and then fell away. It was not the boy's fault that his circumstances were easier.

Patrick started back, kicking a large rock ahead, but it was so heavy it sunk in the soft sand. Half-turnin', he looked at Robert and gave a small smile. "Are you comin' back up?"

A grin spread across the other's childlike face at the offer, and he turned at once to walk alongside Patrick.

"Robert. Will you show me a bit around Gloucester when the time allows?" Patrick finally asked. It was a strange thing, to have a boy wantin' to play with him, someone different from Michael. A fancy boy who was kind. Who even seemed to like him...

"Oh bully! Of course! But – call me Bobby. Everyone does."

"Bobby, then."

"And it's Patrick for you?"

He hesitated. The familiar friendliness was easy and comfortin', but so fast he felt he should hold out for longer. One more glance over at Robert—Bobby's—round cheeks, shinin' with sweat and hope, made him give up any city pretense.

They were all Irish, after all.

"No. Not for all. Paddy's fine if you want."

Bobby grinned, the general delighted smile of one who had few cares and even less to consider as an obstacle.

"Paddy. But just for me, and not for my parents."

He smiled with the secret, and Patrick couldn't stop the returned grin from stretchin' his skin.

They walked up to the front porch and Patrick let Bobby go ahead. As they entered the warmth of the side parlor, the eastern windows created a dark space. Patrick had to let his eyes adjust before he could properly see around the room. Brocades and a carpet covered wide dark planks. Curtains parted crisply at the edge of the room. The wood gleamed with layers of polish, and a glass lamp sat in the middle of the room, casting a softer yellow glow. Patrick looked around for the adults, but Bobby was already ahead of him. He peered around the edge of the small door, then beckoned to Patrick with tiny movements.

"They're havin' a party," he breathed. "Let's go see if we can sneak past to the kitchen."

"Won't we get supper?" Patrick asked, stomach already growling. But to walk around in such finery? Didn't they need to remove their shoes? Should he wash his face just to be in such finery? How could Bobby act without awe, surrounded by so much wealth?

"There should be some cookies put away we might find," Bobby whispered. "And if you won't come along, there's just more for me."

Patrick followed Bobby's lead and tiptoed silently along the back hallway to the cook's entrance. As they neared the kitchen door, Patrick heard Aunt Bonnie's laughter. It was a sound he rarely heard, and he paused at the crack in the door separatin' the hallway from the parlor. The light inside the room was bright compared to the deep darkness of the hall, and he watched, astounded, as his auntie tipped back a drink of whiskey as if she was naturally used to it.

Well, he reasoned, he supposed she was used to it. She was Irish after all, and there were times when she returned from Mr. McClure's and smelled of drink as she would sneak around the shared room. As he'd gotten older, Patrick had figured she kept a flask on her person. It would not be unusual for a woman to do so.

There was no music, but Mr. McClure offered Aunt Bonnie his hands, and pulled her into an embrace before they waltzed around the room. His hand braced widely along her back, and his eyes matched hers intently. Mr. and Mrs. MacHugh stared without joining, her young skin a strange match for his old fingers as they touched, each holdin' a glass in their other hands. His aunt looked so happy that Patrick felt overwhelmed with gratitude to Mr. McClure for bringin' them here, away from the city, away from work, so that Aunt Bonnie could be free to enjoy a bit of whiskey overmuch, and to have a bit of festivities, too. If Patrick ever were to meet his father, he would hope he was like Mr. McClure.

Mr. McClure slowed the waltz, and his legs grazed Aunt Bonnie's skirts, swishin' them in rhythm to his low singing of an old Irish song. Patrick's Gaelic was far from fluent, but he recognized the tune itself.

do shiúlfainn féin I gcónái leat,

Eibhlín a Rún

do shiúlfainn féin I gcónái leat...

Mr. McClure finished the air and leaned in, but before he could watch further, Bobby pulled at Patrick's sleeve.

"What are you staring at?" he said quietly, his voice muffled by cookies.

"Them. Dancin'," Patrick said, still chewin' on Mr.

McClure's slow jig around the room with Aunt Bonnie. What would it be to have a dance with a woman? The vision made him realize how one could display feelin's without saying anything at all…

"Silly nonsense," Bobby said scornfully. "Mam rarely dances. She says it doesn't agree with Da."

The thought tugged at Patrick, and he followed Bobby into the kitchen. "Do you not think your mam only wishes to keep your father from bein' poorly? If he gets a bit winded on a spin, she might not like it."

They were in the depth of the kitchen now, and at Robert's cue, Patrick crouched next to him behind the wooden trestle set up in the center of the room. He took the sweet Robert offered. It tasted like sugar and butter, and he liked the bump of thick crumbs on his tongue.

Robert was still stewin'. "Paddy," he said quietly, in the soft dim of the empty kitchen. "Do you think my da is ill?"

Patrick shook his head. "No, Bobby, not ill. Just a bit older than Mr. McClure to be sure."

"What makes you think that his age matters so much?"

"I don't, really. I was just watchin' it all. I think about such things sometimes. Maybe someday I might be a horse doc – or somethin' like that."

The admission slipped out, a truthful statement but a surprisin' one. Patrick waited for Robert to poke fun, like any of the Boston boys would do for such an odd idea.

"A doc?" He pondered the idea and ate another cookie. "I never thought about becoming a doc. Like a surgeon, or one of those homeopaths – the nice ones? Mam brought one of those for me when I was ailing last winter. Or someone who brings the leeches?"

Patrick shuddered. "No, not one of those. Just...a doctor. A vet – on the horses, likely. I don't know, Bobby. It's just wee fool idea."

"Is there money to be made?"

"Not really. It's more a...it's somethin' that interests me. But I'm guessin' Aunt Bonnie and Mr. McClure—."

There was a bang, and the kitchen door flung open.

"I know there's another bottle in here," Mr. MacHugh said at the doorjam. Robert twisted to Patrick, mouth opened in the shape of a small oval.

"Where did ye put it?" Mr. McClure's voice was less slurred.

"Oh, one of these shelves. I can't see a damn thing without the cook's lamps on."

"What about over here?" Mr. McClure walked past the boys to the shelf nearby. There was a plethora of bottles on the open slabs of wood – brown, blue and clear. He pulled a large one down and turned around to catch the glitter of the light along the label.

He had his back to the wall and faced Mr. MacHugh, but if he looked up and to his left, he would spy them immediately. Patrick had a slim hope that Mr. McClure had had just enough drink to stop minding his surroundin's too much. Livin' in the Boston boardinghouses had given quite an education on the levels of intoxication, but he didn't know how Mr. McClure acted when under the whiskey.

While he read the bottle aloud, Patrick could just make out his face, and the deep brownish shadows that melted along his jaw. In the past year, he had lost some of the extra fat around his middle and his hips, and his pants sagged along the sides of his legs in a low-slung loop of fabric. Mr.

McClure looked and nodded to Mr. MacHugh, they walked out. As they left, Robert let out his air, and then the two boys both stifled the immediate giggles followin'.

"Here you go." Finally finished with the laughs, Robert offered Patrick the other half of the last sweet.

They munched slowly and in silence, enjoyin' the final bites.

"Paddy?"

"What?"

"I think I'd like to be a doc, like you."

Patrick smiled, feelin' strangely alive, as if by Robert agreein' with him, he wasn't so insane after all to have such a secret dream.

In the mornin' after Mass, Mrs. MacHugh suggested a beach stroll before the return to Boston. It seemed a popular idea, and they were not alone on the notion of promenading in church-best clothes. Bobby ran ahead to say hello to some lads at a picnic and see if they'd be for joinin' in a little game of ball along the sand. Mr. McClure and Aunt Bonnie walked behind Patrick, Aunt Bonnie usin' a parasol borrowed from Mrs. MacHugh to keep the sunlight from beatin' on her hair.

Patrick turned to walk backwards a pace to smile. Aunt Bonnie had laughed so much the past hours, as if drinkin' in the last bit of holiday herself. It was strange and delightful to see.

Beyond Mr. McClure's shiny head, the MacHugh's walked slowly. Mr. MacHugh leaned heavy on his wife. His gait seemed strangely limp, as if he was markedly tired. Mrs. MacHugh bent over him, her blonde hair gleamin' with oil, but she did not seem upset, so Patrick turned back to Robert, who waited. The other boys must not have been interested in a game.

"Think we should race all the way to the end of the beach?" he challenged.

"I'm for it," Patrick agreed, feeling adrenaline surge into his gut.

Robert toed a line in the wet sand and they marched up to it.

"And...go!" The shout came behind unexpectedly so both boys jumped as if it were rifle fire. Patrick recognized Mr. McClure's voice, and then he took off in the followin' instant with Robert directly next behind. They needed agility to give berth to the other beachcombers and patrons who were whilin' away their mornin', too. It was quickly apparent Robert was superior in runnin' for all his softer living as he pulled ahead bit by bit.

"Ahoy, Paddy! I'm going to win—!" he crowed as he closed in on the piles of rocks servin' as the start of the breakwater at the far east of the shore. Patrick was only a handful of long strides behind him, but his victory was obvious. Still, Bobby stopped short, pale, as he stared back across the beach.

Patrick followed his gaze, still catchin' wind. Across the sand, Robert's father splayed on the ground, with the wet ground soakin' into his back, and Mrs. MacHugh fell to her knees as the boys watched, the seawater spiderin' up the rough silk of her skirts like a great fingerin' stain.

Aunt Bonnie turned around to look, and even as she screamed out "Patrick!" he was already runnin'. He did not even think about what he'd do, or what was happenin' to Mr. MacHugh. He simply knew he needed to go. He needed to see. He wanted to try and fix it.

Robert appeared at his side, catchin' up at the last

moment. They arrived together, sprayin' sand across his father's pants and into the creases and folds of Mrs. MacHugh's skirt. Mr. MacHugh's face was white, waxy, and sweatin'. Patrick had a strange moment of raw vindication. He had not imagined Mr. MacHugh's ailin' after all. He sank his knees into the drenched ground, his right knee hittin' a rock and the other crushin' a shell. And then there was nothin' but the body—a human puzzle that had an ailment he wanted to discover, for no reason other than plain curiosity.

Above, someone yelled for a doctor. The surf gurgled at Patrick's heels and the raspy, shallow breathin' of the older man on the ground grated on his nerves. Mr. MacHugh's eyes were half-open, dartin' sometimes, and other times going dull as if his wits were leavin'. His body was covered in a thick slick sweat.

"Where's it hurt him, do ye think?" Mr. McClure asked, kneelin' down.

Patrick shrugged, feeling as much at a loss.

There was little change in Mr. MacHugh, so, feeling silly, Patrick just tried a hard pushin' slap and push on his torso. His face filled with a bit more color, but his breathin' was still the same.

"My chest!" he finally pushed out in a voice more strained than Patrick had ever heard. "I can't...get..." He looked like a fighter who'd been gut punched in the slums.

Patrick stared, thinkin' as well he could. The bit of recitation from his biology report filtered into his head. Everythin' living needed air to breathe...Wonderin' while actin', he bent over and breathed hard into Mr. MacHugh's mouth. It didn't bring much response. He considered...could a chest could forget how to work? Perhaps it was an attack on his senses or his humors? Patrick repeated the breathin' in. It did not seem to do much other than keep Mr. MacHugh alive, but that was better than dyin' straight out.

"Move, boy." Short wide hands took over Patrick's on Mr. MacHugh's chest. The newly arrived doctor calmly pumped before pullin' out a shiny instrument. It was a pronged piece with a place for the ears and a flat part on the end, and he seemed to be listenin' to the air and movement of fluids in Mr. MacHugh's body. He nodded, put the item carefully back inside his hat, then made to rub more on Mr. MacHugh's torso except now the man seemed to be breathin' a bit better and his face was not so waxy. His head fell back, but it was as if it was just exhaustion. The doctor leaned forward and inhaled the smell of Mr. MacHugh's breath.

"Remarkable, then," the doctor murmured. "Very good." His words, though quiet, carried enough that Mrs. MacHugh stopped her tiny sobs on the side. "You're lucky I live so damned close to the beach, MacHugh."

The doctor looked up at everyone. "He'll likely pull through, but we need to get him abed," he announced. Patrick finally looked up and noticed how many passerby had stopped and huddled around, their faces both entranced and nervous. All about were men and women starin' and mutterin' amongst themselves. There were men in their Sunday top hats, and women with parasols that huddled so close they hit each other's edges. Aunt Bonnie looked white and pinched and gripped her employer's arm while Mr. McClure watched with an appraisin' gaze.

"Our home is right up the hill, you know, Doc Smith," Mrs. MacHugh stood with the doctor, gesturin' and wringin' her hands all at the same time.

"Yes, yes. We'll all go." He took a step to follow Mrs. MacHugh, gesturing to two men who were usin' coats for a stretcher, but then turned around to Patrick. "You did exceedingly well, boy. Quite an aptitude for such things."

"I was happy to help, sir."

"Have you had some training?" he asked.

"No, sir."

The doc's heavy eyebrows rose. "You'd do well to consider it if you've these skills and have a way to manage some apprenticeship in Boston. Doctors are paving a new way these days."

Patrick gave a bow, his heart soaring even though he felt scared at the same time. It was as if heaven had heard his words to Robert the day before. And just as suddenly, the happiness crashed. He wouldn't be guaranteed such a life. If he was lucky, he'd work with horses, and it was all an Irish boy could really expect.

Robert stood next to Patrick, waitin', but he looked shaken and afraid. Patrick slung an arm around his shoulders and gave a small encouragin' smile. "Come on. The doc will likely have your da up and restin' fine shortly."

"Do you think so?" His voice sounded small and pinched.

"Likely," I repeated. "Else he wouldn't have moved him yet."

"Boy."

Patrick turned around with Robert, not certain who was being hailed. A gentleman in his Sunday best, a top hat made of black silk shimmering in the late light, was starin'. He was tall and heavily mustached, the ends twisted with wax. His eyes were hazel and matched the color of his hair.

"Your performance was impressive," he said intently. "Do you intend to do as the doctor suggested, and further yourself in medicine?"

"Well, sir," Patrick said extra slow, tryin' not to get lost in the shock of the last minutes. "It's a new idea, but I'm sure my auntie might say it's much too fancy and professional for me."

"You might find that it will only take an apprentice-ship with a very good physician who has some extensive training, a medical certificate and a solid patient base to expound on your current knowledge."

He was so formal and intelligent that Patrick was not sure at first how to answer him.

"I thank you for the ideas, kindly," he said at last.

"You think on it. It'd be wasted talent otherwise," the man said. He then turned to his wife, who was waitin' on him. She was much shorter, tiny and quick, with overlarge pearls in her ears glowin' against the sunlight.

The stretcher bearing Robert's father was nearly out of sight.

"Paddy, how did you know what to do?" Robert asked wonderingly as their feet shuffled and crunched along the roasted seashells.

"I didn't. I just...figured somethin' might work. Better than waitin' and doin' nothin'."

"You pleased the doc right enough."

"Maybe."

"You got him to breathe regular again," Robert pushed. "I would like to know things like that."

"Well, maybe you should do what that gentleman said to do and try an apprenticeship with a physician. See if you like it. Your da has the funds."

Robert pressed his lips together. "Da thinks physics are foolish quacks."

The boys arrived at the MacHugh house, and even though the doc was there, the house felt forbidding and quiet. Aunt Bonnie bent over Mrs. MacHugh in her fluffy chair. There was cold tea on the table, and the house was stiflin' and damp.

"How's Father?" Robert knelt in front of his mother's gown, which was still soaked with seawater. The edges of the stain turned white and crusted with dried salt.

"The doctor says he will be alright but needs some good rest. You'll need to help me, Bobby, will you?"

"Of course, Mother," he said gently, and rubbed her fingers with his pudgy ones. "Whatever you need."

They stood or sat, hearin' the gentle tick of the small clock on the mantle, and tryin' not to listen to the shuffle upstairs in the bedroom. Patrick wondered if they'd not make it back to Boston. Another night in Gloucester would not be a terrible thing, if only Mr. MacHugh lived…

Finally, the doctor came down. He seemed less stern, and he glanced around and found Mrs. MacHugh. She rose, her tea paused halfway to her mouth.

"How is he?" she asked, the fear creepin' back into her voice. "Will he pull through?"

"He is not well, I'm afraid to say, Bridget. But I think he's past the worst." The news spread visible relief across the room. He continued. "But he must rest a while. And then you must have him walking a bit every day. The recovery will be quite slow, but if he does not fret over business, I don't see how he can't have himself up and regular in a few months."

Robert stood next to Mrs. MacHugh, frownin', and Patrick realized with a start that his new friend was tryin' to memorize all of the doctor's words. He was genuinely plannin' to help his mother.

The doctor finished his speech, picked up his items without another word, and left, clampin' on his hat with the bulge along the side where his medical instrument was stored.

Patrick watched him go, standin' at the window long after the doc was out of sight. Had he truly done right? He'd saved someone from dyin'? The original elation filled him up fast, a hot balloon fillin' up his chest and spreadin' across his shoulders. It was like something lived inside him, a sense of knowin' or understandin' or maybe just a twinge in his gut.

And if he didn't chase what he knew was inside his blood, where did that leave him?

CHAPTER SEVEN

Jane

August 8, 1883

Patrick is at Danny Svendsen's ranch today, checking on the cattle. As he suspected, there is a sickness marking the cows. It seems to only bother one particular group of them that had been driven south for the winter and brought back late summer. Danny says he is unbothered but Patrick is determined to find a pattern.

His absence leaves me with the duty of chores and errands about town. Even dragging my hands over the dishes, wiping each tin plate thrice over, does not delay the inevitable. Esther has been gone since sunrise to hunt for wild seeds in the pine woods to the west, so I have no one to draw out in conversation. Folding my apron and shoving around the late morning coals in the cast iron belly of the stove, I watch the faint snowflakes of ash rain on the backs of my hands. They are soft and feathery, but they smear terribly when I rub them away. It is like rumors here in Flats Junction. A singular thought or notion or idea, brought on by fire and fear, can turn into something much messier. Just like when Bern was hanged.

I shake the thoughts off and put on my bonnet, determined to face whatever slings in my direction today, whether it be poisoned whispers from Sally Painter, still mourning the deaths of all her children from the last diphtheria epidemic, or Lara O'Donnell's overloud speculation about the fall picnic potluck at St. Aloysius. I put the leather roll of medication and bandages in my basket and pull out the small coin purse Patrick keeps in the top drawer of his study for foodstuffs we cannot grow. We are out of coffee and the brown sugar is nothing but molasses in the bottom of the little barrel. And soon enough we will be out of flour and canned milk.

When I approach the general store, Orville and Anna Pavlock stand at the bottom of the brand-new wooden steps, counting pennies by passing them back and forth, their Russian accents adding a full sound to all the vowels. Nancy Ofsberger flounces out, carrying a bag of nails to repair the corner of the post office's roof that had been scorched in the general's blaze with Elaine Warren a step behind.

"You say it just arrived?" Elaine asks.

"This week," Nancy nods at me as she passes. Elaine swerves around me and the Pavlocks to keep up with the postmistress.

"What did he say? When are they arriving? How long will it take them to get here from California – you did read his letter, didn't you?"

"O'course I did," Nancy snorts. "How else can I give you and Trusty Willy a heads up on your son's plans? Lands, everyone seems to be making plans to come live in Flats Junction. Why—." She disappears into the post office across the alley, Elaine following.

The stairs to the General are made of a mix of green wood and leftovers from Mikey O'Donnell's lumberyard. They don't creak on the joints the way they used to, but now they pop in odd places. The men who helped Kate build back made the porch wider, but they haven't put on a roof on it yet, and the sun heats my shoulders as it leaks into the fresh pine boards. The wood is soft and already shows a tiny bit of wear nearest the door, which, along with Kate's window, are two things that survived the fire, which mostly tore into the old porch and the front of the building, eating it from the top down. The old oak is heavy and scarred black along the side of the hinges, and the window is cloudy along the top, but it was salvageable enough. It didn't require Kate to order out a new one from the East.

The goods inside, though, that's another matter.

I pause for my eyes to adjust to the familiar gloom. The plow is still there, a resolute lump of rusty iron. The foggy glass jars of horehound and hard licorice, lemon drops and cinnamon sticks offer a soft white glitter along the far end of the counter. The pile of old used boots is now stuffed in a battered chest along the wall, and the shelves behind Kate's register, where cloth used to sit in bolts, is empty, as are the racks where spools of lace used to flutter. I wonder if she moved everything over to Sadie's before or after the fire. How lucky, that all the cottons, silks, and brocades did not go up in flames.

"Mrs. Doctor Kinney, how goes it?" Horeb Harvey spins in his chair, clapping bony hands together once.

He and Gil Greenman sit in new chairs built by the cooper, Dag Andersen. They're an odd shape, made from leftover pieces of big barrels. Horeb and Gil seem content to be back inside and no longer playing checkers on a log out front, even though they have yet to get a new checkers game. They still have rocks in front of them, but the checkerboard itself is freshly made and painted blue and white. It looks stark and clean next to their scruffy edges.

"I see you've a new board," I say. "It's lovely."

"Carved and painted by our depot man, isn't it?" Horeb grins, revealing his yellowed teeth, then spitting into a crock at his elbow. "Pretty fancy-like, no?"

"I didn't realize Franklin was woodworking," I say, turning my head. Patrick will want to know this.

"'Bout time that man stopped drinking and beating Bess and put his hand to his old trade," Fortuna, the madam of The Powdered Rose, turns in one great swoop of mauve silk and layers of peach lace.

"Yup," Gil intones from his chair. His voice still scratches from smoke inhalation. He pushes a dark colored rock across the board one space and hesitates. He glances at Horeb, then meets my eye and sits back instead of his usual cheating, his arms across the bowl of his belly.

"If you ask me," Fortuna whispers, except her whisper is so loud it doesn't quite make the definition. "The fire was good for Franklin. Kicked him out of these years of wasted stupor. The man's been a wreck since he lost his arm and his trade, but if he's woodworking again, I say it's for the best for both him, Bess and their three boys."

She wiggles her eyebrows at me, as if there is a secret message to decode within her notion, and then wiggles past me, her wide bosom missing me by an inch. The bump and roundness of my womb takes up more space than I am used to, and the child gives a small twist of protest as I turn. Horeb watches our jostle for the doorway with a gleam in his squinty eyes, and Gil finally gives into temptation by moving that black rock another space.

"Oh, and Jane," Fortuna swings back at the last moment, her corset barely missing Horeb's head. "Have you been to the seamstress yet? That young Helena Salomon – she's already made Sadie a new bodice and it's a design from France that she found out in New York. I didn't know she'd gone to New York – I thought it was Chicago."

"You'll have to ask Marie for the details," I say, winking at Gil around Fortuna's shoulder.

Horeb notices and spins back. "You cheated, didn't you? Goddamn you, Gil—!"

"Ain't."

Fortuna departs with a yank on the door, and I walk further in, searching for the coffee, sugar and flour. Everything is still extra messy, the disorder brought by moving things to re-build and Kate tossing out tons of goods that were ruined either by fire or the remedy to put it out. Most of the white sugar was covered in black water, and sand filled the open tobacco bag. Kate has since ordered in plenty of goods with the money she brought out of her home after the fire, but no amount of willpower and hope will make the trains come faster, the orders fill sooner, or the rails stay sound. On top of the unevenness of train travel and communications, she now struggles against competition she created herself in the wake of the fire, when none could safely buy goods from her, and yet all needed a place to do business. I have heard many say that while they do not like going into the old cooperage and doing business with Yves Gardnier or one of his creepy posse members, the man often has items Kate cannot yet get, as if they procure things from a private stash.

Kate is not behind the counter, so I wander about myself, still looking for where she may have moved the coffee. There's none to be found, and I'm about to give in and ask Horeb or Gil if they know anything about brown sugar, when the faded calico curtain between the back room and the general's main one rips open. With the movement, the fabric gives off the acrid stench of rotted burning. I'm surprised she has not replaced it. Why would she want a memory of the fire such as that?

"What do you need?" Kate asks. She walks to the register and waits without meeting my eye.

It feels like walking through sludge to approach her. We have not resolved the tearing of our friendship, accusations, and anger that runs between us. Though I truly believe she may have been some sort of friend when I first arrived, it is clear it was less about who I was and more about my position as Dr. Kinney's housekeeper. She had worried I was competition...and I made her fears come true.

To be fair, I had not known she and my husband had been lovers until only a handful of weeks ago. I did not understand how much she had craved to marry a man of some stature in order to raise her own standing. I still don't understand this notion, for Kate is perhaps the most powerful woman in Flats Junction. Still, she harbors resentment toward me, for I have disrupted her world. Not only by marrying the doctor, but by keeping her mother close even when

Esther would have left. It seems my very nature is set to oppose Kate's.

And yet, strangely, it is not at all what I want.

"Coffee, please," I say, hoping emotion doesn't creep into my request. Horeb will hear it clear across the room.

"Don't have any yet."

"Then...flour. Brown sugar?"

"None of it," she says.

"Perhaps you should put up a sign, so you needn't answer the same requests."

"That's assuming half the people can read it," she says, tossing her head and looking down at me. She crosses her arms. Today she wears a dress made of bright green plaid—new, and likely the first thing Helena sewed. It has a fashionable cut to the bottom of the bodice, with additional swoops to the fabric across the front and back. It is the most feminine thing I have ever seen on her, and I try not to stare with admiration. It will likely only annoy her. Then again, perhaps she will be even more annoyed if I do not compliment the style.

"Anyway," she says, poking a pin back into her hair. "Who are you to tell me how to run my store?"

"I would never presume to do so," I say, wanting to flee and only grateful there is no one near enough to hear our quarrel. "I'd never tell you how to live, Kate."

She arches over the counter, her black eyes pinning me. "I'd never take your advice, Jane. I'd assume you'd only want to ruin it further than you already have."

Her rancor tears into me, a physical slash across my ribs and under my belly. My tongue feels narrow with words that wish to spill and would only fester the trouble further.

In some ways, she is right to accuse me, for all I did not act against her on purpose.

"I never hurt you with malicious intent," I say evenly, raising my chin to meet her eyes. "You must believe me, Kate."

"Why should I?" she says. "You've taken the one man who would have wed me and made my mother more yours than mine."

"I think you've done enough of the ruining yourself," I tell her.

The reaction is not expected. She pauses completely, as still as stone, before she pales, her eyes round. She pulls up and glances about with darting eyes, and then backs away from the counter with her arms tight around her middle.

"Go see if Yves has what you need," she says, her voice flat but quivering on the edge. "Go on."

Her dismissal is raw and makes me pause, even as my feet follow her orders. Had my words hurt her further? Or was it a truth she has long known and never heard?

I flee the General without looking like I am, and walk the short distance up Davies Avenue to First Street on the north of Flats Junction, hoping the walk stills my pounding heart. There are many people milling about the old cooperage, with Yves himself standing next to the front door. His bald head shines with sweat and his tiny eyes glimmer as he tucks his hands deep into the pockets of brand-new broadcloth pants and a vest made of brocade.

Yves' right-hand man, Arnold Black, picks under his nails with a small knife while leaning against the wall, his eyes catching all who enter. His brilliant smile flashes as Else and Kjersti Henderssen skirt in. They jump a bit to the side when they notice his grin, giggle nervously, and scoot inside. He chuckles and goes back to his knife.

Off to the side, Evan and Natty drink out of a jug they pass between them, and by the stench of it, it's pure whiskey. Evan burps, and Yves rounds from his post at the door.

"Stop drinking zee goods, you fools!" he roars. Natty gulps his mouthful before hastily shoving the jug at Evan. Evan pokes an eye down into the mouth of the jar, just in time for Yves to march over and rip it out of his grasp. He looks around, blank face bewildered, before he notices Yves's purple face.

"Just for zat, you must go now and stack zee flour bags from the back!" Yves barks. "We are to be a respectable business, that is zee plan!"

Evan ambles up, but Natty plants his bottom further on his seat, the liquor making him more defiant than typical. Yves growls, then lashes out, his hand so fast I do not quite see it move. Suddenly, his fingers are in the tender spot right between Natty's voicebox and collarbones, a sensitive spot to be sure, and one that can compress air quickly. Yves glares at Natty, who stares back, breathing out of his nose hard. Everyone glancing at the goods stacked outside begins inching away from the scene—Bianca Brewer actually starts walking backwards towards the street where she'll be safe but still able to see the activity. It's as if Yves's business has become a daily sideshow of entertainment for everyone. Kate may find it hard to lure customers back if there is always this kind of excitement.

Arnold does not move, nor does he look up from his nails. I try to sidle past him, unwilling to witness the exchange. The idea that all of this is entertainment sticks with me as I enter Yves's unorganized clutter, and I see Patty sitting on the boards set up as a counter with her skirts hiked up and two cowboys standing as close to her as possible without actually touching her. Victoria glowers at the men as they eye up Patty's calves and knees, but she's stuck handling money from Harriet Lindsey, who has bought three cones of brown sugar and one of white.

Patty still wears knives around the waistband of her skirt, and Victoria has matching ones in hers. The two look extra painted up, as if they've exchanged beauty advice from Fortuna's girls and then botched it.

There's little room to move, as Yves and his gang obviously do not have a handle on the best way to lay out goods in a store. There are only the few shelves along the one wall, where Franklin must have kept finished buckets and barrels for sale before he lost his arm and his trade. Those are now stacked high with 'magic' yeast and tomatoes and the shelves sag in the middle with the weight of the stamped tin cans.

Old Henry Brinkley pokes around the lard and molasses while his wife Susan gossips in a far corner with Berit Salomon, their eyes dancing as fast as their hands as they chatter in low voices.

I move next to Old Henry and smile at him. "How are you today?"

"Eh. Gout's something fierce, but isn't it always?" he says, then seems to realize who I am, and shakes his head. "But no need for anything fancy or some city medicine, it's just old age. Can't be helped."

"As you say," I agree, refusing to start another argument today. The pause between us is uncomfortable at once, and I jump into it with the old Boston ways of small talk.

"And how is Alice? I will never forget how she made such a fine friend from the moment I arrived. With her little ones underfoot, I scarcely see her these days."

"Yes, well…" Old Henry pushes up his hat and scratches behind his ear, then winces as he puts full weight on his right foot "She's fine enough, I suppose."

"Fine? Susan just said she is poorly these days," Berit inserts herself in our conversation. Susan moves to Old Henry's side and offers him her arm for balance. She smiles slightly at me, the roundness of her cheeks going up in soft folds.

"Alice is ill?" I am surprised, and then saddened. Her husband Mitch has always had Patrick help for everything and anything—from the birth of calves to his own children. "But she has two babies now; is she bleed—." My mouth clamps shut. I had almost starting speaking like a nurse! Discussing blood in public—perhaps I do not have as tight a hold on city manners as I like to believe.

"She's fine," Old Henry grunts. "Just quieter is all. You ready?" He tilts his head at Susan and the door. She nods and they sweep out. Berit smiles at me and goes back to her shopping, adding comments to anyone she passes. A flash of envy shoots through my mind at her ease. What would it be to move so seamlessly among the town? Is it something earned, or something to simply just…do?

After a walk around the store, I am convinced no one has canned milk. This is proven as fact when Victoria drags Yves in to answer my question.

"What is zee trouble?" he asks, coming in at once when she hollers.

"It's the doc's wife, wanting milk."

Yves wipes blood off his knife, looking content with himself as he comes behind the counter. "The milk in the can, we do not have today, but we will do so soon, a day or two."

I look around. "Do you have a storeroom where you're keeping uncounted goods, then?"

Yves laughs, a shrill and nasal sound that sounds like snot bubbling behind his teeth. "Oh, no, see, Matthias is zee one who manages a…ledger as Miss Kate calls it. Books. He is zee one who is doing zee organizing and knows what we have and when."

"I suppose I must do without, then," I say, looking about for Matthias Hummel, though I would have noticed him from the start for the amount of room he takes up.

"I promise to get some of the powder milk first ting, and save zee first can for you," he says smoothly, wiping his hand across his bare scalp and gazing at me straight. "So many of zee details to run a store, to be able to help all zee people so they know they are safe. It is like…it is if I was zee mayor, taking care of all."

"There's been no mayor of Flats Junction since Percy Davies died," old Simon Zalenski drawls, looking up from a pile of squashes. His voice is tremendously overloud, and everyone hears and nods. Yves does not quite turn purple, but his cheeks go a mottled mauve.

I quickly take my handful of purchases, made with Victoria's ham-handed shopgirl attitude, and head to the Brinkley farms for fresh milk as canned is out of the question. Besides, it will give me a reason to stop in and see Alice. Old Henry's words have me worried for her. While I am quite certain this notion does not make me a busybody, it must be how a doctor or nurse feels when they hear of illness. It must be.

124

The walk to the Brinkley farm is not far from our house, so I leave off the sugar, coffee, and heavy bag of flour before heading east. Esther is still not returned, and I note the time before departing. Patrick should not be home yet, if he will make his other rounds, and he had packed bread and hard cheese for lunch. I should have time to see my friend, even briefly.

"Alice?" I call, knocking with one hand as the other grasps the handle. "Are you home?"

"Jane? Is that you?"

She sounds fine. Perhaps Old Henry was mistaken. Alice seems just herself. I step in, trying to be casual, and enter the large space where Alice, Mitch, and their two boys live – the only extra room being a back bedroom. Alice does not move from the stove at my entry, and her toddler, Petey, does not stop running a carved cow about on the floor.

"I have come to get some milk from the farm, but thought I'd see you first. There he is. Little Freddy." I pick up the cooing infant and settle him into the kidney-curve space between my hip, waist, and thigh. Alice's eyes are bright.

"You'll do well, Jane, as a mother."

"I hope so."

"Well, you've got at least twenty other women who you can ask for advice, and another twenty who will offer it even if you don't."

"I know," I sigh into the babe's hair and close my eyes, feeling thankful. Here one has the freedom and the potential to create a family from scratch. To cobble together a mismatched, curated group that supports one another for everything from joy and happiness to utter survival. This is one of the intangible beauties of the west.

I hold the little one and look over Alice, gauging her color and her energy. It will not harm to ask direct, if I do so delicately.

"Doctor Kinney wants me to ask how you're feeling since the birth. The bleeding is gone, and you feel hearty?"

She waves a hand and bustles about, kneading the dough rising on her stove and bending for a thorough clean of Petey's messy face. He scowls at her and swats her hands.

"I'm doing perfectly well. Why? Is Mitch worrying?"

"No..." I lower my eyes. "Should he be?"

"I hope not," she says and then squints out the window at the dark, tiny figures in the far pasture. "It's only...I know he wishes to...touch me again. And I'm not...I mean. I still love him dearly. And I love the boys." She glances at the curled ball of baby softness in my arm. "But I..."

Her eyes suddenly fill and then pour, a cascade of salt water, and she gropes to the table and sits slowly, wiping her face with her apron though it does no good.

"I'm sorry, Jane, truly!" she gasps. "It's only...sometimes I can't get it to stop!"

This is so unlike my laughing, sparkling friend. I stare before I remember I should be calm and comforting instead of shocked. Old Henry had warned of this, after all... For all her hardships, Alice has always been bright-eyed and beaming. This sudden, twisted change is disconcerting. Her shoulders slump and she sinks her head in her arms. Petey silently goes to her and rubs his forehead into her side, but she doesn't move to take him.

"How long have you been so sad?" I wonder, feeling bewildered.

"I...it comes and goes. I don't know. I want to just stop

working sometimes. There are days I wish my parents had never brought us out here – that we'd stayed in Iowa. And I hate the farm work now – with a passion I never did before. And Mitch's family...they are kind, all of them, but I...oh, I don't *know*, Jane. *I don't know*!"

I walk to her and grip her shoulder hard, feeling the deepness of her weeping through the thin summer calico. Without knowing what to tell her, I slowly trace the delicate pattern of the leaves and flowers in the faded pink fabric, and then rub the back of her neck. The touch feels both odd and foreign but also all I can think to do. What ails her, truly? Is she unhappy with her marriage? I cannot imagine Mitch as unkind, but why else would she be so weepy?

The thought creeps toward me, clearing with the noon sunlight. Sometimes a woman can get sad. She might get anxious, and lonely and angry and lash out. Just the other week, Patrick had to treat a backwoodsman from an ax wound. When he had arrived at our door, with his forearm nearly cleaved through and the bandage black with blood, his wife had hopped down from the wagon bed and watched, staunch and stoic as Patrick had bloodied the surgery and tried to connect arteries. When I had asked how it happened, she had looked at me, with eyes pale and dead, and said quite calmly that it had been her ax stroke, and no, it had not been an accident.

What to do with emotion like that? Violent and quiet and sudden? I stare at Alice's wheat-colored hair and at the fine, curling whorls that spray up from her scalp. Surely, she would not lash out at Mitch, who adores her?

It must be the work of the fields she does along with the trials of another babe. And perhaps that she still feels a bit of an outsider with all of her sister-in-laws and Mitch's overwhelming and opinionated family. And perhaps even she doesn't like the way it is so hot these days. But how do I cure this? How to help? There is no medicine that Patrick has on hand to make a woman happy again.

I suddenly recall the herbs in the leather roll at the bottom of my basket. What had the skullcap been for? *Nervousness. A sedative...for removing the trouble of an overeager mind.* Had there been any warnings? A dosage? I know enough that some medications must be greeted with caution for all their strengths.

Leaving Alice for a moment, and still with the babe on my hip, I pull out the leather roll and find the tincture, fit snugly in the small tube of material Esther had sewn in so the glass did not crack when I walked about with the kit. "Would you like to try something? It's not much, made from some of the local flowers around here. It's supposed to help with sorrow, so they say."

Alice brings her head up. "A medicine? For...tears?"

"So they say."

I hope she does not ask me who "they" are, as I am quite sure—as is Patrick— that the notion of Esther's people being a source of medical knowledge will not be met with widespread acceptance, and I do not wish to lie if it can be helped.

There's warm water in the kettle on the stove, kept there for any quick cooking needs. I pour some in a cup and add several drops of the skullcap into it. It turns the water a soft gold. Alice takes it without question, wrapping her chapped hands around the sides of the pottery. She takes a shaky breath and sips a long, slow drink.

"How does it taste?" I ask, curious. Esther and I do not always eat the medicines we discuss. It looks like weak piss.

"It tastes…like lettuce and a sweetness. Whiskey?"

"There's rum," I admit. "But it is the flowers that are important. Do you like it?"

She takes another long draught, almost emptying the cup at once, and leans back. Will it work so quickly, or is simply knowing there may be an answer to her sadness that gives her relief?

She sighs and wipes her face once again. By now the skin is pink and a bit raw around the eyes where she's been wiping constantly. Finally putting her arm around little Petey, she looks up at me and I stop stroking her hair and neck.

"Thank you, Janie. Might Mitch purchase some of the medicine from Patrick?"

"Of course. I'll take care of it. He can get it from me any time," I say, and put my forearm around her collarbones. They feel thinner than I think they should be, and I frown. "And you are sure you're alright? The bleeding is done? Your appetite is fine?"

She manages a wan smile. "It's better than it was. A good cry helps too – I'm sorry I'm not a cheerful host today."

"You're my dear friend," I tell her. It was Alice who was with me in the beginning of the hemorrhage that nearly killed me. She worried over me then, as I do for her now. "And if you like I could tell the Doctor about your woes, too."

Her sensitive mouth draws up and she shakes her head. "Whatever you do, tell him no laudanum. My aunt did that after her last daughter was born and she was never the same again."

We chat about small things then, and I try to help with little tasks for another hour. By the time I tell Alice I must head home, her house feels a bit tidier and she looks nearly rested. As I make to leave, Mitch comes in.

"Mrs. Kinney!"

"Hello," I say, tying my bonnet back on. "And goodbye."

"In for the day?" Alice asks him.

He checks at her cheery greeting. "Ah…yup. You don't mind?"

"No, no. Jane has helped with a few things."

"That sounds very nice, sweet Alice," Mitch nods, his eyes stuck to mine and a plead in them that I am not sure how to read. I decide to plunge in. I've already given his wife medicine. May as well make it official.

"I thought Alice might like one of the little womanly tinctures I've made, what with Freddy's recent birth," I tell him, nodding at the dark brown little bottle on the table. "It is said to help keep the spirits up."

"It works lovely, darling," Alice says, and Mitch's eyes shoot to her, hope rising.

"Does it?" he asks, sounding over eager. "Does it really?"

"It seems to help," I amend. I close the door softly behind me as I go out, hoping that somehow I can pull Alice out of her hidden tears and woes, whatever they may really be. Perhaps she just needs a friend. I know I sometimes feel that, too.

As I pick my way around the broken ground, cracked with heat and cow tracks, Mitch's voice calls after me. I turn, the sun on my back, as he hurries to catch up, a small tin pail with a matching lid clutched in his hands.

130

"Alice said you came for milk, but you didn't get any. Here." He thrusts the pail toward me. As I take it and tuck it into my basket, he switches his weight from one foot, then the other.

"I must thank you. For Alice. She's not been right since Freddy, and…" He looks up and squints at me, the sun full in his face. "I…she's my world. If I can repay…I'll have my father call for the doc. We can pay in cash, for a looksee at the sick cows or something."

"Your father has never wanted help with livestock beyond a competitiveness with the Svendsens," I say, touched regardless with the offer, which is kindly meant. "And he's been vocal about the black measles in town of late, too."

Mitch looks at the ground and scuffs a worn boot along a clump of dried manure. "He…he thinks Doc Kinney killed his best friend."

"His best…" My heart pauses, then thumps hard high in my chest. "You mean Walter Salomon?"

"The doc cut him open and he died."

Does it matter if I argue against this? Suppose I explain the nature of diphtheria, and of waiting too long for a cure, and the lack of iodine in the middle of an epidemic. Would it matter, or are people so determined to turn from science and aid?

"It was…it was a very terrible thing. Walter was so very ill, I don't think anything would have saved him."

Mitch nods, still looking at the dirt. He inhales suddenly and squares his shoulders. "But now you've saved my Alice. The doc's good enough for Svendsen's cows, too, so he's got to be good enough for ours. I'll say so."

His youthful earnestness is even more sweet, and I smile and thank him before heading back to town.

Suppose I really can cure Alice? Suppose it leads to further acceptance with the Brinkley's. And if they begin to support Patrick, that will mean ever more of it from others in Flats Junction, regardless of illness or reservations and prejudice. Would that not be a feather in my own cap, to prove to my husband that the womanly medicines I'm learning are enough to change the tide toward him and his own science? Would that not make a case for my own desire to learn and to heal the sick in my own way?

Alice Brinkley

August 8 1883
Found Alice to be sorrowful and not herself. Sadness and anger
together, unlike her usual cheer. With the birth of her recent child, I believe a tonic for the nerves will help.

Rx

A cup of hot water with four drops of Skullcap

tincture.

September 1 1883
Per Esther's recommendation, an addition to skullcap.
Rx Goat's Rue
A spoonful of leaves steeped in water as a tea.

Patient – henry brinkley sr. –Old Henry

Brinkley farmstead, east of town

Occupation farmer

Dates	
june 1 1879	complaints of gout in both feet
	recall use of colchicine, as mentioned in Virchow's Archiv
	Philipp Lorenz Geiger isolated for use against gout
	~~ask esther davies about chokecherry use?~~
	monitor gout as possible when visiting farm
march 2 1884	note fever and death amid svendsen cattle
	lost several head quickly due to sickness.
	same reported at brinkley farm
	– can this disease travel the air?

CHAPTER EIGHT

Patrick

May 17, 1860

Doctor Burns read the paper every night. He did it slowly, with the same careful method he did for every piece of his practice. His daughter always ate quickly and then went to sew in the far corner. Sometimes Tara would knit, other times crochet. And then there was Thomas, who would take turns bein' extra slow at the table or quick enough to sit for a long time at Tara's side, askin' her simple questions while she stitched just to keep her side attention on himself.

It didn't matter to Patrick. He waited for everyone to leave the table, and then had to clean the plates. He tried to always forget that he and Thomas were the same age, but Thomas liked to remind him. Thomas had a slightly elevated status in the house because he had been chosen by Doctor Burns to be his apprentice. Patrick was only there due to a favor Mr. McClure had called in, and then paid the difference while Patrick did the rest in the form of labor, of which there was a fair amount due to Doctor Burns' wife passin' years ago.

"It's high time we think of some work for ye, boy," Mr. McClure had said. "You have a way with animals, and work as a vet might suit you, seein' as ye have an eye for healin'."

"Work?" Aunt Bonnie had asked, lookin' shocked. "Patrick still has schoolin' to do."

"Ye had a good long schoolin', Bonnie," Mr. McClure had reminded her. "But you were a lucky few. Here Patrick can start to learn a trade when he's not at lessons. You could do with somethin' solid, such as to learn about horses, boyo. At least there is a livin' in that."

"Horses are fine, but I'd rather fix people. Like when Mr. MacHugh was sick on the beach. I could fix him," Patrick had said, speaking bluntly without thinkin' first, but Mr. McClure had just nodded, lookin' far off as he did, thoughts pilin' behind his shining head.

"I can think of a place or two to put ye, Paddy. It's no real trouble."

"You're very kind on all this," Aunt Bonnie had said tightly. "But I'm sure any type of apprenticeship will have a price and we're wound hard enough. I won't spend coin on Patrick chasin' somethin' that's not even a real job. I hate to talk money, Andy," she said, angrier as she went. "But these grand ideas are just not properly affordable—"

"I know that," Mr. McClure patted her arm and smiled at Patrick. "But as I don't have any family here to spoil, I don't mind takin' your nephew under my wing a bit when I can. Consider it my appreciation of your delightful cookin', and the extra paperwork ye do for me, and you workin' the occasional Sunday when I need ye. I don't mean he should stop attendin' Arrott's at the first, but he should look to what he might want to do with himself."

But the lessons at Arrott's stopped once it became clear he couldn't manage runnin' to and from school and still be able to work at Doctor Burns' side. It was no matter, as Michael had stopped goin' the previous months so he could work at the docks and help support his mam what with his da not always bringin' home enough.

The kettle on the small stove set out a jet of steam as it boiled for the evening tea. It was Patrick's job to manage the kitchen as best he could as part of the payment for his place at Doctor Burns' house. He pulled down cups and balanced the kettle along his spare two fingers. It was made of copper, and lighter than Aunt Bonnie's iron piece, but the handle was spun of coppery bronze too, and flushed hot fast under his hands even when he wrapped a rag around.

He hurried to the table and set it out amid the dirty plates. The evening ritual was an early one, but enjoyable. Doctor Burns set down his paper, and reached into his pocket, pullin' out odds and ends of papers, prescriptions, and notes. Patrick quickly grabbed the last of the cutlery and put them in the bucket to soak before jumpin' to his seat at the table at the doctor's left hand. Thomas did not move from Tara's side, which made him the first to fall to the doctor's inquiry.

"Well then, Thomas, how did you feel about usin' the ophthalmoscope?" Doctor Burns had a heavy beard that he kept well groomed, and a habit of strokin' it when he began to question the boys about the day's experiences or their lessons. He was well-known in the doctorin' circles for his wide collection of medical books, and his experience with performin' tracheotomies on children sufferin' severely from diphtheria.

Thomas looked up, guilt flashin' across his cheek-bones, before he left Tara and leapt to his place at the table as well. As an eclectic doctor, Doc Burns enjoyed the new methods available and didn't believe in the old 'heroic' ortho-dox beliefs. He was strictly against the blood lettin' and givin' mercury and didn't believe in the excessive druggin' that marked homeopathic practitioners either. He was also very open to the constant change in the profession and had invested in several stethoscopes, the newest improvement on the ophthalmoscope to combat eye disease, and even a sphygmomanometer to better study pulse pressure. The tools were astoundin', and Patrick felt fortunate every day that Mr. McClure had found a way to make the whole learnin' possible. He dreamed some nights of settin' out his own shingle, treatin' the Irish, and whoever else would have the skill of his hands and mind.

"I would like to draw out the many different eyes we see," Thomas said, settlin' into his chair in a long, easy sort of way. "And list out any complaints along with the draw-ings. We might see similarities in eyes and be able to identify ailments in a new way."

Doctor Burns nodded. "Very good plan, Thomas."

Patrick leaned forward across the table. "Doctor, can we see a lecture? I heard that someone is going to talk about usin' Semmelweis's research to talk about what causes disease and usin' hot water to kill it on your instruments."

There was a pause at the table. Doctor Burns mused on the notion of purifyin' instruments quite often. He often quoted a Doctor Dudley, a curmudgeon who had taught that everything should be boiled. Doctor Burns only used whiskey, but he said it should be just as good, and did a clean of his tools once a week. Patrick secretly thought he also liked how shiny the alcohol made his forceps.

"We shall see," said Doctor Burns, methodically stacking his newspapers and articles. "But now we must mix some medicines for tonight's house call. Patrick, why don't you prepare the first?"

The doctor handed Patrick a note dotted with his horrific handwriting, likely put down while he was walking home. He squeezed his eyes shut and worked to decipher it.

Angels Fevrefuge

Rx	Zinc Digitalis	1 gr
	Sweet of the Sitre	4 gr
	Elixir Tavigerie	3 gr
	Tarter emetie	1 gr

Dose a teaspoonful to patient every two hours in water.

Patrick quickly recalled the receipt. It was one used for those suffering from a difficult fever that had no other obvious symptoms. He went to the cabinet by the hearth to gather the vials, which were labeled with precision. This part was the easy piece of doctor learnin', and both Thomas and Patrick were proficient at it. The rest of the apprenticeship generally meant Patrick and Thomas sat in the shadows and observed how warmly Doctor Burns made his patients and their families feel confident in his skills. He was careful to never over promise the relief or recovery, but did his best, and was not afraid to come home and consult books before headin' back out to a difficult case to try a new idea.

Once the boys finished answering another dozen questions each and stopperin' up a few more bottles, Doctor Burns glanced at his pocket watch.

"Enough for today. Light lamps and we'll go to the Meely's as the last stop, unless."

He always ended his statements so. It meant the unknown. *Unless someone is sick. Unless someone is injured. Unless someone needs something.*

The doctor was forever at the mercy of his patients. Should he be unavailable, there were plenty of other practitioners around who would happily jump into the space left by Doctor Burns, even though they would not be as experienced nor as capable. The two apprentices always went with him, though at times Thomas requested to stay back to keep Tara company. She never spoke up when he asked, and Doc Burns never allowed it.

They stepped out, and Doctor Burns strolled between Thomas and Patrick, his gait unhurried but straight. "Tonight is a good night to discuss your futures, boys, as we walk under this fine sky. It is never too soon to think of it."

"Already?" Patrick did not feel prepared. It had only been a little less than two years. He figured he could still do with memorizin' the medical texts in Doctor Burns' small library. He would like to write out copies of remedies. So much would be reliant on his own confidence, and his own ability to guess and be correct. He wasn't ready to think beyond the next week. Though the trade came easy to him, and he was surprised at how quickly he grasped the concepts, he knew there was so much more to fill into his head.

Thomas inhaled and exhaled sharply. "I hope to go overseas to school next," he said. "All the hospital men send their boys over to learn."

Doctor Burns tilted his head. "And you have a sponsor for that?"

Thomas had the presence of mind to bend his neck. "No, not yet."

Raising his eyebrows, Doctor Burns looked at Patrick. He felt a flush pull up his neck, stoppin' at his jaw. He didn't have a plan, and didn't like bein' unprepared, so he spoke plain, and to the simple heart of his dreamin'. "I was hopin' to stay on here, in Boston."

"Why?" Doctor Burns asked, his voice mild in the gloamin'.

"My aunt is still here, and I wouldn't like to leave her all alone," Patrick said. "She's all I have, and I'm all her own family."

"She could leave with you," Thomas pointed out plainly, as though Patrick would not think of this option on his own. "Wherever you have to go."

"Aye," Patrick nodded. "But she won't want to leave the good work she has, as it pays enough for her to live. I couldn't support us both, at least not right away."

"Wise," Doctor Burns replied. They all walked now in single file along the last of the quay leadin' into the fashionable district along Newbury and Boylston streets, and the brownstone houses. Fruit and nut trees crammed into back gardens, and stone stairs soared higher and higher. There was less noise, too, and Patrick inhaled at the loss of the stench of chamber pots and rottin' manure.

"Neither of you will have an easy time of it in the city opening up your own door, and hanging a shingle," Doctor Burns said, his low voice a calm cadence. "The orthodox doctors will not let you into the hospitals, unless, as Thomas says, you study overseas. Nor will the AMA accept you completely as you did not attend their school, and this regardless of the laws in place saying they cannot ban us from practicing. You will be wrestling countless others for patients."

"Why did you train us, then?" Patrick asked curiously, bluntly. He wondered if Mr. McClure was wastin' his money. Aunt Bonnie would never gloat, but she'd also never let Patrick try somethin' frivolous again.

"There are many who call themselves docs, but few who are properly trained." Doctor Burns checked his watch again, the gilt on the chain glitterin' in the evening sunlight, the last gold rays drippin' off the edges. "If we are all – traditional, Eclectic, homeopaths – going to ask the government, universities and the public to take us seriously, we must have good practitioners. That starts here, at apprenticeships, proper ones. And then it means spreading out across the country and proving, bit by bit, that trained doctors are valuable."

"That is another reason I wish to stay nearby," Patrick said quickly, before Thomas could say a thing. "I want to still be able to ask permission from you to use some of your medical texts if I need them."

It was a compliment to Doc Burns on many levels, but he didn't acknowledge it. "It will be very difficult for you to do, Patrick. There are so many doctors in the city. And you're Irish."

"Take up another trade," scoffed Thomas. "You'll

need it, Pat." He glanced over his shoulder, a sly swipe of a dark head and even darker eye. "I won't go overseas too soon. I want to be close to the action. Some of the boys down at the Medical Society say that the allopaths and traditional docs are specializing their craft, still calling homeopaths heretics. Let them. Their ability will shrink, and they'll need us to sort through the mess."

"You can only do that if you keep up with diagnosin' full-on disease instead of each symptom a patient complains about," Patrick poked Thomas in the lower back, just enough to bug him, but not enough to cause him to trip. It was an ongoing point of argument between the two of them, poppin' up at least once a week. Patrick believed learnin' about all the ailments and figurin' out the puzzle and Thomas thought treatin' each issue individually was the best course.

"Pop off it, Paddy," he said, stoppin' short for a brief moment, just so Patrick collided with his backside.

"Enough," Doctor Burns said. "We're nearly there." He strode a bit faster as the light dipped, and the lanterns about the streets glowed more as the shadows deepened. Thomas fell in next to Patrick.

"I'll always stay in a city where most of the people are," Thomas continued, still on a rant. "When these fancy hospital docs need patients from the masses, they'll owe their income to our referrals. They will have to open up their hospital doors to welcome us in, to bring in the bodies."

"Everyone is talkin' about the science of medicine," Patrick said, his voice going softer the deeper they walked into the finer streets behind Doctor Burns. "What makes you think everyone will not have to start sharin' beliefs about how they practice it?"

Doctor Burns paused in front of a house and looked up at it through the dark gates. "You both may be right," Doctor Burns said. "And an auspicious discussion to have tonight, of all nights. Be prepared, boys." Doctor Burns could be cryptic when he wished, and it usually meant something more excitin' was happenin' than a simple house call. Patrick's heart pattered with a sense of a thrill, now familiar after months of time under Doc Burns.

Thomas glanced up and down the street, which towered with townhouses. He frowned. "Wait. This is Union Park. Isn't this out of your area?" They never went to the fashionable South End. Patrick often wondered if it was partially Doctor Burns bein' stubborn. Alexander Rice lived at number 34 on Union Park, and when he'd been mayor three years ago, he'd helped establish the Boston City Hospital, a place a man like Doc Burns would never set foot. On top of that, the territories between physicians were typically quite specific. Patient stealing was a strictly against the rules. In some places, homeopathic and orthodox doctors could not buy goods or services from one another's patients for fear of recriminations. Sometimes patients couldn't even mix socially, just as Mr. McClure had said years before. It was gettin' ridiculous in Patrick's mind. Something would have to give within the profession. Maybe usin' new science would create a place in the middle where they all could meet and agree.

"This is Doc Halverman's area," Thomas put name to place. "We'll be shunned if we go in. Won't we?"

"Yes, Thomas, usually," Doctor Burns said, putting his hand on the gate latch. "As we've been discussing at length, we should all start working together. Isn't that right,

Patrick?" Why was he askin' each to pick sides aloud? Patrick was still busy mullin' on the whole idea of doctorin' options and now he should pick a side in the convoluted argument.

Before Patrick could answer, the door of the great house yanked open and Doctor Halverman himself was there, flushed and excited. His obvious energy was odd for a serious traditional doctor, and Patrick felt another a surge of excitement.

"Come in! Hurry along, if you please."

Was it a trick? Did he not worry about other doctors seein' them all together? He most clearly did not. There were physicians of all walks inside. Thomas nudged Patrick under the ribs. One of the Bigelow's, a head of the biggest establishments, distinguished by his sleek appearance amid the rest, stood to the side, smokin' a pipe. What was a hospital man doing down in the streets? For all he was also a traditional doctor, he would not normally leave the whitewashed walls of his building to mush around even the best houses of Boston. Patrick was certain he felt as bewildered as Thomas looked, for once less smooth and just as out of place. They were some of the youngest there and they stood against a wall with other apprentices. Each eyed the others with suspicion. None wanted to speak to another, not knowin' where they stood amid medicine and the ongoing ardent discussions.

As everyone milled about without takin' off shoes or hats, Patrick noticed two patients trundled together along the back wall. They sat in various states of discomfort, bandaged and stiff under the white cloth. They looked nervous, and each dressed in the clothes of household staff.

Doctor Halverman began, soundin' truly like he enjoyed lecturing. "As you all know, infection is one of the greatest issues we face whenever an incision needs to be made," he announced, stating a well-known fact. "Any surgery brings vast risk. However, there seems to be some correlation with cleanliness and infection. Some of the docs who are in town from the front lines now swear by clean tools."

"So I've heard." Doctor Burns says, breaking Doctor Halverman's rhythm. He suddenly turned to Patrick. "And so do you, Patrick, isn't that right?"

Had he watched Patrick clean the instruments one late night? Did he spy on Thomas, too? The idea was unnervin', but there was nothing for it but to own up.

"I do," Patrick confirmed. "It seems to make sense to clean them at least after any use, if not right before."

The extra opinions made Doctor Halverman fidgety. "Right. Well, infection can set in easily. And it's not always foolproof, of course, to clean our instruments. There is still much to learn about humors and pus. But I have made a grand experiment – it will change everything. Come, all of you. It's time to reveal."

He led the way over to the patients by the wall. They were heavily bandaged, so much so that it was difficult to tell the gender except by the clothing they wore.

"These two patients are just the latest who have benefited from this," Doctor Halverman gestured. "I will unwrap each, and you will see the state of their injuries yourself. A pot on the stove in their kitchen exploded, sending hot oil into the air and severely burning this cook and her help."

Everyone murmured as Doctor Halverman unwrapped each bandage of the older woman. The cook had needed a large chunk of skin to be sewn together to hide gapin' holes in her arms. Some men turned away, coverin' their faces. Others leaned in. Patrick stepped as close as he could without lookin' foolish. The scar tissue had not yet formed, and the site of surgery was still quite fresh.

Commonly, Patrick now expected to see some red and pink, showin' low level infection, or worse, bright red lines shootin' up to show that the blood had gone poisoned and bad. To have no infection at this stage was a beautiful, unexpected sight.

Doctor Halverman then turned to the other patient. The girl's eyes were wide, darting to all of the men in the room, and her fingers trembled. She was covered in bandages all along her arms and hands, across her chest and neck, covering patches of her face. The first wrap that came away revealed angry, oozin' burns. Patrick was filled with questions, a yearnin'. How was this woman not in more pain? He asked the question without thinkin', and Thomas shifted beside him, likely annoyed with the attention in their direction.

"I've given her enough morphine, just enough," Doctor Halverman explained, not lookin' up as he carefully peeled off the white cloth. The side of the bandage that faced her skin was heavily dappled with blood and fluid. Patrick leaned around the seasoned doctors to peer at the wrappings. All realized there was very little, if any, pus on them. Burns such as that were nearly always a death knell. There was no way to keep infection at bay, no way to keep disease from eating at the exposed meat of a body.

"How old are these burns?" Doctor Burns asked.

"About four days," Doctor Halverman said proudly, and everyone began to clamor loudly at his statement. By now, there would be painful pockets of pus, or a stench of rottin' flesh, the common stink of surgery and old meat.

"Alright, so somehow you are getting the infection to stay away?" Thomas' cynical voice carried through the lower rumble of other men's speculation. "So, you sterilize things. It's nothing magical."

"Ah, not exactly," Doctor Halverman was nearly gleeful. "It's more than that. It's this." He whipped out a large glass bottle. A rubber tube attached to a brass spigot on the top that was also connected on the other end to a large rubber bulb. The Bigelow from the hospital started to laugh.

"This is a joke, Joseph. You dragged me all the way down here to see some ladies perfume? You quack!"

Patrick had never seen a bottle of perfume, as Aunt Bonnie could never afford it even if she had wanted something so fine.

"I've been working on this for a few months," Doctor Halverman said curtly, directin' his annoyance directly at the hospital man. "It will revolutionize surgery, mark my words. It's called a carbolic acid."

"Heard 'bout that," grunted a squat man with a thick British drawl. "I've a colleague in Manchester, wrote me a year or two back abou' how they're usin' it as powder t' treat sewage across th' pond. Angus said the Queen had 'em use it durin' th' Great Stink."

Doctor Halverman pinched his lips hard, and then nodded once. "Yes, true, it is used that way across Great Britain. But the acid is being adopted in France and Italy—has been for a bit, according to Jules Lemaire. He's just published on the use of carbolic acid and how to use it for surgery, and I was able to get a copy translated. I thought I'd try to replicate his theory. I use the acid as a diluted spray on finished injuries, but otherwise my own hands and the patient's body is doused in it before any type of work is done. You see for yourselves – this woman, this patient, would likely be on her way to her death without this."

He was quite right, and everyone knew it. The sound in the room doubled, and many of the apprentices pushed against Patrick to get closer, Thomas at the front of them. Patrick himself wanted to believe it. It would change how medicine was handled. It would give surgery victims a chance at survival – more than they had ever had. It would give burn victims the cleanliness they needed to pull through. He wondered how the hospital men would take the discovery. This might be a catalyst: one of the many moments that could tie all the practices together.

As the others swarmed the two women, Patrick found an empty place next to Doctor Burns, who stood with Doctor Halverman to the side.

"I congratulate you, Joseph," Doctor Burns said. "How long have you been working on this?"

"Months," he admitted, without puttin' a number to it. "It was a bit to get the acid in the first place."

"We'll all want to start usin' it," Patrick said. "Everyone will."

Doctor Halverman nodded, and then stepped away to answer another question. Doctor Burns glanced at Patrick, a crinkle at the corner of his eye. "And what is the best part of this evening to you, boy?"

Patrick watched the tussle of bodies surroundin' the two kitchen staff, with Thomas pokin' a finger at the wounds, unwashed as he was, and the others makin' comments and theories, forgettin' for a few moments they were on opposite sides of a scientific argument.

"I couldn't choose, sir. Both things, I should think."

The answer wasn't definitive, but it seemed to satisfy Doctor Burns. It was only later, when they'd returned to the house, with Tara already asleep, and Thomas snorin' in the narrow bed across the attic way that Patrick realized he hadn't had to elaborate. Doc Burns had understood. Maybe there was a chance he'd pull ahead and make the doctor proud.

Maybe he really could become a doc, for all the things stacked against him. His Irishness; his poverty; his very accent. His lack of supportive family. The entire world of medicine, which seemed to need new ideas while hangin' on tight to the old ways, and doctors who were less welcomin' overall. The lack of books...

He fell asleep listing everything holdin' him in place, until the crushin' weight of the mountain of impossibilities disappeared in dreamin'.

CHAPTER NINE

Jane

September 3, 1883

The flicker of an old candle going to seed dances across the pitted, stained wood of the kitchen table. I glance at the rough surface with the golden flecks of light sputtering across it, and then at Patrick's small clock I've put next to the lantern. He's late. Something must have happened. I've spent yet another fall day going around town, from the General to Yves's, checking on a few minor injuries, and offering advice through a wooden door with a family fighting the dreaded black measles, which has reared again just as Patrick predicted.

My days have found rhythm, broken only by visits to Alice Brinkley to see how the tinctures work for her and to gather advice about childrearing and baby-keeping. There is so much to learn, from boiled bottles to washing out diapers so the stains don't sit. Alice seems better, though not back to herself. I've asked Esther for other ideas, finding my notes to be sparse and spare on the topic of a woman's mind. She has recommended what she called *čhošáša* though she says the other name is goat's rue, and Alice might like it to increase her milk for the new babe, so she is not so tired. It is a plant uncommon to the Dakota Territories, but Esther has planted it from seeds traded with her family years ago. Her mother had gone to Minnesota and brought them back, long before they went to the reservation. She knew exactly where it was, in the back garden of her old, burned house. The timbers were ash and black, crumbling and already moldering into the prairie, but her garden was still alive and growing wild outside its confines. She found the leaves and we dried them over the oven. I'd just made it into tea for Alice at the last visit, and I'm hopeful it will help. It seems the ways of this type of nursing are much more subtle and slow, and nothing like Patrick's sure strokes and confident knife cuts.

I cannot help but look at the clock. It's been a minute. Maybe two. It has been dark for hours. Perhaps I should go to bed? Perhaps a doctor's wife does not wait up, with food off to the side ready for re-heating, and count the moments. Perhaps I ought to put away my project and stop thinking and wondering.

But then I would not be my curious self, I suppose. I want to know what has happened. I wish to hear all the news. I want to be part of his world, even if it is only as a listener. I don't want to be stuck at the broad, pitted table, counting the hours. I want to be at his side, fingering the tools and watching his hands move across a patient's forehead.

Training my eyes back on the hem of the large rectangle of fabric, I stab the needle in and out quickly, weaving it

152

in a wave of bunched denim before pulling the thread tight. It is a simple way to hem and baste, but this is one of the few things I know I can sew without ruining. And besides, the old, stained kitchen table can do with a table linen, even if it is only plain cotton.

A creak makes me pause again, but it's only Esther, shifting in her sleep above and moving the small bed's wooden legs. It's been quiet enough above us these last few months, as the repairs to our porch and its roof are complete and there's no longer the shuffle and bump of men's knees or the thwack of hammering outside. I'm not used to the quiet during the day, and the night makes the lack of noise even more apparent.

The child in my womb shifts, a soft curl and press, and the gentleness of it forces me to stop sewing so I might cup the flesh below my waistband. This babe is different from the first I carried, which did not give much notice of its existence, and laid so still and calm that I suppose I now shouldn't wonder that I lost him. Perhaps an active child in the belly is a sign that all is well. Perhaps the stillness is a sign to fear. I must ask Patrick if there are any books—

The front door shivers on the hinges, catching on the new plank that abuts it. It will tear and wear down soon enough, but for now it does not allow a quiet entry to our hallway. The screen does not creak on the fresh spring, though. Patrick rustles at the hooks. There's the shuffle of his boots, the thunk of his medical bag, and the clink of glass as he goes back and forth from the surgery to replace used vials. I know his rhythm so well now that I can near time how long it will take for him to enter the kitchen. After prodding the fire, I put on the dark oiled skillet and push around the

153

yellow potatoes and glossy onions, with the parsley now so dark it looks like flecks of black char. They'll warm soon enough, and Patrick is taking an extra long time at the wash-bin, anyway.

When he finally enters the kitchen with damp fingers and dusty feet, I am pouring cold well water and setting out bread and jam.

"You're still awake," he says, sounding only slightly surprised.

"Of course I am."

"You don't need to be. Not always. And especially not these days." My husband's eyes flick to my waist and linger. "You must be tired, Janie."

"You once told me your great-aunt would just leave cold food out for you to grab as you had time."

"Aye," he says. He sits without preamble, reaching for the bread and knife.

"Well, I wish to do better. I am your wife, after all. Not your Aunt Bonnie."

Patrick pauses only slightly as I say the name, and then he begins to slather the jam on a thick slice, using double what I would have.

On the stove, the potatoes pop, and the bits of onion sizzle and leak more juice. I pull out the wad of half-burned sheep's wool from my apron pocket and grab down a tin plate, bringing it all to the table in one pass so Patrick does not need to stop eating. He clearly did not eat with his patients or their families, and I wonder if that is because they refused to have him at their kitchen or if he was afraid of infection. I find I'm upset by either, and hope he offers me a third reason.

He does. "I'm sorry I was so late, then. It's only that I cannot keep up. There is another rash of black measles out on the west side of Flats Junction – near the Woodman's and Wagner's farms and beyond. Only a handful are sick, but it's like there's pockets of it. And I still don't..." Patrick looks up from his plate. "You don't have to hear this. Go to bed."

"I'd rather not. Who else will you speak to about such things, if not me? It's been this way from the start, and I don't want to stop now." I take a seat opposite him, and serve myself a slice of bread, too.

He gazes at me across the flickering lantern glow, his eyes searching and then crinkling on the edges as he smiles and reaches to grip my free hand.

"You're right. From the first day you came here, you've been listenin' and learnin'. I prefer it like this, myself." His fingers settle on mine and one spins the band of gold I wear before he goes back to eating. "I mostly worry because Danny said one of his cowboys has it, so now I'm spendin' time at the Svendsen's checkin' on both cattle and man. If it weren't two different things—beast and boy—I'd think it the same disease in some respects for how it ebbs and flows with the seasons. My next worry will be if the Brinkley's..." He tilts his head back. "Speakin' on the Brinkley's. Mitch and his brother George said they'd like me to see the latest batch of sick cows. And maybe see Old Henry's gout."

I busy myself with another layer of jam. "That's wonderful. Maybe they're softening back up to you, Pat."

He is silent, and the sound of fork against metal doesn't resume, so I must look up or let the silence drag stupidly between us. Patrick's eyes are no longer merry, and his long mouth trembles with unspoken words.

I put the over-jellied piece of bread on his plate, with its half-mashed potato chunks and overcooked parsley. As I make to stand and get the water pitcher, his voice pins me.

"Mitch spoke of you."

Sitting back down slowly, I run my hand along a big seam that splits one of the old pieces of wood. It's wood that should not have been pieced together so early, and the green gave way to brittleness and pressure. A sliver catches the middle of my palm, and I pull it back lest I break it into my skin, where it will fester and infect...

"He said you've been seein' Alice."

I meet his frank gaze. "I have. She's my friend, and my oldest one at that." It's a dodge and we both know it. My heart flutters and then sinks into a boiling pit at the middle of my stomach, hard and tight.

"And you leave things. Little bottles and dried flowers. Teas and tinctures. A promise to heal and fix."

"I never overpromise," I protest.

He puts down his fork with deliberate delicacy, as if forcing himself not to chuck it across the room. I wonder if he purposefully shows restraint in this way, when I so often haven't. I had not thought him a petty sort of man.

"I asked you to stop meddlin' in such things," he says, and his voice is low and even. It's so unlike the fiery frustration that can pour out of him, and I find I dislike this control. It feels as though it's the most angry he's ever been with me, and the coldness is worse than the honest heat. I'd rather he shout. I'd rather his arms go stiff and cross and his head shake with emotion.

"I'm not," I say. "It would be meddling if you were treating Alice and I went around you. But you're not."

It's a truth, though he doesn't like it. I press my case. "It's a woman's matter anyway, Patrick. Do you have a powder that can ease a woman's milk? Or stop her weeping? I'm only trying to ease her sorrows. Some women have them, you know."

The doctor leans back in his seat, and the war of his pride and his scientific mind crackles off him. I can sense it in the thread between us, always there and tactile. We know how to speak to one another—or at least poke at one another—and I try, clumsy but with a mind to earnestness, to find footing for us both.

"I have done no harm. It seems to help. And…suppose there are always some who are too afraid of the new science and the city learning you bring. Maybe they'll take me. A woman is less…"

His eyebrows go wide. "Less?"

"I was going to say intimidating, but it seemed an insult to us both," I admit, looking down and rearranging the bread bits on the plank of wood in front of me.

"I understand your reasons, Jane," he says slowly, but there's a note of finality in his tone I have never heard before. "I know you and your mind. But I cannot condone this line of research or hypothesizin'. It goes against everything I've done with my life, all the book learnin', battlin' and scratchin' my way…and fightin' the illnesses, the trials and failures… You must stop. Let Esther's ways be hers."

"Are you forbidding me?" I ask, shocked I am even asking it at all. Horror mingles with bile, a chunky bubble that begins in my lungs and start to push up into my throat, where it sticks on the back of my tongue. "Are you saying I must stop…or else you'll…" I cannot finish. I don't wish to finish the sentence, to give weight and finality to this conversation. I cannot believe it is happening, this refusal and shutting down of my mind, my thoughts. Not again.

"It's for both of us," he says, and suddenly he's pleading, leaning into me across the table, both hands splayed out and palms up, a beseeching and a prayer. "It will only hurt us if you continue. We've been fortunate enough that the only ones who know of your dabblin' in Esther's ways are the Salomons, as they're inclined to us now. Even that is uneasy with them for all they're startin' to look easy at medicine."

"You're saying Esther's ways are nothing. Her people are wrong?"

"I..." He pulls back his hands and runs one through his dark hair, the agitation rearing up again. "It's not what I..."

"You married me knowing I challenge it all. That I want to read and learn overmuch. How can my desire to uncover this knowledge surprise you? Upset you? And suppose it does work. Suppose I find a cure for the black measles—"

"You won't!" he says, too rough and too sharp.

I inhale quickly to stop the sting of tears and bunch my fists with handfuls of my skirts. I've pushed too far, and now do not know how to reel it back in without giving too much ground.

"Let me do this," he says. "I have to do this. I must beat the disease and discover a way to stop it. I owe Widow Haw—Esther. I owe Kate. It's my duty."

It's the wrong words, in the wrong order. I can't untangle them without getting stuck. He wishes me to put aside myself in deference to the woman he'd once wooed? The one who had brought him to her bed first? Am I to return to the ways of the Boston wife, the one who did what was bidden, her voice slashed? Then why did I come to Flats Junction at all?

"And my duty?" I ask, my own anger rising too fast, too hot. "To bow quietly out of the way, to stop my mind from working? I was sure I'd found a man who wanted me to question...who encouraged it." I stand and yank the plates toward me, letting the oil of the potatoes ooze over the edges. "I thought you meant what you said. And now you're just like the rest. Why did I marry you, then? I thought you were different than Henry Weber. I loved you for this. But you're no different at all!"

It is an accusation meant to hurt, and it does. I can see it in the way he winces and hunches his shoulders, but I am not sorry. He has always asked to know what I am thinking, to always hear my story. Well, now he has.

"I don't mean to silence you."

"No? Then what is this? You will lock me up, stop me from helping, learning, researching? What else is there for me, but to play house? I came here for more, to learn more, to be more. And to be more for you. But if you've other duties... If you owe Kate so much—"

"It is not just Kate, Jane. I only mean—"

"Good night, husband," I tell him, turning my back and standing at the stove, my arms straight at my side so he will not see them shiver from the elbows down. The urge to rip and lash out runs through my veins. "I'm sure you are tired after a long day battling this terrible disease, which only you alone might solve. You needn't explain yourself. I have learned my place before. Go to bed."

159

There is a long moment of silence. I can almost feel him chewing on arguments, and all of them are weak. He knows it, and so do I. We can go in circles or one of us must destroy the other, and neither of us is willing to do either. At least, not yet. Has he truly forbidden me from offering old remedies and the folk medicine long practiced by the people of this land? Does he fear the medicines of the Lakota? I did not think it of him. Before I knew Esther, I was the one afraid. I was uncertain of her and her kin when he was the one so jovial, eating their foods and explaining their traditions. He went into their camp with ease. Have we reversed our roles?

And for what purpose does he truly wish to stop me? To give him some standing in the community, some way to prove his medicine and science is needed and not as terrible as some believe? To show to Kate he was a worthy partner, one she should regret?

After another moment, there is a sigh and a shift of a body moving along wood. I close my eyes against his departure, willing my shoulders to stay as iron. As the stairs creak and snap under his boots, I finally give in, sinking to my knees and burying my forehead into my hands. Folding over the bulge of the child, I feel its bones and feet shift as I curl over.

It is our first serious row, and one that is not easily healed. It is too intimate, too personal. Much of it is the long tear that began weeks ago, when I learned more of his story, and how intertwined it is with the town, with Kate. And for all the desire to ruin something in a fit of rage, I find I cannot do it. I'm more sorrowed than angered, and this is something new.

He's right. I don't know much of his own medical skills. I'm a self-taught nurse, learning as I go into homes with and without him to help. Esther has been with me from my first day in Flats Junction. She has grown herbs, gathered them, brewed them and is sharing them with me alone. It is her legacy – one no one else will hold if I don't take it and keep it close. It is an honor to be the vessel for this information. It is a balm to my curious mind, to learn such specialized, lost knowledge. There is so much to discover... how can he ask me to give it up?

The fatigue sinks into my muscles, and they feel filled with lead and balls of bronze. Perhaps if I kneel in the kitchen long enough, warmed by the stove instead of Patrick's body, I will sleep just as well. Sadness rakes through my shoulders, and I wrap my arms around my breasts, shuddering. Might I weep without anyone knowing?

And if I start, will I be able to stop?

Sleep descends slowly, like the sifting of flour. Soft and grey, and the candle on the table lowers to an orange and blue flame, too tired to sputter anymore. My neck is pulled down by a heaviness that is more than fatigue, and I realize I wish to stay in the kitchen not only to cool my cheeks and racing heart, but because I cannot bear to look at Patrick and see any dismay in his eyes.

Perhaps he wishes he had chosen differently.

Perhaps he sometimes thinks of Kate in the sheets instead of me.

Perhaps marriage is not anything like he expected, and he wants to be free of it all...

As I grip my shoulders tighter, his arms come around my middle and curl around the ever-growing bulge of my stomach. He must have removed his boots, and skipped the stairs that creak the loudest, for he has enveloped me before

I heard him, and before I can lift my head. As I do, his chin nestles in my collarbone.

"Don't weep, Janie," he says quietly. "And come to bed. I cannot sleep without you."

"I'm not crying," I tell him.

He continues to crouch behind me, holding both my limbs and our unborn child between his long arms, and inhales with slow measured breaths. When he speaks, it is in languid sentences.

"I wasn't here to heal Kate's brother. Murdoc died of the diphtheria. It was the old doc, the one I replaced after he passed, who could do nothin' and saved so few. And I could not save her father, either. Percy Davies believed in science. He saw the value in it in a way so many did not…or did not want to see in me. He gave Aunt Bonnie and me a place to live. He and Esther asked me to stay."

It is his memories sunk in the past and forgotten, if only so they do not rule his every waking minute, and the unearthing of them is his offering. A truce. It is a hint of his life, long before he met me. It is another piece of the puzzle of Flats Junction, where the past plays out on the future, as it does in most any town and city, and where I live blindly until I learn the rest. The people and the marks they make in Flats Junction are like a pile of sticks, and it is up to those who are alive to decide what to do with them. Do we have a bonfire or build a skyscraper?

Patrick removes his arms and stands us, turning me so he can fold our bodies together into a singular embrace. I lay my head on the soft flannel of his shirt, which smells of salt and carbolic acid, horse and crackling leather. Under it, his heart thuds unceasingly. When I press my face tighter against him, so a button pushes into my temple and will leave a mark, he kisses the top of my head. But he is not done.

"I have fought against the notion that doctors—and I myself—are inept. I have been blamed for more ill than good, no matter the truth of it. Here in Flats Junction...for the first time in my life, I have a place. Percy Davies gave that to me. It is the least I can do, to fight against what killed him. A duty to him. His memory. For his family, even though it won't change anything."

It's then I understand. It is not a battle against Kate, or even his reputation. It is bigger. He rails against those who despise the life he's fought to have. It is a fight for his truth, and his history. His beliefs and for science as a whole. And if I deny him this, if I show how there are other ways to cure and save, he believes I am undermining more than his place in Flats Junction. He thinks I will hinder him. He worries that I am erasing all he has built within himself.

For Patrick, it is a personal battle, in more ways than one.

But it is for me, too. For my own place, and my own voice.

And it seems our battles have set us on opposite paths.

CHAPTER TEN

Patrick

May 1, 1861

Doc Burns drew out a double-folded letter from the thin worn satin pocket of his plaid vest. He handed it to Patrick, the paper crinkled and flakin', the edges bent. One side was torn clean away.

"Do you recall asking me to make inquiries of my friends in England on the status of Irish families?" he asked.

Patrick's heart beat twice as fast, making a hard thump against the top of his chest. He glanced at Thomas and Tara, but neither bothered to listen in. Tara was readin' a new recipt for makin' dumplings, and Thomas was makin' a list – the same one he made every week about his plans to be a well-known rich doctor.

Patrick had requested the favor of an inquiry months ago. He had asked Doctor Burns if the idea persisted that many had emptied out of Ireland. It was brought on by frustration after Thomas had spoken derisively about how many Irish there were in Boston, even with the war declared against the south. The doc had said he would look into Patrick's family as a reward for hard work both as an apprentice and in managin' household chores. Patrick hadn't believed much would come of such a promise. How many years had Aunt Bonnie searched for news of the family? How long had it taken before Mr. McClure had learned of his wife, left in Dublin, and her own death?

"I remember, sir," Patrick said. He took the envelope. His name was scrawled on the outer lip of the correspondence. As he drew out the letter, a photograph fell. It was a black and white, a man and a woman. They stood, staring seriously at the camera, which captured their faces and dress, and even the sparkle in the woman's eyes. He knew, without needin' to ask, that they must be his parents. They were not what he was expectin', but the jolt ran through him just the same.

His da was stocky, roundly muscled and with a wide neck and unruly hair. He was serious, but his stance was one of a farmer, his bunchy hands cleaned but rough. His mam looked like a staunch Irish woman, but even the photograph's age and grime could not hide how she was a woman who must have liked to laugh. They posed in a formal sitting arrangement in front of a mud and rock house, the straw pokin' from the roof above them. A chicken, blurry with movement, was in the far left, near his mam's skirt.

Doctor Burns was quiet, waitin'. When Patrick finally looked up, his skin felt pickled and his eyes were tight. With a sigh, the doctor picked up the letter, purposefully skipping over the long, personal parts of it, or perhaps not reading parts that exposed the prejudice of his acquaintance, and read for them both:

For Marion Burns,

It came to my Attention that there are several Villages simply devoid of almost all People... The locals here have personal lists of these Abandoned Areas in their own minds. I was able to obtain a few Names, and the one – Port, in County Donegal – reminded me you were looking for news of such a Place.

Two months ago, I was able to ride through as a matter of Touring the Countryside with some of the English I am serving... There were only two Residents still living there. It was a Farmer with his ancient crone of a Mother. I do not know how such a Woman survived the Starvation that claimed so many... Still, she was a veritable Fount of Knowledge on each and every Family that once resided in Port. She knew of the Kinney Clan that had lived there.

Regretfully, I report that she confirmed the Death of their Entire House. Buried by one of her own Sons before he left, and the Black Fever killed him too...There were Graves for the lot of them – this Silbhe and Teodóir Kinney and all their Progeny, save, it sounds, for the one who made it to America...The Woman gave me the enclosed Photograph. She said she often saved very special Items in the houses that were left unburned by English soldiers, or that would be Collected by others but left behind at their Departure or Deaths. She said it was to keep their spirits alive, whatever that means to their Superstitions...

Sincerely,
Doctor George Ashley

Doctor Burns finished and set down the letter. Patrick stared at the words on the paper in front of him, unsure how to feel. There was relief, to be sure, that finally there were answers. Finally, Aunt Bonnie could stop wonderin' and worryin' and hopin'. He knew he should feel more upset, but... He had seen children die, and adults waste away. Patrick was trainin' to be a doc. He should not cry over death.

And he had no memory of his parents. He had no memory of siblings, or even of Ireland. Should he feel different other than the quiet sort of silence in his heart? He was strangely peaceful with the news, as if he had been waitin' simply to know their fate.

"I am sorry for your loss, Patrick," Doctor Burns said. In the corner of the room, Tara met his eye, and hers seemed to glimmer. He figured she was rememberin' her own mother, so recently lost. Thomas did not move, and kept his head bent over Tara's stitchin'.

"It's done," he said, and wished to say more on it, but found the words trite or false. "It will mean much to my auntie that you were finally able to discover what she could not."

Doctor Burns nodded gravely, but before any more sentiments could be exchanged, a knock pattered on the door, a hard and swift staccato that only spoke of one thing. *Need.*

Patrick opened the door to a youth. His shoes were covered in the muck and slime of the Boston streets, but even that bit of dirt could not cover his fine linen shirt or the cut of his vest. Even his cap was of the finest, softest wool.

"Please, sir! Is Doc Burns in? We need a surgeon barber, and right quick!" The boy's voice was high on the first and end of his plea and dipped in the middle. Patrick swung open the squat door to let the boy in, but he only stood on the threshold and peered into the kitchen.

Doctor Burns rose and went for his doctoring kit, the bag already packed.

"Come along, then. Patrick. Thomas!" The first was a request, the second a command. Tara did not stir as Thomas stood and moved to join us, though he cast back long looks.

The boy jogged ahead, and Doctor Burns kept a brutal pace to keep up. Thomas and Patrick jogged, but still lagged behind them.

"A horse would be faster," Thomas complained. "And a carriage even better."

"Sometimes feet are the best," Patrick reminded him, pointin' to a snaggle of horses, buggies, reins and shouting drivers on the street as they passed.

They continued to wind up the roads, going higher and into Beacon Hill, the most expensive neighborhood of Boston. Thomas's eyes went round, gleamin' with speculation.

"Suppose someday, a doctor is esteemed enough to own a place like that?" he wondered, pointin' at a house, with its fine stamped concrete and bright red brick. "Tara and I would be grand and host dozens of dinners, with the best of—"

"Tara? And you?" Patrick couldn't help the incredulousness in his tone.

"Obviously!" Thomas said, and his grin looked more like a sneer. "She favors me, and the doc does, too. Can't you tell?"

"This way. Please!" The servant boy's voice was so high it cut through the hum of Boston's many layers. "Hurry!"

Doctor Burns gestured for both apprentices to catch up, and quickly, and the two jumped to oblige. It was time to showcase their skill, and both were eager to help. Thomas and Patrick took turns doing the traditional homeopathic remedies: talking kindly and softly to the patient, listening and taking notes in the files Doctor Burns kept on any and all. They talked to the relatives on symptoms and created an overall sympathetic atmosphere. From there, Doctor Burns gave leave to do what the younger men would as he watched from afar, only jumping in to offer advice when he truly thought their remedies would hurt the patient, which would damage his own reputation.

"This way, good sirs." A butler appeared at the doorway the minute it cracked open. His dark clothes were pressed along the long lines, but the edges rumpled, as if the butler were harried. His pace seemed to show the same, for his footsteps were hurried along a thick padded carpet, woven with golden curls and pale pink flowers on a green and red background. The great house felt like something beyond America, a grand mix of old Europe and new money, with marble or silk on the walls, gilt gold winking from crevasses, and a scurrying of dozens of servants along the edges of each room. Patrick would have stopped to stare at the grandness, had there been a moment to spare.

Doctor Burns took the lead behind the butler, and Patrick wondered if he and Thomas would only watch this time, instead of tryin' their hand at healin'. Thomas usually relied on the old homeopathic remedies. He prescribed several drugs for patients who already displayed particular symptoms. If one complained of a headache, he would give dosages of medicine, decided from past proof in healthy people that would also give a lighter headache. The two, he said, would cancel one another out, displacin' the natural disease by an artificial one that could be more easily healed.

Whenever it was Patrick's turn, he too took on the traditional homeopathic role at first, but when it came time to diagnose anything, he turned to his own knowledge gleaned from pullin' onto a little bit of this and that, much like Doctor Burns did as he needed—and from sources hidden from Thomas and Doc Burns himself.

The sickroom was a woman's place, hung with pale brocade drapes that swept from window and window, hidin' the outside light. The entire floor was carpeted, and the bed a carved panel of sharp rosettes and curlin' leaves. In the middle of it laid the wife of the man of the fine house, her hair damp and dark with sweat like seaweed on the pillow.

"What is the trouble?" Doctor Burns asked the lady's maid who waited at the bedside.

"Fever, and she says a pain deep inside her," the maid said. "She just birthed and is laying in after it—it's only been a few days, but she's…worse each hour."

"How is the babe?"

"Dead, sir."

"We'll take a look," Doctor Burns said gravely. "Tell your master to wait outside the door."

She fled the room, likely nervous in the presence of three men of their profession, and suddenly the only sound was the woman's breathin'. Patrick wanted to reach to her, touch her, decide the best course, his whole body achin' with the need to learn, but Doctor Burns turned to Thomas first.

"Please, sirs. I'm certain it's nothing serious, but I do not feel myself," the woman's voice was breathy and soft.

Her eyes glowed in the dimness of the room, still bright with intelligence. She sat up in bed and pulled the satin overlay across her chest. The ruffles and lace on the edges of her nightgown and wrapper made her look stuffed into the covers, a frothy, foamy pillow of fineness. Patrick though she would look better without all the fuss.

"What do you think?" Doc Burns prompted Thomas.

Thomas stepped up to the bed. The woman didn't twitch as he stared at her. His thick lips puckered in thought, and her eyes followed his movements.

"I believe she is only suffering from a pus-filled infection. We can inspect her, see if she shows signs of mortification somewhere on her flesh. If we don't cut it out, it will spread."

Patrick disagreed. With the babe already dead, it was just as likely the beginnin' of puerperal fever. He was frustrated Thomas did not see it, and that Doc Burns would say nothin' at the first.

"However, if it's blood sepsis, there's little to do," Thomas said. He pursed his mouth and ran a finger slowly along the faint mustache growin' across his upper lip. "And we don't know if it was miscarriage or abortion anyway."

"Abortion? How dare you!" The woman sat up higher and tighter. "Harold and I would never!"

Patrick rocked back on his heels shocked Thomas would make such a presumption in front of the woman herself.

Thomas's eyes met Patrick's and he sniffed, ignorin' the female outburst. "You needn't look so appalled, Paddy. You think just because she's wed—."

"Enough." Doctor Burns picked up the woman's hand and closed his eyes, his fingers on her wrist. "It's fast, but not terribly so. Patrick?"

"Then it might be early childbed fever," Patrick said, steppin' next to Doctor Burns and across from Thomas, offerin' the poor woman a kind smile. She returned it at once, though it looked forced around the curl of her jaw.

A memory bubbled up, one of the readings he poured over behind the house, when he was supposed to be tossin' slops in the bin, but instead would sneak looks at roughly translated notes, given to him privately on the side. He'd often get a chunk of minutes when the doc was readin' the paper and Thomas was tryin' to woo Tara.

Who was it? A German, certainly. Hungarian? Someone in Vienna? The name came to him, an imprint of ink in the white of his mind, swirling with theories and the sharp pine of the new and still-rare carbolic acid.

"Semmelweis."

Thomas looked up from the listless patient, a frown tracin' the corners of his eyes and mouth. "What?"

"Ignaz Semmelweis. He published somethin' this year... I think it's called *Die Ätiologie* ...I've mentioned him before. Anyway, I mean to say, it's an infection, yes, of the blood and tissue, but if she's not too far gone, the antisepsis technique may still work."

Patrick ignored the curiosity bloomin' on Doctor Burns's cheeks, realizin' his error too late, but knowin' it would be the only way to make the other two listen and possibly save the poor woman's life.

"So what would you suggest?" The disdain dripped from Thomas's shoulders and voice. The force of it made Patrick hesitate, but in the space of quiet, Doctor Burns offered the floor.

"Patrick will go ahead, as he has a notion."

Thomas snorted. He dropped the woman's hand, spun on his heel, and walked out of the room. Doctor Burns did not bother to watch him go, and instead gestured for Patrick to continue.

Patrick picked up the opposite and squeezed it very slightly, givin' up another small smile. "It's only there might be something causin' you an illness, with losing the babe. It can happen, and often more than you might think, madam," he said, choosin' his words carefully. "I have a notion that may help stave off any possible illness. If we do nothin' you may certainly get worse."

She would die if it became a true fever. Doctor Burns and Patrick knew it, but it did not help to tell a patient they were close to death.

As Doctor Burns took a seat and began to speak to the lady of her household and other distractions, Patrick went to the door in search of the maid. When it opened, he ran into Thomas's backside, propelling the other apprentice forward. Thomas caught himself after two steps, but not before the husband had to catch him by the elbow or risk being bowled over.

"Pardon. I was just lookin' for the maid," Patrick said, feelin' heat rise to his jawbone and ears.

"May I come in?" the gentleman asked. "This young man says he has already diagnosed my wife."

Patrick glanced at Thomas, and felt his mouth tremble with frustration. "I do not mean to disagree with my fellow, but—"

"He says he must cut her, to release any unwanted humors. Is that not your plan?"

"Certainly not. I have a further notion—"

"A notion, sir, is not a diagnosis." The gentleman sniffed delicately and looked Patrick up and down. "Is that Scots-Irish I hear, then, or just plain Irish?"

The lady's maid rounded the corner nearby, her arms full of snowy new linen. Patrick turned to her at once. "We need hot water – boilin' – and some lye soap – a bar of it will have to do. Chlorinated lime would be even—."

"I have no intention of allowing you to attempt an experiment of some strange theories on my wife!"

"It is the very most current scientific discoveries that has led Doctor Kinney to ask for these items." Doctor Burns appeared at Patrick's elbow. "If you would be so kind?" He nodded at the maid, who scurried off without a sound, her arms still heavy with bedding.

Thomas returned to the room, sweepin' by Patrick. Doctor Burns followed, and the husband, with Patrick last. They stood about, makin' the tiniest of talk, mostly about gentle things, strayin' only into politics and how the new mayor, Joseph Wightman was managin', but backin' away carefully.

When the hot water arrived, along with the lye, the lady's maid stayed, too, so Patrick had a small audience to attempt his experiment. For that was what it was, truly. And experiment to cleanse the woman's inner body tissues as best as could be done and hope he did right enough to save her life.

Doctor Burns opened his medical bag off to the side and began rearrangin' the tools on the bedside table. Patrick caught a glint of the metal of each thing, knowing he'd need some of them, and knowin' he had doused them all in whiskey the night before brought him some measure of comfort. Doc Burns only did a cursory wipe of his instruments otherwise, but Patrick disliked seeing the stains and bits of rust and globs of mucus sit on such shiny tools.

Scalpel, abscess lancet, spatula, a Seton needle with silk. And then the bivalve, with its rounded beak that split in two, which he would use to try to clean the woman's most private parts. Patrick tried not to think of the other men watchin'. He tented the sheets about as best he could for the lady's modesty.

He covered his hands with hot water, turnin' his fingers deep pink, then scrubbed them with the diluted lye, ignorin' the tiny bit of sting. It would be uncomfortable for the woman, too, but better than nothing.

Once he had a solid lather, he began the unchartered task of coating the woman's flesh, both around and inside of her with the lye and water solution, instructin' her to keep her legs bent and hips up. She was still bleedin', but it was slight and pale, and soon it washed away with his concoction.

It was a foolish idea, if he overthought it. Could lye kill whatever illness ate at her insides? Was it already too late? Had the sickness begun?

"We ought to do this once or twice more, every day, to see how you fare. If we are lucky, you will cease your melancholy and feel well enough soon," Patrick said, standin' and wipin' down his hands in the basin of water.

He looked up about to see if Thomas or Doctor Burns had any opinion, but they were both simply watching Patrick's hands, which were still pink against the heat of the water. Clearin' his throat, he focused on the gentleman of the house.

"May we return tomorrow to see how she's feelin'?"

The gentleman chewed on his lower lip, his eyes flickin' between Patrick, his wife, and Thomas. He nodded, once and tight, and allowed his butler to see the trio out.

It was only as they began the walk home that Patrick realized Doctor Burns had called him "Doctor Kinney". He hung back as they arrived at the Burns house, plannin' to thank the man. Thomas stalked in ahead anyway, his eyes cloudy, though his voice sounded jovial as he greeted Tara.

But Doctor Burns turned on Patrick. "Tell Halverman what you did."

He had given himself away with the German. And now Burns knew Patrick had been meetin' with Doctor Halverman. It had been a secret, kept for everyone's sake. What would other doctors say? It was one thing for Doctor Halverman to invite everyone to see his work with burn victims. It was another for a relationship of an Eclectic doctor apprentice discussin' medicine with a traditional physician. Patrick had been careful. He'd kept journals and borrowed translations under his mattress or behind the slop barrel in the back.

"You approve?" Patrick asked, gulpin' the end of the word.

"I'm not saying I do, but I won't stop you. Especially if you're able to bring something new to our patients that works. Let's hope it does, for her sake especially." Doctor Burns inhaled, shook his head, and followed Thomas inside.

Patrick spent the night breathin' in and out in a steady pace. He had clear forgotten the letter about his parents' death, and the photograph. How had that happened? Was he so callous that he didn't care? Or did it mean doctorin' was part of him so much he could forget his own woes for the sake of others? He hoped it was the latter.

He slept uneasily, and when he woke, it was late mornin'. Leapin' out of bed, he clambered down the back attic stairs to discover the house empty save for Tara. He found her sewin' a sampler in the kitchen instead of by the window.

"Where is everyone?"

Tara offered a small smile and stood, movin' the kettle to a hot burner. "My father thought you might want some sleep, after hearing news of your kin and then the excitement afterwards. He said you might wish to go see your aunt and share the letter from Ireland."

It was a kindness, and unexpected at that. Patrick sat at the table and pulled the day-old bread from the middle of the table toward him.

"I'm thinkin' I'll quick run up to where she works and let her know. She should know," he said, already dreadin' doing it.

Tara poured coffee into a chipped stoneware mug, and set it carefully next to Patrick, amid multiple dark rings from many years of coffee mugs set on the worn wood. She sat across from him and picked up her sampler. The design was simple but oddly complicated, a cursive alphabet all in red-dyed thread, which she would, he knew, donate to any school that would take it. Her hands were long and white, with oval nails that shone in the late mornin' sun. It sprinkled through the one large window, dancing across fat dust in the air.

Patrick chewed the last of the bread and heaved up from the table, his limbs feelin' awkward both in Tara's private presence and the emptiness of the day.

"I'll clean the plate and cup," Tara said, also risin' and offerin' a soft smile. "You have been working so hard since you've come here, it makes me feel useless."

"It's what an apprentice is for, at least, one as poor as myself," Patrick said, offerin' up the excuse, though both of them knew it wasn't needed.

He walked the streets of Boston, cleaner and less covered in urine than in his youth thanks to the revered sewers dug everywhere. The lack of open privies was a massive change that seemed to better every day. Patrick wondered if cities were cleaner, or if the untamed wilds were better, where there was less disease, but less industry.

"Paddy!"

He swung around and saw the stocky shape of Michael barrelin' toward him from a side road. He waited, feeling warmth and comfort pile up inside his stomach. He missed his friend, and even though life had taken them on solid different ways, their old friendship felt etched in stone.

"What are you doin' here?" he asked.

"Off to see Aunt Bonnie," Patrick said. "We've had word from Ireland."

"After all this time?" Michael moved into step with Patrick. The sweat and muck on him were straight from the docks. Patrick wondered if the stench was imbedded into Michael's very skin.

"It's not good news," he admitted. Saying the words aloud choked harder than he expected. "They're all gone."

"Paddy – Christ Almighty," he swore. "I've nothin' to tell you, *a mhic ó*." He paused, then moved forward to give Patrick an awkward embrace as they walked. "I'll walk with you to McClure's," he said. "Part of the way, at least. I've an appointment."

Patrick shoved down the gurglin' of emotion in his gut and raised his eyebrows. "Really? You? At what – the taverns are takin' down names for the war now?"

He didn't answer, and Patrick let it be. Together, they headed over the streets toward Mr. McClure's. The evening dusk covered most of the rubble in the street, and it was chilly enough in the spring that a light frost settled over the mud and quenched the stink of rotting leaves from last autumn still sittin' amid the daily dosing of sewage.

And then Michael peeled off toward an alley near one of the Irish bars. In the shadow, a woman in rags stood, apprehensive and stallin', and Patrick pulled at his friend's burly arm.

"You've been spendin' your money on whores?" he asked, incredulous. It was not what he would have expected of Michael. He had always put money forward for his family. Then again, they'd spent so much time apart lately…and was that not the way of the dock men? Patrick tried to cobble old, prejudiced rumors together, but failed.

He squinted. "And if I am?"

"Just surprises me is all."

The woman inched forward, and Michael turned to her. Swiftly, he pulled her close. She looked vaguely familiar, and the lines on her face carved a long, hard life.

"This is Jenny, and she is mine."

It wasn't as though Patrick had much experience at all with women who walked the night, but he was sure Michael knew the way of it: this woman was as much his as the next man with coin.

"If you say so."

"No – Paddy. You mistake me. I'm goin' to marry her." Michael insisted, squeezin' the woman to his side. "Tomorrow. We're marryin' tomorrow."

Patrick was frozen to the mucky road. "Married? Already? And when were you goin' to tell me?"

"Well…you're busy with your doctorin', Paddy."

Worry bundled with Patrick's own sadness, but he wanted to be happy and a fair friend, even if only in words. "*Go néirí an bóthar leat.*" It was all he remembered of the old Gaelic blessing but, Michael brightened under the greyin' sky.

"She'll be livin' with the family, o' course, but it's better than here, and soon enough we'll get our own place," he said.

"Felicitations," Patrick told him again. "I'm glad I was able to hear of it. Ma'am." He tipped his fingers at her, and she stared.

"You'll wish us well, then?" Michael asked. "And come visit?"

"Aye. Why would I not?" he said, shiftin' his feet a bit. He wanted suddenly to go back to the old days, when he and Michael only had small cares. And now Michael was tyin' himself to a woman of the night… Time had changed them both, it seemed.

Patrick took his leave quickly after that, shoving down a strange resentment. He struggled with the news of the family's death, and yet the ones around him could only think of life. Michael marryin'? Was that the way of it always, then? The push and pull of death and promise?

When he arrived at McClure's building, he took the stairs two at a time, and entered without knockin'. Mr. McClure was not at his desk, and the clatterin' of Aunt Bonnie at the stove echoed and bounced on the ceiling from the back room.

Patrick thought again of Michael. He wondered if he should find a strong woman too. One that could handle patient work, or at least keep up a good house. Someone more like Aunt Bonnie, who was formidable, an empress in her small circle of a world. Was there a woman like that for him? Suppose there was. Suppose he found a woman who could manage a house, and cook, and perhaps even help him in his own business of doctorin'. *Suppose…*

"Patrick!"

Aunt Bonnie entered with a rag between her hands and spoke so loudly Mr. McClure appeared an instant later, behind her. The kitchen candles glowed behind them both in a warm, melted buttery light, and Patrick felt his sides clench. He'd be destroyin' their moment of contentment.

"How goes it, my boy?" Mr. McClure asked, looking over him from hair to shoe. He always seemed particularly pleased with how Patrick went on. It added some scrim of pressure to his every step, and sometimes made him hesitate when he would normally push back with Thomas and Doctor Burns. Yesterday's outspokenness with the woman's health was new. But he had felt so strongly…

"Well, I've some news to be sure," Patrick told him. "Michael is marryin' he says."

Mr McClure smiled. "There's some good news in the day, then."

"Is everythin' alright, Patrick?" Aunt Bonnie cut directly to the heart of the visit. Her eyes narrowed, taking in every thread on his pants and shirt, lookin' for a scratch that wasn't there.

Patrick drew out the photograph of his parents and set it on the scratched oak of the desk. Mr. McClure spun it around so he could see it better, frownin'.

"Doc Burns helped me out with some of his connections in England and Ireland. He was able to find out about my mam and da." Patrick spread his hands open and then clapped them behind his back. Aunt Bonnie stared at the photograph. Patrick couldn't tell if she recognized his parents, so he plunged ahead. "His acquaintance made some inquires over in the old country and he discovered they're all gone."

"Gone?" Aunt Bonnie picked up the photograph. "Gone where? To America? Canada?"

Patrick shook his head, findin' the words strangled, so he spit them out, soundin' shorter than he intended. "No, Auntie. They're all dead."

"Dead?" Her one knee buckled, and she put the other on the desk. There was a tremor in her fingers, and she looked away, toward the kitchen, blinkin' a little.

No one moved, and Mr. McClure kept his eyes on the floor for a long while.

Finally, Aunt Bonnie turned her head, and met Patrick's eyes. "That is a blessed thing that we finally know their fate after all these years," she said, her voice steady but softer than usual.

"They died likely of the great hunger. Or because the English wouldn't let them leave, even though they might have tried, or they were sick…" Patrick stopped himself, knowin' he was speculatin', babblin'.

She came over and put her arm about him. She could only reach around his middle. He stared down at the top of her head, where the grey shot through, pepperin' and streakin' her scalp. Had she always been so small?

"It's all fine now, Patrick. Done and dusted. They are at peace, and likely a better peace than most." Mr. McClure said from the kitchen doorway. He had a dark bottle of whiskey in his hand and gestured with the other. "Come."

He set out three of the tin cups, and poured a generous amount of alcohol in all of them.

"*Mhà na h-Èireann beanntan thu. Mhà i lochan agus aibhnichean gad bheannachadh. Mhà an Sealbh nan Èireannach enfold thu. Mhà na beannachdan Naomh Pàdraig feuch thu.*"

Patrick's Gaelic was poor, but the cadence recognizable in a way, and they lifted the dull tin glasses solemnly and drank down the hot, spicy whiskey in long gulps. They stared at one another for a long moment, that seemed short but to drag, and Patrick felt the pull of returnin'.

"I should get back. Doc Burns gave me the time to come but…"

"Go," Mr. McClure said, smiling just with his eyes. "Thank ye for tellin' us."

Patrick turned and took his leave. He tried not to slam the door, and closed it slowly, softly behind him. As he eased the latch, he heard Mr. McClure's voice filter through the wood.

"Are ye truly alright, then, *mhuirnín*?"

His term of sweet endearment made Patrick pause. It did not bother him mightily that Mr. McClure took an interest in his aunt, and truthfully, they were both as close to a mam and da he'd ever known. He'd often, as he had grown older, wondered at Mr. McClure's occasional touch or small kindness toward Aunt Bonnie. Perhaps he had loved her all along.

The clock chimed as he let himself back into Doctor Burns's house. There was a snort from Tara's corner, revealin' just Doc Burns himself, but no Tara and no Thomas.

"Ah, there you are, Patrick," he said groggily. He inhaled heavily and stood, a medical book falling to the side.

Patrick crossed the long narrow room and bent to pick it up. He turned it over to read the title. It was one they did not use in their trainin', and as he peered at the letter pressed words on the dark cloth cover, he realized it was not a medical book at all, but a treatise.

"You're readin' *Beiträge zur Biologie der Pflanzen*?" He tried his hand at the now familiar German. "What about?"

Doctor Burns smiled a little. "I'm trying to keep up with the times. You are not the only one to cross battle lines. Our little world of medicine is about to get trickier."

"How so?" Patrick frowned and set the book on the edge of the chair. It balanced, teeterin', and then stilled.

"Beyond what's happening in Europe, there are rumblings within the AMA, leaking into the Massachusetts Medical Society. They don't like us – Eclectics that is – just as during the war between the states, when the army medical boards wouldn't even allow Homeopaths into service."

"Congress supports us, they say, though," Patrick protested. "And the newspapers – whenever they say much on medicine – tell those Orthodox docs to be tolerant."

"You've been watching. I'm glad. And it doesn't really matter. We doctors are a group onto ourselves. I have a feeling the Society will want to clean up the profession. It's time to look at what everyone is doing and adapt."

"You want us to look at chemistry now?" Patrick felt his mind stretch with the possibilities. The trade—the doctorin' profession—was changin' so incredibly fast.

"I'm saying we should consider treating full diseases instead of each individual symptom. You know I generally follow a little bit of everything," Doc Burns amended. Patrick had long wondered if Doctor Burns was in fact that most unusual American type of doctor – an Eclectic, by both denyin' and usin' bits and pieces of the two main factions of the physicians.

"Can we try sterilizin' our tools after each use – the way they say?" he asked. "More than just occasionally. Maybe every time we use them. I had them cleaned before we went out yesterday. Have we made an appointment to go back? See if it worked?"

Doctor Burns paused. "You're not political like Thomas, with a fire in your belly, are you, Patrick?"

His deep tone made Patrick pause all movement, nervous though it was. "I have no inclination to politics nor class, if that's what you're askin'."

"It's only an observation. A difference between apprentices," he said, standin' slowly. "Perhaps I have erred in allowing a mix of opinions."

Patrick stood too, upsettin' the treatise on the table. It flapped upside down with his swiftness. "What do you mean?"

"It's only we went to the Wilbur's today," Doctor Burns started, and it was the apology in his voice that gave it away, even before the confession. "I thought he might continue your lead with treating the poor mother, but Thomas said cutting was the best choice. He thought to drain the bad humors from Mrs. Wilbur. There is still the agreement that humors cause most illnesses in many of our circles, and I thought, given her weakness, he may have the right of it."

"But—but the tools weren't cleaned again!" Patrick said, aghast. "And no need to cut! Did she have a fever? Was there pus?"

Doctor Burns spread his hands expansively, then they dropped to his side, as useless as sausages. "What we are doing…it is on the edge of all medicine. My opinion, and yours. And Thomas's. It is all speculation. Any who says what we do is pure facts is a fool. There is only one way to find out. You know this, Patrick. Experimentation is the entirety of our profession. To believe it is anything but is to fail."

"She will die!" Patrick said, his face feelin' as though it melted with shock. "How could you—why would you—what will you do when that young woman dies?"

"You think Mrs. Wilbur will die?"

Thomas had opened the door behind them both and stood on the threshold with a small smile leftover on his face. Tara ducked under his arm and entered, a basket saggin' on her arm with turnips and potatoes, wilted lettuce and the peek of an orange.

Patrick turned on his heel, the worn edge of his sole makin' him slippery. "You know she will. There was no abscess, no pus. Jesus, Mary and Joseph! What did you slice?"

Thomas strolled in, castin' his hat on the table. He watched Tara and cocked his head, appraisin' her figure. Doctor Burns grunted and shifted, shielding his daughter from view. Thomas rolled his eyes slightly under the hood of his lids and twisted to Patrick.

"Don't worry. Besides, they won't blame *me* if something happens." The implication was heavy, filled with derision and disgust. Patrick could only imagine how Thomas approached it. Had he said it was Patrick—"Doctor Kinney"—who prescribed such an act? Had he twisted the memory of the harried staff and said it was Doctor Kinney who would heal their mistress? Had Doctor Burns said nothin', or just not heard the slide of the words, so easily spent and so quick to destroy a life?

And all the frustrations of playin' second fiddle, of his Irishness, of his work to save and to be thwarted by nothing by pride, the letter from Ireland, his parent's sure deaths, and even the small thing of cleanin' up after another apprentice… it all boiled up and spilled, hot and messy, into his mind and through his veins.

Patrick did not think before he lunged. The punch landed so perfectly he felt the softness give and fluid weep between his knuckles. Tara's scream was so high it went beyond hearin'. Thomas roared and leapt backwards, stumblin' and clumsy, his fist to his head, coverin' his eyeball, where blood and wetness poured. He shouted and yelled, cursed and wept, all at once.

Patrick stared at Thomas, then at his hand, which was covered in the milky fluid of an eyeball, forever burst and gone.

As Thomas sank to his knees, and Tara wrung her hands, Doctor Burns spun and grabbed Patrick by the bicep, his fingers pinching so hard they burst blood vessels in Patrick's arm.

"Get your things. Now."

Patrick couldn't move, appalled and vindicated in the violence. What had he done? He was to be a physician! To save and cure, not ruin… And yet. A seed of anger uncurled deep in his gut. He felt an eye a small price to pay for his name, perhaps forever ruined in the city of Boston. His future, in ruins in a single hour's work.

"You're done. You cannot be my apprentice, not with this," Doctor Burns said, pushing Patrick to the attic stairs. "Hurry."

Patrick turned, his feet like bricks, as the doctor went to Thomas's side, and Tara slowly pulled her hands from her face. He hiked up into the dusty slanted room and yanked the handful of belongings toward him, stuffing them into the same box he'd used when Mr. McClure had dropped him off near three years ago. Everything still fit inside the single small crate, which felt both practical and sad. How had he kept so little?

He grabbed his other shirt and the collar, the last copy of *The Lancet* and his spare pencil stubs. Folding it all between his worn wool jacket and the spare set of socks, he took the stairs down one and a time, scarcely believin' it was to be the last time. Shame filled his bones, hot and fierce. What would Mr. McClure think? Would Doctor Burns return unused funds to Mr. McClure for the time not spent under his roof, or had Patrick destroyed it all?

Doc Burns stood by the door, his hat on, and a hand on the latch, waitin'. Tara boiled water in the black kettle on the stove, while Thomas sat at the table with a rag to his eye, the spare one weepin' salt and anger.

He met Patrick's stare, and lowered the rag so his puckered eyelid was stark and purple-red, a glaring accusation written in flesh. "You think you're just going to leave? You think I'll forget?"

Patrick's voice strangled him. He had so many thoughts fightin' for their own words, but none made it out. Doctor Burns put a hand on his wrist and pulled him out into the street before Patrick could even form an apology. He wasn't sure he would mean it, anyway. The sting of what Thomas had done, the cuts he'd made in Patrick's name... if the woman lived, it would be a miracle. If she died, it would be blamed on a "Doctor Kinney". Was an eye enough a price for a life?

"I'm taking you to the stables at the hotel." Doctor Burns didn't need to elaborate. There was only the one hotel, located up on Tremont Street. "The horses are managed by a friend of mine, Georg Stassen. Parker gives him full reign over the animals and the hired help there. May as well use some of your learning toward a trade, and a surgeon barber is better than nothing."

They strode, too fast, toward Beacon Hill. Patrick's mind whirled and reeled and his heart felt like it would burst out of its very shape. How had it come to this, and so fast? He knew his position with Doctor Burns was less stable than Thomas's, but he hadn't realized it to be so tenuous. How would he tell Aunt Bonnie? Would the work pay or be another apprenticeship? Was he done forever as a doctor? Was his profession dead inside his hands and mind before he could start, all because of a petty dislike from his fellow apprentice? Because Mrs. Wilbur would die and his name be attached to that and Thomas's half blindness?

They stopped outside the Parker House, and Patrick was left outside the hotel to whirl within his mind as Doctor Burns went into the hotel stables ahead of time, his shoulders pulled back so far his belly seemed doubly long.

In the moment of breathin', Patrick tried to find his air. In a matter of mere seconds, his world and his life had upended in smoke. Everything he'd worked for, everything he'd dreamed of in the dull grey of each mornin'...all gone.

189

He'd be a vet? A 'surgeon barber'? What would Doc Halverman say when Patrick could not show his face? What would come of his name and his passion? His drive to fix and cure and save? How could he do what he felt was his need—what he needed to do, or go mad with the wantin'.

A stout man, grizzled along the edges in both hair and clothin', arrived at the double stable door with Doctor Burns. Patrick started out of his shredded thoughts and glanced up at the sun. It had shifted enough to the west that at least an hour had already passed.

"This is he," Doctor Burns said. "A fine apprentice, as I said, Georg. He will do you well and learn fast."

The kindness in the words almost broke Patrick, and if he had been younger or less hard in the ways of the Boston streets, he might have begged Doctor Burns to reconsider, even as he knew he could not go back. He could not face Thomas.

Instead, Doc Burns only shook his hand, brief and quick, and then moved off into the teemin' mass of arrivin' guests and horses, leavin' the horseman to stare Patrick up and down, as if he was horseflesh himself, before crookin' a finger and drawin' Patrick into the fetid air of an animal barn, and far away from carbolic acid, shinin' tools, and dyin' patients.

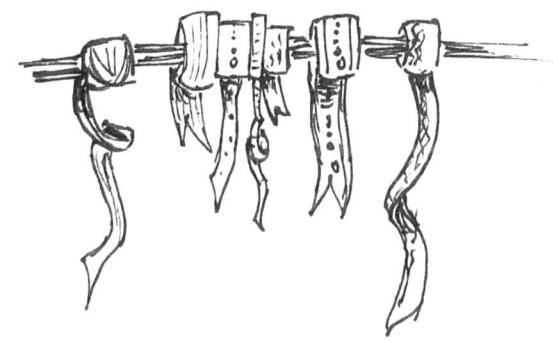

CHAPTER ELEVEN

Jane

September 14, 1883

Spools of ribbon drip from a wooden dowel along the window of Sadie and Tom Fawcett's summer house. When I enter the small space, they all flutter in whorls of pink and green, brown and yellow. The silk ones flow like water, and the velvet ribbons are fuzzy and weighted by their very fabric. I reach out in spite of myself to graze my fingers along the ends of them, stopping just short so I don't dirty the bits of lace Helena Salomon has pinned up for viewing.

I'm not the only one stopping in on my way to or from Yves's makeshift mercantile or the post office. Sally Painter, pinched and grey and avoiding me like I carry the plague, fingers a bright plaid before settling on something darker. Lara O'Donnell's bosom takes up far more space than should be allowed for one woman, but it's her voice that fills the room.

"Now, now, Sadie, you've the seamstress in your very own backyard and have placed an order for two dresses off the first. The least you can do is allow me a new dress in between them."

"I think given my generosity I may get my two new dresses before anyone else." Sadie stands closest to the small table Helena uses as a counter, and behind which the young woman herself stitches a mound of matte silk in the palest blue. Sadie inspects a handful of feathers, each brighter than the last. As Helena sits, basting yellow ribbons onto the silk, her eyes remain on her work, but flicker slightly as she peeks up. A small smile twitches at the corners of her mouth. I think at first she means to simply look pleasing to her customers instead of wearing a frown a concentration, but then I realize she is holding mirth, and look quickly away in case I am tempted to chuckle, too.

Lara maneuvers carefully around stacked folds of cloth and a barrel of muslin. She plants her feet in front of Sadie and crosses her arms across her breasts, a feat in itself. She shakes her head.

"The idea to bring in a seamstress was our joint idea, Sadie. We took out the newspaper ad together. We both told Kate we'd be patrons."

"But Tom and I have invested in the plan," Sadie says, attempting to look sincere but only coming off as smug. She has a glow to her cheeks again – one that has been missing since the death of her infant daughter. I will have to tell Patrick that the cure was not medicine at all, but something to do that excites her. Maybe Alice…

"Excuse me, Jane," Susie Henderssen inches past, her hands clutching a square of dark purple velvet. She holds it up to the light of the window, inspecting it for any tiny moth-eaten holes.

"Only because Kate didn't ask me first," Lara argues. "Mikey could have built somethin' fast – we've spare extra lumber everywhere in the yard and he doesn't just sell it. He can make things."

"Just like my Tom built all these shelves?" Sadie waves her hand airily at the whitewashed shelving behind Helena on the far wall.

"Tom didn't build those. I have it on authority that the Salomon apprentice boy did it."

"Hardy didn't have time to build anything here. He was too busy working on the Kinney's roof. Isn't that right, Jane?" Sadie rounds on me, and I look up from the fashion plates Helena has spread out on her bed.

"I confess I didn't pay attention to who was on my roof," I say, feeling caught between the two powerful women's eyes. "But he was over often enough."

Sally Painter sighs heavily and puts down the bolt of dark plaid. "It's all beautiful, Helena, and your work is very lovely, but I'll have to ask the Reverend if I can buy the length."

"Don't worry, Mrs. Painter. I'm supposed to get new shipments every four months or so with the latest styles from my connections out East. When that arrives, I will have to discount that fabric," Helena says, looking at Sally directly and smiling with confidence beyond her years. "I can save it for you if it's still here when that happens. It would be my pleasure."

"Very kind of you," Sally says, looking surprised. I wonder if she does not expect such a kindness from a member of St. Aloysius Catholic Church, given her husband is the Reverend at the Lutheran St. Diana's. Or perhaps she has been so stuck in her own dark space of anger and pain with the loss of all her children in the diphtheria epidemic that she has forgotten how good people can be, when they wish, to one another. She departs, shooting one last poisoned glance my direction. I ignore it, though I feel the prick of it inside my chest anyway. If only Reverend Painter had come for Patrick sooner...if only... And now we must live with Sally's rancor over our heads, for she blames me the same as him, as if my husband's profession has bled into my own life and skin.

Sadie and Lara turn up their noses at each other, but then both shimmy over to the fashion plates I'm perusing. Helena brought back several from her surprise trip to the east coast and promises more in the future so trends do not take years to reach Flats Junction any longer.

"Are you certain the bustle is comin' back, Helena?" Lara asks, turning over a page of *Godey's Lady's Book*. A few of the etched images show a high bustle in the back of the dress, with the side pulled into puffs and deep folded apron-like draping along the front. "And it's not a very soft-lookin' one, is it?"

Helena does not stop her stitching, the swipe of her needle a flick and slide of silver in her hands. The thimble flashes back and forth. "It's like a shelf, a structure. I brought out some of the metal bands and am having my mother copy them. No sense in ordering those when we can have them made up the road. She thinks it may be too troublesome, but I think she'll manage it. And anyway, I need to finish the gowns first."

"*Gowns* she says," Lara smirks, but it is without malice and said as a truce to Sadie. "I'll be washin' dishes in a gown."

194

"Soon all of Flats Junction will want a gown," I agree, running a finger down the page of *Peterson's Magazine*, a monthly out of Philadelphia with slightly different designs than *Godey's*. The sleeves look unnaturally tight, the collars high like previous years, and the bodices long and stream-lined, with excessive trimmings of ruffles and flounces and shirring. The fabrics noted in tiny print are similar to what Helena has packed between crinkled paper—plush and satin brocade, and even an embossed fabric rolled with leaves. I will never be able to afford such luxury—or even have Helena make me a dress—but it is nice to dream.

"We'll have to have Kate do a few more festivals as a place to wear our finery," Sadie says, smiling at Helena.

"What am I doing?"

Everyone swings around as Kate enters, a grin playing across her face. She nods at Susie and offers a bigger smile to Helena, who stands. Her body leans toward Kate for a brief moment as if she wishes for something bigger—an embrace or a clasped hand—but she quickly sits and takes up her sewing as Kate approaches. She glances at everything with a proprietary eye, and I remember that while Sadie has pro-vided the space, it is Kate who has bought all the goods, from the cotton to the thread.

"We thought with all of Helena's beautiful work, we need a few more times to show them off," Lara explains. "Another festival or two. Flats Junction can do with some revelry."

"I don't know," Kate says. "With the new recruits at the Fort pouring in, I have a feeling we'll end up drawing more of the Army than in previous years."

"How is that bad? I've nine children and over half are young women. They could do with seeing some men and havin' a choice. Helena herself needs to wed, and soon," Lara remarks, and winks at Helena.

The girl flushes a pretty soft rose, and bends her head lower over the yellow ribbon, but then looks up with sparkling eyes. "With Flats Junction becoming such a spot on the map, and all the fine dresses now, we could hold balls like they do out east."

"How do they do them?" Sadie asks, pouncing on the topic, her hands clasped at her throat. "What do you wear?"

"Well, I saw one, once. People could mill outside the great houses in hopes of glimpsing the wealthy, or—in my case—the dresses. But they start at eleven at night. I heard there's at least eight courses for dinner, which is served around two in the morning."

"Gracious! Dinner in the middle of the wee hours?" Lara puts a hand to her heart. "It's the very hour of devilry!"

Helena's mouth twists. "You depart at daybreak, too."

"It goes all night?" Sadie looks less thrilled. "But what about work the next day? I suppose we could do it on a Saturday, with Sunday—"

"No one should miss church after a night such as that!" Lara argues.

As they dive into the specifics, Kate slips next to me, avoiding even looking in my direction and bends over Helena. I'm close enough to catch her words, as she murmurs, "And what were you doing awake and on the streets of New York and Chicago at eleven at night?"

Helena's jaw tightens and she lifts up her chin, a new type of light in her eyes, and she refuses to take the bait. The girl is full of youthful defiance, but there is a confident worldliness too, which seems to sour Kate slightly.

Kate turns to the room and inhales loudly, then announces, "The train has brought in the last of the supplies I ordered to replace what was ruined and burned. You can all start shopping again like usual and on the regular."

"Oh, has it?" Susie Henderssen looks up from where she has been laying different colors of silk ribbon against the fur of the purple velvet. "That is good news, Kate."

"Yes, good news indeed! Will you be bringing in other goods this time?" Sadie asks. "Smoked oysters and champagne?"

Kate looks oddly uncomfortable for a brief second, then shakes her proud head and puts on her sales face. It is the same look I recall from the very first day we met, when I had just walked off the train and into town, dragging my trunk through sliced ice and frozen mud.

"We'll have all of that in Flats Junction in short order," she says. "And more. I'm going to get electricity here, come hell or high water."

That announcement makes the room go still. Even the rustling of Helena's pile of silk stops.

"Electricity? How?" I say. I am, as usual, the first to question Kate. She does not look at me as she answers, instead tilting her head at Sadie and Lara.

"Deadwood's getting it. If they can go that far west, they can start to splinter off to smaller towns. I'm figuring we can get enough interest around town to invest in it, we can get it." She nods at Lara and Sadie, and I realize her point in this. The women often start the seeds with their menfolk.

I stare at her, taking in her silhouette. Her ambition always makes mine pale. I thought marrying a Boston man for his household and not for love was to be strong. I believed a whirlwind affair early in my widowhood to be risqué. And I thought to forge my way pregnant and alone to the Dakota Territories ambitious at the very least, if not a bit desperate. But Kate's plans always feel grand. She is the one who orchestrates the festivals, she made a fashionable seamstress business possible. And now she wants to mastermind electricity?

"Don't you think if something like this was feasible, the menfolk would have discussed it by now?" I ask, standing up straighter as if that might make me tall enough to look her in the eye.

"The menfolk haven't even thought about this possibility," she says, waving a hand into the distance. "They're too busy running their businesses."

"Without those businesses, there wouldn't be a Flats Junction," Lara says, her neck reddening. "It takes everyone."

"I'm not saying it doesn't. Just that sometimes I get an idea, and I'd like to run with it. Make the town grow even bigger."

Sadie narrows her eyes. "Do you have any idea the cost?"

"Not yet. But I will." Kate nods at Helena and makes for the door. "So, make sure you stop by the General now. I'll see you there."

"But what will Yves do?" Sadie asks, echoing my own next thought. "Where will he go, now?"

Kate swings, her hand on the latch and her eyes dark. "What does it matter?"

"If Yves dismantles his store at the old cooperage, he may very well go back to mischief. It's a fair problem," I say, hoping I sound as gentle as I mean.

She rounds on me, the lines carved on both sides of

her mouth as she frowns in my direction. Before she can be dismissive, I push on.

"You've just said yourself with the Army and new recruits the town may get wilder instead of more refined. There's many coming from all over already—"

"From all the world over," Sadie mutters, her nose wrinkling.

"America is supposed to be land of opportunity for all," I say.

"But surely not *all.*"

"That's true, Kit," Lara adds. "He can't just be told by you to pack up."

"Let me worry about it," she says, turning the handle, her body itching for the escape.

"You're not the mayor or the sheriff, Kate," Sadie says, almost laughing at the silliness of the idea. "You can't kick Yves out of town. Not on your word."

Her lips thin, and she stands taller. "It was with me that he was invited to Flats Junction, and he and I have an understanding."

The way she says it is strong and without quiver, but all of us women glance at one another in unspoken exasperation, the thoughts running between us. *Kate is unmarried. She does not know men. She has been too long in charge of her own future. She will see...*

"Anyway – Kate." I say, rushing before she can flounce out. "If there's already a lapse in genteel ways in town, and what with the terror of July 4ᵗʰ—" Lara and Sadie suck in their breath at my mention, and I reverse the direction at once. It is still a sore subject, Bern Masson's recent hanging by a mob, and Kate goes white under her golden-brown color. "All I'm saying is, properness depends on no posse in the area, no deaths without a trial. Yves back on the loose changes everything. We wouldn't want the electric bosses to hear rumors of such chaos—they might back out of bringing electricity here for fear of sabotage."

I don't mention the old rumors, which laid blame for broken rails and lost trains and their goods at Yves's feet, and, by default, Kate's as well. I won't hint at the skeptics, who still think he had a hand in starting the fire on the General Store in order to set up his own highly lucrative business. I don't remind her that she must tread her ambition carefully or risk losing whatever support she has—whether that is based on her own merit or the ghost of her father—because she knows, too. I can tell by the way she holds her shoulders, and the clench of her fingers.

"And you'd be the one to know about being proper," she says softly. "That's what you've always been, haven't you? The proper Boston widow."

"I tried to be," I say. "And now I'm the doctor's wife. Doctor Kinney and I will support you in your bid to bring electricity."

"Tom and I will, of course," Sadie jumps in. "And he'll make sure Nels Henderssen does, too. What else are employees for?"

The mood in the room lifts and swells around me, and I feel buoyed. It is as if I belong and my life flows in unison with these women.

"If Nels and Clara are for it, I'm sure my Jarle will be, too," Susie pipes up.

"Mikey and I will do whatever is best for Flats Junction," Lara says.

Helena finally glances up as she finishes off the edge of the ribbon basting. "Well, if it's going to get busier, I'll need that Model 12 Singer sewing machine to keep up with demand."

"A sewing machine?" Lara asks, looking intrigued. "I think the Horowitz's have one. Trusty Willy was talking about it last time we ate at The Golden Nail."

"It may be helpful," Helena says, shrugging with one shoulder and then bundling up the blue silk. "Alright, Sadie. Time for a fitting."

"Oh, right!" Sadie flicks her palms at all of us. "Out now, all of you."

Lara glances once more at Helena, her eyes slanted, before hustling out. Susie follows, and then it's Kate and me vying for the doorway. She gestures sardonically for me to pass first, her gesture at first odd until she points her gaze at my gently rounded stomach.

"Are you thinking this one will survive?" she asks, but there is no anger in her question. The gentleness in her tone seems out of place after the barbs we've shoved at one another all these months.

"One can only hope. It's a foot in the grave however one looks at it," I say, a shiver zipping up my backbone in memory of my previous miscarriage and its bloody aftermath.

"Well, we'll all want to hope for a healthy birth, as a sign of some of the doc's abilities," she says, her voice sliding lower. "Wouldn't want any bad bits of wondering to surface."

I glance at her sharply, uncertain of the threat under the words. "If you mean about the doctor and myself—"

"Those too," she says. "Though I squared those up when they first started. No, I mean Pat's practice itself.

Between dying babies, the diphtheria, and black measles running unchecked, he needs to watch himself."

"You know as well as anyone that he cannot easily cure black measles!" I say, heat swelling under my ribs. "Your own father—."

"I'm only repeating what I hear, so you know it, Jane," she says, finally meeting my eyes completely. I find hers unreadable. "That he's likely the one carrying the black measles, since he goes from house to house, and people get sick. He has just anyone over to dinner. Who knows what diseases are carried on and where."

"Just anyone!" I jerk back, memories reeling. "Do you mean to say because Moses Thompson has eaten at our table that he's given the sickness to Patrick, and he then gives it to patients? We know little enough about the illness, but anyone can see it makes no sense. Kate, you yourself had Moses over—"

"Not recently, and not at my introduction," she says. "And I'm not the one who says it."

"Why are you telling me this? To warn me?" I ask. "I already know the doctor lives on the edge of a knife. The black measles isn't doing him—or anyone—any favors."

"Then maybe he should figure it out," Kate says, shrugging and shaking her head at the same time. "Or stop trying to treat it at all. Sometimes you can't fix things."

She rotates on her heel and heads west toward the general. I watch her go, the weak sunlight reflecting as white shimmer in her black locks. It feels awkward to admit that she's right. Sometimes it does seem like Patrick's battles are hopeless. And sometimes, no matter how much one wants to change the course of an illness, a reputation, or even a life… it cannot be fixed.

CHAPTER TWELVE

Patrick

September 8, 1861

The horses had their own smell. It was sweet and sour, warm and moist. Patrick didn't know if he'd grown used to the stench of their feces or if it truly did smell better than the shit of the slums. Or maybe it was because he worked nearer the Anglos on the Hill and everything smelled better, looked cleaner and felt richer. The hotel, being the first one in Boston with indoor plumbin', was considered extraordinary.

Patrick worked the low jobs, paid only with a few coins once he'd proven his worth. But Mr. Stassen was fair and honest, and especially exactin', as all Prussians seemed to be.

He smiled, and whistled, and the horses' ears perked and turned with his sounds. Even the new ones that came in with guests usually felt comfortable quickly. With the high-bred ones he did his best.

203

"Alright, *Junge*, vee must to get you set mit dis one's leg," Mr. Stassen said, soundin' pleased. He had discovered Patrick was decent with anythin' close to barber work, which had been a surprise overall. Patrick himself didn't know he was good at it, either. While it was often dirty and bloody, he could do a lot of wound cleanin' and joint testin' easy enough. He'd learned more than he could ask already, with Mr. Stassen takin' a shine to him. But it was dangerous often enough, so he didn't tell Aunt Bonnie many details just the same. Besides, she threw up her hands when he told her and Mr. McClure of his failure with Doc Burns, omittin' the worst of Thomas's injury. Neither of them cared much for the details now, so long as he earned a wage and kept out of trouble. Patrick wasn't sure if he liked the freedom or if their disinterest grated on him deep inside.

He followed Mr. Stassen, takin' a seat on a leather stool in the narrow stall. It only wobbled slightly after Patrick had nailed a piece of wood to the second leg. The straw below was crispy fresh on top of damp earth.

The horse nosed Patrick's shoulder after he sat. Mr. Stassen was strong, and he held the horses well, even when they were skittish. But this time, the soft brown mare was docile, and she only twitched when Patrick touched her foreleg.

"Her mistress, she say she do not know what it vas," Mr. Stassen said. His deep, rumblin' voice was slow whenever they were with horses, and Patrick tried to match any movement of his fingers to the rhythm of it. "De *alte Fledermaus*, she do not know vhat to do mit her poor beast, und she say it were a rock, but rocks not make the holes in da animal skin."

204

There was a hole the size of a copper penny in the horse's leg. Mr. Stassen said nothin', and Patrick knew it was yet another test. He felt around the puncture and did not sense warmth. Even better, the animal did not seem to mind his touch. It was either a fresh wound or healin' already, and well.

"It looks shallow, sir," he said quietly, and just as slowly.

"Dat is a mite small comfort. Da poor beast, she vill need some extra meal tonight. Very vell, *Junge*."

The test was done. It was simple compared to some. He recalled a time when he had to sew an entire flap of skin back on. It wouldn't have been so difficult had it not been on the horse's forehead. Mr. Stassen had complained for days about his sore muscles from holdin' down that filly.

Mr. Stassen wiped down the side of his face and looked at Patrick as they stood along the wall opposite the now calmly munchin' horse. "So, do you like dis, de vork mit de horses?"

It was a philosophical question, and not anything like the practical information he barked or the chores he set. Patrick watched the mare eat, and tilted his head, feelin' the unruly hair ticklin' his neck. Aunt Bonnie needed to cut it.

"I like it."

"You vish to be a horseman, like me, Pat?"

Patrick shrugged. Whether or not he wished this, it seemed his career would move along now in this vein. There was little about wishin' or choice. He was old enough to understand that his role could be more than just workin' in a stable. In a small town, he might be more valuable. He could keep expensive horses, cattle and oxen in workin' and marketable condition. This, in some ways, was his last aim, now that doctorin' people was out of the question.

"Vell, dere is the time to tink on it, ya?" Mr. Stassen clapped him on the shoulder, gave it the smallest of squeezes and went shoutin' off for the other lads.

"Harry! Octavo! Albert!" His shout sent shadows scurryin' and the rest of the stable boys lined up. Patrick had been there longest, and had the most experience, but he still lined up, too. Harry was another Irish lad, new in from the streets because he had an uncanny way of dodgin' around rearin' horses and a quick way with a bridle. Albert was fresh off the boat from England, his family some unknown sort of religion they kept to themselves. And Octo was dark—olive-skinned where Patrick was fair. His family came from the interior of Portugal, though Octo had been born in Boston. He kept his head down most of the time, as if tryin' to keep people from noticing his heritage.

"So today, we vill have da usual customers," Mr. Stassen said. He rattled off the names of hotel regulars who stayed for business every month. "Octo, you take Mr. Payne. And Harry and Albert, da new ones. Patrick, I know you vill vish to see your friend Mr. May."

Eagerness welled in him as he heard the name of one man in particular who regularly stopped into the hotel. He quickly put out a particular brush that he knew Mr. May's horse liked best.

"You think he'll bring his wife?" Albert poked his head around the door.

Patrick made a face. "No. He never does."

"She's so pretty though – I saw her the one time, all tiny like a—"

"Al-bert!" Mr. Stassen swung by and whacked Albert on the ear. "No talk. Work."

Patrick didn't care to worry on Mr. May's wife, who he had never met. Mainly he wished to see the man himself and the quiet, generous energy he brought, and how he would sometimes speak as if Patrick were almost an equal. Sometimes, Mr. May would bring up doctorin', which seemed to be one of his hobbies and passions like many men of means, and Patrick would eat up his words as though they were fresh kraut. There was very little talk about the profession in general circles otherwise, and while sometimes he ached to talk about what he had learned with Doctor Burns, he knew keepin' quiet was the best course. No one would expect an Irish boy to tout fancy knowledge from a German medical pamphlet anyway and would cuff him for impertinence. When he walked home or to Mr. McClure's, he would read the shingles of the many who hung one out to gain patients even if they weren't proper doctors. And if Patrick was honest, he was keepin' an eye out for Thomas's, wonderin' when he'd get his certificate from Doc Burns…if Thomas would get one at all with a single eye…

There was one street that six doctors were vyin' for the attentions of the passerby, each promisin' more cures or better service than the other. Some kept up with vigorous druggin' and bleedin', and there was a prominent German who practiced some sort of 'homeopathy' and had an apothecary filled with a huge number of funny bottles.

Octo's charge cantered in first. Mr. Payne was brusque and tight and his mouth was typically set in a cruel line. He bolted off his mount and shoved the reigns at Octo, growling as he did. "Boy. Be sure to shine my harness this time or I'll have you thrown out for your negligence," he sneered, as if he actually had the power to do so. None of the boys were ever quite sure if the threats they heard were good or just words.

Octo knew to keep quiet, but as he moved by, Mr. Payne in all his haughty grandeur made a swipe at the lad's back. The backhand startled the horse, and the animal reared up and sent a shrilly scream. Octo let go of the reigns and dashed into the box and the darkness. The horse reeled and Octo screamed high before the sound cut off. Mr. Payne fell to the floor as he stepped back and onto a pile of horse apples. In the shoutin', Patrick felt his blood surge. He rushed forward, the first to reach the animal's flank but he missed the reigns as the animal spun again.

"Goddamn stable shit!" Mr. Payne yelled, which only aggravated his mount more.

Patrick stood over the man, who seemed incapable of getting himself off the dirty floor, and hoped horse wouldn't rear again, or he'd smash onto his master's legs.

"Hush!" Patrick said to the horse, who ignored him and started to spin, lookin' for an exit. He put his hand on the animal's side, hopin' touch, if done with stealth, would calm him.

"Dat's right, boy." It was Mr. Stassen, and Patrick's surging heart paused. He started to rub his hand up toward the animal's face.

"Dat's goot, very goot," Mr. Stassen's low voice continued, and the ears flicked toward it. "So slow now, and very soft, so you might not hurt dis man on the floor." Mr. Stassen sidled along the back of the horse, into the animal's view. "Very pretty horse, yah. Patrick," he continued in the same tone. "You vill vant to slowly grab the reigns as I take the bridle und together we vill get him in."

"Octo's in there," Patrick nodded forward. He could just make out the stable boy's face half-buried in the hay. He did not seem to be movin'.

"So, to da next stall then ve take him."

In one movement, they took the horse's head from either side. The animal calmed enough that they could lead him into the next box over, even though it was not prepared. As Mr. Stassen locked the door, Mr. Payne finally pulled himself to his feet.

"What kind of stables do you run here anyway?" he said. Anger and humiliation raked his voice. "Causing my horse to fright!"

"They have very fine stables." A new voice pierced the dusty gloom. Mr. May had arrived. "How do, Mr. Stassen?"

Mr. Payne glowered all about, uncertain if he should pick a fight in the company of another gentleman. Gruntin' and muttering' he stalked out, leavin' an audible sigh in his wake.

Patrick moved into the first stall quickly, followed by Mr. Stassen. In the cracklin' yellow straw, Octo sprawled out, his left arm at an odd angle and covered in blood. He was awake, though, his dark eyes flittin' back and forth.

"Does it hurt?" Patrick asked, kneelin' in the damp ground. "Can you move it?"

Octo paused, thought, and tried to shift. He winced and the white under the warmth of his skin went grey. He shook his head. "I can't move it."

"What about your shoulder. Can you move that?" Patrick asked, very aware, suddenly, of Mr. Stassen breathin' over his shoulder, and the shadow of Mr. May behind them both. "I'm not seein' bone in the blood here, so that's well." He pointed at the bloody mess of the arm.

Octo cradled his arm tightly to his side, afraid to try again.

Patrick inhaled as the trainin' poured back into him, kept locked up inside until needed, and now it all felt easy. "Well, it's probably broken. I'll do you a splint, and clean you up, if you want to go have a lay down at the back."

There were cots studded into the wall where the stable boys all slept, and Mr. Stassen helped Octo to stand, which the boy did, gingerly and faintly.

"You can fix dis, den, *ja* Patrick?" Mr. Stassen said, glancin' at Patrick with speculation. "I vill help you when he is rested, and first, there is someone vaiting on you I am tinking."

The trio exited the stall. Mr. Stassen walked slowly with Octo to the back of the stables as Patrick turned to assist Mr. May. The heat of the moment still shot through his body, and he worked hard to calm his breathin'.

Mr. May smiled at Patrick as he walked his horse to the next waitin' stall. "How have you been these past weeks, Patrick?" he asked.

"Well enough, sir."

"Your aunt is still in good health?"

"Aye. And Mrs. May?"

"She is quite well." He said the same of his wife each month, though sometimes a shadow passed over his face as he did.

Mr. May leaned against the stall as Patrick began to brush down his horse – one he called Wiltshire out of some sort of sentimentality for old English ties. Though he must have been tired from his long ride from Gloucester, Mr. May always took an interest in the care of his horses. He trusted only Patrick or Mr. Stassen, and still he stayed to watch.

"Before I forget," Mr. May straightened and pulled out a folded paper. "I've a letter from Bobby for you. He knew I was heading down for my usual business and asked me to bring it along."

Mr. May also was good enough to sometimes act as letter courier, though Patrick thought he did the services more as a favor for Robert's father, Mr. MacHugh, who seemed eager that his son had a friend in Boston. The connections between Mr. MacHugh, Mr. May and Mr. McClure were wrapped up in outlayin' Gloucester politics. Patrick didn't pay much attention to the threads, unless it meant news from his friend.

Mr. Stassen moved nearby as Patrick brushed down Mr. May's horse. The stablemaster checked the other horses and soon bent over a horseshoe. He took it off a spirited mount that didn't take to his cleanin' nor cared for Mr. Stassen's s desire to remove a shoe and check for a rock under the loose iron.

Suddenly, just as Patrick finished brushin', Mr. Stassen shouted aloud. The horse he was checkin' yanked, pitching him forward. It was slow and fast at the same time; one hoof came down, hard, right in the center of Mr. Stassen's middle. Patrick moved fast, unthinkin' and on instinct, grabbin' the halter. Somethin' whizzed past, the speed of it nickin' at his hair.

Grabbin' the rough rope that held the horse's halter, Patrick pulled on the leather, remindin' the animal that it still had a bit in its mouth, and the pain of it brought the stallion to an abrupt pause. He twisted the ropes tighter, securin' them harder than he likely needed to do, then turned to Mr. Stassen, who was lyin', winded, on the ground.

He groaned, and a hand went to his middle. *"Himmel, arsch und Zwirn!* Right in de middle! Ach, Paddy, I'm *a kotzen!"*

The warning, which Patrick did not understand anyway, came barely in time before Mr. Stassen spewed his last meal all over the floor. The horse, already skittish, burst out a high-pitched protest and tried to shy again, but the new ropes, tied with Patrick's bunched fingers, held.

Patrick went to his knees, old piss and mildew of the main walk sinkin' into the broadcloth. Actin' on impulse, he unbuttoned Mr. Stassen's shirts, realizin' as he went that he didn't know what he was doin', but understandin' he had to see what had happened more than anythin' else. It was a curiosity that burned in his very bones, and his blood was still up from Octo's accident and the knowledge he'd be settin' an arm to rights already.

The fabrics pulled open. First there was the wide expanse of a chest, dusted with thick blond and grey hairs. Under the swell of Mr. Stassen's ribs, in the soft flesh of the belly, a large purplish red mark bloomed already.

"We might call for a surgeon," Patrick said. "Just to take a look. He can take a look at Octo, too."

"Da barber, he just like to cut me up," Mr. Stassen protested, but he sounded like he was wheezin'. Patrick watched the corner of his mouth for the dreaded bubble of blood, but none arrived.

"I won't let him," Patrick promised. "But let me fetch one or two of the lads to sit with you while I run out."

He made to stand, already forgettin' the horses and Mr. May, just as Mr. Stassen gripped Patrick's arm. "Look for Joe Chilling up Cambridge Street, yah? He's like to be da kind…he don't cut so fast. And there is a chance he won't care…he will see to Octo maybe, even if da boy is of the wrong color, *ja*?"

While Patrick had never needed to run for a barber, and he wished he could fix Mr. Stassen himself, he was out of his element, with the reminder of Doctor Burns ringin' with his every step. *We are guessing. It is speculation and experimentation at best. Anyone would be a fool to pretend otherwise.* Patrick had no finished trainin'. He had no medical certificate. And he had witnesses should he do anythin' to Octo or Mr. Stassen.

He plugged into the muddy chill of the street and made a straight path to the shingle of a Joseph Chilling, only needin' to ask directions twice. The barber was already outside his place, comparin' barrels that must have been straight new from the cooper judgin' by the greenness of the wood. He did not live in a boardinghouse, but his own mean little front space was shared by six other men doing various trades, from blacksmithin' to leatherwork.

He glanced up as Patrick approached, and immediately stood straighter. He was a lanky man, with long thin legs and almost silly long arms. To match his body, his chin and nose were long too, giving the impression of a creature more than a man.

"Hotel stables. It's Doctor Stassen." Patrick used the formal, official title of the hotel vet to carry urgency. "He's been kicked by a horse, and I can't make any sense of what bleedin' is goin' on."

213

Patrick didn't need to elaborate. There was only one building that was known as a 'hotel' in Boston. Without speakin', the man went inside and came back out with a wide roll of linen tucked under his arm while shoutin' directions in Germanic tongues behind him. Patrick assumed he was speaking to the stout woman standin' alone in the back of the open lower level, perhaps the one who rented out her space to all those tradesmen.

As they hiked back, Patrick was grateful for Chilling's long strides, even though it meant he needed to jog next to keep up. While they moved, he eyed up the bundle Joseph Chilling carried. Narrow metal poked out, gleamin' in the half cloudy afternoon, strikin' a silvery pewter against the stained yellowed fabric. Anticipation and fear shivered down his spine. He did not wish anything to be wrong with Mr. Stassen, but he was eager to see a surgeon barber in action. This was somethin' he could watch and learn something new. It was as if he was still trainin' to be a doctor, just not in the way he'd once imagined learnin' the work.

Arrivin' at the stables, Mr. Stassen had not moved, but he was still alert and awake, which Patrick took to be a good sign. Mr. May sat on one of the benches, keepin' up a stream of talk, which he paused as Joseph Chilling strode in.

"Joe, dere ya are," Mr. Stassen said with a grimace. "Dat dere big dope of a horse done kicked me. I'll teach him, soon as I can!" It was an empty threat. No one dared to hurt the customer's horses, least of all Mr. Stassen.

The barber knelt down in the rank hay, and brushed his hand lightly across Mr. Stassen's chest, moving the shirt fabric back again. In the short time that Patrick had been gone, the bruise had grown, and was a deep purple red, with tendrils of red fingerin' out from it.

214

"It was only a matter of time before a beast got you, Georg," Joseph said calmly. He put his hand on the bruise, barely touchin' the skin, and Mr. Stassen winced with either anticipation of the touch or with pain. Immediately, Joseph Chilling drew back his hand and shook his head. Patrick felt as though the diagnosis was too quick, but then the barber looked up and asked sharply, "Is this how it looked when you last left him?"

"No," Patrick said. "It's gotten bigger. Darker. The streaks of red weren't there."

Joseph Chilling glanced back down at the skin, and his mouth twisted up in thought.

"I'm not going to cut right now," he finally decided. "It's too risky, and there's no sign of needing it. There is a chance it will heal on its own, and likely if I cut to let out any pus or humors, or the excess blood, the wound will fester."

He bounced back on his heels, crouchin' in front of Mr. Stassen. "There's some talk here and there of how infections start, one of them being the tools themselves." He gave a little snort. "I'm not sure what I believe, but I know, and you know Georg, that any cut is a risk."

Patrick had to bite his tongue, wantin' to shout that he believed the same. That he truly thought it made sense. That his own life had been damaged by one who thought the opposite. But he dared not and shoved the emotion deep into the pit of his stomach. Maybe later, if he could get Mr. McClure alone, he might confess his frustrations...

Mr. Stassen pulled himself up to a sittin' position, the movement stiff and careful so that he barely shifted his torso. The action still made him go white.

"So, should I try to valk it avay?"

"No, not for a while. We'll want to let you lay off yourself for a bit. Can someone cover your duties?"

Mr. Stassen jutted his chin toward Patrick. "Dat one is coming along nice in the training. He vill make a goot vet, or a goot horseman, vhat he chooses."

Joseph nodded, narrowin' his dark eyes at Patrick, too. "Well, then, do you think you might settle things in the stable until Georg is back on his feet?"

It took Patrick a moment to realize that the surgeon was talkin' directly to him. He started, suddenly aware of Mr. May's eyes, too. "I should, sir. Will he be off work long, do you think?"

The man stared at the bruise on Mr. Stassen's chest.

"It will depend," he hedged. "If the bruise stops getting too dark, and if it starts to turn colors soon – yellow, maroon, and the purple begins to fade – then he can get up as soon as he likes. But if it stays or worsens, come and get me, and we will try to let the blood out."

"How soon will I know which it is?"

"You'll know soon enough if it is worse. It will get black, and swell. I'd say you might be up to bloodletting yourself, boy, but you haven't the tools."

His off-beat compliment stirred pride in Patrick's breast, and he stood a bit taller, for all it was a vain thing. Though everythin' in him cried out to try his hand at healin', he dared not put it to the test.

Joseph Chilling took Mr. Stassen off to his quarters in the back of the stables, one long arm under the stablemaster's overwide shoulders. Patrick watched them go, feelin' the air out of his lungs. Was he officially in charge, now?

Mr. May quietly stepped nearby. "Will you go help the young boy, now?"

Patrick had not forgotten Octo. The lad's injury had festered in his mind, even has he had made their employer the priority.

"I will. It's sprained at least. Maybe broken, but not a terrible fracture."

"And you have no qualms about his heritage?"

"He's Spanish. Or...something of the like. What does it matter?" Patrick knew prejudice existed in every walk of every street, but he knew enough that it never did anyone any good. Besides, he and Octo were equals in the stables. There was no need to let him suffer on account of his language or his parent's nation of birth.

Mr. May's eyebrows went up. "I shall watch and assist if you need me."

Patrick paused, and looked at Mr. May's fine, brushed suit up and down. The man removed his hat and placed it carefully on a straw bale. He spread his fingers out, showing old calluses.

"I insist. Allow a man some practice in his preferred hobby."

They walked back toward the bunks. Octo laid flat, as if still and stiff in death, but his chest went up and down, hitchin' half the way. Patrick brought a lantern closer, as the rear of the stables was always extra dank and without any natural light.

"How you feelin'?" he asked.

Octo turned his head, but kept his body still, the arm bent over his belly. "Fine enough, Paddy, but it's starting to ache something fierce."

"I think it's broken, and swellin' now to hide the break," Patrick said. "It's the same with people as horses, though we don't need to put you down as we do the poor beasts."

Octo managed a small grin. "What are you saying?"

"Let's put you in a wrap until the arm stops puffin' up and then I can feel what ails you. I'm not promisin' too much, but I think I can get the bone and arm straight enough, so you won't have trouble using the arm later. That's the hope, anyway. I don't want to say it will be perfect."

"Whatever you have to do, I trust you." Octo slowly swung his legs out so he could sit on the edge of the flat bed. Patrick pulled a strap from some of the extra bridles and took Octo's spare shirt. After wipin' off whatever blood was still wet, he began bindin' the arm so it stayed in the protected cradle of Octo's preference, but was pulled against the boy's chest and supported. He'd seen Doctor Burns do such a thing a few times, as broken bones were common enough. He just hoped he remembered how to do it right.

Wrappin' the fabric under the leather strap, the contraption looked unlikely to lead to healin', but Patrick knew the swellin' around the wound would make anything else impossible.

"I'll take a look tomorrow, and bit by bit, we'll heal you up," he promised Octo. "But now you should rest. There's no good in bumpin' that arm."

Octo nodded, and slid back into bed, his eyes starin' up at the ceilin', glassy with pain and fatigue. Patrick watched for a long moment, before rememberin' Mr. May.

"I'm sorry, sir. There was no need to get your hands into the injury."

"That's quite alright, Patrick. It was good of you to let me watch."

They walked back through the stables, toward the entrance together. Mr. May strolled, even amid the muck, his hands behind his back. Patrick watched out of the corner of his eye, wonderin' how he might copy the walk, and then realizin' there'd never be time nor a place for him to walk so unhurried. He'd likely keep his odd, long stride and be inelegant all his days.

Mr. May inhaled and turned. "MacHugh says he'll be coming to Boston soon; likely I'll travel with him if the timing allows."

"Will he bring Robert?"

"I'll ask."

There was a long pause, and then Mr. May cleared his throat. "How do you think my Wiltshire might hold as a war horse?"

The question was unusual for only a moment, before Patrick realized Mr. May was thinkin' about the war between the States, just recently tippin' to boilin' in earnest.

"I...are you askin' about whether he can stand cannons?"

After a pause, Mr. May nodded.

"Likely better than other horses." Patrick thought of the high-strung breeds and their equally difficult owners. "But he'll still shy."

"That's what I thought," Mr. May agreed. "But he'll have to do."

It wasn't Patrick's place, but he was surprised Mr. May would consider leavin' his business and his wife for war, but perhaps he had not made a full decision yet.

"Will you go?" He shouldn't ask but couldn't help it. He liked Mr. May, almost too much. And while Patrick knew attachments were ill-conceived, it seemed sometimes he couldn't help connectin' with others. He wondered if that boded well for his work as a physician or not.

"They say tens of thousands of men are fighting just from Massachusetts," Mr. May said absently, speakin' into the dusty, dim silence of the stables.

Patrick knew enough about the fightin'. Mr. McClure lived vicariously through the newspaper stories and often spoke of it over Sunday dinner. He often referenced the Battle of Malvern Hill, a source of pride for Mr. McClure as Cass's 'Fighting Ninth' regiment had distinguished itself as a true Irish force. That was back in spring, but lots of people talked about it still.

Mr. McClure considered himself fully American as well as an Ulsterman, and wished he were down south, helpin'. But the army had turned him away, much to Aunt Bonnie's obvious relief. Mr. McClure was too old.

"All I know is what I hear," Patrick said, pettin' Wiltshire once more. "Half our Irish boys are dyin' in the tents from illness alone down there, so they say."

"You're likely correct," Mr. May said softly. "Though it is what the coloreds have dealt with, living down there, treated so meanly. Do you have feelings, one way or another, Patrick?"

That he would ask about abolitionism so baldly gave Patrick a chill. Sometimes such words were liable to get a man killed, and Patrick was no good hand in a street fight at the best of times. But this was Mr. May, who was clear on one side of the argument. A deep desire to show his astuteness to politics, to show his education, reared inside his mind.

"I don't think anyone should be intolerant of anyone, to be sure," Patrick said, soft and lightly. "Those southerners think they own a man or his wife because they think someone with darker skin is less than human, and that's plain stupid. A man is a man, whether it's dark skin, Indian blood, or with a lost leg in battle. I won't be thinkin' otherwise."

A long pause drew out the worst of Patrick's fears. He shouldn't have been so bold as to answer. Maybe Mr. May was testin' him. But then Mr. May sighed and smiled a tired sort of way. "You've always been smart, Patrick, from the moment I first saw you. I'll trust you on the horse."

Patrick wished he wouldn't – for all he knew, the horse might throw the man at the first shot of a musket, but what was he to say? Mr. May looked to him for advice, and if anyone knew his horse well here, it was Patrick. Still, he hoped Mr. May would choose to stay back, instead of ridin' his proud stallion into the foamin' madness of battle.

observations
at the stables
Parker house - boston

Octo

broken arm
bound until swelling down
clean break, it feels, so used four strong sticks and wrapped arm
rendering it unmoveable from elbow to wrist
hope the fracture of ulna will heal straight
uncertain if he should move fingers - causes little pain he says
seven weeks after injury
pain is mostly gone, as is swelling
tissue thin and wasted, but with use will be strong again

healing likely. due to age? octo's italian blood?

georg stassen

kicked in the chest by back legs of horse
ribs bruised, pain with breathing
dark bruising at once
streaks of red present quickly after injury

per rx of dr. joseph chilling

watched for darker red, more lines, worse breathing.

suspect broken ribs, nothing to be done but wait?
bruise turning yellow
on edges by day five

CHAPTER THIRTEEN

Jane

October 8, 1883

"At least there's no river deep enough around here," Berit Salomon says, nodding her queenly head in the direction of Flats Basin River, which is little more than a creek. "Then you won't worry of taking a wading bath and drowning the baby in the womb."

"And don't forget, you shouldn't get a haircut," Anette Zalenski reminds me, nodding at her mother. She and Berit share a smile, each echoing the other in their uncanny likeness. "It can affect the babe's vision. No one wants a blind child."

Everyone refrains from speaking of Harriet Lindsay's new baby, who is indeed blind, but whose fault for that seems to lay solely with the parents themselves, particularly Alan Lampton, who never proposed married to Harriet, though they have lived as if married as long as I've been in Flats

Junction. I meet Marie's eye, where she leans casually against the low edge of her tinner's bench, an elbow propped on one of her gleaming, oiled machines.

"Well, all that is very well," she says, the corner of her mouth lifting in a small smirk, though she avoids my gaze as if I might cause her to laugh. "But if we followed all the rules and notions, none of us would ever leave the safety of our bedrooms, nor see another throughout our birthing. I work until I cannot, and you see my children are fine and grown. And Thaddeus has been in the room during birthing Garik and well beyond and after." Marie pauses, then nods at me.

"That's true," I say, feeling passion rise in my breast-bone. All these rumors and odd traditions, which are not rooted in science or old medicine, but some strange super-stition…I would like to stop it all, and it might begin here, speaking among the women. "Out east, it is widely believed a mother must be left alone completely for nine days after giving birth, and no one must be in the room—only the father, once, for a few minutes—else disaster will strike. I have seen myself this is false."

"What about reading?" Anette asks, looking intrigued. "I didn't read a stitch for three days after each child, not even the papers Jacob brought from town."

"What about reading might harm you after birthing?" I ask, opening my hands and spreading my arms, careful not to knock over a tall tin coffee pot Marie has on the counter.

Anette looks down, where she has arranged Marie's cookie cutters in order from the largest, a house, to smallest, which is a dainty star. She frowns slightly, a look I have never seen on her clear brow, but then she shrugs and grins and shoots Marie a feisty laugh.

224

"Well, I'll remember that next time, then. Winter's here in full force, and everyone knows what a farmer likes to do best when there's nothing to be done outside."

"Clean the barn?" Marie asks.

"Is that how you put it? I was thinking along the lines of a bed and me, happily—"

"I should see Kaspar," I interrupt, more for Marie's embarrassed red cheeks than anything else, though I suppose I do not want to hear details of Anette and Jacob Zalenski's marriage and their robust preference for one another. "I've only just stopped to do so."

"Yes! Yes, of course," Marie says, relief tangling in her words. "You know the way."

I head through the blacksmith shop, feeling a bit lost for leaving the comfort of the women's chatter, but also still embarrassed in spite of myself. It seems I struggle to find a cadence that works, walking between decades of a proper Boston woman and a rougher western one. There have been times I found myself embroiled in a sexual conversation between the women, and I revel in the sense of belonging. But other times, Anette's poking makes me far too uncomfortable to partake.

Thaddeus shoots me a cross between a glare and a nod over his forge. Nearby, his youngest son Natan sorts sticks of raw iron. I take the great oak door into the kitchen, where it is only Hardy getting a drink by the table and little Garik sleeping in a trundle bed along the back wall.

"Mrs. Kinney!" Hardy says, wiping his mouth quickly and plunking the tin tankard on the boards, remembering only at the barest last minute to be quiet about it. He glances at the sleeping babe, who sighs slightly before settling into a deeper sleep. I suppose a child born in such a big and loud family does learn to sleep through most noises. It makes me wonder how my own babe will do, with slamming screen doors and knocks at all hours. Will I go running at the slightest whimper, or learn to be immune to most of his sounds?

"I'm here to check on Kaspar."

"He's itching to get back to smithing, so I'll go with you," Hardy says, leading the way before I can wave him off. "Just looked in on him myself and all, and the skin is over the bone, can't even notice it no more, but seeing as you are the real nurse, you got the right of it."

He pushes the door open to the bedroom. Kaspar is already sitting up in bed, looking settled around a tray of bread and jam, with the family's small pile of books propped up in both hands.

"Hello, Mrs. Kinney," Kaspar says, his voice bright. "Come to see my arm? It's feeling better every day. I've been sitting in with Pa and the boys, doing the bellows to help with my good arm. Think I'm better yet?"

I set down my leather roll of medicine and take a seat on the side of the bed. He gives over his arm with something like pride, and I inhale with relief. "I see your mother has kept your bandages clean."

"Not her. Mother's not too much for bedside help."

"It's me," Hardy says from the door, where he leans and watches my hands unwrap the bleached linen. "I got old Mrs. Salomon to make over one of the old sheets into strips. And then the iodine every day, morning and night."

"You?" I twist, wincing at the pinch of my womb.

"Mrs. Marie said if I didn't mind and could do it right."

I finish unwinding the bandage, which was clearly placed that morning. By the time I get to the bare skin, it's definitely healed. Though parts still crack and ooze just by movement, large swathes are a deep reddish pink, puckered with tightly woven scar tissue. As I lean in, I look for any signs of infection, pressing gently along the edges of the entire wound first as Patrick has shown me to do. When Kaspar doesn't wince one bit, I push further into the wound, slowly working toward where the skin had burned near to the bone.

"What are you poking him around for? Pus?" Hardy asks.

I glance up at him, surprised at his understanding. "Yes, actually. Or pain." It's only at the very tender part, which still leaks a clear fluid, when Kaspar sucks in through his teeth. But there's no yellowing, and I chew on the inside of my cheek, considering.

"You say iodine, every day."

"Twice," Hardy says.

"And new bandages?"

"All the past oh, six or seven weeks. Twice again."

"I think, then…" All the warnings from Esther pour into my mind, snippets of reminders and caution. *Apply inside the wound if it be clean. Do not use too much. Do not give to women. A poultice is easiest.* But I don't have a poultice. I only have the oily tincture she and I made. The leaves themselves would also be too hard to be precise. Apply inside the wound. If it's clean enough, that is. But if Hardy is telling the truth…

Is this how the doctor feels every moment? Wondering and guessing? An experiment and a hope? Is there any part of patient care that is a certainty? He always acts as if

227

he knows, with a confidence softened by carefully placed acknowledgement that nothing is sure.

But I could hurry the healing so much faster. It would get Kaspar back at the forge, helping Thaddeus and keeping the family's business running.

The decision is made even while I wonder, as my fingers pull the vial of comfrey out of the little pocket.

"What's that?"

"Essence of comfrey. It's a plant, in season around here spring and summer, and it's very good at healing quickly."

"Why wouldn't you do it right away?" Hardy is near on top of me, leaning over my shoulder, his breathing hot on the back of my neck. I want to shift away, but there's no room, and besides, I find the boy's fascination intriguing.

"One doesn't want to use it too soon. You can seal infection inside the body and kill a person from the inside out in such a way. Once you know it's all clean – very clean – you start by dripping it into a wound. When that's healing up well, you can rub it on the outside."

Hardy frowns. "Is this the kind of medicine the doc uses, too?"

"Similar enough," I hedge. "And there." I dab the oil into the open pieces of the injury, then look up at Hardy. "Did you see?"

He seems to realize how close he is, and pulls back, but not away. "Alright, yah."

A rustle of skirts outside the door reveals Marie, who holds Garik on her hip. I hadn't heard the baby wake, which makes a shiver of doubt fizzle through my skin. If I can't hear a baby's cry, what kind of mother will I be?

"Hardy, what're you doing bothering Mrs. Kinney?"

"Sorry Mrs. Marie." Hardy, red up to his ears, shuffles his feet. "I just thought that, with the bandages, I wanted—."

"You wanted to show off to the doc's wife. So, then. You have. Be off, the fires won't keep themselves lit."

"He's done well," I say. "And before you run off, Hardy, can you get me some of that fresh linen you mentioned?"

An eager light flashes across his wide face, the blue eyes bright under the pale golden flop of hair. "Yes, ma'am, right now."

He dashes past Marie, who rolls her eyes only halfway before meeting mine.

"After all he's been given, orphan that he is... If the boy put half his mind to blacksmithing the way he did over Kaspar's arm, fussing over the iodine."

She stops when Hardy slips back into the room, watching him bend over Kaspar's arm again and carefully re-wrap the new linen. I stand to make more room for him, and over his back, I meet Marie's gaze. Her head tilts.

"If Kaspar truly can swing a hammer again," she says, so soft I can hardly hear her. "Maybe..."

The quiet moment crashes with the clatter of feet and the whirlwind of Helena Salomon, fluttering with a newly trimmed hat and matching ruched ribbons on her bodice in the shade of a summer sunrise.

"Mother! There you are! Why aren't you in the tin shop?" she asks, her voice commanding even if breathless.

"Checking on your brothers. Both of them." Marie juts her chin at Garik and then Kaspar. "Suppose I was in the privy? Would you come hunting for me then?"

"I wouldn't open the door on you," Helena amends. "I'd just yell at you from the outside."

"What do you need?"

"This!" Helena pushes a scrap of paper at Marie, who peers at it close and then further away. I make a note to mention spectacles to her the next time I can slip it into the conversation without making her prickly.

"What is it?"

"It's a needle case, but with little sections inside, to divide out my different needles."

"You want a different space for each needle?" Marie shakes her head. "Just stick them in a stuffed sock."

"Mother, please," Helena sniffs. "I'm not having an old sock in the dress shop. Plus, this will keep them from rusting."

"Copper'd keep them from rusting better," Marie says, shifting Garik as he grabs at her ear.

"But you can make it?"

"I've figured out how to use all those fancy attachments you brought from the east. I can figure this."

I watch the banter between mother and daughter, noting the way their hips and shoulders turn toward one another, an easy familiarity and push-pull of emotions and frustrations, all colliding together in their conversation. If I have a daughter, will I be able to raise her and watch her make decisions without my say? Will I ever see her as an equal, as I see Marie attempt to do with Helena?

"There, all good, see, Mrs. Kinney? Can't you take a look?"

I pick up Kaspar's arm, who seems to be enjoying the additional activity in his room, as his grin has only gotten bigger with each passing minute. I suppose he's spent far too long huddled up in bed, far away from the usual noise and action of his father's forge, and the gossip that comes with it.

"It looks as well as I might do," I say, offering Hardy the truth and praise at the same time. He goes red again and side-steps out of the room to head to the forge. As he passes Helena, her eyes flick to his and hold. They turn to look at one another for only a fraction of a moment, but it's long enough. If I knew the Salomons well enough, I would comment or tease, but I fear Marie might be angry at the apprentice's interest in her daughter, even though Helena has turned herself into an active businesswoman and clearly can handle herself in worldly matters.

"Don't encourage him overmuch," Marie says, coming into the room and looking over Kaspar's arm. "Thaddeus doesn't give praise, and it won't do to have him expecting it."

"Father praises us," Kaspar says, inspecting his arm. Given his ease of movement, I'm hopeful the scar tissue won't cause him too much trouble. "Sort of."

Marie gives her head a quick shake, the wild black and grey of it swishing along her collar. "Well, then. The man's idea of a kind word is backwards, but he does try, I'll give him that."

My first marriage to Henry Weber was cold and practical, a precise properness punctured with the cancer that killed him. I'd bent myself into the Boston businessman's wife to fit what was expected of me, hiding the rabid curiosity under layers of manners and self-imposed rules. When all of that failed to stick, and I found myself a widow, I did not grieve the life I had lost—or perhaps more exacting, I did not mourn my husband. There were bland and tight words between us, without affection, and our frigid sheets owed much to our lack of a passionate understanding. I never expected a kind word from Henry, other than for him to comment on my ability to coordinate a dinner for his business partners. He did not know me, or did not wish to see me, and I think much of that matters in a marriage.

But Marie speaks of Thaddeus's lack of gentle language with something like laughter in her voice, and Kaspar's dark eyes twinkle as if he is in on the joke. Perhaps that is the difference, then. They know him, and under all the hard gruffness, there is something soft and kind indeed. I suppose it means I never truly knew Henry Weber. Or there was nothing soft below the surface of him. I shall never find out.

I roll up my kit and turn to Marie. "I'll be back in a day or so to see how the new medication I put on is doing. If it heals as I hope, I can use more, and we can finish up his healing. Now that much of the flesh is binding itself, this next cure is safe to use."

She frowns with light interest, but another clatter outside in the hall makes her turn as well.

"Is Kaspar's room the place to be today?" she asks, sounding annoyed. "Who now?"

"I don't mind," Kaspar says, grinning and fair bouncing in his bedclothes.

It's the last person I expect to see.

Kate, waving a dark bottle, and looking distracted as well, only drawing up short when she spots me behind Marie.

"Oh." Her voice strangles itself, and I realize why when I spot the label on the bottle.

"Iodine?" I ask. "Did it just come in?"

"Kate's been dropping it off weekly," Marie says, missing Kate's wide eyes completely as she glances at me. "Ever since the first day Kaspar's been injured."

"You've...had iodine? For how long?" I step toward

232

Kate, though Marie is a barrier between us, made wider by the babe in her arms. "Since when? Patrick's been waiting, begging, doing without for—"

"Just another reason showing how important I—the General is to Flats Junction," Kate says, trying too hard to be conversational. "I can get in things like iodine."

"But not share it? Not sell it unless it is convenient to you?" I press Marie's shoulder, hoping to get past and closer to Kate. "How long have you kept it from the doctor? How many people died because of it?"

"What do you mean, died?" Marie asks. "What does iodine have to do with it?"

"It cleans all wounds, especially before and after surgery," I say. "It would have saved your Urszula after the operation."

Marie goes white, her lips flatten, but she only folds them over her teeth. Her scarred knuckles strain against the bones as she fists her hands under Garik's bottom.

"You assume so much," Kate snaps. "You think I would let children die? What do you think I'm doing now?" She shoves the bottle at Marie, but my arm shoots out and grabs Kate's fingers, the bottle caught between our palms.

"I think you might spite Patrick because of me. Why not with this?"

Kate's jaw works its way back and forth, and I suddenly feel my shorter height against hers. She could plow me into Marie with a jerk of her arm or drop the bottle and let it spray along the worn boards at our feet, staining them forever.

Instead, she lets the bottle fold itself into my fingers, huffs, and stomps out.

I stare at the small brown bottle, and the black words stamped on the white label. It's still warm from her hand, the liquid inside sloshing soft and with a splash. So much life can be wrought out of something so small.

Marie inhales. "It saves, you say?"

I nod, blood pulsing through my temples. How long has she kept this from Patrick? How much has she had on hand all these many months of sickness, of surgery?

"You should take it. For the doc. We still have a larger bottle with enough to get us by. If he needs to do another cut, if there's diphtheria again this fall, and more children…" Her voice goes raw and rough on the edge. "Besides, we owe you payment yet for Kaspar's care."

Her gift only propels me after Kate as fast as I can after muttering a farewell, and I go out through the forge so I can only nod again at Thaddeus instead of being stopped to hear the latest gossip from Berit Salomon.

Kate's at the back steps of her rooms behind the General, looking for all the world like she's trying not to flee. A woman racing through the streets causes more and more notice as Flats Junction settles into its roots, becoming a respectable town more each month.

"What do you want?" I call. "Kate!"

She pauses at the bottom of the steps, the fabric stiff across her shoulder blades, and then she turns, looking for all the world like she's the one being wronged. "Want?"

"Yes! Do you want Patrick? Is that it? Or do you want him to fail because he is not yours? Or is it all of Flats Junction to bow at your feet, as if you are some queen of old? Or do you simply wish you were someone else entirely and despise the rest of us because we seem happier?" The

234

questions are jumbled and pour out, long puzzled over since I first met Kate and began to piece together her place in town. She has remained an enigma to me, and, I think, to everyone. I don't even think the doctor understands her, not fully. I wonder if she knows herself. Perhaps that is the root of it. If a person does not have a solid footing in life, can they ever be content? "What, then? What do you want?"

"I don't know," she says, cutting me off, her candidness so unexpected it feels like being slapped. "I don't know. Everything?"

There's no way to answer such an expectation. No one can have everything. It is impossible. Is it this desire for the impossible that makes her who she is? How does one live inside such a mind?

"Kate—"

"How-do, Kate. And Mrs. Kinney, as it were." A shadow of man and horse casts over us, too large and tall for life. We both look up. Kate squints into the sun, but my bonnet tilts just enough that I can see across the brightness to Moses Thompson's shiny, earnest face, split by his wide grin.

"What? You need coffee?" Kate asks, sounding ever more wrung out. "Everyone needs coffee. You know where it is."

"I surely do, and the like," Moses says, getting off his horse and slapping the reins with a practiced loop around the railing of Kate's back steps. "Word is already flying around the taverns and the Winters mess hall that the General's up for business, like. Hear Yves isn't too pleased. You watch for him, right, as it were?" He asks the last to Kate directly, his voice a notch lower as he seeks her gaze.

"I know how to handle Yves," she says, but her mouth compresses and she crosses her arms around her stomach.

"So you have," Moses says. He glances at me. "I still think fondly of your cooking, Mrs. Kinney, near better than mine in all the ways, and you know I'm a fine cook, and the like."

"We'll...I'm certain Doctor Kinney would be happy to have you over again," I say, uncertain if Patrick indeed would feel this way, but finding nothing else to fill my line.

"Grand. Maybe Kate will come, too?" he asks, sliding his head to include her.

"No." Kate squeezes herself tighter.

"There's time. Alright, it's my turn to keep the fire and the brew lit in the bunkhouse tonight, so I'll just get the coffee and leave the money on the till, as it were, Kit." He takes the back stairs three at a time and disappears into Kate's private back quarters so fast she doesn't have time to stop him.

When she spins back to me, I try not to let my surprise at Moses's familiarity with her quarters show. I suppose it is not up to me how either of them spends their time, but I can't help commenting.

"He seems like a good man."

"Don't go getting ideas," she hisses at me, her eyes darting around the street. "He's too easy with the way of things, that's all. He thinks just because he and I are similar, because we both—" She cuts herself off, then starts again. "I've made pacts with men before, and they don't work. None of them do. It always ends up with death or loss."

"Loss? Other than Patrick, I didn't think you'd had anyone who..." The clarity slams into my entire body. It surprises me that it does not stop the child in my womb, but the babe just turns and rearranges between my hip bones without a care. "Was it you and...did you have a candle for Bern?" What are the odds of it? She hankered for Patrick, and then Bern, two men who courted me, wished to marry me? Why me and not her? Because of my coloring? Because I am less fire and she is too much? Perhaps she has more than the one reason to be angry with me, and now, of course, Bern is gone and dead...

She snorts. "I owe no explanation to anyone, least of all you."

"Oh, stop it," I say. "You have to let your anger go at some point. You can't keep carrying on with this grudge, keeping medicine away when we order it. You have many men interested in you. That Chen Wang fellow makes eyes at you constantly, and if you and Bern Masson, well, I mean... or you and Moses—"

"I want nothing to do with Moses Thompson!" Kate says shortly. "It won't work, Jane, so just stop your matchmaking there. It ain't enough. I had it all figured when Pat came to town, when he and I pledged—and then when he courted me the whole summer of 1881, I was sure I had what I needed. A good man, a kind one. A white man who could add his strengths to mine...and then you took it all."

"If I recall," I counter. "It was your own hard-hearted stubbornness that turned Patrick away."

She ignores the blame, too caught up in the hotness of her words. "Do you know how few men want to stand next to a woman like me? One who has a business, and who does not have pale skin and light eyes? I only belong here, where people know me. I can't go anywhere else, and I can't just be with anyone, and I would've thought you'd be able to figure out that on your own. Now go away, unless you're actually going to buy something."

I think of the bottle in my pocket, a gift from Kate to Marie, and Marie to me. Ought I offer to pay for it? But then I think of the children who have died as the doctor did without, and I think Kate owes more than a single bottle of iodine.

"I'm sorry," I say quietly. "I'm sorry for everything. Is that what you need to hear?"

She stares at me. "Small words are never going to be enough, and you and I both know it. Some things cannot be healed."

In this, I think she is wrong. From what I have learned and seen, I am quite sure, if we wish it, humankind—men and women both—can heal most anything.

But we must wish it.

CHAPTER FOURTEEN

Patrick

October 23, 1861

"The Army is different about docs, you know. They like them," Patrick told Robert MacHugh. "Or doesn't that talk reach Gloucester?"

"I never really paid much attention to it." His friend, fresh from the trip into Boston, wandered around the stables, touchin' things Mr. Stassen would likely wish he'd leave alone, if he were around to say so. Mr. May puttered over Wiltshire after bringin' Bobby down from the hotel, both freshly re-dressed after the drive from the north.

"Well, it's all changin' with the war. Army men say the generals listen more to the docs, and the docs have figured out how to stop some of the infections."

"You notice all that?"

"The papers say." Patrick shrugged, suddenly feeling silly he paid attention to such stories. Somehow all the stolen snippets of stories in the broadsheets at Mr. McClure's table, the chatter of grooms and hotel guests, all comments about the war had impressed upon him the situation at the front and the changin' station of physicians. They were still a dime a dozen in the city, but it was becomin' apparent that some were better than others. There was one doc's work that still made the news at times, though his work had long since finished. Patrick heard Mr. McClure read about it – how a Doctor Ffirth had tried to prove that yellow fever was not so contagious and came from some unknown source. He'd put black vomit on fresh cuts on his skin, vaporized the liquid stomach discharge and breathed the steam, and even swallowed fresh vomit too, and had never gotten sick. Patrick had almost vomited himself listenin' to Mr. McClure, but none of that dampened his eagerness to learn more...if only... He looked up just as Bobby made to touch Mr. Payne's horse.

"Wait! Get back!"

He was too late. Robert's hand spooked the tense animal, and the front legs jerked along the boards of the stall, bangin' fierce.

"Woah!" Robert yelled, which was the wrong thing to do, makin' more noise. Patrick shoved him aside just as the horse reared and attempted to break down the wall.

"Get back, damn it!" he shouted, standin' between Bobby and the bouncin' horse. There was nothing to do but stand without movin', though both their chests were goin' up and down faster than the animal's kickin'. It was like eatin' one's heart.

After a long moment, Patrick sliced a glance at Bobby from the side. "Just away and we'll head back."

Robert followed his lead. Walkin' slowly, they were able to get away from the snortin' horse, and bumped into Mr. May, who had come out from Wiltshire's box, and was watchin' without a word until the two were safe and near. Robert himself busied his hands with the hangin' of tacks Patrick had just finished, likely embarrassed by the ruckus he'd caused.

"You don't think about yourself, do you, Patrick?" Mr. May asked, his eyes rakin' over the pair.

"Sir?"

"This doctoring you mention. You'd do it to help people, wouldn't you?" He had been listenin', it seemed, and Patrick felt warmth rise to his ears. He shouldn't be speakin' of the profession. It was lost to him, and the sooner he remembered it, the better.

"I suppose, but it's a fool's dream. Bobby speaks of it to tease me."

"There are apprenticeships," Mr. May pressed, warmin' to his favorite pet subject. "All the trades have them. We can never have enough lads learnin' the trades of all kinds."

"Yes," Patrick said, not mentionin' how Aunt Bonnie thought doctorin' not a trade at all, especially after the issue with Doctor Burns. He hoped Mr. May wouldn't dive into the topic too much, as he would hate to reveal his shame and his loss. The entire memory festered inside him, a hole he tried to fill and cover with each passin' day.

"And you won't join the war? Learn the doctoring there, as you mention?"

"Too young, sir, though some of my friends have tried," Patrick said, thinkin' of Michael and his multiple attempts, all of which ended with him turned away and stuck back breakin' his body at dock work. Michael had said next time he might not tell the truth, that boys younger than him were gettin' into the Army on account of the money offered.

Besides, he had a steady job at the hotel stable now, and what good was Patrick with a gun? He would be better in the hospital tents, and yet held back. Rumors flew in the trade. Suppose one of them had heard of the death of Mrs. Wilbur? Suppose they'd heard the whispers, linkin' Patrick's name with her demise? He couldn't risk it, even if it meant buryin' himself among horseflesh.

Mr. Stassen had gone with the Army himself – a man of his skill with horses was quickly given a position taking care of the officer's mounts. Each week, the news of the war seeped into the talk of all the people comin' in and out of the horse boxes. It permeated the streets, and the emptied tents in the North End, where many of the Irish boys and men abandoned their lot and joined the Army. That was all the talk – the empty Irish quarter – Mr. McClure and Aunt Bonnie spoke of it often.

With Mr. Stassen gone, Patrick's slightly elevated wages helped pay the rent. Even with Aunt Bonnie still workin' faithfully for Mr. McClure, her rent went up with each passin' month. Now that the boardinghouses were emptyin' of unruly groups of Irish, the landlords scrambled to make up profits that they were used to gettin'. The women and children, if they were lucky, received cash from their menfolk in the Army to make ends meet, but it was still no guarantee that the money would arrive, or be enough, in the end. And that was the gist of it. There were never enough funds for livin', let alone becomin' a doc's apprenticeship.

"Well, that's something to discuss. An apprenticeship," Mr. May said.

Patrick hadn't realized he spoke aloud and pressed his lips together from givin' away his feelin's. "It's a dream is all, sir."

"Dreams matter. Especially now. I'll get Bobby back to Gloucester at the end of the week, but I won't be back next month."

"We'll see you the month after next, then. I'll keep Wiltshire's box clean."

"I'll be fighting," Mr May said, his tone final. "I must. But you're still young. You should do what you want if you can keep out of the war. Try your hand at being a true physician."

"I appreciate your confidence in me, sir," Patrick said, wishin' Robert would stop rearrangin' the tack all wrong across the way and more desperately wishin' Mr. May would leave his dreams to himself. Such a thing was beyond Patrick now.

Mr. May, who nodded once, quick, then put a hand inside his dark jacket and pulled out a brown envelope. "There is enough there to get you two years with a proper physician or through the months of a college if you'd prefer that way. At least, that is what I've been told as I made inquiries. I'd suggest you search for one that is more a... homeopath, instead of a traditional doctor. The heroics are going out of fashion, but mind the homeopath is one that is not quite so strict on Hahnemann's theories."

Patrick stared at the envelope, and then back up, shock rippin' through his body. He glanced around, but it was only Robert nearby, and Robert did not care for money—Mr.

243

MacHugh had plenty. His friend did wander near to peer at the narrow package.

"A patron? Whew, Paddy! Now we can be apprentice docs together! I'll move to Boston, I will, and I'll be a physician like you will be." Robert grinned at Patrick and then Mr. May. "Awful kind of you, sir."

He was so very wrong, but Patrick would not correct Robert. He had no heart to tear his friend's hopes in the first moment they were uttered.

"I'm grateful," Patrick said, astounded. "But sir, it is too much. Surely in times like this, your family will be needin' the money. I'm just…a stranger."

"I've seen you nearly every month for years, Patrick," he reminded. "And I've seen you put yourself out to save a body many a time."

"I'll not take it, sir, I'm sorry." Patrick stepped back from the narrow package, as if it would catch fire. What would Aunt Bonnie say, acceptin' such charity? She would ask what they would be beholden to, and what the gift might mean, comin' from someone outside their community. And Mr. McClure? Patrick couldn't wager his opinion.

Mr. May gave a little half shrug with one shoulder, annoyed at having to explain his actions, perhaps. "My wife and I have had no children, and I'd put money aside for them. I'm…well, I'm no fool. I may not come back from the war. I wish to be generous with my funds. Please, take it."

He stepped forward so the envelope hovered inches from Patrick's chest. Slowly, he reached up and took it in two fingers, holding it as gingerly as he could, though the weight of the banknotes was unexpected. As soon as it lay in his palms, Patrick stared at the small fortune in his hands, thinkin' of all the meals it could buy, all the niceties he could give Aunt Bonnie. But then he realized it would be ill-bred to use the money in a manner Mr. May didn't wish. He wanted Patrick to put it toward education. For whatever reason, he saw some potential in offerin' such an inheritance.

"But…" Patrick tried to find another reason why he couldn't take the money, but the reasons were slippin' away even faster than his words. "But I'm Irish!"

"How does that matter, Patrick? I know you well enough now, and this war is changing everything. You're young, with an open mind for learning and a knack for healing. Don't be wasting it."

Already Patrick thought of his first purchase, even before he counted the cast. There was a physician's kit for sale in the apothecary, and it cost dear—a full twenty-two dollars—but it would last Patrick his lifetime if he cared for it properly. Even without a practice he missed the weight and shine of the tools he'd used at Doctor Burns's. No amount of time seemed to erase that loss.

Patrick walked Mr. May to the door, fillin' the man's ears with gratitude, Robert trailin' behind with a leftover grin on his face. Patrick would have to break to him the news later, and without an audience, that doctorin', for him, was a lost chance.

Just as he thought it, Doc Burns appeared and blocked the late afternoon sunlight. Both Patrick and Mr. May squinted against the buttery yellow sun, and the ochre edges of light, but Patrick placed the voice before the face.

"There you are, Patrick. I'm glad to catch you today."

The jolt of the voice and the familiarity of the face rushed back on Patrick. He could not believe the jerk of his knees and heart at the sight of his old mentor and Tara next to him, lookin' as if she was freshly bathed and the sweetness of summer lived on her brow.

Behind him, Patrick could feel Robert's body still, and his breathin' came fast. Patrick would have reached back and pinched his friend hard had he not been standin' in front of Mr. May, but as it was, Tara too looked past Patrick's ear, her eyes locked on Robert's face.

Doctor Burns failed to notice the charged link between his daughter and Robert MacHugh, and instead nodded in deference to Mr. May before turnin' to Patrick.

"I've come to say good-bye," Doctor Burns said. "I'm off to join the war effort."

Mr. May jerked next to Patrick, an involuntary movement of eagerness, before the gentleman pulled himself back.

"Mr. May, this is Doctor Burns. He trained me in the physician arts until I came to work at the stables," Patrick said, worry buddin' up as he made the introductions. Would Doctor Burns hold his peace? Or would he betray Patrick in his carefully structured life? Would Mr. May demand back the funds, realizin' his hope in Patrick's future was misplaced?

Yet it would be far more suspicious if Patrick did not make the introductions, and he finished them off, explainin' Mr. May and Tara alike to one another.

"You are of the medical persuasion, then?" Mr. May asked, looking polite and excited at the same time.

"Indeed, I am. There are great medical advancements to be made on the battle lines," Doctor Burns said. "I feel a duty to go and see some of it myself. Try some experimentation. Also, I thought you might wish to hear it directly, Patrick—Tara and Thomas are to be wed."

Patrick had not expected to hear Thomas's name, nor the news of the engagement. It was true that Thomas had always made it clear his interest in Tara. Patrick himself saw the young woman as a sister, and as such he did not see Tara's interest in Thomas.

Her eyes settled on the ground at the announcement, and her shoulders hunched. Patrick wagered that Robert's own body did much the same in the shadows of the stable.

"I see. My congratulations. It is recent?"

"It is. With me off to war, I wanted Tara to be looked after, and well," Doctor Burns said, lightly puttin' an arm about her firm shoulders. "Only just decided last night. But that is all very well. I'm off soon myself."

"I am as well," Mr. May said. "Perhaps we will journey together."

"Indeed." Doctor Burns looked at Mr. May squarely, as if they were equals. "I shall look for you in the march south. So very good then, Patrick. Be well."

"Be well yourself," Patrick returned, a lurch in his gut as he watched Doctor Burns and Tara turn away. Would he ever see the doctor again? Or Mr. Stassen? How many would the war tear away from the livin'?

"Well, that's a fine thing, to know you are already making headway with physicians about town," Mr. May said, lookin' pleased. "I am certain I've made a good investment in you, Patrick."

Patrick smiled weakly, unable to meet Mr. May's eyes. He instead watched Doctor Burns melt into the crowds, Tara a colorful pillar next to him in her bright green and pink dress. Robert stepped up beside Patrick, his own vision glued to Tara's back, his eyes watery.

Was Mr. May's 'investment' worthwhile? Patrick did not see how it could be, but yet he had to do well. He had to do something with himself, if only to make Mr. May proud. To carve a livin' out doin' what he loved. What he knew was livin' in his hands and mind. He would use Mr. May's inheritance to save lives. He'd go to college, get a certificate, heal and save. He would make the man proud. He'd make a difference.

CHAPTER FIFTEEN

Jane

February 21, 1884

I feel the weight of my babe in the turn of my ankles. It is as if water pools in the long ligaments of each toe and boils up so the lasts of my boots squeeze every inch of my flesh from the bottoms of my heels to the middle of my calves. Patrick says I must watch how fat my feet get, and though it seems to get better each night. By the time the day ends and I bank the fire in the shiny black of the stove's belly, I am certain my feet have burst or the laces will instead.

Esther says I am showing signs of a difficult birth, but of course this is not what I wish to hear. It is the last thing Patrick will want to hear, so I notice she does not mention her worries when he is home.

Still, there are many hours we sit at the table and sift through the seeds from last year. They are such fat beans, shaped like the kidney in Patrick's *Anatomy Physiology*

Hygiene book, but white, which the doctor says is not the color of a true human one. We have flat golden seeds of squash and wrinkled balls for the peas. I would have sent out for more from the east, but I do not think we have the money for such a frivolous thing, and who knows if Kate or Yves will be bringing in seeds.

Or, I suppose, if Kate will bring in seeds for me.

I wonder if Esther knows of her daughter's odd moods and reasonings. Sometimes I think she understands Kate perfectly but will not speak of it in deference to Kate or because it is not the way of the Sihasapa. There is much of the Lakota I do not know, even with her careful teaching.

She brings out folded packets now, carefully preserved in leather pockets. She lost whatever she had kept in her house fire years ago, but the garden behind the ruin and the plants in the front still sprout up, almost happy in the newly burned earth around them. She has gone down every month through the fall before the crackle of winter to collect the seeds of many herbs. Now she opens the handmade packets on the wide planks of the table, and the pebbles and narrow whisps of the various plants spill along the seams of each tiny bag she's built as she needs.

"This one is lady's slipper," she says, stirring the minis-cule tan-colored seeds with a stout finger. It looks like coarse sand. "The root is used for anxiousness but also if you are having trouble sleeping. I have seen it used for pain in the womb or stomach, too."

"Would the root truly work if one is with child as far as I am to help me sleep?" I ask, running my palm along the expanse of my overstretched stomach. "I doubt it!" My last pregnancy did not take me this far down the path of future

250

motherhood, so my surprise at making it past the last weeks feels as though I have already surpassed certain death. This also is something I do not tell the doctor, for he acts as if I may be made of spun sugar for how suddenly he will look to me if I just gasp with the splatter of hot oil from the skillet.

"Today we shall also make the teas from what we dried all summer and fall," she says, leaving the seeds on the table and standing to touch the faded edges of the yarrow hanging over the eastern kitchen window. "Sometimes it helps to mix a few together for best results. I do not remember all of them, but some are well-known to my people and I would share them with you."

"Before you forget?" I tease.

"Before I go."

I drop the small roll of leather on the table. She speaks with such defined surety, and I suddenly feel left to sink. Esther has hedged this subject for months. I had thought she might stay at least until I am done birthing children, until they are grown a little. It is a jealous thought, one more self-serving than caring for her own desires, yet I know too that I love her as a daughter ought to do, truly and without doubt or rancor. She knows this of me, too, yet seems to feel she cannot stay.

"You know I—we—do not keep you here on charity. We hope you stay as you are the only family either of us has here in Flats Junction."

She does not smile or nod to this, absorbing it instead as the truth and accepting it. She brings down the herbs to the table and begins to sort the blossoms and the curled, feathery leaves of the yarrow into piles. Their dried stems rustle like crisp straw left too long in the fields, brittle and easy to snap.

"I have spent each season with you—only spring is left—teaching you what I remember. I should go."

"We are not afraid to have you here with us," I say, coming as close as I properly dare to acknowledge the danger the doctor and I hold close by having her under our roof. "And the fire to our porch in July had nothing to do with you. I'm certain of it."

"You don't know, Jane. Don't pretend you know."

"I know enough of the matter to believe you are not a threat."

"Others may say different. It only takes more cases of black measles in town for the older families to remember my Percy died of it. They will say I am bringing it, and the cry against me will become louder each day. They will say I give it to Patrick, and he brings it to homes. They will come up with any number of excuses. It is the way of it."

I watch her nimble fingers twist the leaves off the stringy nettle next and I reach to copy her. The clumsiness of my hands is more obvious by the thickness of each joint's swelling, which seems to worsen each week. She offers more so I can shred the tough stems into a pile of long frayed ropes, which smell green and dusty.

There is nothing I can say to dissuade her.

The reality of that hits me. I have tried and failed to keep her with us, and it is a tear in my heart to know she still does not feel she can stay. It is also true that I cannot refute her words. She is correct. Flats Junction may hold many good souls, many who would not ask her to depart, if anything for love of me or even respect for Patrick's request. And many such people are powerful enough that their voices carry weight. But there are not enough of them, in the end.

I have seen the bloodlust of a mob. I saw the body of my old beau strung up like meat to be butchered. I would never have suspected it of my own neighbors, to be crazed with the insensible desire to see someone—anyone—pay for damages, to cry for an answer and find it without reason. Perhaps I have become too trusting, forgetting that until Flats Junction grows and becomes more a city, intolerance sits just inside the skin of a person, ready to burst forward at the barest scratch of the knife. Perhaps, too, it is the way of all people, no matter where they live and what they have seen. I suppose, as Patrick might say, it is our biology to be so, though I find the idea and thought unbearable. It means we are unredeemable at the end.

And it means Esther is truly correct about why she cannot stay. The people here will not let her. I must not be blind to her truth.

"You are right," I say quietly, into the dry coolness of the kitchen, where the tendrils of winter curl along the edge of the room where the stove cannot reach. "And even though they say such wrongness about Patrick himself, they will lay blame easier at your feet for the smallest thing. It seems it comes about for anyone who sticks out."

Yet Kate manages to slide under it all. I suddenly wonder if that is why she clings so tightly to the General Store. It is the lifeblood of Flats Junction, but perhaps for her, too.

"It is not only the fault of those who wish to run me out for my differences," Esther says, calm and gentle as always. "I myself cannot live with feet in both places, straddling the two worlds forever. I must choose one."

253

"I suppose I understand," I say, thinking that I could try to, but it would be an impossible reality to say I do completely.

"And without Percy, my foothold is not strong enough here," she finishes quietly.

It is something in her tone, going hoarse at the end, that stops me. She has never said so before. In the past, her reasons have been that she was no longer needed. She would say Kate did not want her. That she needed to see her own extended family, and took herself off to the reservation with no real plan to return quickly.

This is the first time she has mentioned her late husband. Perhaps that is the root of it. Everything here only reminds her of what she has lost.

"You and Percy built Flats Junction," I say. "You did, together. It's your legacy, this town, even more than it is Kate's. She's building more on top of what you started. If you leave it, you are giving it up."

Her eyes take on a shine. "It is kind of you to see it this way. My way of it would say I should go, to make room for the next to grow."

"There is wisdom in you," I tell her, gripping her hand across the table so suddenly, so she cannot pull it away. "There is value in that, immeasurably so."

"It is always good to have a purpose." She turns her hand under mine, squeezes it gently, and then releases my hold on her. "I will stay until your child is born, but then I will go, and we will not argue this again."

There is little more to say, and much to do after this. We sweep together the fragments and crushed petals, putting them inside a small cloth and rolling it. I take chalk to mark

254

it, so I know what it is, and mark in my little book the uses. Tucking it up behind the white sugar cone on the top shelf of the pantry, I pull out the pan of soaked beans and grab turnips and potatoes from the crates.

Esther unwraps yesterday's bread and begins to toast it inside the oven, turning it on the fork with a rhythm I envy. The doctor announces his return by banging the screen door and the great oak door with a double slam, and then another hard click. I pause slicing the turnip skins and frown. He does not go into his surgery as is his usual, as he takes such care to clean and wash his tools first thing. He's in his study, with a closed door.

I look up, turning toward the hallway. Esther hears it too, and she takes the knife out of my hand.

"I will finish this now," she says.

I give up the kitchen entirely and walk down the short dark hall toward the doctor's small office. In the quiet, the sound of a match scrape is overloud, as is the pop of the sulfur when it catches to light the lamp.

"Patrick?" I ask, putting my mouth closer to the door jam.

He does not answer, and I touch the handle, finding it unlocked. I walk in slowly, uncertain of his mood and wondering what could have brought him home so early and to act against his careful routine.

He does not look up when I enter. He is not even at his desk or at the bookshelf pouring over a book looking for a remedy. Instead, he is on his knees, bent over one of the old crates shoved along the back of the wall. It is where he keeps his dusty patient files, ones that no longer need filing as the patients are dead or gone, or leftover from his Boston days.

"Do you need anything?" I ask, and finally he looks up, his eyes tight around the edges and his mouth a thin line. For a moment, he looks nothing like my husband, and it makes my heart stutter. "Is everything alright?"

He folds himself backward, crouching, his elbows dragging on his knees, which are now coated in fine dust from the floorboards, one of my never-ending tasks to try to keep clean.

"I just thought I'd see if I'd written anythin' that can be used as a remedy for the measles."

"The black measles? You've said there's no cure. You don't even know how it infects to start."

"No, the usual. The red—the regular."

I go to lower myself to be near him, clumsy though I may be, and he immediately stands up, pulling on my hands to bring me back up before I can get too far.

"Don't get down, Jane," he says. "Here, take my chair." He guides me over to his own larger chair that waits behind his desk, a fair cry more comfortable than the spindly one that sits across from it. He perches on the desk itself, swinging a foot in an impatient tick.

"I'm not fragile," I say, lowering myself down and grateful for it anyway. Even short times on my feet seems to aggravate them.

"No, but you are my wife, and carryin' my babe, and I may treat you with special care, can't I?" he asks, a small smile trembling through his frown.

"You may, and gladly."

"It's only…Fort Randall's recruits comin' in from all over, some from the cities, and there's word some of the fellows are struck down with what sounds like the regular measles."

"That's good, though. It's better than the other, isn't it?"

"Yes, and no. The red is more curable in some ways, at least, there are some understandin's on how to manage it. But it's far more catchin'. It can kill a whole fort of menfolk in a month if left to chance. I sent word to the new commander that I want to visit, and if I do, I wanted to have some sort of medicine on hand."

"Not at your expense!" I say, shocked the doctor would offer such a gift.

"No, no, the Army's, to be sure. I'm just hopin' he'll let me, and quick. David Fawcett should be comin' around with an actual report."

"Whatever you decide to do, it'll take too long to get it in from the east," I say. "Even with the trains not breaking down as much lately."

"It won't matter if I can't figure what to do." He sighs and crosses his arms. "I just don't want men comin' in from the fort and mixin' with folks in town and then we've yet another epidemic on our hands. I don't think I can manage another one. There's been no rest."

He rubs the skin between his eyes carefully, and strangles the ends of his hair, gestures wrought with frustration. I suddenly feel that I still have not been helpful enough to him, but now is not the time to bemoan my woes and ask him for praise.

"It is almost too much to ask, to handle the politics of the government and its army, to educate while healing," I say, leaning forward and covering his knee with my palm. "To worry on it all and try to cure everything, even without answers."

"It's part of the profession," he says, covering my hand with his. "I just wish it was not so difficult sometimes."

"Did you find what you needed?"

"Mm?" He starts tracing the back of my fingers with a single one of his, a delicate touch that sends delicious shivers up my arms and makes my womb tighten around the child.

"From your old files. Did you find anything about the red measles?"

He keeps tracing, running his thumb along the inside of my wrist. "No, not enough to matter. It's only I haven't had to deal with it directly myself. I think there's somethin' in one of the books. I'll look for it later."

"I can help you now."

"Isn't there supper to be gettin' on?"

"I'll ask Esther if she might finish it. This is more important." I rise, but he keeps hold of my hand, drawing me near so that he can splay both his hands across the inches of my stomach and rest his forehead in the hollow of my collarbone. He inhales with a hitch and lets it out slowly.

"You can't catch it, can you?" he asks, sounding shaky in the muffling of fabric. "You've had the measles?"

"No. Does it matter?"

His head jerks up, his eyes direct. "Aye, it matters. A sickness like that, it can kill grown men. Think on what it'll do to you—and to the child."

"Have you had it?"

"I've had the cure."

"Which is what?"

"Already havin' it."

"Perhaps it's not as bad as the rumors," I say, running a hand along his cheek and through his hair. He leans into my touch, a sign he's either amorous or truly exhausted. "Maybe it's something else entirely."

"That worries me even more." He stands up slowly, with some sign of soreness from a long day on the saddle, but that does not stop him from pulling me near as my overround belly allows, wrapping his arms about my middle as far as they will reach and tipping across the expanse to kiss me with such tenderness I feel tears crinkling on the corner of my eye.

"What is it?"

"I just..." He runs a hand along the edge of my stomach. "I don't want to be one of those men who finally finds the woman of his heart, only to lose her and the child in birthin'."

"You'll be able to help. You've done so before," I remind him. The reminder does not help, though, and only makes him frown. The memories of the stillborn birthing and following bleed rain down on us with my mention, and I wish I had not spoken.

"You've only about two or three weeks left?" he asks again, for the hundredth time. "You're sure?"

"As certain as a woman can be."

"Hm." He kisses me again, and then walks to his shelves of books, a mix of mostly English tomes, with a few in German and two in French. I have never asked how he accumulated so many, and in such various languages. I do not think he can read them well, and perhaps just uses them for the Latin and the diagrams. But then again, the doctor knows enough Lakota to get around, so perhaps he knows more than I expect.

And how does a poor Irish boy from the Boston slums learn such things?

CHAPTER SIXTEEN

Patrick

October 16, 1862

Patrick rocked the old iron kettle on the one-burner iron stove. He glanced around, a habit he'd started since rentin' out the small place on the street level of a two-storey apartment in the South Cove. It was a single room, with his personal bed doublin' as a patient's table. The square table in the middle was also his desk and had two mis-matched chairs—one belonged to Michael and his Jenny, who had no children to use it yet. There was a single window, which Aunt Bonnie had hung with a large, starched flour sack for privacy. His eye fell on the dirt packed between the floorboards, which were scuffed so deeply that the knots had popped out. The empty holes left even deeper gauges to fill with street grime trudged in from the handful of passersby. His neighbors were not shy about pokin' in a head to see who had taken up residence. All but one had scoffed when they learned he was not only Irish, but one who had taken the three months of medical schoolin' and planned to be a doctor. Part of it was that the location was on the cusp of Charlestown, which had few Irish livin' there yet. The other part was that the other visitor had been Mr. McClure, who had walked the space as if it were a fine manor and spoke to Patrick as if he saw him as an equal, even complainin' of an ailment or two.

The only thing left to do was hang his certificate, earned the same time as Robert MacHugh, who had the means to stay at a fine boardinghouse with two square meals while he looked for a place himself for a practice. And then he had to do somethin' about the sign out front, which was currently nothin' but a plaque with his name and the rod of Asclepius.

He could have something done up with a carvin', and pay an ironworker to twist up a hanger, but it seemed a frivolous use of Mr. May's funds to do somethin' so fancy. The medical kit, the medical school courses—for all they were generally for allopathic medication use, so different from Doc Burns—and the setup of the business itself, from paper and pencils to a leather bag and square case to hold glass medicines. And then, of course, the subscription to *The Lancet*, which he traded for a chance to suffer through *Virchow's Archiv für Pathologische Anatomie und Physiologie und für Klinische Medizin* and pick apart the *Philosophical Transactions* out of London's Royal Society. It took painful attempts to piece together the Latin from the German to cobble together what had just come from Europe. Sometimes he had to give up, swallow his pride, and ask for a rough translation. He thought it gave him an opportunity to learn beyond what everyone in the States could readily read from the *New England Journal of Medicine*.

"Paddy? You in?"

Patrick spun in a circle, his gut clenchin'. "What do you want, Thomas?"

Thomas ducked in, wearin' a vest in the latest and most fashionable cut. Patrick suspected him of overspendin' at the tailors. But then again, Thomas was able to enter many of the finest homes in Doctor Burns's list. Maybe it had somethin' to do with the clothing.

"I came to see how you did," Thomas said, tossin' his hat on the worn table and peerin' at the patient files with a keen eye. Patrick put his new leather doctorin' satchel over the top to hide the names, and Thomas laughed. He understood, and it rankled Patrick somethin' fierce all the same.

"What else, then, other than to steal my wee list of patients?" He decided to call it so anyway, even if there was only Mr. McClure and his old notes on Mr. May and old Doc Stassen. He liked to leave out some of the papers if only because it looked as though he had many a case if a new one might come to call.

"I'm looking for help with a patient."

Patrick's eyebrows went up. "You don't like the way I work. Why would you want me comin' into the room to contradict you?"

"I like to give some of my more discerning patients some options, to show that I am not being unreasonable."

There seemed to be a catch, but Patrick couldn't see it. To be asked to give a second opinion was not an uncommon ask among the profession. But yet...

"Thomas, it won't work. You believe in treatin' a symptom on its nose...if someone is tossin' up their food, you give them somethin' to do the same, hopin' they cancel each other out. In school, I was taught to listen, to treat the symptoms as a whole with a fix, not a counter. Your patient and their family...they'll be more confused than anythin'."

"Nonsense," Thomas said, sounding almost jovial. "It's a straightforward thing. You'll see. They simply want to hear the diagnosis from multiple sources."

"Why not ask someone in your own circle?" Patrick still could not dive into the notion without questions. It seemed too smooth and any other respectin' doc would ask someone who practiced in his own vein.

"The truth of it?" Thomas collapsed into the better wooden chair and adjusted the patch over his lost eye. "They're money but they're Irish. And I'm not. And you're the only doc I know who's Irish."

"Just an opinion?"

"Just so."

Patrick's curiosity grabbed him. It was too hard to pass up, and a small piece of him hoped this was a road into healin' and makin' amends with Thomas. It had done him no good to have damaged the man for life, and even with the years lost in the stables, and Thomas' years of experience ahead of him now...he did not know if that was enough. Had Thomas forgiven him, thinkin' he'd served enough penance?

"I'll come 'round in a day or so," he said, makin' a decision.

"Because you're so busy?" Thomas asked, soundin' just as snide as when they were young lads at Doc Burns's table. "I can see you've patients lined up and around the back."

"I've my own schedule, and I won't disrupt it for you." The urge to sound important strangled his reason for a moment, and the challenge curdled the falsely pleasant slant of Thomas's mouth.

He sneered, grabbed up his hat, and sniffed. "I'll see you in Jefferies Point tomorrow at four. It's the third house on the left after crossing Neptune Street."

He departed without botherin' to fully shut the door. Patrick followed him out and glanced up and down the street. Thomas's retreatin' back disappeared around the bend as the crowd of the mornin' wove around him.

Patrick sighed and went back into the room. It was odd to live in such a solitary way after years in the boardinghouse with Aunt Bonnie, then sharin' the attic with Thomas at Doc Burns's, then with the lads at the stable before bunkin' with Robert at medical school. The last two weeks alone felt a luxury but also made him itch. If he was truthful, he'd always imagined a house full of noise, same as he'd always had. Aunt Bonnie to be sure, when he could find a place big enough. A wife, someday. The notion of a woman to wed was an odd and faraway vision. Also then there'd be children callin' up and down the rooms makin' lots of sound. Anythin' else felt strange and empty, and he kept listenin' for noise. Would he ever get used to the quiet?

He took a nail he'd borrowed off Mr. McClure and aimed for a vague place on the wall with his iron pan, hopin' he wouldn't hit a thumb and leave it unusable for tomorrow's round with Thomas. And Bobby. He'd pick up Robert on the way, too. It would at least be good for his friend to get some additional practice. Though Bobby had more formal schoolin' from up in Gloucester and had gone straight to doctorin' school with Patrick, he hadn't had an apprenticeship, leavin' his practical skills a wee bit lackin'.

He closed an eye and missed the nail the first time, puttin' a slight dent into the plaster. Wincin', he inhaled and took another try, finally gettin' the nail in. He pulled the certificate out of the waxed paper and debated putting a small hole in the top in order to get it on the wall. He would have to find a frame for it, but he'd felt that, too, was an unnecessary expense. But now, looking at the nail all alone, and thinkin' about the hole he'd have to make...

Maybe he'd go get something when he went to make his visits of the day. Or maybe Robert would know where to go.

He replaced the certificate in its sheath, took up his hat and the readin' material of the past weeks as well as the most recent *Lancet*. There was no small amount of pride he took in lockin' up behind himself, and he thought maybe he could be allowed some vanity as he looked up to where he planned his sign to hang.

Some of the docs used canes to look fine as they walked, doublin' it as a weapon if needed. But those were the doctors who had not grown up in the Irish slums. Patrick knew the strength of his hands all too well – and seein' Thomas only reminded him of it. Sometimes he could still feel the way the eyeball had exploded under his fist... Sometimes he woke in a cold sweat, a nightmare of Thomas standin' over him with a blade and a plan to cut out both of Patrick's eyes in return. Sometimes he couldn't help but shiver, feelin' like his judgement was still out there, waitin'...

"Hey Pat!" Helmut Mittelmann called, wavin' from the Bavarian bakery on the corner. His wife shook out dry laundry in the window above, her large bosoms spillin' from her traditional blouse and makin' Patrick feel unnaturally warm under the collar. He barely glanced up when she hailed him, and hurried past before Helmut would ask him if he wanted yesterday's bread and hold up the rest of the day with a long discussion about the copula of the House of the Angel Guardian's new quarters, just built over on Vernon Street two years prior.

And then he hit Beech Street another block over and the smells hit him full-force. Human feces and dog, cat and horse dung mixed with meal slops and chamber pot piss, old beer and rancid meat. Even with all the changes he knew about medicine and how more docs thought about cleanliness, he had to wonder how soon before large changes happened in the cities. Maybe there was something to movin' away, if only to be away from the festerin' slop of the streets.

At the doctorin' college of medicine in Maryland, he and Robert had kept their room clean of dirt as best as two young men could without more than a broom and a few rags. It was still odd for Patrick, given the differences in their economic upbringin', that Robert followed Patrick, usually choosin' to listen to Patrick over others. It made him think twice, to be sure he wouldn't accidentally lead the other astray. It made him feel extra responsible.

He kept thinkin' on Mr. May, too, and couldn't wait to tell the man about his progress. In the four months since he last set eyes on the man, he'd done exactly as promised and then some and wanted Mr. May to be proud. He'd even left word with the lads at the hotel stables, in case Mr. May should come back lookin' and askin' for him.

The first stop was at old Doc Chilling's. The surgeon barber still plied his trade on the same street, with the same landlady, and still looked as long as a beanpole.

Sometimes, Chilling would bring Patrick to some of his operations. It wasn't often, only if the timin' allowed, but so far there'd been a removal of a tumor, a particularly gruesome lesion, and a setting of a bone that had broken the surface of the skin. The last time, Chilling had even allowed Patrick to finish the stitchin' himself. All this was in exchange for Patrick's *Lancets* when he finished readin' them, as Chilling didn't take with subscriptions. He thought them highly suspicious, especially comin' from overseas, but didn't mind usin' Patrick's once they arrived in the States.

"Ah, Paddy. How goes it?" Doc Chilling asked, curving his bony fingers around the handle of his fork as he poked into the contents of his midday meal. The smell of old meat and burnt carrots filled Patrick's nostrils, but he refrained from wrinklin' his nose. It was somethin' he'd decided to do particularly, as he thought it a sign of a good doc who wasn't so reactive to stench.

"I've brought the *Lancet* for you," Patrick said, holdin' it out. "I've finished it."

"And what have you gleaned from it this time round? Anything of note?"

"Always, but I wouldn't want to spoil the surprise. When next I visit, we can debate, as I'm certain we'll disagree on half." Patrick nodded at Chilling's plate. "I'll leave you to dinner, then, and be on my way."

"Hold on, then, man," Doc Chilling said, standing up with his kerchief still tucked into the loose collar of his shirt. "Didn't want you to go without this." He turned to one of the crates on a low table and pulled out a thin package, oddly shaped.

Patrick unwrapped it at once, unwillin' to wait. It was heavy and spoon shaped, and covered in intricate, scrolled designs. The silver of the instrument gleamed so brightly Patrick blinked.

"A tongue depressor," he said, turnin' it in his palm, testing the great weight of it. It was fine – perhaps the finest thing he would have in his kit. "English?"

"It is," Chilling said, sittin' back down at his plate. "Not one of the new folding designs, I'm afraid, just a classic '50's style, but the fine silver will last you a lifetime."

He was not wrong, and it was one of the tools Patrick did without. A tongue depressor could be anythin' – a wooden spoon, the handle of a spatula, a book folder. Thomas, he recalled, had one of horn, and Robert had acquired one of ivory.

"It's too generous a gift," he said, curlin' it into his hand. "And why?"

"I've another just like it, and you've been helpin' me on my patients, plus all these *Lancets*. Seems the least I can do, even if we aren't exactly eye to eye on some doctorin' notions."

Patrick glanced at the silver again. It seemed too fine, yet a sunburst of pride bloomed inside his stomach with Chilling's backhanded praise.

"I've been forcin' myself as an apprentice on you, is more like," he said. "But I'm grateful, and gladly." He slipped the new piece into his pocket, where the heaviness strained the seams of his vests stitchin'.

"As am I," Doc Chilling said, stabbin' a hunk of yellow potato and holdin' it up to the sun with one eye closed, as if testin' how accurately it had been sliced. "I'll be seeing you soon, then."

"Aye," Patrick said, noddin' his farewell and settin' his hat on as he walked back out into the clamor of the street.

His next stop was to return the *Virchow's Archiv* journal to Doc Joseph Halverman, whose house was on a much finer street, up from Roslindale. He still felt odd climbin' the great wide brick steps to knock on the polished oak door, as if he had a place in such a fine neighborhood. Doc Halverman's maid opened the door, a mousy woman of tiny height, but with a formidable width and a near-impossible to understand accent.

"Der Doktor es im die studium," she said, not botherin' to look Patrick up and down as she did the first few visits. She half-lead him to the open door a few paces into the front hallway before bustlin' on toward the back of the house, where the bangin' of pots and a cloud of steam billowed out.

"Doctor Halverman?" Patrick called as he knocked and entered at the same time. He felt the courtesy important, even though it highly likely the man had heard the commotion at the front door.

"Patrick," the doctor greeted, but didn't look up from a stack of bristling papers and a two-inch thick ledger. He'd put on some weight since the first time Doctor Burns had brought Patrick and Thomas to see the healing methods Halverman had used on burn victims, but still crackled with the same energy of scientific experimentation and zeal.

"Returnin' your journal," Patrick said, carefully settin' the pamphlet on the very edge of the wide desk. It reminded him of the one Mr. McClure kept, though much glossier, as if polished with fine oil every day. He might want to mention it to Aunt Bonnie, though she would likely think it too fancy and fine a thing to do on a desk in a tenement.

"Very good, Patrick. You're always timely. Take good notes, ya?" Doctor Halverman still did not look up, making notations as he scrolled the numb of his pen down the top sheet. His own accent was barely there, as if he'd taken great pains early on to sound as American as possible. Patrick envied the round tone of Halverman's voice, and sometimes practiced when alone, though he always felt damned silly when he did.

"I did," Patrick spun his hat and wandered the study with small steps. Doctor Halverman had shown him one or two things in the study, but Patrick had not dared to press.

"And what of the other journal, the one you also read?" Doc Halverman finally sighed and leaned back in his chair, the pale blue-grey eyes finding Patrick. "The one you share with Chilling down on Cambridge Street. What did you make of the article on the stones in female bladders, and the lithotomy?"

Patrick spun on a heel, wipin' the guilt from his brow as best he could. "How did you know?"

Halverman shrugged, twistin' his pen between two stout thumbs and forefingers. "Even though we still do not work together, the doctors talk. There is always idle chatter, Patrick."

"I didn't think you paid much mind to it," Patrick said, hopin' he wasn't draggin' up any other old memories. He never knew how long and deep the stories ran, and who might decide it was time to start believin' them. Other than askin' – and havin' to answer – questions about the rumors Thomas must have spread outright, Patrick couldn't be certain when his luck with a doctor's patience might run out. What had he heard? *Thomas says you kill women in childbirth…*

270

Doctor Smith can save anyone, but never call that Kinney fellow, he'll bleed a body dead... It was only a matter of time before the established doctors heard the street gossip. Or, worse, when they all might decide he was not worthy to work among them no matter what methods he followed and make him scrape a livin' once again with horses, no matter what fine certificate he had from the medical college.

"I only find it interesting you are so widely spread. A surgeon barber, a traditionalist, and me—an orthodox. And this after you worked with Burns for a time."

"How else are we to combat disease if we don't share?" Patrick said, pullin' out the first defense. "You yourself share. It's how we met."

Halverman tilted his head to the side. "Ya. This is true. And it is why I like to keep you around, Patrick, even if I cannot make you my apprentice. Who else will I debate with, in any rate."

He gestured to the leather-bound chair across from his desk, and Patrick took it, feelin' his heart bump a bit unwieldly. It was true he walked a fine line, and never knew when it would crumble, but he thought himself enough of a good judge of character that he'd created a patchwork of doctors who would abide his unusual friendships.

Besides, it was not as if he was established enough to matter. For now, there was some relief in being unknown. It allowed him to walk the veil between the different layers of the trade.

"Let me ask you this, then," Doctor Halverman settled deeper into his own chair. "What are your opinions on smallpox cures. Have you heard what happened in Chancellorsville, where some of the southern soldiers tried to

271

inoculate themselves. Unsurprisingly, it didn't work. Do you think it will ever become a trouble here, people trying to heal themselves through untried and untruthful odd methods?"

"Aye," Patrick said. "We're no better off here."

"But America is the land of might and opportunity. It is all new here. You do not think that stands for something? We should have physicians in every neighborhood. Or battlefield, as it were."

"It stands to reason that diseases of the old countries will come here, and will prosper, same as the people. It works the same, like rivers or...or our new pipes in the sewers. What flows one way will go back again, aye?" Patrick enjoyed the verbal sparin'. It was the only time he felt in his element, and almost an equal. It was heady, though he tried not to let it go to his head. "And yet, there's new changes comin' to medicine every year. We'll survive the waves, I'd wager."

"There's word of other diseases, particular to the west," Doctor Halverman said, lookin' amused. "Are you sayin' they'll come east, then, with the tide of the people?"

Patrick hesitated. The west was a strange land in his mind. He knew pockets were long-settled, older than even some of the oldest homes in Boston. But between the southwest and the northeast was a massive expansive wild place where his mind imagined rampagin' savages and countless graves, vast mountains that crashed into the sky and homes that looked like ants under the impossible width of the prairies.

"There's no documentation of western illnesses plaguin' other parts of the territories comin' east," he said. "It might be possible, but I'd think a massive migration of people comin' back would be required."

"Suppose it is just one thing," Doctor Halverman persisted. "One person. And then suddenly, pffft! An epidemic, without the books to help us. Without European minds to offer ideas. What then?"

He spoke of an end of ages and a search for unnecessary trouble, it seemed to Patrick, and he rummaged through his mind to find an answer or an idea. He came up empty.

"It seems we're borrowin' trouble where there is none, speculatin'," he said, hopin' he didn't sound too defensive.

"But that's where you're wrong, boy," Halverman said, leanin' forward to grab his pipe and tobacco box. "It's half our work to speculate. How else to consider the possibilities? How else to consider what's happening? Your man Chilling gives you a chance to put your hand to patients, and you'll eventually be so busy with the ailing that you won't have time for social calls such as this, but in the quiet, there's always more learning to be done. Never stop asking questions, and expect those around you to ask them, too. Expect it. Without questions, our minds grow dull, and we lose a chance at a scientific discovery."

He puffed on his pipe and stared at Patrick, darin' him to argue. He couldn't. He agreed with everythin' Doc Halverman said, right down to wantin' to be surrounded by curious folks, folks open-minded and desperate to learn. It was how he felt, as if a burnin' lived within him, always seekin' and searchin' for answers and ideas.

"You're sayin' we should be tolerant of each other," Patrick said, changin' direction. "And we should be open to all possibilities. And consider the unknown."

"Exactly."

"Doktor?" The maid barged into the room, her double chin quiverin'. "A man ist im der back. He ask for you."

Doctor Halverman sighed, but not with too much annoyance. "Alright, Helga, I'll be there in a moment." He set his pipe, still smoking slightly, in its carved holder and stood. Patrick stood likewise, grabbing up his hat from his knee and walkin' to the hallway first. He knew both wealthy and poor alike came to Doc Halverman, dependin' on what kind of cure they thought they needed. And the doctor never turned away anyone, no matter their coin.

"It is always good to see you, Patrick," the doctor said, clappin' a hand on Patrick's back. "Stop by again in a few weeks. I'll be finished with the *Archiv* by then."

Patrick saw himself out, feelin' a bit dazed. Doctor Halverman had pressed some weighty ideas, more than usual, and he wanted to go home and think on it. But he was half to Robert's place, and needed to let him know about the next day's patient call. If he admitted it truthfully he just wanted a friend there as a buffer between himself and Thomas. Maybe Bobby would see it, though Patrick knew his friend wouldn't call him out.

Robert wasn't home, though, which was a bit unusual. He didn't have a girl to see, as far as Patrick knew, though he supposed Robert might and just hadn't spoken of it, if it was somethin' new. He left a note under the door, givin' the time and place, and went home a wee bit anxious that Robert might not get it, and Patrick'd have to face Thomas alone after all.

But when four o'clock rolled by the next day, Robert was already there, lookin' a tad sheepish around the edges.

"Sorry to miss you, Paddy," he said, glancin' up at the houses and gates with interest. "I was out."

"So I saw. No matter, I was seein' people myself anyway." Patrick glanced around, wonderin' if Thomas wouldn't show after all. The houses seemed too fine for Irish, though he knew some did rise above the discrimination, and usually brought as many of their own with them when they did. Still, he was surprised Thomas asked for the opinion at all. Surely these people would want an English-American over another Irish. Wouldn't they want somethin' to raise their own esteem to their neighbors?

Robert spun about, then paused. "That's our man, then?"

Patrick turned and looked down the street. Thomas strolled, lookin' dashin' and very much the gentleman doctor with an entirely different suit, never mind the eyepatch.

"That's him."

Thomas approached, his smile creasin' the skin under the lost eye crinklin' as if he had a very kindly way about him.

"Patrick. You're on time," he said, sounding surprised, but turned to Robert before Patrick could swipe back at the incorrect jibe. "And you are?"

"Doctor Robert MacHugh," Bobby said, stickin' out a hand and hidin' the last of his Irish accent, though he clearly couldn't take back his name. Thomas shook the offered hand with some heartiness, and then nodded at the third house.

"Here we are."

They were let in by a proper butler, who took all their hats in one hand and ushered them as a group into the sickroom. It was a large enough room, filled with a frilly bed and dark polished wood, overly floral-patterned wallpaper and narrow windows hidden with dusty drapes. Patrick stifled a cough at the stench of old bedding and unwashed skin, not to mention the staleness of the air itself.

An elderly maid sat beside the sick man, who looked yellow in the lamplight. He was sleepin' though his eyes twitched behind thin lids. The maid closed the book she was readin' and hopped to her feet.

"I'll be gettin' the lady o' the house then, aye?" she asked, her voice round with Ireland.

"No need to disturb her yet. I've brought Doctor Kinney and Doc MacHugh to see to Mr. Joseph first."

The names seemed to draw her up, and bright eyes flicked between Patrick and Robert. Thomas made a tiny movement with his brows, as if urgin' Patrick to do somethin', so he settled for a quick incline of his head and a fast smile.

"If you might wait outside the door, we'll let you know when to run to your lady," Patrick said with as little condescension as possible. The maid's face did not register his accent, but she seemed to soften around the edges, curtsied, and hurried out.

The minute the door nestled in its frame, Thomas let out air. "How much says she won't wait at all for us to call her and has gone straight to her missus to say I've brought the Irish docs?"

"I can find out for you," Robert offered, and flung open the door without waitin'. Patrick's heart bumped a wee bit, but it was for nothin', as Robert turned back in with a grin. "Glad I didn't take that bet, then."

Thomas shrugged, and then gestured to the man under the bedclothes.

"Eldest son of the Irish attorney," he said, spreadin'

his hands wide into the room. "Can't say I'm thrilled about treating the son of a judge, but duty calls."

"What does it matter what the father does? It's your patient, man," Patrick said irritably. "What's wrong with him?"

Thomas shrugged again and dropped his arms. "You tell me."

It felt a game and a test, as if they were back under Doctor Burn's eyes, fightin' for approval. It made his blood race and the pressure of his heart rise, as if he and Thomas were runnin' neck and neck in a race and there was no way to know where the finish line might be.

Joseph Murphy the younger lay without movement as Patrick sat beside him, Robert hoverin' at his shoulder.

"Have you done a full body examination?" Patrick asked Thomas.

"As much as I could. You know when people are wealthy how they feel about getting undressed. I've only his word and his wife's, before he took to his bed."

Patrick was not surprised. "Symptoms?"

"He said he'd had no troubles or health issues in years. But lately his head aches, and he's felt weak or numb." Thomas stood at the foot of the bed, arms crossed, as if expectin' the lad to leap up and offer additional evidence. "He was quite the dandy before this. Frequenting all manner of places and women, drinking heavy and spending his father's coin. I've put it on the drink, but he seems young for it to be a trouble, being only in his late twenties. Then again, he is Irish."

Robert stiffened at the slur, but Patrick was used to it from Thomas. He puzzled over the pieces, and the lack of information.

"And how long has he been like this?" Patrick asked. "Did he suffer an episode?"

"From what his wife says, he was unable to move his leg one day, and from there he has become more and more confused, as if he's losing his wits."

Patrick stood and began to categorically list all the disease information he'd gleaned at college and from the various journals. He thought and discarded a dozen notions, feelin' more than a little annoyed he couldn't have been brought in on the case earlier.

"He can't remember things?"

"I can't decide what's more a sign of his disease," Thomas said. "The weakness and head pains or the change in his memory. It seems a wasting illness if ever there was one."

Patrick had a list of questions to ask but wasn't sure if Thomas would know the answer. If Thomas had no ideas or suspicions, he likely had not thought to ask certain particulars. He would have liked to know if there had been hearin' loss or vertigo. He chased the edge of an idea, one that seemed plausible, but would require some explainin' and without the proper laboratory, he'd only be speculatin'.

"It hurts," the man whispered. "The light hurts, Mona." He breathed in once, twice, and then slipped back into sleep.

Patrick frowned, then stalked to the door. When he opened it this time, the maid was waitin'. She dipped a curtsey, which felt odd, as if she was givin' him deference.

"If you might fetch your lady," he said. "That'd be grand."

"O' course. She's not too far." She bent a knee again and hurried off.

Patrick turned back to the room to see Thomas and Robert watchin' him with expectant airs.

"Well?" Thomas asked, leanin' forward. "You best not offer the hypothesis to Mona straight off in case you're wrong."

"There's a chance she might give me the last of the clues," Patrick said, glancin' at the sick man again. "If she's feverish or a rash, or sufferin' a few other ailments…"

Robert's face was twisted. Patrick knew the look – one he'd seen often during their joint schoolin' when they'd worked together to solve questions from the teachers. Thomas simply looked put out.

"Stop stalling and tell us, Paddy," he said. "Unless you really mean to offer the lady of the house a guess and nothing more."

"It's not a guess!" Patrick said hotly. "It's a strong hypothesis."

"And?"

Patrick shot Robert a glance, and Robert shook his head. He wouldn't speak up, and Patrick didn't blame him.

"Fine, then," he said. "It's the old disease. Ricord spoke of the many stages of it when he disproved John Hunter's little experiment."

"Ricord? The Frenchman?" Robert asked.

"He was born in Baltimore," Patrick corrected. "Though yes, he's been in France these past years."

"Decades," muttered Robert.

"What are you saying?" Thomas asked. "That this is… what, the French disease?"

"I suppose that depends on where you're standin'," Patrick said. "The French disease, or Italian. The Polish disease, the German disease. The Turks will say it's the Christian disease. It's the same one, no matter the name."

"But then—"

Thomas was cut off when the maid barged in, followed by Mona Murphy. She was slender and held her shoulders back while her corsets propelled her stomach forward under layers of bodice lace and a bustle that draped carefully behind her.

"Well! So many doctors," she said, her accent faint enough that it was only noticeable to someone who remembered what it might sound like if full. "I do hope there's some solution."

Patrick approached and looked at her closely without trying to narrow his eyes. And there it was: a glassiness around her pale blue-green eyes, one side of her throat swollen under the tight collar, and patches of hair missing, though artfully hidden as well as her maid might do.

He shook her hand anyway, tryin' not to cringe and then gave the smallest of nods to Thomas and Robert. He'd gloat about it over a pint when they left.

Mona Murphy bent over her husband, assessin' his health. Findin' it lackin' yet, she hummed displeasure and spun.

"Well?"

Thomas stepped forward, his chest expanded. "It's the French disease, madam."

Patrick gulped so hard he was sure it was audible. Robert started, his eyes bugged out briefly. The maid's mouth went tight.

Mona Murphy fainted dead away.

That evenin', Thomas gave a reenactment of Mona's response after his third beer at his rented room near Doctor

Burns's place, where Tara lived alone until their wedding. Thomas's cheeks glowed and a bead of sweat slowly trickled from under the eyepatch. Robert, subdued, nursed his first drink carefully, elbows on the smoothed wooden table. His eyes kept dancin' to Patrick's, but neither felt they could speak while Thomas was near. In the snap of his shoulder blades, Patrick's own anxiety bled into his arms and down his back, as if a hot knife was held to his spine.

What could be said, now, that would not cause a fight?

The three of them had gotten Mona to bed, and Thomas left his instructions for future care. He'd taken the envelope from the butler as they'd gathered their hats, and offered to buy beer on the way back.

"I'll live like a king off the Murphy money now," he said comfortably. "They'll need me for treatment, and won't dare to have another doc come, for fear of the news of their disease spreading further."

Robert scowled into his ale, and Patrick resisted tossin' his own drink into Thomas's smug chin. He wanted to shout that it was his notion and should be his cash. He wanted to punch Thomas, but couldn't, not with that damned eye patch remindin' him of what happened last time he'd lost his temper.

"Thomas?"

The door to Thomas's rooms squeaked, the hinges flaky with rust. The three men were first greeted with the gentle curve of a woman's hip, and then the soft smile of Tara Burns, though her cheeks flushed even brighter when she saw them all.

"Oh! I didn't know you had company, Thomas," she said, her voice even, but her eyes seemed to sparkle as they landed on Patrick. He grinned at her in response, but when she kept smiling, he realized her eyes were not for him, but for Robert.

Robert swallowed just loud enough that Patrick could hear him, but Thomas didn't notice. He was too busy leanin' far back in his chair and wavin' at the stove.

"Put it on the warmer. And since you're here, you may as well serve us. Give you some practice being my wife."

Tara paused only slightly, but Patrick had been long enough at Doctor Burns's house that he noticed. Robert stared into his cup, and hunched lower, and Thomas went back to drinkin'.

"When is the weddin'?" he asked the room in general. Thomas shrugged. Tara looked nervous. Robert glanced at both and sat up a bit straighter when there was no answer from either.

"Her father wanted it soon," Thomas said, thumpin' the legs of his chair hard on the ground. The bang was rewarded with a muffled shout and the poke of a broomstick handle from the tenants below. Thomas ignored it and waved at Tara. "What are you waiting for, woman?"

Tara shot him a bland look, one of so much indifference it seemed to slap Patrick across the jaw. In that single glance, he realized how much Tara disliked Thomas, for all she'd never treated him poorly, either. How had Doctor Burns missed so many signs? Had he simply been desperate to get her settled before he went to war? Patrick himself would have been a kinder choice, for all he only saw Tara as a sister.

As Tara warmed the soup and sliced the bread, Thomas listed out what he knew of syphilis, drawin' out Bobby. As Robert offered more information than Thomas, Patrick saw Tara's eyes flick between the two, measurin', and he knew

282

Robert would come out on top. Not only was his friend of a sweeter nature, he knew much more than Thomas, who likely had never cracked a foreign journal in all his studies. It showed, and to the daughter of a physician…it mattered.

"And anyway, with such knowledge and the funds it'll garner me, I could even look at going overseas. Getting some additional lessons from the doctors there," Thomas said, clearly usin' the facts Bobby had just given as if they were his own.

"Overseas?" Tara swung around from the tiny stove. Her skirts, full and ruffled on the bottom, brushed the black edge, leavin' a smudge. "When?"

Thomas waved a hand and took a swig of his beer. "Who knows? I'm to be paid handsomely by the Murphy's for a good while, I'd wager. You'll be a wife in style, maybe even live in a place near Moore Street."

If he expected the idea to light Tara up, he did not know her. She turned back to the stove with a shrug of one slim shoulder, and her dismissal sent Thomas to his feet.

He gripped her elbow hard. "You'll look at me when I'm speaking!" he hissed.

But he'd forgotten there were two others in the room. Patrick would've vaulted over the table, but Robert was closer, and he had an arm around Thomas's throat faster than Patrick could shout.

"She's not your wife," Robert said calmly. "Not yet anyway."

Patrick's muscles quivered under his shirt, as if achin' to be allowed loose. He inhaled so hard through his nose he was certain the cartilage cracked. Thomas did not yield, his fingers twitchin', and Patrick moved slowly toward Tara.

He took the wool out of her hands and gently shimmied her away from the stove by his body alone, even without actually touchin' her. "I'll handle it. I've done so many a time before," he said.

"You always were a hand in the kitchen more than most men," she said, slidin' away from the shiny black surfaces. "You never burn a thing."

"Go on home, Tara," he said. "And we're grateful for the victuals."

Thomas made a grunt as Tara moved to the door, testin' Bobby's hold. But then Patrick stuck out the meat fork so that Thomas couldn't move without gettin' a belly of metal.

"She's best off home, Thomas," Patrick said, too casual and not carin'. "Robert, why don't you walk her home, make sure she gets there safe?"

Robert looked as if he'd been gifted the world, but eased Thomas out of his grip slow just the same, as if hopin' against hope Patrick meant it. With Thomas stuck between the table and Patrick's kitchen weapon, Bobby was able to step to Tara's side, where she waited for him. Patrick had half expected her to bolt, but knowin' Bobby was comin' with her seemed to have stayed her step.

"I'd be happy if Robert would step out with me," she said, the use of Bobby's front name paired with the words of courtin' enough to make Thomas choke aloud. He made to lunge and feint to avoid the meat fork, but Patrick followed him.

"It's the old slum days," he told Thomas casually. "Just can't help but be quick to fight, it seems."

Thomas's chest heaved and the high points of his cheekbones turned deep red.

Bobby cleared his throat, his cheeks flushed as well, but with a rose-pink. "If you'll take my arm, Miss Burns."

"Call me Tara," she told him, flashin' Bobby a bold look from under her lashes as he opened the door up wider. "And I do hope you won't leave me wondering if you'll walk with me more than just tonight."

Patrick caught Bobby's incredulous eye. He grinned at his friend and shrugged a shoulder, while keepin' the iron fork aimed at Thomas's belly.

"Sounds like you've best get courtin'," he said, and was rewarded with both Bobby's grin, Tara's tinklin' giggle, and Thomas's growl.

"Thank you, Paddy," she said. She took Robert's arm and gazed at him as they stepped out. The spark between them wasn't lost on anyone, and when the door shut, Thomas turned his one good eye on Patrick, his face white.

"You think that's anything?" he growled. "She's just playing. She'll come back to me in the morning."

"Oh aye?" Patrick was certain he knew Tara better than that. "And has she been the grovelin' type before?"

The pointed question hit home, and Thomas worked his throat, and then made for the door once more, likely to go on after the newly minted couple. Patrick swung up the fork.

"No need to go disturbin' the lovebirds," he said. "And I wouldn't mind testin' a theory on curin' wounds to the gut, if you care to try your luck on whether I'll 'accidentally' stab you."

"How long are you planning to hold me hostage?" Thomas asked.

"Oh, an hour if I must," Patrick said. "They need time for a kiss on the front step. Come off it, Thomas. It's not like you love her."

"But she was supposed to be mine," Thomas said, his voice blank and flat.

Had Patrick not already taken Thomas's eye, he would have worried he'd made an enemy. As it was, Patrick figured he was already in for a penny. What did it matter for a pound?

notes from Philosophical Transactions

<u>London based
english</u>

Bernard, experiments.
the liver creates sugar? sugar found in the vena cava and
hepatic veins, but not in the portal as proof.
 article in January 1861 journal -
experiments continued on liquid carbonic acid

the lancet, sept 27, '62
polypi of the uterus
report from a dr. tanner

bloody discharge via vaginal channel led to anemia
how much blood loss causes anemia? differ per patient?
growths can cause bleeding sometimes, or sometimes none at all.

nitrate of silver on hand

Virchow's
Beiträge zur Lehre von den Entzündungen seröser Membranen

translate? theory of inflammation of.....membranes?

would a theory be practical to use, or an experiment?
tell patient it is only a theory and not yet studied?
suppose germany has different medicinals available for
said inflammation?

burns

homeopathy / homeopathic practices
symptoms only ascertained by discussion and relationship with
each patient
Eclectic leanings?
like cures like
if a patient is complaining of an illness in the brain, give a dose
that will provide the same feelings in a healthy body - they ought
to cancel out
much is empirical and sporadically based.
bedside manner perhaps the most effective piece of knowledge

Halverman
allopath, not a hospital man
open leanings to eclectic minded
orthodox and traditional physician and philosophy
does he prefer any title? does one matter more than another?

consider
/orthodox allopaths and homeopathy combined as thus /

after receiving a medical license, offer proper receipts as burns
did, and the experimentation in limited environs as halverman

would use of caution paired with willingness to be good at bedside and ability to be open to use of medication formed by
experiments of allopath traditionalists and hospial men plus use
of surgery when needed only - as chilling once said, to keep cuts
at a minimum unless desperately needed...is this the true receipt
for successful doctoring?
/

surgeon barbers, both
Stassen applies knowledge of anatomy to horses only
chilling will operate on animal or human alike.
it seems best to be an eclectic leaning physician.
orthodox and homeopathic sects will never agree. best to find
middle ground.

CHAPTER SEVENTEEN

Jane

March 3, 1884

It seems every day starts with a knock on the door this week, and every time my heart leaps into my throat and rattles. Twice it's been family members asking for the doctor to see to their sick, both times it was something manageable—a high fever in one and a deep accidental knife slice for the other. One knock came from a woman who said she'd a double case of black measles in her house, who came so late that her aunt and cousin were dead before Patrick could arrive. Danny Svendsen stopped by with Moses Thompson to say he'd lost another twenty head of cattle to the odd disease. And this last knock comes so early that I have only just poured us coffee and it's still too hot to sip.

"I'll get it," I say, and walk swiftly down the hall. I'm only able to do so because I was already standing. These days, moving from the table bench makes for a cumbersome and unwieldy maneuver that makes me feel ridiculous and quite ungainly. Patrick can be up and back in the time it takes me to get up at all.

Esther turns the egg pie on the stovetop, checking under it to see how brown the crust is, the top a fine gold of fresh yolks. She's added some additional herbs to this particular bake, saying there are some to aid with childbirth. She said it like she knew my time was near, though it would not be difficult for anyone with an eye to think so, too.

Marie stands on the fresh porch, her work apron on and her scarred hands already a pale green-grey. Her face looks tight and her mouth hard, and when I meet her gaze, she shakes her head as if we share a womanly secret.

"My fool of a husband thinks my son is ready to work," she says, looking at me as her jaw works over itself. "He says it's high time Kaspar get himself out of bed and back to the forge."

"Oh?" I don't catch what she wants. "And...did something happen to Kaspar?" The boy's arm is still freshly mended, it's true, but since using the comfrey, I've noticed a marked improvement. Patrick will poke at what I observe and based on my explanations, he agrees the scars are strong and the healing well on its way beyond concern.

"Not yet," Marie says tightly. "But I don't want to wait for it."

In the wildness of her tone, I can see it in my mind as well. The newly mended skin ripped apart with one wrong move, the slip of a hammer with a hand still not at full strength, and the following potential infection.

"I'm not starting over with him hurt," she said, pressing. "I want the doc to tell Thaddeus what is manageable."

"And what makes you think Thad'll listen to me?" Patrick asks. He has come silently behind me, and now places a light hand on my shoulder. "If anythin', it might make him contrary just to prove me wrong."

"I think we've all moved on from such pettiness," Marie says. She plants her feet wider and crosses her arms around her middle. "Tadeusz told me what you've discussed about other matters, too, so if you think him about to make a point using our own son…" She raises her eyes to look at the roof. "He rebuilt your house with you, doc. He'll listen."

I slide a glance at Patrick, surprised he's pushing back on this. "I can go, too," I say. "I've been treating Kaspar."

His mouth slips up and he nods. "We'll be there right off."

"No need for rushing," Marie says, holding up her hand. In the creases of her palms, soot or metal dust traces the lines of it. "If you wait to come a bit, Thaddeus may not immediately realize I came to get you. I could do without his annoyance until he pieces it together." She tilts her head at me with a glint in her eye. I feel the familiar tingle of a joyful tiny spark inside, something I get whenever one of the women in Flats Junction think to include me in their circle of female notions.

"We'll eat breakfast, then, and be there first thing," Patrick agrees.

She nods once and heads off back toward Soup's Corner. Patrick closes the screen and the main door in order to keep the chill out of the kitchen. He follows me back in and sits down at once to drink his coffee, which now is a perfect temperature for the gulps he prefers.

When I take my seat again across from him, a tendon twinges in the curve of my hip bone. It is incredibly awkward to be so pregnant. I must sit sideways at the table or stretch quite far to reach it. Walking has turned into some sort of waddle, my feet turning out to the side, and my bones feel like they're creaking with the extra weight of fluid and child. Patrick says everything is progressing as it should, and his eye falls on me even now as I'm doing nothing but trying to get comfortable on the wooden bench.

"Maybe you shouldn't come with me to the Salomon's," he says. "You've been walkin' around town all week instead of restin' up for your birth."

"So do all the other women," I remind him. "Everyone works until they can't." This is mostly true, with only a few exceptions, such as Sadie Fawcett, who doesn't work during the day anyway, unless one can count flouncing around in Helena's latest creation or gossiping at the General Store.

"And half of them lose their babes or their lives," he says lowly.

"Please don't remind me."

He looks up from the egg bake Esther sets down in front of him, guilt and fear flashing across his eyes.

"I'm sorry, Janie. I just don't want you thinkin' I can perform miracles if things go badly at the last minute. There's still so much…"

"You pulled me back from death once before," I say quietly.

Esther shoots a glance at me when she takes a seat next to Patrick. Her mouth goes thin, one of the few signs of emotion she will ever show, and I wonder if she is remembering my hemorrhage as well – does she think I am tempting fate by speaking of it? Or is she only remembering the terror of watching me fade?

292

"I was lucky," he says. "You were."

"I've married that luck," I say lightly, trying to pull the conversation out of the darkness. I cannot think of all the possibilities. I've spent too much time dwelling on them already. Alice told me, at my last visit, that she would go into birthing listing everything that she was told could go wrong by her many sisters-in-law and then thinking backwards how literally none of those particular fears had come to pass for any of the near uncountable births of her nieces and nephews. I was trying, perhaps without much success, to do the same. I did not want to be reminded that pregnancy was viewed as having a foot in the grave…

As I think of it, another twitch tickles in my side, not unlike when one walks too fast for too long. I shift position on the uncomfortable seat, reminding myself it will not be long now and all the odd aches and pains that surface with my condition will be gone. A part of me cannot wait to have my body be my own again. I had not known a full-term pregnancy would be so very uncomfortable, and for all the fears a child-birthing bed holds, there is something driving me there as fast as I might go, if only to breathe freely again without the press of a foot under my ribs.

Esther finishes first and rises. "I will do the dishes," she says. I watch her take her plate to the wide counter under the kitchen window and find myself standing, perhaps a bit too fast, and bring my own over to join her.

"What will I do when you leave?" I ask.

"You have kept a far grander house than this one," she says, a soft smile on the strong planes of her face. "You will manage."

She says it with confidence and finality, and it makes my stomach clench. I do not want her to go. And how is it I crave this? Had Henry Weber and I had a child in Boston, my own mother would likely have only come down from Rockport to glance in the bassinet. I cannot imagine Ruby Hobbs doing much more than that.

"Let's go, Jane," Patrick says from the kitchen door. He's put on his hat already and grips his medical bag. "I figure we can stop at the Salomons and then check on Doris Tucker's laceration."

Doing rounds together is one of my favorite parts of learning the nursing trade slowly but surely. Often it means I cannot offer the same remedies or herbal concoctions I've learned from Esther for fear of undermining Patrick while he's in the room itself, but I do learn much. And I do enjoy time with my husband.

We walk together, my arm threaded with his elbow. The doctor's pace is slower with me so attached, he doesn't seem to mind. If anything, he goes even slower than needed, so that it is a stroll more than a walk, as if we are a couple out to see the city parks of a Sunday. Our heads bend of their own accord against the wind, but it is not as terrible as the deep blizzards, and I ignore the tug and pull of pregnancy with the freshness of the air brought by the coolness. It is a dangerous time of year, to be sure, but with the crisp winds, all the summer stenches are bleached.

"How are you feelin'?" Patrick asks. He has not yet asked it this morning, and it has become a habit. "Any bleedin'? Any sharp pain? Cramps?"

It amazes me that only a few short years ago I would be appalled and embarrassed by such a conversation. Yet the doctor has always put me at ease from the beginning, and he has never shied from asking the difficult or unseemly questions. I've noticed he also is a bit more blunt with me than other women. I prefer it, for it reminds me he sees me more as an equal, even when we disagree.

"Nothing that seems out of the ordinary," I say, thinking to the morning's twinges. "Nothing that is unnecessarily uncomfortable."

"Good."

We pass the Lampton pigsty, which is churned muck even without snow to make it slush. Harriet Lindsay comes out to throw slops and waves at us, then goes back in as the pigs go crazy over the food. The sound of their squeals can be heard two streets over and three across, but no one minds too much given that Alan Lampton provides a pig for every festival all year.

"Do you think they will ever wed?" I ask, glancing back at the door where Harriet had disappeared. "She gave up being a schoolteacher for him."

"They don't belong to the same church," Patrick says. "And with neither of them Catholic or Lutheran on top of it, neither Father Jonathan or Reverend Painter wishes to be the one to marry them."

"Here I thought it was because they've been 'living in sin' all this time."

"No," he says. "It goes beyond that. Even with all the preachin' of love and acceptance, there's still lines to be drawn on religion. I don't think that will go away so easily, even out in the wilds of the western territories."

Our discussion on the politics of faith is cut when we arrive at the smithy. The sound of three hammers is further joined by the faint ping of Marie's own work in the adjoining tinshop. The cacophony makes me wonder how any of them have any ability to hear. Do they not get a ringing in their ears after years of such clamor?

"How goes it?" Patrick asks, overly loud, but he times it so his voice lands in the odd bare space between pounds and slams on metal.

Thaddeus swings from the anvil, his eyes near hidden in a scowl and a hammer half-raised in use. Kaspar peers from under his dark hair, looking for all the world a bit uncertain. Natan turns from the fire with a cheerfully red slab of metal only to have Hardy take a step back right in his way.

"Look out!" I cry, sounding shrill even to my own ears. "Natan!"

Thaddeus's torso twists and jerks at my scream, dropping the hammer. It hits the destroyed earth of the smithy with a dull thud. Kaspar freezes, still clutching his own hammer and tongs, and Hardy reaches to grab hold of something—anything—as he pauses mid-movement. What he grabs is Natan's arm, bringing the boy's arms down, and with it, the sweltering metal. It lands across Thaddeus's shin, where it hisses. The acrid smell of roasting hide hits my nose and I clap a hand over my mouth.

The doctor is already moving toward the big smith even as Thaddeus curses and kicks the metal to the corner of the metal shop.

"What are you doing, grabbing blind like that?" he roars at Hardy.

"I—"

"You weren't looking again, were you? Not seeing, not moving in the lines!" Thaddeus draws shapes in the air, marking the flow of the workshop's deliberate layout. "This smithy can easily handle all of us! You'll be covered in more than just a few burns!"

As he rails on, I notice fresh pink and red marks on Hardy's arms and wrists. None look terribly deep or troublesome, but I see the blacksmith's reasoning. Natan and Kaspar sport only a few even though their years in the shop must double Hardy's.

Patrick takes a knee in the dirt at Thaddeus's side. The smith steps back, bumps into his anvil and swears again. "What are you doing, doc?"

"It landed on your shin, Thad. I thought I'd take a look at the burn while I'm here."

"It's nothing," Thaddeus grouses. "No worse than anything else I've had."

The doctor raises his eyebrows and doesn't get up. Thaddeus huffs a single, drawn-out sigh and plants his foot against the anvil stump. I come near with the bag Patrick had dropped, prepared to pull out gauze at the very least.

"I wear leathers, trade them with David Fawcett for iron work," Thaddeus says. "I'd be a fool not to do so what with only fool apprentices about to help." He glares at each of the boys. "Why are you standing still? We've orders to fill and we're not a little behind."

Patrick stands up as Thaddeus yanks up his pant to the knee. While the leather is burnt black to a crisp and is already peeling apart where the red-hot metal landed, the skin underneath has only a pale-pink mark.

"See?" Thaddeus says, sounding not a bit smug and lowering his foot.

"Well, there was no harm in lookin'."

"And at least you didn't immediately accuse him of wanting to chop off your foot," I say, hoping the tease lands properly. Patrick looks a bit askance, but Thaddeus only snorts and shakes his head.

"What do you need, doc?" he asks instead, folding his arms. "Or is it my wife to do work for you?"

"Actually, we're on the way to see Doris Tucker, but thought to see how Kaspar's doing."

The shuffling in the tinshop comes closer, and suddenly Marie is leaning on the doorjamb between the two shops. Her arms cross as she waits. Thaddeus narrows his eyes at her, his mouth under the grey and black beard going flat. He turns his back to her deliberately and tightens his arms further.

"He's doing fine, as you can see. Back to work. All healed up."

"May I look?" Patrick asks. He moves forward without waiting for Thaddeus to approve, perhaps because Kaspar is old enough to speak for himself. The boy willingly sets down his hammer and rolls his sleeve with eagerness. To show off his battle wound or to show how well he's healing is anyone's guess, but Patrick hasn't seen the injury in months and is overly curious by now.

"It's healed fine, doc," Kaspar says. "I can move it and all."

"No ache in the bone where it was showin'?" the doctor asks, taking Kaspar's arm in both hands. "What about twistin' the skin. Can you do everythin' without trouble in the forge?"

Kaspar hesitates, his eyes flickering to Thaddeus, then Marie, and then finally me. But it's Hardy who steps up next to Patrick, gazing down at Kaspar's healed arm with something like ownership.

"He's not got his full strength, and all," he says. "But that'll come. It's healed up real good with the medications. I put them on twice a day."

"Medications?" Patrick asks, at the same time my heart plummets. What was I hoping? That he would not find out? That the boys would not speak up? Perhaps I had thought Hardy would not be interested in speaking about how he healed Kaspar, thinking it womanly work he did only for his friend.

"Mrs. Kinney gave us oils and such," Hardy says, his pale blue eyes snapping as he bounces on his feet. "I cleaned with iodine in the beginning, changed the bandages just as she said, and then when the timing was right, I did the comfrey."

"You're using comfrey," Patrick says, his voice toneless. He nods at Kaspar and releases the arm. In the bow of his head, I know he's fighting his feelings, whatever they may be this time. Anger? Frustration? Mere annoyance? I steel myself and draw up my chest.

"It has worked marvelously," I say. "And much quicker to heal than without."

"Mm." He takes his bag from me and checks the latch of it for no reason other than to keep from meeting my gaze.

"We haven't settled the payment," Thaddeus says suddenly. "That's why you've really stopped by."

Marie stirs from her post, but Thaddeus is already moving into the house. "I'll have something in a minute."

He bangs through the heavy oak door separating the smithy from the living quarters. In the sudden quiet, all three young men glance at each other uncertainly. Kaspar shrugs and picks up his hammer, only for Marie to step in.

"So he's alright to use it?"

"With care. Don't strain it. It'll take some time for the scars to stretch more like skin and for the bone and muscle under it to get strong again. Hardy's not wrong. You don't have your full strength yet."

The doctor flashed a glance at Hardy, as if seeing him for the first time.

"I'm glad you stopped by," Marie says, coming closer and wiping the grime off her hands on her long-marked apron. It has small flecks of tin embedded into the middle of it, sharp shards that have stuck to the leather and poke out like tiny spikes. "It puts me at ease to know he's going to be alright."

"Well, and it's true we're off to see Doris. Her brother-in-law had her choppin' onions and she near sliced off her entire finger," Patrick reports.

"I heard it was her thumb," Marie counters.

"Forefinger," Thaddeus says, re-entering and handing Patrick a copper coin. "Got it straight from Matt himself. Said it would have ruined the entire batch of soup had it had anything else in the pot when she was slicing over it. As it were, he just rinsed all the onions off and put them back."

"Are you saying Matt Winters is serving people human blood?" Kaspar asks, his eyes wide.

Thaddeus swats at his son and points back at the fire. "Bellows."

"People would certainly be angry to hear it, but it's not technically true," I say. "Though I should hope word like that isn't getting out."

"What's getting out is Yves Gardinier telling everyone he's running for mayor," Marie says, shoving her hair further back into her kerchief. "Heard that one yesterday."

"There's been no mayor in Flats Junction ever," Thaddeus says. "Not even a proper way to vote."

"There's talk of it, what with the railroad and Fort Randall getting bigger."

"Percy Davies was as close to a mayor as we've had," Patrick adds quietly.

I glance at him, wondering if he's given up on his annoyance with my use of herbs, but he doesn't spare me a look, so I cannot read him. He sets his bag on Thaddeus' anvil as if planning to stay a moment, but he only bends down to re-tie his boot lace.

"No one will allow Yves to be mayor," I say, thinking back to the uncomfortable itchiness I feel walking into his ad-hoc store. He's still in business, Kate and he seem to have some sort of strange truce, where she has the everyday goods and he still somehow has both local produce and the very fine things. It's said The Prime Inn will start serving oysters on the regular now, and all because Joe Greenman has a plan with Yves.

"No one will allow anyone but Old Henry Brinkley to be the mayor," Thaddeus says, his tone reasonable with a touch of something else. I sneak a peek at him, where he rests his hip against the anvil with his arms loosely crossed this time and realize he's leaning forward into the conversation. "No one will allow for anything too new if we're going to have politics in town. We've survived this long without it, some will be against it in general. Nearest thing to keeping the peace will be to keep things as close to the same as they are."

"Old Henry has been more like the sheriff, or even something like a judge," Marie says. "Like when Bern Masson was hung."

The sentence itself hangs in the forge. It is a strange cloud, one that hovers over many things in Flats Junction, and certainly certain conversations. It seems I cannot dodge it, and most others cannot either—yet for me it is something else. I'd come close to considering the man for marriage before changing my mind, and I never found peace even before Bern died. There's also the other pieces, left scattered since speaking to Kate. Did she hold a candle for Bern? Had she yearned for him? For how long? Before or after Patrick had courted her in that summer and fall of 1881? And even beyond that – had Bern cared for her?

"Bern's death wasn't enough," Patrick suddenly says. In the realm of politicking, it is as close to a contentious thing I've heard him say in all our time together. "It won't be, not until people feel safe again."

"Or until their memories fade," I say.

"Arson's a hard thing to forget," Marie says. "How long before you feel secure in your own home, Jane?"

I bite my lower lip, my teeth scraping the corner of my mouth. I have not thought of it one way or another, if only so I would not consider how unsteady I feel.

"I am...no less safe than the General," I say, choosing to divert the question. "It seems anything or anyone can go up in flames."

"Some still say the General's fire was the fireworks themselves," Thaddeus says. "But that doesn't excuse your own place, doc. That was pure arson."

"As was Esther's house all those years ago."

"Are you sayin' it's the same person?" Patrick wonders. "And if it was Bern, he wasn't always doin' it alone. He wouldn't."

"How are you so sure?" I ask. I'm suddenly hot and uncomfortable. I don't like this conversation. For all Marie seems inclined to opinions, and Thaddeus overeager to share his thoughts, it is not typical for me. I am not one to hear gossip, and I do not know what is allowed.

"You were courtin' him," Patrick says, turning on me. "You likely know Bern better than most of us. Do you think the man would act on anythin' on his own preferences?"

There's a deep press inside my hip bones, not unlike the one at breakfast, and I inhale hard. What are they implying? That Bern was not the arsonist? That he had others helping? Or...

"And how did Kate Davies know to point to Bern anyway?" Marie asks the hardest question yet that no one has dared to mention. It is as if we are all quivering with it, and yet she has been brave enough to ask it aloud. I swallow a retort, fearing I will betray the bit of confidence I have shared with Kate.

And yet...what do I owe her?

She would say everything. Kate would say I am beholden to her forever for marrying Patrick. It is as if he had no part in the decision, when it was he who followed me to Massachusetts to ask for my hand. She would say she lost everything by me coming to town, that her chance at raising her standing as a married shopkeeper disappeared when I arrived. I cannot imagine her admitting to her own part in the mess of it—her hard and shiny and stiff-necked proudness that made Patrick finally see their profound differences.

"Maybe Kate saw somethin' we didn't," Patrick says, still finding the good in her anyway. "She was high up on the balcony durin' the fireworks. She might've seen Bern settin' fire to our porch at the very least."

"She may be part-Sioux but she can't see in the dark," Thaddeus said, lifting his eyebrows. "It was dark on the east side of town, doc, with the fireworks setting off more than enough bright right in front of us all. No one was seeing through that."

"Maybe she knew something," I blurt. All eyes spin to me. Patrick's eyes blow wide. Marie's teeth snap and Thaddeus's chin lowers, his beard settling across his overlarge chest.

"Like what?" Marie wonders. "What would Kate know about Bern?"

"I didn't think you two spoke," Patrick says, looking confused and a bit windblown about the edges. "Or are you only speculatin'?"

"I..." Now that I've started, I struggle to find a dam for the words. They quiver on the edges of my tongue, and I can feel the pull of the child, as if the earth is stretching for it. It's a gentle push, a nudge, a clench of my waist, and then it is the sound of a waterfall. And yet it is a private one, as the birth waters flood the smithy floor and drench my chemise and socks.

Marie's face twists into a cross between worry and mirth. She glances up at her husband and shrugs a shoulder.

"Perhaps it's always your fault, Thaddeus. This is two women who have gone into labor in these metalshops, and you're always there to see it."

"So are you, woman!" the blacksmith growls.

"I don't count," Marie retorts, coming to support me under an elbow. "I was the one birthing last time."

Patrick puts both hands on my stomach, then one under it as if testing the weight and the location of the babe. He cocks his head as he pushes. The infant does not move as it usually does when he checks it so.

"Can you make it home, Janie?" he asks.

"I...think so?" I don't sound certain and am not too far panicked that I miss Marie and Patrick exchange a glance.

"If you hurry, you'll be fine," Thaddeus says, sounding suddenly urgent. It is an odd thing from such a massive man, and when I look up, I see he looks as worried as I feel. The smith takes a step further from me and almost runs into Natan, who once again is holding a hot piece of iron. Natan yelps, Hardy spins, and I let out what sounds like the moan of a woman in throes of pleasure. I flush hard, but perhaps no one can tell, for I feel hot and stretched, and this is only the beginning.

"You won't make it if you're feeling pains that fast," Marie says. "Don't listen to Tadeusz, he's never borne a child in his life."

"Maybe we can get a cart," Patrick says, but he sounds doubtful, and has pulled out his stethoscope to listen both to my heart and the babe's, as if we are in his home surgery and not standing in the middle of a public workshop, with the stares of three youths on us.

Hardy inches up and peers into Patrick's bag. "What do you need, Doc Kinney?"

"I need—" Patrick jerks when he realizes who asks. "Don't touch anythin' in there – it's all been sterilized!"

Hardy hunches his shoulders and glances at the kit's contents and then his grimy palms, quickly wiping them further down his stained trouser sides.

Another push, faster and stronger, clenches both sides of my hips and presses down, and my thighs shake.

"She won't make it back," Marie says, firm and calm and certain. "Doc, she won't."

"I'm sorry!" I say, but it comes out no better than a wheeze.

Patrick's mouth trembles once, and when his blue eyes meet my brown ones, I find him looking at me with something akin to trepidation. I reach out, planning to touch his cheek, to tell him I will be fine, but end up clenching his shirt, the buttons sinking into the soft flesh below my thumb. It is unlike the last time, when the pain came slow and easy and like a haze. These are hard, insistent. I am racing towards motherhood, and I am not prepared for the sprint.

"Jane," Patrick says. "Can you—"

Still clutching his shirt, my knees buckle with the next pain. It is hot and white and stretches upward into my spine. Perhaps the bones of my back are breaking. Perhaps I will never walk again. Perhaps this child will be the end of me.

"My bed. You must," Marie says. I do not know if she speaks to me or to the doctor, but it's Thaddeus who booms over my head.

"Our own sheets, woman? Are you mad?"

Marie does not bother to answer him. Or perhaps she does, and I simply do not hear it as the blood rages from ear to ear, as a roar that sounds like nothing, but everything fills my mind. Patrick half-walks, half-carries me the handful of steps out of the forge and into the Salomon's living area. There's no

Berit there, nothing but a banked hearth and the smell of the morning's toast, and yet when I walk through the room, the smallest details shout. A crock painted black, with a red rooster and bright blue and yellow flowers. The glint of a nutmeg grater's silvery tin on the mantle. A brown family photograph of the Salmons taken before their Urszula and Thaddeus's father passed on…when had a photographer been to town?

And then I'm through the next door and into the short hallway where the bedroom doors branch off, and Marie attempts to shoo Patrick out of the room.

"I've seen my wife undress before," he protests. "And I don't trust leavin' her now."

"I'm strong enough to keep her upright," Marie says. "I'm stayin'."

I want to jump in, keep the peace between them, but as I open my mouth, I only gasp. It is a helplessness. A weak moment. I do not like it. It is as if my mind has fled, and I wonder if this is perhaps true panic, the true departure of senses, when one is so afraid that all reason flees.

This birthing is my nightmare returned. It is a dance with death, the end and the beginning, the reminder of failure. It is a rebirth and birth all in one. Such notions hit me full force, colliding with the pain.

I look at the doctor, who has been a rock before, even in his own uncertainty. I want to hold him, clutch him near, shout at him, and yet I find all I want is to close my eyes against it all. Patrick refuses to look at me as he unpacks his kit, laying down the bright instruments: scalpel and specula and obstetrical forceps. His fingers shake as he moves, and I realize he cannot bear it – he cannot bear to watch this birth, and yet he must. It is his own nightmare, too.

For the first time in many months, we are as one in our fear. I find some strange comfort in that, but I cannot tell him so, for the next pain tears through my womb as if it wished to split me in half, and all I can do is scream.

CHAPTER EIGHTEEN
Patrick

June 1, 1867

Bobby and Tara married at the new St. Mary Star of the Sea Catholic church, just north of the square on a fine spring mornin', and Patrick was one of the few there to witness it, along with Tara's neighbors, and a few of Bobby's other acquaintances in Boston down from Rockport. Patrick battled feelins of pride as he watched them wed. Bobby'd courted for near five years, as was proper, enough time for Bobby to build up a practice to keep Tara in fine style. Doc Burns didn't seem upset his daughter had exchanged one doc for a different one, and Patrick even had the feelin', as his old mentor shook his hand and winked once, that Doctor Burns preferred Tara's choice all the better.

His steps sounded overly loud on the wet stones as he walked to his first patient after the weddin' breakfast at the Burns house. The cobbles huddled unevenly under his feet and sometimes the cracks were so wide his soles slipped between, twistin' the side of his foot. He didn't dare take too long to mince about, though, not when called to a birthin', and besides, he didn't want to lag too far behind the boy he followed to Bay Village. His stomach full of weddin' cake and tea, he felt as though he had luck on his side for all patient work.

He recognized the lad—the son of one of the families who lived above the butcher's a street down from his rented room. He'd treated the boy's older sister for a bad rash and had lived on the potatoes and carrots offered in payment by the mother for most of a week. Patrick missed the boisterous noise of his childhood tenement, but he'd found the comradery of a small jumble of streets and houses clustered close to be near the next best thing.

"This way!" the boy called over his shoulder. He scuttled to the back of one of the large neoclassical homes on Fayette Street. Patrick followed, enterin' the kitchen and at once enveloped in yeasty steam. A woman, covered in flour, with overlarge jowls and a body so immense he caught himself starin', peered over a kettle near as wide as she, scowled.

"What's that, boyo?"

"Mr. Larsen had me get a doc straight away, m'm. It's the lady, she's time!"

The cook's face cleared. "Ah! Finally!"

There was no more time to gawk at the kitchen's creamy tiles or dangling cookpots, or even notice the other staff in the gloom of mornin'. The boy hurried Patrick through the basement maze and up two flights of stairs before creeping through to the main area of the house and up yet another.

At the first door on the upstairs hall, the boy stopped

and nodded. Patrick drew in a breath, gripped his leather bag hard, and knocked firmly. Once, twice, and then a final time.

The oak swung open toward the inside, and a man with a face pale and shinin' like wet wax glared, wild-eyed, into the hall. His dark eyes, sunk under the forehead and a heavy lock of black hair, found the boy first.

"Didn't I send you—"

"Doctor Patrick Kinney, sir," Patrick said, jumpin' in quick. "I've come at once."

Mr. Larsen started, as if struck. His hand on the knob tightened, then a gasp and muffled half-scream seemed to break him.

"Well, then, my wife is laboring. See what you can do," he said, brisk and hard, openin' the door wider to the bedroom.

Patrick walked in with his back straight and steps quick. The smell of mucous and sweet but thick scent of birthin' fluids hung in the air, as well as the sharp tang of smelling salts and dense, overused rose and jasmine perfumes.

"This is the doc you brought, Tommy?" Mr. Larsen asked, soft but not too quietly. Patrick wanted to swing around to explain himself, but that would not serve a purpose, and he had every intention of doing right by this woman, so that he could prove he knew his mettle. Mrs. Larsen lay in a bed of frilly champagne satin with chartreuse ribbons, with lace-covered pillows under her sweating neck. The bulge of her unborn babe roiled under the frothy nightgown, and her hair plastered to the edges of her cheeks and in her ears, which stuck out a tad more than what might be fashionable.

"Mornin', Mrs. Larsen," Patrick said, settin' down his kit. "How are you feelin'? Pains comin' often and quick?"

"Often, yes," she said, her voice a soft breathlessness. "And quick."

"Your first?" he asked, openin' his bag on the mahogany table at the side of the bed.

"Her third," Mr. Larsen said from the open door, watchin' Patrick's movements. "Though, God willing, her first to survive." At his clipped sentence, Mrs. Larsen's breath hitched, and a tiny, choked sound escaped her throat.

It explained the man's tightness about his eyes, then, and the need for a doctor straightaway. And, also, perhaps why they did not have a family physician, if they mistrusted any who had failed in the past. It made Patrick doubly certain to do a proper job of it.

"I'll just do some measurin' of breathin' and heartbeats – yours and the baby's – for a bit, see where we land," Patrick said, keepin' his own voice low and calm.

Mr. Larsen watched the first bit of the process, but once Patrick had turned out the instruments and began countin' seconds, he left the room. The man also sent in a maid to sit in the corner with some sewin', a little mousy thing with thin shoulders and skinny ankles. She reminded Patrick a little bit of himself back when he was younger, but she winced every time Mrs. Larsen made a noise.

After cleanin' his tools and his hands with the new liquid carbolic acid, he bent to carefully determine the status of the birthing. There was nothin' out of the ordinary from what he could see at first look—Mrs. Larsen's heartbeat and the babe's were steady and strong—and he wished he could ask what had happened in the past. Knowin' if the previous births were stillborn or too early or sickly would give him some sort of map. But such a question seemed too delicate to ask, especially given Mrs. Larsen's current state of pregnancy. She seemed to breathe with a rapid sort of inhale, and he took her hand into both of his, findin' her gaze.

"You must inhale slowly and with care," he said, pattin' her fingers. "Focus on that."

"I'm afraid, doctor," Mrs. Larsen said. "I think about the coming pains and then I can only be afraid."

"I can understand it," he said, smilin' and keepin' his voice low and even. It was one of the few homeopathic tactics he used to make the patient feel at home. It was like becomin' a confidant quickly, which helped with any later decisions, and it never seemed to fail.

"Can you? You've birthed a child?" That her humor was intact seemed a good sign, and her next breaths were smoother.

"Ah, you've caught me, then," he said. "I admit I haven't."

"At least you're man enough to admit a failing," she said, and her eyes sparked before darkenin' with a coming contraction.

"Ease through it, Mrs. Larsen," he said, continuin' to pat her hand. "Is it very painful, or just a lot of pressure and squeezin'?"

"No pain, just pressure," she said, gaspin' through it.

Patrick checked the timing and began to count the spacing. He searched for something to talk about, and found himself pointin' out the weather, the stitchin' of her bedding, and the pattern of her drapes.

As the contractions lengthened and quickened, he checked her progress again, findin' her body fit and handlin' the whole birthin' without issue.

"Do you think it might live this time, doctor?" she asked, gaspin' through another pain. "Do you think this time I might do right by Mr. Larsen?"

Here was his openin', and Patrick refused to miss it. "Were the other children born livin'?"

"Yes," Mrs. Larsen smiled sadly. Her brow glistened with drops of sweat, glistenin' like thick dew. "Both girls, and both drew breath, but they died shortly afterwards. One lived three days, the other a week."

Her back arched with another pain, and Patrick went to support her shoulders.

Both children lived? And longer than a few hours.

It could mean some sort of deformity all her children would bear. It also could have been due to the previous doctors comin' in with dirty hands and tools, givin' infection and illness to the new babes from the moment each met the world. Again, Patrick felt frustration bubble up, but he shoved it down. This would always be his lot – not knowin' what happened before. There was only now. This woman, this birth, this baby. He had to do his best and not speculate.

"It won't be too long," he told the wee maid. "Will you want to tell your master?"

"He won't come," Mrs. Larsen said, soundin' strained with containin' her bodily convulsions. "He says it's not a husband's place."

Patrick decided not to comment his own opinions on the matter. He didn't have an accurate one anyway – he had no wife. He liked to think if he did, he'd be there for her, even if he wasn't a doctor with an interest in the medical piece.

It didn't take long before the head crowned, and the shoulders slipped free of the pelvic bone. Patrick's eyes were for signs of trouble, lookin' at the babe all over from the moment the last of the toes showed. The newborn was a perfect male, unblemished in any way. He held the boy up and smacked him, so the arms jerked out and a piercin' cry echoed through the room, lusty and dry. Mrs. Larsen propped herself up on her elbows and smiled, her eyes crinklin' at the corners and her sweat already drying on a smooth forehead.

"Alive?" she asked, sounding shocked and hopeful and worried and pleased and a thousand other emotions. Patrick wiped the child down as he wailed and nodded, bringin' the babe to the mother as quick as he could.

"A son, Mrs. Larsen," he said. "And he seems perfectly healthy right now."

Her eyes sparkled suddenly. "I do pray he stays so."

"God willin'," Patrick said, standin' over them. He watched her hold the child with reverence, touching each finger and nail with a tentative slide, as if the boy would shatter and break at any moment.

He went back to inspect Mrs. Larsen's body, holding the sheet high so she would not see his brow furrow as he inspected the blood still oozing from her. It seemed to be not too much, but he felt it still seemed to be a bit more than he preferred. Suppose he ought to—

"I heard a babe cry," Mr. Larsen announced, bargin' in. "Very well. Stand aside, then Doctor Kinney, I've brought a real doc to make sure my wife is well looked after."

Patrick dropped the sheet and spun, only to see Thomas walk into the bedroom behind Mr. Larsen.

"Thomas?" he said, soundin' strangled even to his own ears.

"Ah, I didn't know it was you here, Pat," Thomas said, lookin' as surprised as Patrick felt. "Was asked to come see about a birth."

"It's done and over already, and well done at that," Patrick said stiffly, feeling his pride bristle and prickle. He gestured to Mrs. Larsen. "Might I congratulate you on your new son, sir." He narrowed his eyes at Mr. Larsen, who seemed a bit at a loss. Perhaps he had expected to find his wife still laborin', or that Patrick would be wringin' his hands, uncertain of what to do.

The man took small steps toward his wife's bedside and leaned over gingerly. "A boy, then, Melinda? That's very fine." He slowly sat on the edge of the bed and peered closer. "Dark hair, like mine, eh?"

Patrick left them to the moment and went to look at the blood loss again. He wondered when the placenta would show. It would be best if the woman would nurse, or if he could press gently on her stomach to induce the crampin' needed.

"How goes it with her, then?" Thomas was at his side, speakin' in hushed tones. "She bore it well?"

"The birth was fine," Patrick said. "I am just watchin' now for the rest of it."

Thomas cocked his head and looked at the bleedin'. "I'd yank out the placenta by the cord. If you do it fast enough, it comes out alright."

"Too many possible outcomes to go by force," Patrick said quickly. "If it tears and leaves a piece behind, it will fester, and she'll die of the rot of it or you'll make a big tear inside."

"I've never seen it," Thomas retorted. "And I've delivered countless."

316

"As have I."

"Irish women in the slums birth differently," Thomas said, a bit louder now. "You want to clear the body of birthing debris, of course. Lest she bleed overmuch."

Mr. Larsen stood at the words. "I'll have Doctor Smith do the rest of the treatment, then. Thank you, Doctor Kinney. My butler Mr. Harding will see to your payment."

"I'd rather stay, if you please," Patrick said staunchly. "I'm not certain of Doctor Smith's methods and would like you to be certain of the risks."

"I'm certain Doctor Smith knows what he's doing," Mr. Larsen said, soundin' even more stubborn.

"It'll be no extra fee for me to stay and assist him," Patrick pressed, feeling panic rise. He knew Thomas and his hasty ways. He'd do somethin' rash. He might not even sterilize his hands. He might…

"I'll be sure to let you know how it goes," Thomas said smoothly, picking up the sheet. "I appreciate your interest in the patient."

Patrick swung to look at Mrs. Larsen. "Madam, you are the patient in question. I would do as you please."

Mrs. Larsen, still in the glow of motherhood, but no less astute for it, swung her head between the three men. She even peered briefly at the little maid still sewing in the corner, the quiet chaperone. Patrick suddenly had a wild notion of shakin' the little girl and having her come to his defense, tellin' the others that he ought to stay, for he had done such a swell job with the birthin'. But what would Thomas and Mr. Larsen say to such a testimony? It would carry no weight at all.

"Whatever you wish, Alfred," she said at last, soundin' blissful and tired.

Patrick was ushered out by Mr. Larsen, then, who hurried him along the packin' of his medical bag. He tried to see what Thomas was going to do, but there was no time before he spun out of the room and left by the front door, after being given payment by the stiff-shouldered butler. He didn't even bother to count it and clutched the papers in his fist as he walked, flat and hard against the daylight back toward his little rented room.

All he could do was fight anger and resentment. What had he done, other than the right thing? He'd given the woman a perfect birth! Was it because of his Irish name, and the slightest bit of an accent? Was it because Mr. Larsen had already planned to ask for Thomas for this birth? Was it because—

"Doc! Doc Kinney? I been waitin' for ye, sir!"

He'd made it home, and a boy bounced up from the slight stoop in front of his door. Shoving down fatigue, he bent at the waist to peer under the lad's cap.

"What is it, boyo? Who's sick?"

"Mr. McClure. He sent me!"

It was the last name Patrick expected to hear, and he spun on his heel and took off at such a brisk pace it was near a jog. Not for the first time did he wish he had enough coin for a horse and a space at a public livery to board one. The boy half-ran at his side, pantin' and shoutin' at other boys he knew as they crossed the streets toward Mr. McClure's building.

When they arrived, he remembered at the last moment to slip a twenty-five-cent postage paper to the lad and took the creakin' stairs two at a time to Mr. McClure's floor. Aunt Bonnie swung open the door at his quick knock, her face pale and tear-stained and strained.

"Aunt Bonnie? How is he?" he asked as she stepped aside for his entry.

"An—Mr. McClure's taken a faint, but it's worse than the ones in the past–he fell, hit the stove hard, and I...I didn't know what to do."

She sounded hoarse with buried hysteria, and he knew Aunt Bonnie would not be so distraught without good reason. Patrick recalled the ailments the man had mentioned when he'd visited the little practice and paused at the door between office and kitchen-bedroom.

"Mr. McClure has had issues in the past with faintin' I know. He'd told me it was nothin' worth worryin', and it has been years since he fell over last. But after seein' a few patients over the years, I now wonder if there's somethin' to do with him inside. Humors or heart. Did he tell you anythin' of note, or is he not speakin'?" He hated to ask but had to do so.

"He was in bed last night when he felt pressure and pain in his chest and was still there this mornin' when I arrived...and then he fell on the oven hard. I got him to bed, just barely. And now he can't get up, Patrick. He's fadin'."

When they walked through to the living quarters, Patrick was filled with memories and familiar scents. There was the smell of oil lamp, Aunt Bonnie's cookin' and coffee and tea. His eyes adjusted to the dim interior and he still remembered to sidestep the leg of the stove on his way in.

As he approached the bed, his eyes traveled over Mr. McClure's body. Had he always been so small? Had he shrunk so much in the past few weeks? He tried to see the man as a patient, but in truth the vision wavered. He was a body to examine and at the same time the fatherly man of Patrick's life.

"Mr. McClure? I'm here. It's Patrick," he said, sittin' on the edge of the thin mattress. It groaned with the extra weight, the springs creakin' below.

Mr. McClure's eyes opened. Aunt Bonnie had tried to straighten the bit of hair on top of his head. She brought over a damp towel from the stand nearby to bathe his waxy face, and suddenly it felt like double sight. Patrick had seen this look on a man's brow before. It reminded him of Mr. MacHugh on the beach in Gloucester so many years ago.

Patrick took up Mr. McClure's wrist. His breathin' had a wheeze to it. Removin' the stethoscope out of his inner vest pocket, he focused hard and listened and counted. He tried to find some peace for his own panic. This was his first patient-not-a-patient. This was the first time he had to try to cure one dear to him. Could he do it? Could he let go of the emotions warrin' so deep inside him he was sure he'd get a stomachache if he kept it in too long? His head pounded with too much blood and his fingers twitched with uncertainty.

And worst of all—how would he manage if he could not help?

There was an odd rhythm to the beat of Mr. McClure's heart, as though part of it was not beatin' at all. And then there was the blisterin' burn along the side of his neck, where he had hit the stove when he went down. Patrick thanked heaven for small favors—at least he hadn't gashed in his bone and died on the spot.

"Where does it hurt inside?" he asked.

Mr. McClure weakly pointed to the area of the chest near the breastbone, right by the sternum.

"I had horrific aches last night," he said slowly. His eyes opened and closed with a strange pattern. "Down my

320

arm," he indicated to his left. "And I nigh fainted again." He shifted and winced. Patrick listened again to his heart. As he counted, he noticed a scratchy rhythm too, and it was slowin' audibly.

Patrick's own heart sank.

He looked at Mr. McClure's ashen face and realized with a strong, hard jolt that there was nothin' he could do. He did not even have much by way of pain medication to ease the discomfort. Nothing he had read in medical journals or discussed at the table in Doctor Burns' house or at Doc Chilling's side was enough to fix what ailed Mr. McClure.

He would either come about or he would die.

"Patrick," Aunt Bonnie was back at his side, and Patrick felt her hand on his shoulder. It was tiny, weightless. He shook his head slightly, and her palm dropped away, leavin' so much space it felt like the weight of the sky.

So this was what it felt like to lose a loved one.

It ached and seared and left a black hole.

Patrick looked up at her and then, almost woodenly, stood so she could take his place. Mr. McClure was dearer to her, for all he was the only father Patrick had known. He was more to her, and she to him. Patrick would be a fool to deny it.

"He knows," he said to her. "You do, too."

"But can't you—"

Patrick shook his head again, once, tight and fast.

Her face tightened, as if he had thrown vinegar on her, but then she turned to Mr. McClure and said briskly, "Andy, Paddy says you must just bide your time."

"Ach, it's the end," he rejoined with his unflappable calm. Patrick exhaled at his easy acceptance, but Aunt

Bonnie's eyes filled. Mr. McClure tried to raise a hand to wipe them even though his strength was nearly gone. "Soft lass, you know it is. I'm old enough as it were. I only wish…"

He paused and his breath turned into a rattle. Patrick watched his chest rise and fall under the thin blanket and then, somehow, he continued.

"I know I could never marry ye as I wished…and your memory is beholden to your husband as well…but I do love ye…"

Patrick tried to draw in his gapin' mouth. Now was not the time to make a bother at a bedside confession. He'd been there for a few deaths to be sure, but something this personal? He felt hot under the collar though his hands were clammy. It took a moment to remember he still held his stethoscope. He gripped it tighter, the rubber windin' around his fingers.

"Paddy…take care of her, will ye? And any others who need it, no matter who they be…you're a good doc, Paddy…a good boy…"

For a moment Patrick thought Mr. McClure would go on, but he fell silent, and without knowing what else to do, he leaned in and took another listen to the heart. The beat was faint, completely erratic, and falling fast.

Putting his hand on Mr. McClure's forehead, which felt oddly condescendin' to do to the man who had raised and clothed him. He gently pressed on him to lay deeper into the pillow. Mr. McClure struggled to push back, his voice fainter.

"I'm sorry I could not provide much more for ye," he whispered, and suddenly Patrick wondered if he was speakin' to Patrick himself, or Aunt Bonnie, or his long-lost wife still in Ireland.

Time stretched and shrunk.

He lost track of it.

Hours and minutes wrapped themselves around his mind and he simply held onto his aunt or Mr. McClure as they needed.

And then, somewhere between Aunt Bonnie calling out his name and Patrick wipin' his brow again, Mr. McClure passed away, just like that.

Patrick sank to his haunches next to the bed, and looked at Mr. McClure's face, lopsided and doughy in death.

Aunt Bonnie said, strangely, brokenly, "Andy..."

For a long moment, there was nothing but silence in that space, an odd, singular experience that brought to light the faraway slam and shout in the hallway, the soft fall of a small log in the stove belly and the shallow, controlled breaths of his aunt.

"What now, Aunt Bonnie?" he asked quietly.

"I don't know," she said, her voice rough with tears that would not come. "I hadn't worried on it. I thought there were years..."

"You'll move in with me. I can make space on a wall for another bed."

"Paddy, there's hardly room in there for you, let alone your practice," she said, still thinkin' of others besides herself. He loved her for it, he realized. And it made him want to be like her. To give back. To make good on Mr. McClure's request, and Mr. May's, and all those who had seen fit to be kind and do good by him.

"Stay as long as you need. It is the least I can do," he said, soundin' firmer than he felt. "I'll stop by the coroners on my way home, and we can sort his office and things together this week."

Aunt Bonnie nodded, wipin' her eyes with the edge of her apron. "I'll wait here for him, so I can be sure they do as he would wish."

She meant the right preparations for a layin' out, as there would likely be one with all the Irish neighbors. And then a Mass and a burial. Patrick's shoulders dropped a bit as he thought of all the responsibility to come—the wake and the meal, the whiskey and the stories. He would have to take a role, even as he was not blood. The thought both thrilled him and made him sweat. He'd not thought of that, either, just like Aunt Bonnie. He thought he'd have years…

And then there was the other bit.

Aunt Bonnie…married?

He puzzled on that on the way home, walking half-blind in the late afternoon sun. The shadows were grey and purple between the buildings, and the sun was rose and gold dependin' on which street he was on. The smell of piss and vomit, horse dung and cooking meat, rancid and peppered, swirled around as he wove between carts and flower sellers.

Aunt Bonnie had been wed?

He couldn't believe it. Could one go along believin' a person was one thing only to discover they were somehow something else, something more complex, something layered?

Because he was lost in thought, he did not notice his neighbor's eyes, nor the handful of men and women slowly start to follow him.

He did not hear the silence.

But he noticed his door, which had been ripped off the hinges, and then his new little wood sign, with his name and the symbol of his trade, torn down and trampled, the bits

324

of paint and color the only way to know that was what the splinters were at his feet.

"What is this?" he asked, feelin' his blood pulse and then freeze. He spun to face those who watched. "What has happened?"

"Couple of boys come, they have the clubs, they ask for you, and then they tear it apart," said Helmut Mittelmann. "I not know they want to hurt, to make it bad, or I not tell."

"Did they say why? Who?"

"They say they come for a Mr. Larsen. He say his wife dead, and you why, and you a bad doc."

Helmut shrugged and snorted, dismissin' the notion, and the others nodded, their eyes and nods giving Patrick support, but it was not enough. Not anymore.

Patrick closed his eyes and swayed, catchin' himself on the door jam. Thomas! Damn him! He had done it...he had pulled the placenta, and she had bled out. Patrick knew it! He...

It was too much in one day. He needed a moment.

He needed...sleep.

He could not breathe, and he thought he might be sick right there on his doorstep. Where would he take Aunt Bonnie now? How could he have a trade? Make a livin'? Save lives?

Everything he touched came to ruin and death.

Perhaps he should not be a doctor, after all...

CHAPTER NINETEEN

Jane

March 3, 1884

The push and pull of blood and bone is hard and weighted and heavy. My pelvis widens, the blood pumps, and my veins strain to bursting as I hold in the swell and crest of each hardening of the belly.

"You must breathe," Marie tells me, lofty in her knowledge of many births. I want to snip at her, tell her I am no stranger to birthing, but my chest feels like it might explode if I ask too much of it. Breathe, she says!

"Marie's right," Patrick says. He is distracted by his tools and his care for cleanliness. Even as I am spun in circles by my own body, I recognize his fumbling. It is unlike him to be so scrambled. I wonder if perhaps he worries over me and this birth. Or is it that he has become so used to my help he does not know how to be at a bedside without me?

Taking their advice, I force a deep breath in and out.

The knowledge of coming pressure does not help, for I seem to seize up in preparation, making the actual pain worse. My mind feels fuzzy along the edges, and I am restless and listless at the same time.

This is nothing like my last labor, when I bore out a stillborn and bled afterwards.

This is feral and primal, a tear and a press.

"Marie—have you any extra sheets or blankets?" the doctor asks.

"I'll have Thaddeus go for them," she says, and moves to shout out the bedroom door.

It is an odd, disjointed thing to be birthing in a bed not my own. Even stranger to be bearing down in a room where not too many months ago I helped Marie herself give birth to little Garik. I suppose I must count myself fortunate to be in a place that has seen so many successful children born to the world.

"Steady on, my love," Patrick says in my ear. One of his hands holds mine while the other presses on my stomach, waiting and counting. "You're doing well."

"I am?" The words are squeezed out, faint and soft and like pebbles.

"It's as fair a birthin' as I've ever seen," he says. I have no cause to doubt him, and do not think he will tell a falsehood at this moment. "But I won't be leavin' you as it is."

Marie returns with Hardy as a shadow. The boy holds a mound of linen and blankets, and Marie directs him to put them on the narrow bureau.

"Berit is always over-ready," Marie says, wry and bemused as she glances at the abundance of blankets. "If only I were as prepared for life."

"How goes it, Doc?" Hardy asks. He creeps closer to Doctor Kinney's side and peers over the shiny instruments Patrick has laid out on a clean towel. It is one of his oldest, edged with a tiny lace from his late aunt. It gives me a strange start to see a memory of his Aunt Bonnie in the room, as if she is here. Or perhaps he is using such a cloth as an especial homage, in the hours before his first child is born. The idea is tender and dear, and I hope to remember to ask...

Another press of my hip bones silences all wondering and thoughts, and I gasp without meaning to be so loud.

"It goes fast, I think," Marie says, standing over my legs at the foot of the bed.

"It is not her first," Patrick reminds her, and I wish he would not bring up the ghost of memory. It is not a good one.

Hardy dances on the edge of the room, but no one seems to think to ask him to leave. He is light and quick, though, and for all his height and long limbs, he does not take up too much space. Instead, Patrick hands him a cloth.

"Clean your hands and be prepared to grip Jane's," he says. "Hurry on."

"Are you counting her pains?" he asks, doing as he was bid.

"The minutes between and the seconds of," Patrick says absently. He raises the sheets and my knees go up on their own accord, as if my body knows how it must move in order to survive. Marie goes to the door again and shouts for water and washcloths. My eyes go up as Patrick's fingers move intimately, his head hidden under the blanket.

The grain of the wood above seems to move like worms or snakes. The edges blur. I try to count the knots

328

in the boards but keep losing track. Every time I get close to ten, my body clenches. It is a tensing from my thighs up to my neck. Perhaps my neck may crack. Is it possible to break one's head over the pain and pressure?

What part of childbirth means death?

Why exactly do they say…a foot in the grave…?

"It is comin' quick," Patrick says, his dark head rising from the linen. "It won't take too long, now."

"That's a good turn, then," Marie says. She hesitates, and then reaches for the same cleaning cloth Hardy used. "So then. Here. I will take her hand." Her bunchy, calloused palm takes mine across from Hardy.

Hardy does not budge from across the bed. Instead, his eyes are trained on my face and then the doctors, and roves back and forth too fast.

Everything is too fast.

My limbs quiver and shake, and I cannot seem to stop it. I worry it is unnatural, and then remind myself I have not attended enough births to know what is so. All fades and ebbs, a web of fluid and heartbeats. If I stood, I would fall, for even laying down everything is dizzy and dim. A soft grey cloud pillows my sight.

"Patrick," I say. "I am not ready."

He looks up and his eyes slice mine. They are clinical but merry, a war I did not expect to see. He is both the physician and the father, the surgeon and the lover. I wish I might reach to him, but both my hands lay captured.

"Neither am I," he says softly, and his confession makes tears split across my eyelids and down the crevasses of my nose. Or perhaps that is sweat.

I cannot tell much of the world anymore.

It is a good thing he offers me a piece of comfort, for the next pain rocks me upwards, so that I half-sit, half-strain against Marie and Hardy's hands. They press back, a balustrade against my own strength as my shoulders turn to stone and my fingers curl and bury into their flesh.

The actual birth itself is a relief and a sob and a fracture of pain.

Patrick is no longer my husband. He is the doctor, and he is all business as he pulls our babe from my womb and carefully places the infant, blood and mess and all on the faded fabric of my chemise. I want to remind him it is not proper to allow so much gore, and that the cotton will be stained, but there is no push within me to press.

Instead, I clasp the babe near, searching the unfamiliar lips and swollen eyes, appalled at the whimpering and snuffling, feeling all elbows once again.

"Here, Jane. He will not break." Patrick replaces Hardy and folds my arms properly. The words are an echo of early ones, and I close my eyes against the memory.

When I open them again, the doctor has gone back to his vigil between my knees as he handles the other, earthier demands of a birth—sinew and scissors and cords—and Marie approaches with hot water and cloth from the doorway. Hardy leans back, finally looking as though he has come from a trance, or at least seems uncertain. He had been so steadfast in the thick of it…I want to tell him to be proud of his ability to withstand blood and screams, but Marie takes the boy from my grasp with sure hands and a motherly smile.

"He is a fine one," she says, pressing him against her round bosom. "Lusty and already hungry."

The babe roots at her softness, and she quickly washes him with warm water, just as Patrick looks up and once again meets my eyes straight. It is something I have always noticed with him and all others, a frankness that stems from an earnestness to do right and well. When he looks so direct at me, though, it seems we share something else. He sees me, for my curiosity and my faults, and yet there is a gentle curve to his gaze. It is small, but somehow reminds me I am something else to him. Something more.

And now we share this.

He comes to take the baby from Marie and looks down at the bundle. His shoulders go down a full inch, and his chest rises and falls so fast it seems the small boy heaves as if on a pitching ship. Had the doctor truly been so overcome with nerves? Or is he simply overcome with emotion? Patrick has long wished for a full and noisy house...he has said so to me many times.

The sweat cools on my forehead and around my ears, drying in the hollow of my throat. I want to hold my child again, but do not wish to spoil the moment for his father. Patrick glances over the bit of the baby he can see, and seems to find it enough and pleasing, for he hands me our son with a twinkle in his eye and a smile quivering on the corners of his mouth.

"What'll we name him?" he asks. "For your father or mine?"

"Both," I say, not caring too much either way. I clasp the boy near again, and the baby swishes his head back and forth against my neck, smashing his tiny nose into my skin.

"Maybe just your father," he says, even softer. "Téodóir was my own da—Theodore for English."

The name hits me like a slap. It is the same name as my one-time lover, long lost to circumstance and my own careful detachment from Boston life. I do not want any reminders of my sister's husband's cousin who took me to bed in my early widowhood and whose unnamed son lays in the earth next to Patrick's aunt in St. Aloysius's cemetery.

"Something else, then. What about your other father— Mr. McClure," I say. "Andrew? And Rupert for my father, then."

Patrick looks as though I have handed him not just the moon, but also perhaps the stars. He leans back, though he keeps a hand on the boy's downy head, a finger tracing the curl of the tiny ear.

"Andrew it is," he says, and then he smiles. It is such a smile I cannot help but return it, and it seems as if my heart has broken into pieces, fractured and offered to both him and our child.

"I'll get you something to drink, now that the trials are over," Marie says, unfolding her arms. "And I'll tell everyone of the safe birth and Andrew's arrival. Come along, Hardy."

"But…will you need any more help, doc?" Hardy pauses at the door.

"No, I'm just watchin' a wee bit more," he says, suddenly seeming to remember there is still the remaining piece of birthing to do. "No need for you to be here for it."

Hardy looks as though he would prefer it, but Marie jerks on the youth's arm with a hard glare, and leaves Patrick and me to ourselves for the first time in…I do not know how many hours have passed.

I suddenly think about how joyful Esther will be when

we return home with our son. I find I cannot wait to tell her, more so than even writing a letter to my own family. I will write my Aunt Mary, too, and hope she still lives and will receive it. I will tell so many...

"You must offer him your breast," Patrick says, cracking into my musing. "It will help."

"Help? Oh, he's wishing to nurse." I pause at the implication. I've seen Marie nurse her own child in this very room, exposing her nipple to air and child as if it is the most natural thing to do. Still, there is some strangeness in showing myself in such a way, even in front of the man who has seen me in all nudity.

"It's not just that. It will help with the end of this," he tells me, pulling the sheet over his head again to continue his doctoring. If there was any reason to be hesitant before, it seems a point lost given the muddy earthiness of our situation.

I pull down the front of my shift and try to blunder through allowing the child to nurse, hoping I recall how to do it properly given the scant moments I've seen it done.

The babe seems to know what to do, so I let him at it without too much fussing. Patrick notices and nods his approval, and presses on my deflated stomach with a palm as Andrew suckles. There's a throb deep below and inside my pelvis, and soon a gush of fluid and slipperiness.

"Good," the doctor says, looking fully relieved at last. "There we be." He goes back to my legs, and then shakes his head. "Thad wasn't wrong. We'll owe the Salomons sheets at the very least."

"I've the spare," I say, staring down at my son.

My *son*.

The word repeats and bounces and pulses in my mind. I am a mother. More than a wife, a widow, a housekeeper, a nurse.

Mother.

What an odd thing to be thrust on a woman. It is as if giving birth is more than giving life to another, but instead an entire rebirth and metamorphosis. Change and unchanged. What a strange lot women are given. We are meant to create such change, from the very depths of our anatomy. We are meant to transform with it. And yet we are also the rock upon which community is built and re-made, just like childbirth itself. Perhaps birth of child and village both are part of our nature. I have never thought of it as such before, but now the parallel is stark.

The working of Andrew's jaw is a sawing back and forth, and the pale blue-green of the veins in his temple curl and disappear into the fine sheen of skin stretched across his skull. I'm struck by the wonder of this moment, the gift, the undeniable reality.

"Are you happy, my love?" I ask, peeling my eyes from my son's curving cheek.

The doctor's head rises from my ankles, where he mops what must be the last of birthing blood.

"Happy? You're askin' this now?"

"Are you?"

"Of course I am, Janie. You're safe and well, and our son is born and healthy with a solid chance of survivin'. What more can a man want?"

I want to ask him if he's happy he never wed Kate. I want to ask him if he's satisfied with me as his wife, as the mother of his children, if he is pleased with his lot in life.

334

Perhaps he is only fulfilled in this moment, with a birthing well done and his child new to the world. I wonder if he is truly happy with my questions and my mind, and if, in the depths of his being, he forgives my medicinal dabbling and my nature.

In my boneless exhaustion, I cannot find it in me to beg for his words. I reach out a hand and he takes it, holding a rusty cloth in his other. There is a ruby crust in the half-moons of his nails, but his hands are warm and the pads gentle.

"I love you," he says, frank and earnest and delighted. "And I thank you for this."

He bends to kiss first my forehead and then my lips, and it is to this scene Marie enters, followed by Berit, both bearing trays. Thaddeus looms behind them, hovering in the doorway. Patrick straightens, and I hastily throw the edge of the blanket over my bared chest.

"Coffee and some beer," Marie says, putting down her tray on the dresser. Berit sets down a smaller one piled with slices of toasted bread and a crock of butter, still wet and newly pulled from the cold stream behind the smithy.

"Beer for you," Berit tells me, handing over a clay mug. "It will help bring the milk." She encourages me to take several sips. I nod up at her as I drink. The beer is malty and froths along the creases of my gums, tasting of hops and last summer's wheat.

"I'd like to get Jane home, so we aren't here overnight and puttin' you out," Patrick says to Thaddeus. "Think someone at the General has a wagon hitched up?"

"I'll send one of the boys to go see," Berit says, smiling so wide that her eyes nearly disappear in the fine wrinkles of her feathery skin. "Congratulations, Jane."

She slides past Thaddeus, who slowly enters the room with his arms crossed, looking down his nose from his great height at the bundle in my arms. I feel exposed, but not outlandishly so. It is important to keep reminding myself that our roles were reversed mere months ago, when it was Marie in the birthing bed. That helps me from feeling too improper.

"So then," Thaddeus says. He stops and clears his throat, tightening his arms. "All went well. Seems you're not as much a sawbones as you used to be, doc."

Patrick glances at me, quick as silver, and then turns to Thaddeus. "I thank you for your fast hospitality. My wife and I...it's a boy." He cannot help it. The grin appears in his voice, so infectious it attaches to me. My smile brings one to Marie's dark eyes and when she laughs even Thaddeus's mouth turns up under the beard.

"And Hardy was grand," Patrick adds. "The lad has never shirked from the sight of bleedin'. He's a natural with it."

"He helped with Kaspar," I say. "He's likely the reason your son is back at the forge."

Thaddeus's eyebrows go up. Marie nods, her head tilted to the side. "He took over the care of the arm, that's certain."

"He's a waste with the fires," Thaddeus says bluntly. When everyone stares at his candid comment, he lifts a shoulder. "It's no secret."

"He tries very hard," Marie counters. "You can't fault him. It's not like he chose to be a blacksmith's apprentice."

"We could take him," I say, and then wince. I'm feeling oddly magnanimous in the glow of birth, and it makes me feel a swell of goodwill and helpfulness. What do I mean to say? We sometimes struggle to make ends meet if people are all healthy or feeling particularly against Patrick – and we've a newborn. How will we keep a growing boy?

Patrick, however, does not frown at me as another husband might. Instead, his face is open, his stillness a sign of his thoughts racing in circles.

Thaddeus shifts his feet. "So then. You want an apprentice, doc?"

"I...would not wish to take away your own help, Thad."

"Natan is a solid smith already, and Kaspar will be well enough once his full strength returns, thanks to you and Jane as it is. Hardy will work hard, and he's taken a shine to your profession."

"He always has," Marie says, sounding bemused. She glances down at me, and then bends to tuck in another corner of the blanket, allowing herself another peek at little Andrew.

"I'm sorry to speak so quick," I say softly to her. "If you need the boy for the forge, to keep up with orders, it's understandable." But the menfolk overhear me, and both shake their heads.

Thaddeus clears his throat. "I feel responsible for him since taking him in as Kate asked. Least I can do is see him settled in work that suits him."

"It's expensive to take on an apprentice, especially one without any means," Patrick says, then holds up a hand in the face of Thaddeus's glower. "But I'm not askin' you to cover his cost, Thad."

"I'll help pay for some of his board, when I can," the smith says, glancing at me and fading a little. "If you're up for it as you be, Jane. It's more work for the women to take on a youth. But...*tak*, *yes*, I'm asking, doc. Will you train him?"

Patrick is quiet for a long moment. In the quiet space, Andrew sighs. I wonder when I might stand. I'm suddenly itchy for my own mattress and the smells of my kitchen and Esther's gentle voice. The sounds of the forge drift through the open door. Flies find their way in, circling the untouched toast. If I just listen with my head to the side, I can almost hear the rush of the day's train coming. It will bring people looking for goods, and more men for the fort and the whispers of war and troubles from the East. It will bring fine oysters for Yves and tinplate for Marie, and perhaps some of Patrick's medical supplies and, if he's lucky, a letter from Robert MacHugh with books on measles.

Patrick comes back to life. "Jane. It's your notion, but I like it. Especially with the babe—it'll be harder for you to be my extra set of eyes and feet with the little ones attached to your skirts." I smirk at his mention of more children already. "Will you feel right if we have Hardy live with us? He's young to start, but he can help around the house, too. If he has no formal trainin', it'll be takin' me longer than usual to have him settled as an apprentice as it be."

"And he will want this? Will you ask him?" I look up at Thaddeus, who snorts.

"Haven't a doubt he'll be pleased. You've seen him around the doc."

"If the town keeps growin' as it has been, we'll need more doctors eventually," Patrick says, nodding. "And though I have had expectations that my children would follow my steps, I've no guarantee that they will. And...he's an orphan, like me. Someone must give him an opportunity." There seems to be the crux of his opinion—to continue the pattern of his own life.

"So then. It's settled," Marie says, bringing my dress from the chair and giving it a single hard flap. It does nothing for the creases and wrinkles, but she goes to the petticoat next and digs my socks out of my shoes.

"He's still…" I waved a hand at the babe. He seems to be suckling in his sleep, but I have no notion what to do next. Marie comes around and slips her pinky into his mouth and he releases, settling into an exhausted sleep. It makes me wish to do the same, suddenly, and I wonder what hour it is. I have lost all track of time and sun.

Thaddeus departs in a faint whiff of charcoal and smoke, and Patrick packs up his tools as Marie helps me into my clothes. It is an odd thing to put my dress on without the bulk of the babe within me. The bodice folds in empty curls. It's even odder to stand with his weight in my arms and not between my hips. I'm loose-limbed and watery about the knees.

Natan and Hardy are at the front of the forge with Franklin Jones's wagon, and Franklin himself at the box seat. Half the back of the wagon is filled with goods from the depot out for delivery, and though he has offered his wagon, he glowers at us when we appear.

Hardy, on the other hand, is brimming. "I'll pack my things and be right over," he says to the doctor. "I'm to start straight away, Mr. Salomon says!"

I glance at Patrick, feeling the air go out of my lungs. So much change, all at once? But Patrick looks pleased and a little anxious, and I decide not to press and push. Besides, perhaps all this bustle and need will have other results…

"Well there, Doc and the missus. I hear there's a new babe." This is gruff, but not unkind, and I'm suddenly hopeful that here is another who might come around to Patrick in the end. If only we would be so fortunate, to overcome the rancor in the corners of town...

"Thank you, Franklin," Patrick says quietly, and helps me carefully into the back. He bends his head low. "It'll be bumpy but short, and better than you walking the whole way."

I nod as he takes a seat up by Franklin and we wave and call our numerous thanks as the wagon bounces east toward home. We owe the Salomons more than sheets, and my mind already turns to baked goods and other small tokens of my gratitude, though as I think it, I realize they do not expect any of it. The knowledge of their good-hearted giving washes over me. It makes me wish to weep. Somehow, amid all the trials and troubles, we have found true friends. However grudgingly Thaddeus may offer it, it runs deep and is honest. Marie waves extra fast from the forge door as we jostle off, while Thaddeus only watches with his usual half-frown. The boys disappear into the darkness and fires and soot. I wonder if Hardy will miss the time with others his age or if he will be glad for the change and a chance at a trade he clearly finds intriguing.

Andrew makes a squeak. I look down at him and wonder at the pucker of his mouth and the fine downy dark hairs on his head. We have a son. We're gaining an apprentice. Patrick is finally, finally coming into his own in Flats Junction, and I am with him.

In the wonderment, all time is lost. Suddenly we are at our gate, and Esther is waiting for all of us at the door.

CHAPTER 20

Patrick

August 23, 1876

The raid, the Crow, the screamin' was over. Quiet descended slowly, a filterin' of sighs and whimpers, and the changin' of the sun and moon. Patrick had not slept. He paced the floorboards, scrubbed partially of the blood of amputation and arrows, and wondered how on earth he'd get himself and Aunt Bonnie another carriage out of Flats Junction.

And the men he'd doctored? Were they his patients, now? Did he owe them his time?

Harry Turner slept behind the counter while the mornin' light pierced the General with a bright pale buttery glow through the one unbroken window of the store. His white hair glinted like spun candy as the sun snaked into the gloom.

The patients groaned or mumbled with various degrees of volume, but Harry didn't stir. It had been a long night, and Patrick was still awake. Somehow, so was Aunt Bonnie. It had needed nightfall for the shootin', shoutin' and reelin' horses to stop, and by the time he'd finished wrappin' up the last man dragged off the street, word had started to spread, and two more injured were brought in by their relatives and put into Harry's private quarters.

Surveyin' the damage he'd done, Patrick saw a floor stained with blood, a bundle of soiled linen and rags, and his tools, gleamin' once again in the white gold light of mornin'. Aunt Bonnie proved herself a competent nursemaid in a pinch. She approached again, but this time bearing a well-worn tin coffee pot, hopefully full of coffee.

"I do not think he will mind I used some beans," she confided, pouring a steamin' cup. "He's got several bushels of the stuff in back besides what's out here."

Patrick's eyes trailed over the men in the front room. In all, three amputees, but the rest would be manageable with cleaning and care. He wondered how the Indian man did with his arrow wound. Harry had mentioned that the man was Blackfoot Sioux – at this time, not a tribe botherin' the town. He'd said they'd stopped bothering Flats Town after the Sioux Uprising ended in '68.

Whether it was planned or no, though, the Sioux's Crow enemies caused havoc. As most of the town was built with fresh timber, Patrick had no doubt that would be beyond devastatin'. Outside the General, townfolk picked up the pieces already, but there were still no children playin' in the streets.

The windows let in a cool breeze, dampened by a subtle thickness of settlin' dust and a whiff of stove smoke. Some-one nearby cooked bacon for breakfast. Patrick's stomach clenched in protest, but he sipped the coffee instead, and then bent over one of the young men who had stitches across his arm where two arrows once lodged. He made sure the wound drained, plannin' to clean it when the patient woke. It was said the Indians were exceptional bowmen and could fire nearly six arrows within a minute. Perhaps this young lad was lucky he was only hit twice, and in a fixable area.

"Hey Doc?" The words were a ragged rasp from the far corner of the room.

"Aye?"

"Think you can let me up? I got cattle to worry on and my wife can't do it with the children too."

Patrick pressed his mouth together and set down the coffee. "Let me look. I worry if I send you off too soon, it will open or get infected."

"Infected, truly, eh? What's infected?" The man, hardy and weather worn against the sun's heat looked skeptical but lifted his leg dutifully. Patrick pulled apart the bandages, made from sheeting material Harry had yanked down from his bolts of fabric yesterday. He wondered, briefly, if the man would charge for the use of all his supplies. Some of the food bags servin' as make-shift beds were soaked through with blood, the contents completely unusable.

The gash on the man, deep and cut horizontally across the back of his right calf muscle, still dripped watery blood, but there was no telltale blistering of yellowy discharge or pus. "You need to heal it so it's not oozin'. Could we send for your wife to at least see you?"

"Still won't get the steer 'round," he said rationally.

"If you go out now, you'll likely limp the rest of your days, and won't get the cattle in much anyway."

343

"You're saying if I push myself now, the long-term outlook ain't so grand? Short term loss for a better future, s'right?"

"Somethin' like that," Patrick said, re-wrappin' the wound.

The man sighed. "When Turner awakes, he can go fetch Molly. He knows where I live and all."

The General's door swung open without warnin'. The breeze and the bell tinkled softly, but it had the desired effect.

Harry woke quickly, attuned to the sound of the bell. His white hair stood up on all ends. Patrick pivoted to see an average gentleman in relatively fine clothes, a dusty bowler on his silver shot black hair. A watch chain gleamed against the deep green of his double-breasted vest, and the fine muslin shirtsleeves rolled up to stay out of the way. His boots shone, but the edges were already dusty.

"What is goin' on here? *Damo*!" He surveyed the gore around his feet, then crouched next to Nels and settled his chin into a cupped hand.

"A relative? I would have a word with you," Patrick said, steppin' up and prepared again to explain why he had amputated the leg.

The man stood with wiry speed. "Who in Christ's name are you?"

"That be a doc, come on the carriage through yesterday." Harry Turner's voice drawled out from behind the counter.

"A doc? Really? From where?" The man was shorter than Patrick by several inches, but his confidence overwhelmed. His posture, and even the slight widening around his middle reminded Patrick of Mr. McClure. Suddenly, he very much wanted this newcomer to like him.

"Boston," Patrick said, offerin' his hand.

The man shook it once, slowly, eyein' Patrick up from travel boots to hatless, frizzy hair. "Scots Irish, then?"

"No. Irish only."

The short fingers looped into his suspenders, barely visible under the vest. "Your accent sounds a bit Scottish."

"My aunt's employer was from Ulster."

"There it is," he nodded. "I'm Percival Davies." The introduction was given warmly, but without further explanation. The surname only offered his Welsh roots.

"Patrick Kinney," he said in return.

"And you're a doc?"

"Just passin' through. Couldn't bear to see the hurt layin' in the street, though."

He raised his eyebrows. "Most would."

Patrick tried not to get his blood up, but his neck felt extra warm under the collar. "I'm a doctor. It's my callin'."

"Heading to Yankton or westerly?" he asked. The pryin' seemed to be acceptable to everyone else in the room. Patrick only hoped Percival Davies wouldn't ask about his history too much, or for references. He and Aunt Bonnie had left Boston in such a flurry...

Patrick sized up the damage of the bodies. He wanted to clean out some of the wounds better, but also knew he and Aunt Bonnie couldn't keep takin' up the space in Harry Turner's General. The people would need to be moved back to their own beds.

"I thought westerly, but no rush," he answered finally. "Is there an...inn for me and my aunt?" he asked, as Aunt Bonnie came out from the back room.

Mr. Davies shook his head, rockin' back on his heels. "There is, but it's part brothel to be clear. You're welcome to stay with me, Doc Kinney. Harry can send you by." He spun on his toe without waitin', nodded again to Harry Turner, and left just as unexpectedly as he had arrived. Patrick let out a breath, surprised he was holdin' it, and glanced at Aunt Bonnie. She shrugged and bent to offer water to one of the patients. At least they wouldn't waste their coin...

Once everyone was stabilized for the mornin', and two more picked up by their relations, Patrick stopped movin' for a moment in the back with Aunt Bonnie and Harry. They hovered over cups of coffee.

"I cannot thank you enough, Harry, for your store," he said, repeatin' himself again. "How will I repay you? You've whole bags seeped in blood out there."

Harry took a sip of coffee, the mug bumpin' under his long nose and leavin' small red half-circles on his flat cheeks. "No different had the Crow burned the place down, though then I'd be left with nothing. I can suffer a few bags. Besides, this is the first raid the Crow have done in Flats Town in likely five years, so it's not like I'm losing much overall. My woman, May, may she rest in peace, would say we're fine lucky for such a long stretch these months."

Aunt Bonnie swallowed her coffee too fast and coughed. "It happens often out here, otherwise?" Her eyes didn't cut to Patrick, but he knew she was shootin' him meaning under her words. She'd rather go back Chicago-way or someplace more peopled. But the truth of it was Patrick was runnin'. He wasn't sure if it was from Thomas or the ugly falsehoods of Boston or just needin' a place fresh and his very own, away from the prejudice of the Irish slums. It was just a big ache in his chest and shoulders, and he itched with it.

"The Sioux and the Crow are enemies," Harry told Aunt Bonnie. "Crow and Sioux are mortal rivals. Always run from the Crow, regardless."

They were interrupted as more families arrived, looking harried. Patrick offered the most competent looking one of each group the basic instructions on care for the wounds, assurin' them that he'd do his best to come by in the next day to see how things fared.

Soon there was only Nels left, who tried not to moan. Patrick offered some of the precious opium, but he dreaded facin' the man's family especially if Nels was drugged on laudanum.

"Will Mr. Davies be alright with my aunt and I staying on with him for a night?" Patrick asked Harry, as they moved blood-soaked flour sacks out back for Harry to spill out the worst of it and then salvage the remainder.

The bristled eyebrows shot up. "Oh that he will have. He's the banker."

"His house is near?"

Harry's head shook back and forth like a dandelion in the wind. "You can't miss it. It's nigh a solid three storeys high. All decorated like a cake too, some of it."

"Sounds pretty," Aunt Bonnie interjected, coming up with another flour sack in her arms.

"Oh, it's pretty alright," Harry said. "Percy Davies keeps the town together, especially in times like this. Backbone of steel, that one. Still, not altogether perfect, if you catch my drift." He glanced at Aunt Bonnie, then wiggled his eyes at Patrick purposefully before leanin' forward. "I'm not of a mind for gossip, really," he said. "But he keeps a woman, you know."

Patrick shrugged, uncertain as to the trouble, but Harry pressed more urgently. "He hasn't married her. Can't, you see. He's got a wife back east yet."

As much as Patrick could understand the concern, he had firsthand experience with such arrangements and found it hard to be intolerant of it in others—he couldn't rightly be angry about it or cast judgement. Not when Aunt Bonnie and Mr. McClure... They were interrupted by a shrill scream. Patrick dashed back into the General Store.

Nels's wife had arrived, and had her eyes glued to the space where the leg used to be.

"Darling!" She fell to her knees, eyes dry but lips tremblin'. "Nels, we were so worried!"

He roused as she fell onto his chest, face buried in the sun-blackened neck. His hand came up to stroke her hair gently, his hand tremblin' only slightly.

"There now, Clara."

She sat back on her thighs and brushed the hair from his forehead. "I thought you were killed."

"I ain't," he said. "But surely would like to get home."

"The Brinkley's let me use their wagon," she said, her face set and determined. It was only because Patrick stood so near that he noticed her lashes were wet. "I can get you home and tend to you. Mother can manage the little ones for a while. And I have you."

Clara shifted so her husband could get onto his foot. Nels staggered, and Patrick dropped to a knee to be sure the stitchin' hadn't slipped, and to be sure the bandages would hold the jostlin' of a wagon ride. Already he considered how

348

to get a wooden leg out for Nels, craftin' a long letter in his head to Chilling. Chilling would answer, he thought. Probably.

It took Patrick, Harry and Clara to get Nels into the wagon, and Clara assured the men she would need no assistance at home, even though Nels's face was paste. "You know I have help within hollering distance," she said calmly, lookin' only at Harry Turner.

"You'll come and check on me, doc." Nels surprised Patrick with his request. "Make sure it all heals well?"

"You can count on it."

Patients. A whole lot of them. It was better than Boston—to be needed so much, to have houses to call upon, injuries to see. What would it be like, to be able to set up a practice in the west, truly? Patrick hadn't really thought about it. Their journey was just a vague notion of west and onward, waitin' for the right time and place to show. He and Aunt Bonnie had nowhere else to go, and any town with a doctor wouldn't need him on principle.

As if able to hear Patrick's thoughts, Harry turned as Nels and Clara drove off. "We don't have a doc," he said, matter-of-factly. "Used to, an old curmudgeon who ran off any new young snapper wanting to test the waters here."

"Why'd he leave?"

Harry snorted, then spit along the side of the stairway up to the general. "Didn't. He died of the typhoid himself, less than six months ago."

"I see," Aunt Bonnie said.

Patrick could feel her tryin' very hard not to look at him sideways and with intent. He felt his own reaction—a strange leap in his ribcage and deep in his belly.

"Well, one doc's like the next, ain't they," Harry said casually. "You best get off, then."

Patrick took the General's steps two and a time down, feelin' oddly full of vigor. But Aunt Bonnie's back was straight and rigid as they crunched along the dried ruts of the road. The midday light was fierce and hot, clear like polished glass.

In the quiet bustle of the street, she finally spoke, all blunt and firm and anxious.

"Do you mean to stay long, Patrick?"

He inhaled, breathin' in small bits of dust and dung. "A little while," he admitted. "I should keep an eye on the injured, the ones I've amputated at the very least."

"You want to stay longer, though," she half-accused. "I heard through those broken windows what Mr. Turner said. There's no doctor in Flats Town."

"No…but then again, it's not a very big town. Might not support a doc fully," he reasoned, but his mind raced. There was no chemist, nor vet either, so the more he'd offer by way of service, even in exchange for home goods, might suffice…

Aunt Bonnie's hand stopped them a few feet from the brown and scraggly yard of Percival Davies' home. "I am afraid of this place," she said. "I have been afraid nearly since we've left Boston, and it's not easier here." She glanced around the weeds and the rutted street. "I know it's the only way to give you a chance to make somethin' of your doctorin'. Just…" She sighed and released his forearm. "Just let's see if we can discover a bit more about it before we – you – decide."

"Of course," he promised. "That's partly what I'm hopin' to do while we stay here at the bankers."

The Davies house stood out ostentatiously from the others. The top storey had painted curls along the eaves in yellow, pink and white. There were multiple windows, all filled with leaded glass, and drapes in each. Percival Davies himself stepped out as they walked up.

"Welcome!" he said jovially. "Come in."

He opened the door and watched Aunt Bonnie glance over the fine carvin' of the porch.

"You like the fixin's?" he asked and shook his head. "Did those up for Bets, you know. Not that it matters."

Aunt Bonnie for once had no scruples. Maybe she wished to know more about their host before spendin' a night under his roof. Or perhaps she was simply too tired to worry about social niceties.

"We heard you have a woman," she said. Her tone was dry but friendly, and the man passed her a grin. He seemed relaxed, and not the hard-nosed political figure Harry Turner had described. In any event, Patrick was glad for her boldness.

"Nay, Bets will die surrounded by her lace and ribbons in New York," he said simply. "Her choice."

Bouncin' through the door, his voice, mellifluous as a bell, carried through the hallway. "Esther! Our guests have arrived!"

A shadow spread long against the white daylight of the back room. Patrick blinked. The woman was stately and quiet, her eyes warm and black, and her dark hair streaked with steely white strands. Her height was the most surprisin'. Her chin was at Percy Davies' eye level, but he gazed up at her with a mix of pride and adorin' devotion.

"So! Miss Kinney and Doc Kinney her nephew," he introduced, slidin' his thumbs into the ends of his suspenders.

She nodded and smiled, and it lit her face. "You'll want a place to freshen up and put your belongings."

Esther was efficient, and they were put in guest rooms upstairs at once. Patrick heard the splash of water in a basin across the hall, where his aunt washed grime and blood from her hands and face before dinner. He glanced down at his own fingers. Blood dried black and flaky under his fingernails, and he was sure he looked a bit wild around the edges.

His shirt was stained with blood, too, so he stripped and put on his spare. The caked gore on the sleeves had the familiar 'good old surgery stink' as the barbers liked to call it. He'd have to wash it soon or risk ruinin' the shirt for good.

"Excuse me?" The words came the same time the knock. He tucked in the shirttails and pulled on his suspenders before openin' the door, expectin' to see Esther.

He couldn't help starin'. A woman waited, but it was not Percival Davies' lover. This woman stood glossy and tall and straight—a young woman bloomed and with a defined tilt to her chin, which she lifted at his gaze, a challenge and an invitation. She was dressed smartly, with polished shoes and a well-cut dress formed around a corseted waist. She shoved pins into shiny black hair and raised her eyebrows as she looked him up and down.

"I am to ask whether you need anything else. A towel or more water?"

He blinked, then remembered his voice. "I don't, thank you."

She nodded and closed the door for him, leavin' him feeling knocked about. Taking a breath, he went back to the water, scrubbin' with the sliver of soap. Never one for much style or fancy dress in the best of times, Patrick enjoyed the casual attire of the west. But now in the banker's formal home, in the presence of a beautiful woman... He felt conscious of his lack of necktie, among other things. He certainly didn't look much like a serious doctor, that was certain.

Delicious scents, unfamiliar but mouthwaterin', drifted through the rooms. He was hungry, he suddenly realized. Famished.

He walked carefully through the parlor to find the kitchen, noting the carpet under his feet, and the mix of furniture. Some pieces were beautifully carved and tufted with patterned silk, and others were hand-made wooden pieces, polished and practical and covered in hides. It was an unusual parlor, but in a way a balance of what life was like in the Territories. One foot in the gentile east, the other in the unruly west.

"Doc. There you are." Percival Davies's voice cut through the slanted light. He stood on the far side of the room, half-hidden in gloom and dust-floated air. A foggy glass filled with copper liquid swirled in his hand. "Join me, you look as you could use it." He held out a second drink, and Patrick crossed to take it, not knowin' what else to do.

Percival knocked the top of his glass with Patrick's and drank deep. Patrick eyed the liquor with distrust and sampled it, hopin' he wouldn't choke as he swallowed.

"We've been without a doctor for several months now," Percival said without preamble. "Through the end of the winter and into the spring. Now summer nearly." Shaking his head, a sleek intense look glazed over his face. "Shame, really. A town as big as Flats Junction without a doc to help the sick. Many have died."

Patrick's first question blurted out before he could ask it delicately. "The raid. That happen often out here?"

"The Crow attacked Flats Junction simply because it is here, and it was a whim. Their real purpose was to go after the summer camp of Esther's people." He pointed out the western window toward a field. At the far end was a leafy expanse of forest where thin ribbons of chalky blue smoke spiraled up toward the clouds. "It's their traditional camp," he continued. "The Crow are the natural enemies of the Sihasapa, and usually the skirmishes are confined there. For some reason, this time, they came into town to cause trouble with us whites. And then the Sioux—her family and the others—rode after the Crow to drive them out of Flats Town. You saw how that went over—everyone panicked. And with the damn book comin' out soon, it's only going to get worse."

"A book? How will a book change what's happenin' in Flats Town?" Patrick asked, strugglin' to keep up. He took a deep drink of the whiskey and then wished he hadn't. It made his throat close up and start to go up his nose, which burned and made his eyes water.

"The bloody fool Custer will end up getting' us all killed out here. Or worse, start a war. Do you know he was out here – in the Territories – just last year and published all about the gold to be had. It's why there's more people everywhere these days, not just in Flats Town, but further west, toward the sacred lands in the Great Sioux Reservation. Damn them all," Percival finished fiercely. "It's all their land, and we're lucky to be on it."

"Of course," Patrick said quickly, hopin' he would be able to cover his ignorance. There was only so much one could learn while travelin' west, and he never knew whether what he heard was truth or gossip anyway. That said, he didn't know Percival Davies any more than the next village banker. But the fact that his lover was Sioux, and he had a child with her, made him a far more reputable source to get information about the politics of Dakota Territories. He decided to try his hand at speakin' on it, hopin' the man would offer his opinions. It would help Patrick understand what manner of man ran the town, and what it would mean to stay.

"I thought the Peace Treaties – the Medicine Lodge one in the late sixties, and the workings of President Grant, mean that they want the Plains to stay as property of the Indians. What will Custer's book matter?" His grasp on government policy might be weak, but he tried to read a newspaper when he could. It helped with his travels. Last year he'd read about troubles in Kansas and Texas with the Comanche and Cheyenne tribes, so he and Aunt Bonnie had gone north...to Flats Town, it seemed.

Percival gave a witherin' glance and poured himself more drink. "You don't really believe that if there's gold to be had that the greedy out there will stay away, Indian land or no?"

"But if white people start diggin' around the reservation, and in this sacred area, don't you think they'd have some sort of retaliation comin' at them from the Indians?"

"Exactly."

Jesus, Mary and Joseph. If what he said was true, then the West would explode into another set of skirmishes, if not outright war. Though Patrick didn't enjoy the notion of frequent Indian raids...battles would mean work. His services would at least be needed.

"Father. The meal is ready." The young woman stood at the parlor door, now wearin' an apron.

The banker nodded and set down his drink. "You've met my daughter Katherine, Doctor Kinney?"

"Briefly, Mr. Davies," he said, and tried not to stare at her beauty—the flawless pale cinnamon skin and eyes that swallowed the light and glowed.

"Ah, aye." The man paused at the door by his daughter. "And call me Percy, if you will. Formalities are not so deep out here. Come along. Esther will have a feast, and your auntie is already helpin' her out with the vittles."

The dining room was connected to a kitchen, and the spaces reminded Patrick a bit of the MacHugh house in Gloucester. The nostalgia hit him full force for a moment as he thought of Robert, and wondered how he did with his marriage to Tara. Thomas had departed for Europe, so would be out of their way, and he was sure Bobby and Tara were dotin' on old Doc Burns. He ought to write Bobby... maybe once he was settled. He realized, with a pang something like a heart palpitation, that he was seriously thinking of stayin' and never goin' back to Boston. As he gripped the back of a chair, Katherine brushed past with a covered porcelain dish. If he wrote Bobby, maybe he'd mention her too, if only to say how there was beauty in the west.

"Cornbread, of course," Esther said, as she unwrapped a steamin' cloth. Mr. Davies made a noise like a smack with his lips. There was also water cress, and bowls of mushrooms and turnips, meat pressed with chokecherries Esther calls *wasna*, and other more familiar things, like roast and potatoes. She spoke about the unusual dishes without needing a prompt, as if expectin' Patrick and Aunt Bonnie to want to know. Two long lines ran parallel along her mouth, from her nose down toward her chin as she spoke solemnly, but they only served to make her entire face look more refined. She seemed ageless, mysterious, and yet almost motherly.

Very little was said after the food was passed about and everyone ate. Aunt Bonnie's foot hit Patrick's, and her eyes flashed to his briefly. He knew she was appalled they'd not said grace, but he only lifted a shoulder. Should he have forced it? He felt out of his element, dazed and exhausted, and yearnin' for a bed and a steady rhythm to his days. Now that it may be at hand, he found he craved it, and wouldn't do anything to upset the chance.

"Flats Junction needs a doc."

Percy's words struck the silence, hard and hammerin', and without warnin'. Patrick stopped with a fork halfway to his mouth, and set it down carefully, meeting the man's gaze.

"I gathered that," he said.

"No, but we need a good one. One that can do more than hack off a limb or pull out an arrow. We need one that can support Flats Town as a whole, if you catch my meanin'."

His heart leapt, but he attempted to keep calm, and refused to look at Aunt Bonnie, in case her worry caused him to falter. "I was concerned that a small town might not be able to support a full-time doctor." If Percy was being blunt, Patrick would be, too.

Percy made a contorted, comical grimace with his expressive mouth, wiped it and leaned back in his chair at the head of the table.

"We don't have room for a citified doc, to be sure," he said firmly. "But one that can do some apothecary work, and maybe some barberin', and of course managin' any livestock."

"How did the old doctor manage?" Patrick asked.

"Oh, old Doc Gunnarsen was a bit of a farmer himself. Could half live off the land, and the rest of it was from patients."

It was no time to be coy. "That's all well enough, but I've no hand in farmin', ranchin' or otherwise. My only trade is as a doc."

Percy glanced at Esther. She didn't move, though her dark eyes slanted at him from her food. Patrick shifted in his chair. It was as if he awaited some sort of judgement, and he felt strained in his own skin. He wanted time to speak to Aunt Bonnie. He wanted to walk the width of the town itself...

And he wanted to be done runnin'.

Done with the wanderin'.

"Well, if you have any relatively decent knowledge of beasts – horses and cows especially – and then also of people, that's a start," Percy said slowly.

"I do have trainin' as vet, and some as a chemist," Patrick said, tryin' not to come off overly confident of his abilities, but also not sound too green.

"You needn't try and sell me on your credentials, Patrick," Percy said, wavin' the hand curled around his tin water cup. "I only want to make sure you're able to take care of yourself enough. If you can act as vet, and offer medicines, and also handle the settin' of bones and limbs and basic doctorin' I don't see why you wouldn't stay on."

"I plan to, a few days, if you can spare your hospitality," Patrick said, uncertain if he should offer anything more concrete. It was happenin' so fast and easy he felt the wind knock out of his lungs.

Percy slung an arm to include the whole room. "Our house is yours, for as long as you need. Hell, we'll even get the bodies to help you build your own place."

It sounded like an offer.

An ask.

Patrick glanced out the window. Flats Town proper went south, and the room's view was only broad prairie with a homestead far in the distance. The sun had dipped lower but shone a steady mid-afternoon light. Everything glowed dun and white and yellow. Heat sizzled along with insects buzzin' and buried in the tall prairie grass until the tree line, where trees kissed the edge of a field.

"We would—the town would—be obliged," Esther pressed into the quiet. Her voice, already low, was husky and forcibly emotionless. Next to her, Katherine laced her fingers together, and her eyes met Patrick's. There was somethin' in there—hope and fire and somethin' fragile. It made him want to sit with her on a porch and unravel her thoughts. He wanted to know her, to learn what made a young woman like that so very proud and yet brittle.

"You haven't had any other offers?" Aunt Bonnie asks. "No other doc wished to stay?"

"There were others before Doc Gunnarsen ran them off, fresh from the east," Esther said. "With new ideas, other ways to heal. And besides, we buried our boy this past spring. Perhaps, had we a doctor of any kind, he would have lived."

Patrick's blood lurched at this disclosure, even though there was never a guarantee a doctor of any type of experience could save a lad.

"Besides," she continued simply, as though revealin' her child's death was no more than a listing of tragedies. "I would like a doctor here who can treat many people – no matter the nature of their heritage."

"I understand," he said, and leaned forward, his elbows on the table.

"Well then, man, you will seriously consider stayin' here, then?" Percy asked lowly.

All the troubles of Boston floated through Patrick's mind—the broken wee practice and damaged sign, the disgust of prejudice, the loss of an apprenticeship. He wondered what it would be to finally put down roots, to belong, to be needed and not run out of a town or hated for his accent or last name.

He met his aunt's frank gaze. She tilted her chin and raised a shoulder. He was the man of their tiny family now—the one earnin' the money and makin' the choices. It still sometimes felt odd to speak without her say so.

Yet if there was to be a decision about this, it was his to make. And she was offerin' it.

"I would be glad to make Flats Town home," he said, feeling the weight of the words glue him to the chair. Even when Percy and Esther's palpable joy vibrated in the room, and Katherine smiled at him so brightly it shot stars into his heart, and even with the promise of a house and patients… even then it felt like he'd signed his life away. It felt unreal. Would it really be where he could make a mark?

After dinner and a round of whiskey in celebration, he pulled himself up the stairs to go to bed. The fatigue of the past days ate into his bones. He opened his bedroom door just as Aunt Bonnie jerked hers open from the other side.

"You've chosen, then," she said softly. He could not read her face or her eyes in the gloaming, but her voice was tight and forlorn. "Here, where Indian raids will give you work, and where we'll be killed at any time."

He had no energy for a fight. "They could come to any western town. We're no safer here than anywhere else."

"Hardly a comfort, Patrick."

Walkin' over to her, he put his hand on her shoulder. If he were still a youth, he would bury himself, but the years for going to her for comfort were gone. Now it was up to him. "I want to do good, Aunt Bonnie. I want to help people with what I've learned. And I want to do it without hindrance. That might be here, as they'll have me. And if it is, then I'll be glad to have a place where I can take care of you, as I promised Mr. McClure."

It was the first time in months Patrick had said the man's name, and his aunt went stiff under his fingers. He continued, pressing his case. "I've done a poor job of it these past years. Every time we come close to findin' a town where we might settle, there are too many other docs, or ones that won't tolerate me, or not enough work to keep us fed and sheltered. If it made sense to go back east to Boston, I would. But that's not the best way of it either, and we both of us know it."

He dropped his hand, listenin' to the shufflin' below the stairs, where Esther and Percy spoke together in their parlor. He decided to go for it all, and hoped his aunt understood.

"You warned against this years ago – that this wasn't even a trade, too hard to make a livin' off bein' a doc. Maybe you were right. But I don't know what else to do. It's all that lives in my hands and mind. It's what I crave."

Her chin came up and she deflated, suddenly shrinkin'. It gave him a pang. Couldn't she see how travel had worn her? He needed to find a place to give her last years some solace.

"I know I said that, Patrick, but you are very good at what you do." Her voice was both annoyed and resigned. "I'm glad you didn't listen to me. Forgive an old woman her worries. It's your work and your life now…not mine. I'll be glad to stay. We will do fine."

She sighed and entered her bedroom. The door latched with a metallic click. Patrick stood in the hallway alone, feelin' out of place and full of thrill at the same time. He'd found a home for himself and would carve a place. He'd be the doctor for Flats Town. He thought of all the people he had to meet, all the patients who would need him. Excitement bloomed in his chest, warmin' him all over down into his fingers.

It would be like he'd once dreamed—makin' a difference, findin' cures, usin' the talent that could not help but burst out of him, even when it was not always the right time. Offerin' medicine, searchin' for the answers to an illness, bindin' a wound. It was something he could not deny, never could.

He inhaled, and then felt certainty melt into his marrow.

He'd done it, then.

He was a doctor, through and through, and now nothin' would stop him from medicine.

Nothing at all.

CHAPTER TWENTY-ONE

Jane

March 3, 1884

Franklin doesn't speak to either of us as he drives the wagon to the house, but the fact that he's driving at all, holding the reins with his one hand as he guides the wagon, is something to celebrate. I curl Andrew closer to my breast, a hand under his bottom. It's a marvel that his head fits into the crinkle of my elbow. One would think such a place too angular and hard to nestle a newborn's skull, but it somehow curves perfectly.

"News travels fast," Patrick says aloud, and I lift my head to see Mitch and Alice Brinkley waiting on our new front porch, their wagon waiting off to the side and the horses tethered with feed bags. Esther pauses halfway to opening the door for them and her eyes widen with shock.

"Perhaps it's only chance," I say, and shift on the wagon board. The dampness of fluids under my skirts makes me want nothing more than a bath in the tin tub upstairs. Still, Alice's face fills with light when she sees me, and my own spirits are yanked out of fatigue. She seems much better each time I see her, and I do hope she's still drinking her teas… And then I realize she will want to see the baby, and I will be able to start showing him to folks. Joy runs through my veins, a starburst of delight and awe. I have been a daughter and sister, wife and widow, housekeeper and cook, but now… *mother*. For a moment, I wonder how I will fare with this new role, particularly with Esther so certain she will depart, but there is no time for questions or worries because Alice has approached with sparkling eyes and outstretched arms.

"Thank you, Franklin," the doctor says, and offers the hand opposite the one Franklin still has, and though the man hesitates, he takes it and shakes Patrick's palm once, fierce and fast.

I hand Andrew carefully to Alice, who coos as she sway-walks back toward the porch where Esther waits. Her body leans and yearns and stretches toward my babe, and she bends over Alice's arms at once. Mitch and Patrick help me out of the back of the wagon, using both of their arms as if I am made of glass and porcelain, and already broken at that. I want to wave off their over-chivalrous care but find my knees wobblier than I wish and the fatigue of the birth itself finally bearing down on my limbs. It seems a woman gets a spurt of anticipation after the birth, as if nature does not wish her to rest, but to be filled with uplifting emotions that keep her awake for a bit, until it wanes and leaves her wrung out, like a much-used dishcloth left to shrink in the sun after a washing.

"A boy, then?" Mitch asks us both, as I put all my weight to Patrick's elbow as we walk to the porch. Behind us,

Franklin hails someone as he drives off, and the muck from his wheels churns the street into deeper ruts.

"Aye," Patrick says, sounding proud and thrilled. I glance up at him and he meets my eyes. They crinkle at the corners when he smiles. Perhaps now that we have a child, he will be less exacting of me. Perhaps he will allow me to still be his wife and the mother of his babes, but also the nurse, the healer…this strange growing thing deep in my belly that is more rooted than anything I have known. As I think this, I remember the wild licorice, saved by Esther and myself for after birthing a child, and I suddenly crave stewing them. Is this how Patrick feels, always, when confronted with health and wellness? When he's given a trouble his mind at once goes to how to heal and save and fix? If so, there must be a way we can meet on our philosophies.

I'm pulled from my brooding when we reach the porch, and Alice and Esther ask how well the birthing went, and if I am in much pain, or if there was much difficulty. Patrick answers the questions with scientific airs, though I just smile and shake my head, taking Andrew back into my arms from Esther, who'd plucked him from Alice. What is it about women, that we desire to hold infants and children? It is something ingrained in us, as if our biology screams for memory of it, whether we crave motherhood, or have it, or only remember it.

"I didn't mean to bother you on a happy day, doc," Mitch breaks into the feminine chatter. "But my brothers and I overruled our pa. You gotta come see the cows."

"They've the same? Anemia, bloody urine, and the like?" Patrick's shoulders sink an inch. "If it's like at Danny Svendsen's ranch, I can only diagnose. I haven't been able to figure on a cure."

Mitch shrugs. "At least be sure it's the same thing, then. So when you find a way to heal them, we can be sure to be part of it."

Patrick shoots me a look, one of dread and warning, but also resignation and relief. He dislikes not being able to cure people or animals, and when he comes up dry, I know he takes it to heart. Thinking of the previous epidemics of diphtheria, his lack of proper medicines, his battle against the seasonal black measles, when he has laid his head in his hands or on his desk in frustration and near-defeat. He has never yet given up, though, and I mean to match him.

"Come in," Patrick tells Alice and Mitch. "Jane should sit a bit."

We enter as a group. In the kitchen, Esther puts on a late pot of coffee and begins to boil water for tea. I sink gingerly on the wooden bench, and Alice slides next to me.

"You seem...happy," I say to her, low. "Are you doing well?"

The corners of her mouth curl, and the smile meets her eyes. "I have more better days than not," she confides. "I notice when I do not follow the instructions you gave me, and Mitch has noticed it enough to agree I should do as you say. He came for the doc about the cows, but I came to get more of the sorrow tea if I you have more?"

The success of my treatment, that I could chase away the melancholy from her mind and heart, swells deep under my ribs. As the men stand and talk in the hall yet, I wave Esther over and ask her to get the packet of vials she and I keep stocked in the far corner of the pantry, behind the cones of brown and white sugar.

She brings them over, and I sort through with one

hand, until Esther takes over. She plucks out the skullcap and goat's rue and then also one I recall—barely—as cudleaf sage.

"This will calm you," she says, smiling at Alice, her voice gentle. "And it will help."

"I hadn't thought of that one," I admit, feeling the euphoria dip. "I am still learning, I suppose. There's so much to remember."

"I will help you," Esther says. "With that and this little one." She reaches for him and lifts him up again. "And if you like, I will make you a cradle board, so you may take him easily with you to visit Patrick's patients."

"Oh, like a sling?" Alice asks. "I have used that."

"A bit different. A sort of pack," Esther says, bouncing Andrew lightly as her hips sway. "You will see. It is useful."

"There is more," I tell her. "Hardy will come to live with us. He's to be Patrick's apprentice and start to learn the medical trade."

"Hardy, the orphan boy? The blacksmith apprentice," Alice remembers. "Why?"

"He prefers it to the forge," I say. "But it will be another bed to make up, and a growing boy to feed, and oh! He must get a horse..." I trail off, suddenly consumed by all that must be done—diapers and dinner, floors and filing, nursing people and my boy, a youth to manage and the garden that must be planted. And yet under it, a great hunger to sit next to Esther and learn all her herbal knowledge and pass it along to help Patrick. There are sick cattle now, of course, and there will likely be another sickness come winter. There will be more men at Fort Randall, which will likely only bring more violence and injury. And the change of the season will bring the black measles back, too, which is the bane of Patrick's existence.

It seems my life is suddenly overfull.

"A baby and a boy, all in the same day," Esther says, sounding amused. The kettle on the stove burbles, and she hands Andrew back to me so she can pour tea and hand me a cup of it.

I glance at the leaves in the steaming water, and her hand folds over mine on the handle.

"It is bitter, but good," she says meaningfully, and I suddenly know she has given me the remedy I craved when I first stepped on the porch. I deflate onto the bench and lean against the heaviness of the table.

Esther hands Patrick and Mitch matching cups of coffee, and then heads upstairs for bedding for Hardy. We'll have to put him in the kitchen until we can build a cot in the surgery or something else.

"How will you keep a boy fed?" Alice asks. "They eat a lot. My nephews can inhale double what a grown man will eat in a single sitting."

Yes, there will be worries of money, more than usual, but then again, I will have my garden, and with Hardy staying, we'll certainly make it bigger. "You have taught me how to can and preserve vegetables," I remind her. "And we will just have to manage. Everyone does."

"Yes," Alice says, her voice gentle. "We all do." She means life in general, I am sure, but also her own suffering, and mine, and all that must be done to survive. We are all in it together.

"Well, then, Jane, "Patrick says, "if you, Alice, and Esther will be fine for a bit, I'll go with Mitch to the Brinkley ranch." I twist to watch him throw the last of the coffee down his throat. He winces at the heat of it.

"I suppose you ought," I say, standing. The act feels easy enough, and I hope I get my full strength back soon. There will be little time for me to lay abed with this new babe. My sister would take a week at least, if I recall correctly from my mother's comments, but that is for women who make an easy life.

Patrick heads back to the front door, Mitch in his shadow. Alice and I follow, just as Esther comes down the stairs with her arms full of blankets and quilts.

"I'm wonderin' if all the new horses are bringin' cow sickness," Patrick muses to Mitch, as he slaps on his hat and gives me an absent kiss on the cheek. "All the greenbacks comin' out to Flats Junction and makin' their way to Fort Randall. Beasts generally infect other beasts."

"Horses to cattle?" I ask, unable to help myself and needing a distraction from the steady ooze of fluid from my womb down the inside of my thigh. "Is that possible?"

Patrick considers, but before he can speak further, our little tableau is interrupted by a hail from the street.

"Kate! How goes it?"

It is not one of us, though, but Moses Thompson, riding past on his horse from the direction of the bunkhouse and on a direct collision course with Kate as she strides toward us on foot.

She frowns in his direction and refuses to answer, instead marching past our low gate and up the path to the porch. She wears a new dress today, one of green and purple stripes, and the stitching is so fine it looks city made.

"I'd come to tell you that, what with the new fine

goods brought in with the spring rails," she says, directing her plans mostly to Patrick and the Brinkley's, "I'm holding an official grand opening in a month. But if you wouldn't mind telling Widow Hawks to stay home for it. Wouldn't want to cause any difficulties."

"Now, Kate, we've been over this," Patrick says, but I put my free hand on his bicep and squeeze. He presses his long mouth together and inhales slowly.

"Your mother may do as she pleases, I think," I say, and ignore the clench of Kate's jaw as I do. I wonder if Esther has heard her daughter from the depths of the house. "But we will pass the word of your grand opening as we see patients."

"We'll tell the family," Alice says, smiling carefully at Kate. "Do you need a cheese or pies? Tina makes the best."

"I..." Suddenly Kate looks uncertain. Perhaps she had not really planned on so much support or does not know how big to make her grand opening. Perhaps she is trying to do too much and is afraid of another repeat, where festivities result in the destruction of her home.

I wonder if there will be fireworks in Flats Junction ever again.

Then she tosses her glossy head and smiles. "Certainly, bring all you wish. We can make it a grand opening and a grand celebration."

"A celebration, and the like?" Moses ties his horse and comes up to greet us. He notices the bundle in my arms and his dark eyes widen and then shine. "Oh, I see!"

"It's for the grand opening of my General," Kate corrects him. "Not for Jane's babe."

"Two reasons to be happy, then, as it were," he says, ignoring the acid in her tone.

"We will be there, Kate," I say. "I will bring vittles, of course."

"Fine," she says, and nods once before spinning on her heel. Moses grasps her wrist, but not tightly, and turns her around. His eyebrows go up, and he does not seem to mind how she glares at him, or how violently she wrenches herself from his fingers.

"You didn't see the new child, as it were," he reminds her.

Kate's gaze slides over Andrew's cheek and the jumble of blankets, and for a moment, I am certain she will crack and weep and wail. Perhaps she wishes to, or perhaps she thinks offering a softness to me and to Patrick will be a moment of forgiving, when she is still not sure she wishes to be so.

How long can a woman hold a grudge against those who wronged her, even if it was not meant in malice? Sometimes I think we are closer to healing, and other times the pain and the words of anger between us is a canyon.

"I see it," she says.

She sets her teeth and turns back to the road. Moses watches her go, and sighs, shaking his head, but it is with a strange sort of understanding.

"Well, and congratulations indeed, Mrs. Kinney. Doc," he says, and, after watching Kate cross the street, he makes to his own horse and heads off toward the Svendsen ranch to the north.

Kate's back is straight, and she moves like water, much like Esther does. Do strides and a person's gait come with inheritance? I will have to watch to see if Andrew moves like Patrick.

As Kate takes First Street, a lumbering figure detaches from Soup's Corner and walks alongside her, though he seems indifferent to her as he holds two bowls of soup. It is one of Yves's posse, and it makes me wonder how Kate will manage to rid Flats Junction of the posse's lecherous presence. How will she run a general store properly, when Yves has set himself up as a pirate king in the old cooperage, with a corner on the market of the finest things the train can bring through town?

I suppose it is not my trouble. There will be other worries, like how Patrick manages with an apprentice, and how well I can keep my newborn fed and healthy. Andrew sighs, and I shift my stiff elbow.

"Here," Alice says, turning to me. She lifts up the babe. He curls his body together, as if he still believes he's smashed within me. "Put him up against your shoulder." She settles his tiny face into the crick of my neck.

Patrick and Mitch are already up on the board and untangling the reins when Hardy, a bundle of belongings in his fist, careens around the south corner of our street. He pauses at Sadie and Tom Fawcett's and peers around to the summer house in their yard, offering someone a small wave before he arrives at Mitch's wagon, flushed and brilliant-eyed.

"Doc! I can go, too, right?" he asks, chucking his bundle into the back of Mitch's wagon without waiting for an answer.

"It's cows, boy, not people," Mitch says, but not unkindly.

"I'm supposed to learn it all," Hardy says. "I think. Yah?" This to Patrick, and then to me, hope and joy and a crazed sort of amazement written all over the broad face.

Patrick grins at everyone and puts down a hand to yank Hardy up. "Aye, you're best to learn it all."

Hardy clambers into the back but leans on the springboard so he's right between the two men. "Right. Where are we going?"

Mitch yells for the horses and they start with a jerk before finding their pace. Alice turns back for her coffee and to help make a meal, her steps light as she hums the refrain for *I'll Take You Home Again, Kathleen*.

I stare out at Flats Junction for a moment, absently patting Andrew on the back, as a whistle blows in the distance. There's a high chance it's bringing more Army recruits, more troubles, more disease. I suppose that is how it will always be—change coming toward us, danger growing and fading. All we can do is try to inch forward with knowledge each day.

My baby sighs from tiny lungs, a sound particular to newborns, I think. It will all take some learning, just as Hardy must also do. Patrick spent a lifetime doing...and I find I am less anxious and more excited to begin.

Learning. It is our existence here, as life continues, and comes in all shapes and forms. It is different kinds of medicine and experiences and experiments. It is stuffing our heads full of knowledge and possibilities.

It is all Patrick has ever wanted.

It is all I have ever wanted.

Kate

March 3, 1884

I'm fuming when I leave the Kinney house, but mostly because Moses Thompson seems to think he's got some sort of sway on me. Who does he think he is, acting like a husband would, and all comfortable about it as he does.

He thinks we're alike, and I know he's wrong.

I twitch at the fabric of my skirt, and the marvel of my dress's beauty pulls me out of my rage a bit. It was the third dress Helena Salomon whipped out after Lara O'Donnell went out and actually bought a sewing machine. It came all the way from Britain, used already, so it was not the full forty dollars, but thirty. That still means Lara spent more than Sadie fixing up her summer house, so Lara had the first machine-made fine dress with Sadie the second and me the third. I find I'm somehow in the middle of more politics than less these days, and I need to get the General fully operating and putting Yves out of business slow-like so he doesn't real-ize it at first. Then he'll get bored, and maybe go rile up the fort and the local tribes around it for some excitement and leave Flats Junction alone again.

Maybe he won't run for mayor, like he's threatening. I've heard that one, too.

As I think on Yves and his disgusting and untrust-worthy presence even when he's not within eyesight, Matthias Hummel appears next to me, hulking and block-ing the sun and spilling soup from the Yang brothers over both his hands.

I want to tell him to go off and away, but Yves's make-shift General is also on Second Street up the way, so I can't very well be angry he's walking back to the posse's local stronghold.

I should've taken the other road, but I wasn't sure if Moses would have doubled back to walk me, and I didn't want to walk past Sadie's house in case she saw me and wanted to talk about me investing in the latest fabrics out from New York. I've already invested in the seamstress busi-ness, and I've other ideas for my funds once I get the General operating as the only store in town, just like it used to be before the fire. I mean to do more than Percy did. I mean to be bigger than my father. And that's clearing out Flats Junc-tion of people like Yves and the competition he's brought since I set him up to handle overflow while the store was rebuilt after the fire.

I want to take over one of the inns and turn it into something respectable and fine. I've got to convince Toot Warren to turn The Golden Nail into a finer restaurant, like they've had up in Deadwood as Fortuna says.

I reach my back steps, but Matthias is still a step behind me. I'm sure if I spin to tell him off, he'll knock soup all over the front of my new dress. Hiking up the stairs, I hear him follow, and sure as anything, he comes in and sets the soup on my table as if he's planned it. What is it with menfolk, always trying to help without my asking. Is there something about me that seems to beg for assistance?

He walks through into the main room of the store, and while I'm staring at the soup as if I could make it disappear with my glaring at it, I hear the grind of the rusty plow. I hurry after him only to see him dragging the old thing back to where it used to sit before we—the men—replaced the worst of the burned floorboards.

After he shifts it, his eyes float around the room, settle on me, and he moves past without touching a single bit of me. He leaves one bowl of soup and takes the other, seeing himself out the door without a word. Ridiculous man. I suppose he was only seeing where things lay in the General, so he can report back to Yves and try to beat me out of more sales.

How will I maintain control over Yves in the coming months? How will I keep the new recruits from Fort Randall from giving him too much business? I must make some deal with the commander at the fort and do all those business plans burning a hole in my pocket. If a woman could be a mayor, I'd run for it. As it is, we'll have to hold some sort of election soon enough. Flats Junction is getting too big to be lawless. And if I can direct the votes, I can make sure someone who wins will run Yves and his posse out of town. Or, at least, make them less liable to cause trouble.

Or maybe I'll work with Yves to make sure the Fort doesn't meddle overmuch in Flats Junction. Maybe I need to make sure the government doesn't get too much control over these parts. Once that happens, I have a feeling my voice will be cut off. Before that happens, I need to make sure I'm too powerful for it to stick.

There is the fort to consider. Business there, I think.

And electricity. I can get it in. I must. It's better than being a mayor.

The train whistle blows long and hard and bright outside, and I shove the pins in my hair again before heading out to the depot. Franklin will have the goods organized—he's been changed since the General's fire. Bess doesn't walk around with bruises anymore, and I haven't seen him drunk in months. For all that went wrong the night I had Bern light the General's roof on fire during the fireworks, some things came right. Even Kaspar Salomon is said to be working the forge again, so the worst of it has passed.

I approach the depot by dodging a small flock of chickens, newly escaped from Nels and Clara's backyard, and wave at Meggie and Tilly, who hang out of The Powdered Rose's upper window as they air out their skirts in the crisp spring air. The train is just pulling in as I climb the steps to the depot, and it belches black smoke into the blue-white sky. I am sure there will be the trinkets I've sent from the east for Helena and more of her fine machine-stitched gowns. As I wait for Franklin to begin unloading, I watch the folks tumble off the train. Cracked leather bags and small trunks bang after a young couple. A dusty cowboy looks hungover as he limps off and pulls his hat down against the prairie's glare. A dozen army recruits in rumpled navy wool, all wearing mismatched boots and looking hungry for adventure spill out, followed by a gentleman in a fine wool top hat.

He approaches and at first, I wonder why he's singled me out. Then I realize it's got to be my fine dress. I must look important, surely. I straighten my spine up, hearing it crack along my midback, and try not to look as pleased as I feel for being recognized as someone of note.

"Looking for an inn," he says, and his accent is clipped along the edges, like an Englishman's might be. He meets my eyes, and my heart jerks a tad when I see he's only got the one—the other is covered by a fine linen patch. He reaches to shake my hand with a smile. "Thomas Smith, madam. At your service."

The End

Historical Note

Middle books are always tricky. You need to push the plot forward without rushing it, and allow space for characters and situations to breathe. Little interactions can add up to explosive arguments, which change the course of the book and the plots themselves. That said, *Medicineman 1884* serves two purposes: to continue the story from *Outcast 1883* and to offer a significant background to medicine in the nineteenth century. Much of what happens here in *Medicineman* continues to layer the many intersecting characters and sets the stage for growth and for future storylines to come together.

A plethora of very obtuse, long-forgotten, and dense research was part of this book, some of which has taken me off on tangents to write other projects and to have more fun learning than I've had since college.

What was interesting in reading incredibly boring books about medical history was how much strife existed between doctors and how fluid medical beliefs were at the same time. On top of the changing science, there was a massive lack of trust of science between patient and physician. Yet I believe there were doctors who listened and shared amongst one another and made a difference for their patients – otherwise, we would not be where we are today. I thought to make Patrick Kinney that kind of doctor, who almost obsessively wants to learn and gather knowledge. Sometimes it gets him in trouble. But it also makes him more open than most, which can become a personal conflict for him as time and experience unfold.

Science, medicine and history offer a complicated view of the transformation of medical practice in the 1800s. Huge leaps were taken in public health. In the first half of the century, medical practitioners were often women. If they were not women, they were everyday farmers, blacksmiths, and fishermen who would offer to set a bone or stitch up a laceration as a sort of side gig or as needed. The profession was considered...not a profession. In fact, parents hoped their children wouldn't go into the field as there was no clout, power, or even respect among people for doctors. One could hang out a sign saying you were both a seamstress and a doctor without anyone questioning it.

In short, we knew very little about science and the medical community was divided. Patrick's struggle against his ethnicity as well as his calling to be a physician is an echo of that very quiet, little-known push and pull of medicine during most of the 1800s. He became a doctor in those crucial few years where doctors went from being just anyone to someone who read books and who went to medical school (even if school only lasted a few weeks!) in order to receive a license (medical licenses were new in the mid-1800s). It was a fascinating time in world history as well, when the discovery of bacteria as pathogens and germ theory exploded on the scene in 1865, and for once was met with support. Patrick references Ingaz Semmelweis, who had a massive amount of proof showing handwashing could save thousands of woman in childbirth prior to '65, but who had not been taken seriously by the international medical community, and was in fact ridiculed regardless of his empirical proof that cleanliness mattered. A few years after his death, germ theory proved him right, and it changed medicine – even if that change didn't happen overnight. Prior to this, those who thought clean hands and tools were important were often ostracized from the entire community, just like Semmelweis.

On top of the quickly evolving discoveries, Patrick's journey happened when doctors fought amongst themselves. Orthodox or allopath doctors were the original "doctors" who built the American Medical Association (AMA) in an attempt to dominate the industry and keep patients away from botanical or homeopathic doctors, who had differing views on how to work with patients and prescribe medication. This rift meant patients of conflicting doctors couldn't even work together or be seen talking to one another. Accusations of patient stealing ran rampant, and doctors kept to their territories if they didn't want a fight. This strategy meant the changes in medicine didn't spread easily between doctors, though it must have happened slowly as eventually the two sides came to the realization that they ought to work together and find common ground (for a while, those who tried to find middle ground were called Eclectics – physicians who used a little bit of orthodox medicine theory and a little bit of homeopathic – essentially taking what they deemed the best of both practices). I made Patrick one of these, whether or not he would have called himself so, as I like to think for him to be as open-minded as he typically is, it would suit.

This fight to become a doctor, though, is also what puts him at odds. American science didn't get interested in native medicine and traditional or natural medicine until nearer the 1900s, when the government sent out people for field studies to discover what the tribes used in medicine and to report back. Before this acceptance, Patrick would see Jane's dabbling as a full-on rejection of everything he had worked so hard to accomplish, though his push-back on this is ironic, given what he had lived through as a youth muddling through the mess of the trade.

Everything mentioned, from the medical journals, their articles, particular doctors and their books, diseases, and their treatments are all historically accurate, as are the Boston neighborhoods and street names, and physician tools listed. Even the herbal medicine Esther/Widow Hawks and Jane use are listed with their proper Lakota name, use, and availability in the Dakotas at that time and season.

Other details, from the cost of Helena's sewing machine to how the Army transported their injured on the prairie are all true, as is the methods of dealing with birth (different though they are) that Patrick, Thomas and Doc Burns use. The lack of hygiene and washing of instruments was prevalent, even after the Civil War for a long time. In short, if one survived an injury, illness, or stint inside a hospital, one was quite lucky.

As I've mentioned before, there never was a town called Flats Junction (or Flats Town) where I have it sitting on a South Dakota prairie, but there very much was a junction of train tracks where the Milwaukee Road railroad lines crisscrossed near Fort Randall. Fort Randall itself did exist on the Missouri during this time, as did all the foodstuffs brought west that Yves hoards in his "second" general store. All the kitchen tools, food, and clothing were also available in the years spanned in this novel.

It was an adventure to be sure to list out as much as I could about history and science and medicine and herbs

within the confines of a novel. I hope you've learned something, or at least have a fire in your belly now to go look
something up. It is just another chapter in the Flats Junction
saga, with more to come, as the women in the west try to
twist the town to fulfill their deepest heart's desires.

With joy—Sara Dahmen
buried in very old medical journals, Wisconsin

Author's Acknowledgements

This book has had several names (Becoming Doctor Kinney, for one) as is usual when writing a novel. It's also had many renditions. One version was completely from Patrick's point of view, starting as a baby in Ireland. My publisher heard that first attempt at a writer's conference years ago and was one of the few who said, "I know what you're trying to do, but there's a better way to do it." Thank you, Ben, and your team, for making this novel a much better version of itself.

I changed the verb tenses, the timeline, and the structure more times than I can count. I thought maybe this book was best as a side novel someday, to offer backstory. But as the Flats Junction books have built upon themselves, this last version came into existence—both a look back at medicine and history and juxtaposing it against the ongoing drama happening in "real" time for Jane and Kate and Marie. In the end, these books are about them—how they, as the women, truly built the west, tamed it, and built it into something resembling community while keeping its wild heart alongside their men and partners.

So as we continue to build this saga, I must thank Ben Coles and all the editors, production team, and cover designers at Promontory Press for helping with every aspect of these books. For Craig Anderson, my first line editor, who has to suffer through the earliest drafts. To my manager,

Noah Jones, who sees the big picture when it comes to anything I write. To Bonnie Nadell, my book agent, who always sees the potential in all my books. And to Laura McDonald, my talent agent at Gersh, who gets that half of my world is writing and the other half is coppersmithing, and supports every piece of it. And, as this is published while we're under contract, I must thank John, Steve and Lonna, Andrew and Tanya, Marty, Leslie and Miranda, for putting so much work into the television development of the Flats stories. It's a major property and not an easy road to build anything in the entertainment industry. It wouldn't even be this far without your unending aid and enthusiasm.

I'm so thankful for my friends who consistently read my books or shout their existence into the void. For my family—both blood and chosen—who show up for book signings and overbuy each novel.

To my children: Will, Hannah and Jack, who understand that "mom has to write!" and leave me alone without a peep of complaint whenever they walk into the office and get 'the look'. It still amazes me that writing is actually my day job!

And as always to my husband John, who believes I'm a worthy writer and it's more than a hobby – it's a passion, a vocation, an obsession – and supports me every step of the process. It was John who said to go and publish. Had he not pushed and believed the books to be worth pursuing officially, they'd all be still gathering dust on my laptop. None of this would have happened without you, my love.

Bibliography

Black Elk, Linda S. *Culturally Important Plants of the Lakota.* Sitting Bull College, Fort Yates, ND; 1998

Bynum, W.F. *Science and the Practice of Medicine in the Nineteenth Century.* Cambridge University Press, Cambridge; 1994

Chevallier, Andrew. *Encyclopedia of Herbal Medicine.* Penguin Random House, New York; 1996

Dungan, Miles. *How The Irish Won the West.* Skyhorse Publishing, New York; 2011

Erbsen, Wayne. *Manners and Morals of Victorian America.* Native Ground Books & Music, Asheville; 2009.

Gilmore, Melvin R. *Uses of Plants by the Indians of the Missouri River Region, Enlarged Edition.* University of Nebraska Press, Lincoln; 1977

Hertzler, Arthur. *The Horse and Buggy Doctor.* Harper & Brothers, New York; 1938

Moynihan, Ruth B. et al, Editors. *So Much to be Done: Women Settlers on the Mining and Ranching Frontier.* University of Nebraska Press, Lincoln; 1990

Obenchain, Theodore, G. *Genius Belabored: Childbed Fever and the Tragic Life of Ignaz Semmelweis.* University Alabama Press, Tuscaloosa; 2016

Ryan, Dennis P. *A Journey Through Boston Irish History.* Arcadia Publishing, Charleston; 1999

Starr, Paul. *The Social Transformation of American Medicine.* Basic Books, New York; 1982

Steele, Volney. *Bleed, Blister and Purge: A History of Medicine on the American Frontier.* Mountain Press Publishing Company, Missoula, MT; 2005

Tanner, Dr. Clinical Remarks on the Polypi of the Uterus. *The Lancet.* September, 1862; (Issue 2039): pages 328 – 329.

Utley, Robert M. *The Indian Frontier of the American West 1846 – 1890.* University of New Mexico Press, Albuquerque; 1984

Webb, James. *Born Fighting: How the Scots-Irish Shaped America.* Broadway Books, New York; 2004

Wilbur, C. Keith. *Antique Medical Instruments.* Shiffer Publishing Ltd., West Chester, PA; 1987

The Flats Junction Series

Tinsmith 1865
Widow 1881
Outcast 1883
Medicineman 1884
Trader 1884
Stranger 1886

For more information,
visit www.flatsjunction.com.

To connect with Sara,
visit www.saradahmen.com.
Find her on Twitter at @saradahmenbooks,
on Facebook, or Instagram at @sara_dahmen.

To learn about Sara's cookware line
inspired by her research for Flats Junction,
visit www.housecopper.com.

Printed in the USA
CPSIA information can be obtained
at www.ICGtesting.com
CBHW081929091223
2508CB00006B/21